I0636200

Thundering Sunset

THUNDERING MOUNTAIN RANCH
BOOK SIX

NICOLE NEISWANGER

Calico

publications

Copyright © 2025 by Nicole Neiswanger

All rights reserved. No part of this book may be used or reproduced in any form or by any electronic or mechanical means, including AI generation tools, information storage and retrieval systems, without written permission from the author, except for the use of brief quotations in critical articles and book reviews.

This is a work of fiction. Names, characters, places, and incidents are products of the author's imagination or are used fictitiously and are not to be construed as real. Any resemblance to actual events, locations, organizations, or persons, living or dead, is entirely coincidental.

If you purchased this book without a cover, you should be aware that this book is stolen property. It was reported as "unsold and destroyed" to the Publisher and neither the Author nor the Publisher has received any payment for this "stripped book."

For questions or comments about the quality of this book, please contact us at calicopublicationsllc@gmail.com.

Publisher: Calico Publications, LLC
Cover Design: Covers and Cupcakes, LLC
Editor: Telltail Editing
Digital ISBN: 978-1-960600-15-8
Print Edition ISBN: 978-1-960600-17-2

For my father, Doug Fleming,
Your unwavering support and love means the world to me. I was
certainly blessed with the best parents and couldn't be more lucky.
Love you always.

One

December 1902

Michael wiped the sweat from his brow as the heat from the fire roared in front of him. He flamed the fiery blaze bursting from the forge and inserted a heavy metal rod. The rod turned orange and then a deep red as the high heat seared it. When it reached the right temperature, he pulled out the rod and shaped the metal with his hammer, his muscles bulging from the force of the blows.

Once it was the desired shape, he inserted it into the metal bucket of cold water. The water hissed as the heat was extinguished, steam rising and drifting toward his face. He tilted his head to avoid being burned by the rapidly climbing moisture.

Church bells rang, telling all who could hear that it was noon. He was at a stopping point, so he placed the metal rod on the bench behind him and the hammer on the wall rack. Michael pulled off his heavy black apron and hung it on the hook next to his tools before dunking a metal cup in the bucket of drinking water he kept handy and drank deeply of the warm liquid. He would've preferred icy water to the heat that burned around him, but as thirsty as he was, he wasn't too choosy.

After he'd gotten his fill, he wiped his mouth with the back of his hand, probably further smearing the dirt and grime on his face, but he didn't mind. Michael enjoyed what he did. It was satisfying work, and he did well for himself, especially being in the heart of Helena. His older brother, Ben, wanted him to work on the family ranch, but he enjoyed working in town.

He'd never wanted to be a rancher. Cow chasing just wasn't something he was particularly fond of, especially once he got a taste of city life. Michael was in the thick of things in Helena. He had plenty of work to keep him busy and friends with whom he socialized regularly. Ben thought he needed to settle down with a good woman, but Michael wasn't in a hurry. There was no need to start a family, not when he had plenty he wanted to do before then.

"Hello," a familiar deep voice echoed from behind him.

Michael turned and grinned. "Hey, what are you doing in town?"

It was as though he had conjured his older brother with his random thoughts.

"I had business at the bank, so I thought I'd stop and say hello. You're still planning on coming home for Christmas, right?" Ben leaned up against the door to Michael's smithy. He was bundled up in his thick sheepskin coat, leather gloves, and a worn Stetson.

"Of course." Michael pointed out the window. "As long as the weather holds."

"Elizabeth will be mighty upset if you don't show."

Michael chuckled. Ben's wife, Elizabeth, liked to have everyone close by, especially around the holidays. Any chance she was given to have everyone home, she took advantage of it. Michael didn't want to disappoint her, so he'd find a way to go to the family's ranch.

Michael ran his fingers through his hair. "Tell her I'll try to be there by Christmas Eve." He wasn't sure how he'd make it work, but he'd find a way.

Ben frowned. "That late? She was hoping to have everyone there the whole week."

"I'd like to, but I've been busy here of late and can't take the time."

"What happened to your help?" Ben looked around the corner, likely expecting to see the young man he'd hired earlier that year.

"He up and quit on me two weeks ago. Found the woman of his dreams." Michael had tried to talk him out of leaving, but he'd been determined to go. "Without his help, it's been difficult keeping up, so unless I get help soon, I'll be lucky to be there for Christmas Eve and Christmas Day."

"I understand, but try to make it if you can. I wouldn't want to disappoint her." Ben slapped his hands together. While it was warm inside the smithy, the raw air blowing outside was enough to send pinpricks so fierce you'd rather be dragged by a horse than stay outside too long.

"I'll try." Michael picked up his thick coat and pulled it over his shoulders. While he'd been burning hot a moment before, the chill could sneak inside his bones mighty quick if he stayed still long enough. "You here long?"

"Just overnight. Need to meet with the lawyer and order a few supplies. The weather isn't looking promising, though. I told Elizabeth I'd stay the night so I don't worry her by traveling in the dark. Not sure I can get out of here before the snow blows in, so I might be here longer than I'd planned."

"You staying at Luke and Louisa's?"

Their brother Luke and his wife, Louisa, had moved back East so Louisa could attend medical school. He and Ben were keeping an eye on their place, Thundering Ridge, while they were away.

"No. The family that was renting the place took everything, lock, stock, and barrel. There ain't a stick of furniture left."

"What happened to Luke and Louisa's furniture? They didn't take it when they left town."

"It's stored in the attic, and I'm not inclined to pull down a mattress and frame for the night."

"That makes sense." A breeze whipped through the open doors, and Michael tightened his coat.

"But I promised Luke we'd keep an eye on his place. I want to check on it and make sure nothing needs repairing before I try to rent it again."

"You're welcome to stay with me, but it'd be on the sofa back there." Michael pointed to the two small rooms at the back of the smithy.

Ben crossed his arms. "Yeah, I've seen your sofa. It's lumpier than the rutted road to the old homestead. I'll take a room at the hotel. Besides, you snore louder than a freight train coming down the tracks."

Chuckling, Michael shook his head. His place wasn't big or particularly comfortable, but it sure beat having to pay for a room. "Not sure how Elizabeth sleeps through your caterwauling, but if you change your mind, you're always welcome."

Ben grinned widely, likely knowing he was right. "I appreciate that, but I ain't above paying for a bed at the hotel. Would you like to have dinner later?"

"Yeah, I'd like that. I'll meet you at Mimi's Diner? It's gonna take me at least that long to finish today." He pointed to the pile of work waiting for him.

"Sounds like a solid plan." Ben left, the wind picking up the flaps of his coat and almost taking his hat with it before he disappeared out of sight.

Michael's belly rumbled, a reminder that he hadn't eaten in some time. He strode to his combined office and kitchen, where it was a tad warmer than outside and where he could rustle up something to eat. The space was cozy, with a small cookstove next to a small wooden cabinet where he stored canned beans, canisters of flour, sugar, cornmeal, and rice with two shelves above that held his metal plates, cups, a few utensils, and a chocolate cake a neighbor had given him just the day before.

His small desk played a dual purpose, where he'd spend most days catching up on paperwork and eating his meals when he had a free moment. An old brown winged back chair that had seen better days but still greeted him like an old friend sat across from his desk and next to his bed. It was covered with a thick red and blue quilt his ma had made him when he was young. It was one of the last things she'd made for him before she passed.

He'd left the smithy's wide doors open, along with a sign out front telling any customer to holler if they didn't see him. As much as he would've liked to close the doors to keep the heat in, without an assistant, there was no choice but to keep them open. He wanted it to be clear to everyone in town that he was still open for business.

Grabbing a loaf of bread, he cut two thick pieces, slathered cold butter on them, and found a few pieces of ham from dinner the night before. He settled back in his chair and put his feet up on the small stool he had just for that purpose. After a few minutes, the rumbling in his stomach ceased.

As he took the last bite, cursed screams and the dull thud of wheels crashed outside. Horses neighed, people screamed, and footfalls pounded along the dirt road.

"What the hell?" He jumped to his feet and rushed outside, just in time to see a carriage wheel fly past him. A small buggy had crashed mere feet from his fenced-in corral.

He ran to calm the horses, who squealed and pranced in fear. They shook their heads and rose on their hind legs, trying to release themselves. He grabbed the bridle of one and held it still as another man calmed the second horse. After a few minutes, the agitated horses settled. Once that was done, Michael turned and saw a tangled mess of a blue skirt, ruffled white petticoats, and trim ankles encased in black cotton stockings. He should avert his eyes, but he couldn't help but enjoy the view.

The unladylike cursing coming from inside the carriage ruined the image. Pulling away from his not-so-innocent thoughts, he scrambled to the edge of the carriage to help. He had to swing his body sideways to avoid her kicking legs as she tried to sit. Because of the angle of the seats and her awkward position, she wasn't able to gain enough leverage to heave herself out of the carriage.

He grabbed one of her ankles, and she shrieked, "Unhand me, you... you reprobate!"

Startled, he stepped back. "Just trying to help, ma'am."

"I don't need your help," she muttered, along with a few mumbled curses.

"As you wish." He smothered a grin at her angsty tone. An elaborate hat covered her face, so he couldn't get a good look, but what he did see was something to whistle at.

She continued to struggle in the carriage, trying unsuccessfully for a few minutes before finally stopping. She huffed and then sighed. "Well, don't just stand there. Help me out, would you?"

"Don't want to overstep, ma'am." He certainly didn't want to catch more of her ire.

"You aren't overstepping. Just get over here and help." Her irritated tone conveyed her inability to do it herself.

"But you said you didn't need my help."

"Forget what I said."

"Oh no, ma'am. You made it quite clear you could get out on your own." He was being obstinate, but the women in town had been increasingly disagreeable of late. One of those famous suffragettes had descended on Helena just one month ago, and since then, women had been strutting around town, holding signs and exclaiming they didn't need a man, that they needed equal rights, and that anything a man could do, they could do as well.

Not that he disagreed with 'em, but if you tried to hold a door open for one, you likely took your life in your hands due to how irritated they became over simple gentleman gestures. He'd been taught to do things proper like and wasn't sure what to do with the women who thought his behavior was unseemly.

"Humph." She unsuccessfully tried once again to climb out of the carriage, but the angle made it impossible. Finally, she sighed and pushed her hat out of the way. "Would you be so kind as to help me out of the carriage?"

Grinning, he stepped forward. He'd made her suffer long enough. "I'd be happy to."

With that, he reached in and grabbed her tiny waist, lifting her effortlessly up and out of the carriage. Her black hair, the color of the midnight sky, tumbled down her back. As he helped her gain her footing, her trim body slid against his until her feet hit the ground. She used his shoulders for leverage, and for a brief moment, he stared into her silvery blue eyes.

She sighed breathlessly, and ungentlemanly urges coursed through his body. He hadn't held a woman in his arms in years, much less one as lovely as her. She reminded him of someone, and it tickled the back of his brain, but the conscious part of him had just been replaced with a fiery round of lust, and all he could think about was kissing her plump pink lips.

She stared at him for a moment before trying to ease away, but he hadn't released her waist. He didn't want to, but common sense prevailed, and he regretfully let go, retreating to give her room. He had been raised to be a gentleman, and his ma would've slapped him upside the head if he had done anything to besmirch her honor.

"Thank you." Her voice certainly didn't scream sincerity.

"My pleasure, ma'am. Are you hurt?"

"What? Oh, no, I'm fine." She yanked off her hat to push back the locks of hair that had fallen across her forehead.

"Are you sure about that? The carriage hit the ground mighty hard."

"I *said* I was fine." She glared at him. Something akin to fury flashed in her eyes.

Well, all righty then. She's a feisty one.

"Didn't mean to imply anything, just wanted to make sure you weren't hurt. I'd hate not to call the doc to get you some help if you were injured."

"Why is it that men always assume we aren't all right if there's been an accident? If we say we're fine, then we're fine." She slapped her hat against her thigh and then rested her hands on her hips. Her elaborate hat was filled with feathers, ribbons, and bows that bulged out from the rim and rested next to her as though she had a baby on her hip.

"I assumed nothing, ma'am." Although she was right. He had.

"Didn't you? And quit calling me ma'am. I'm not my mother."

"Yes, ma'am."

She glared at him, annoyance flashing from her eyes. He wanted to chuckle, but her gaze made it abundantly clear that that would be a dangerous idea. The woman didn't appear to appreciate his humor.

"Hmmph." She then dangled her hat on the nearest fence post, turned away, lifted her thick black hair, quickly twisted it, and shoved a few pins inside to keep it in place. Her skirt had torn and was hanging haphazardly from her waist, but she didn't seem to notice, and he wasn't sure he wanted to tell her. The gentleman in him knew he should say something, but she definitely wasn't receptive to him. She placed her hands on her hips and surveyed the scene in front of her.

Before he could stop her, she bent, pulled the back of her skirt through her legs, and tucked it into the waist, which only tore the back of her skirt farther. The rip reverberated through the air and startled her. She groaned, looked behind her, and tried to assess the damage.

"Your skirt's torn, ma'am."

"Well, why didn't you say something? And I said, quit calling me ma'am."

He shoved his hands into his pockets and rocked back on his heels. "Didn't think it was my place to tell you, as you appear to be quite independent. My ma always told me to treat women with respect, ma'am." He was saying ma'am just to aggravate her, and it was certainly working.

He could see the consternation in her blue eyes as she struggled with how to respond. A blush crept up her neck and into her cheeks. She tightened her hands into fists and was likely trying to decide if she wanted to punch him in the nose.

She glared at him and then reached behind her, trying to tuck in the ripped section of her skirt into her waistband as best as she could, but as she struggled with the angle, she only made it worse.

"Ma'am, if you'll let me."

She looked at him for a long moment before nodding. Trying to hold back his laughter, he reached for her small waist, pulled up the edges, and tugged it into her belt, so it didn't gape behind her. Doing the best he could with what he had to work with, he finally got it in place so that her underclothing wasn't privy to the entire world. He wanted to be the only man to see her that way, and he was going to do his best to see that happen.

Marie was horrified. What started as a bright and hopeful day had turned disastrous. She had begun the day excited about the suffragist meeting, but it hadn't ended as planned. After another disappointing meeting with her suffragist sisters and the lackluster response they were getting, her carriage had careened uncontrollably down the road until it crashed in front of the smithy. Then, to make matters worse, she hadn't been able to maneuver herself out of the carriage without *his* help.

What aggravated her more than the failed meeting was the fact that she had to ask a man for assistance. She was an independent woman who didn't need a man for any reason, except when she was in that unfortunate position, apparently. She hadn't had the arm strength to push herself out of the carriage.

The man had broad shoulders and a scruffy beard but the darkest of brown eyes. They twinkled as if he were trying hard not to laugh at her predicament. If she hadn't been so frustrated with the events earlier, she might have been more inclined to laugh. The situation was quite hilarious, but the events of the morning were nothing to laugh about, and she was in a foul mood.

Marie tried to glare at him, but a smile lifted the corners of his mouth, and it brightened his face. It was unfortunate that his beard covered his chin and cheeks. She wouldn't mind seeing what the line of his jaw looked like under all that black hair. Was it chiseled? Were his cheeks pronounced? Were his lips full or thin?

Stop!

She wasn't interested in men and hadn't been for years. They served no purpose other than to ensure women didn't have equal rights. In fact, having a husband was tantamount to having a prison sentence. They controlled everything.

Some women had some say in their marriages, such as Eloisa Scranton and Greta VanKleef. Their husbands were prominent supporters of women's rights, but they were the exception. Many women trying to join the fight had husbands who were adamantly against their participation, and as such, they hadn't gained as much traction as Marie would've liked. At the rate they were going, it would take years before Montana granted women the right to vote, and she didn't want to wait that long. She wanted it to happen now, but she didn't have that much control.

She pulled on the lapels of her jacket and straightened it as best she could. Good manners dictated she be courteous for the help he had offered, but a small part of her was infuriated that he had offered before she had asked. Why men always assumed women were helpless was a question that haunted her at night.

"Thank you, Mr...."

"Michael Seymour, ma'am."

He was one of the Seymour brothers. She thought he'd looked familiar, but his scruffy beard hid his appearance, and she hadn't recognized him. Marie had only met him once, the year before, when his brother Luke had found himself in a bit of a pickle. Luke and her brother, Walter, had been embroiled in quite a mess before things had thankfully resolved themselves without too much bloodshed, although if she remembered correctly, he had been responsible for saving his brother's life.

"Ma'am," he said again.

Marie was flabbergasted that it was him, but she also bristled at his continued insistence on calling her ma'am. She had already mentioned more than once that she preferred not to be called ma'am, but he was being stubborn and insolent.

As she gazed at him, she wondered if he wasn't doing it just because she didn't want him to. She remembered Luke saying on more than one occasion that his brother was the jovial one in the family, always making jokes and trying to lighten any heavy or somber mood. Was this his attempt at poor humor?

"You need to quit calling me ma'am."

"Certainly, Miss...?"

She ignored him and stared at the carnage of her carriage. Some men had taken Princess and Rufus in hand and were calming them, but it was obvious her unsettled horses wanted to flee if given half the chance.

Marie didn't understand what had caused the accident, but she had felt something snap, and it'd startled the horses enough that they had bolted unexpectedly. Marie had tried to stop them, but no amount of pulling on the reins or yelling had stopped their erratic, uncontrollable running.

It hadn't taken long before Marie had hung on for dear life, praying no one would get hurt as the horses dragged the broken carriage and Marie behind them. Eventually, a wheel must have hit a rut, causing it to flip on its side before it careened to a crashing halt. She had been thrown forward into the cavity of the carriage, luckily staying inside. She had tried to protect herself, but she'd still found herself stuck with her head, arms, and chest at the bottom and waving her legs in the air. It had been the most uncomfortable position, but she'd been alive and spared any lasting harm.

Marie shuddered at the thought of what could have happened. She wasn't necessarily concerned with herself, but if any children had been maimed or killed by the scared horses, she wouldn't have been able to live with herself.

But she was alive with intact limbs and no obvious injuries as far as she could tell. Walter wouldn't be too pleased if he found out she had ruined his best carriage, but it certainly wasn't any of her doing. She hadn't caused the accident and hadn't even been going very fast, but that would be of little concern to her brother if he thought she had been reckless.

Living with her older brother had its advantages, but his over-protective behavior was trying. If he thought any misdeed had occurred, there was no telling his reaction. He'd likely try to keep her from continuing with the suffragists, but she was determined that no one and nothing would stop her until the women in Montana could cast their vote. Until then, nothing could stop her from doing what she was destined to accomplish.

Approaching the fallen carriage, she took stock of the damage. One wheel lay twenty feet away, in several pieces. The carriage itself was on its side, just a mere foot or two from the open doors of the flaming forge in the blacksmith's shop.

She grasped the side of the carriage and pulled at it, making no progress, when muscular male arms appeared next to hers and pulled. She wanted to protest, but as Michael intervened, she surmised she couldn't do this alone, although she would never admit it.

Together, they righted the carriage, even though it leaned

precariously without the one wheel, and it appeared the other wasn't in better shape. One thing was clear, however: there was no way she was going to take it home tonight. She'd have to come up with a plausible excuse as to why Walter's carriage was at the livery.

She guessed it was sheer luck that the carriage had crashed to a halt in front of the Thundering Sunset Smithy and Livery. Michael was just the person to fix her carriage, and she'd have to hope he would.

"Your carriage is gonna need some work," Michael said.

"Yes," she muttered. "That's clearly obvious. I'm glad your eyesight hasn't been damaged." He was either really smart or a know-it-all. Neither one was something she wanted to deal with today.

"If you'd like, I can pull it into the back of my barn and see if I can fix it."

"How soon until the repairs are done?"

He stroked his scruffy beard and then walked around it, clearly examining what he was dealing with. When he came around to her side, he said, "It'll probably take me at least a week."

"A week?" She muttered a curse word under her breath. She couldn't hide this from her brother for that many days. There would be too many questions, and she wasn't an expert at lying. In fact, most times, if she tried, she failed. It was better, to be honest.

Michael lifted an eyebrow. "Both wheels sustained damage. The one that's still attached looks to be in decent shape, just need to make sure the spokes aren't broken. The other one, however, is completely useless. I'll need to build a new one." He knelt in front of it and pointed to a spot on the axle. "The axle's broken as well."

"Ugh, I don't need this today. Is there any chance you can fix it any faster?" She had no other mode of transportation. Princess and Rufus were nothing more than carriage horses, and she had never learned to properly ride either. She also had multiple meetings this week, and it would only complicate matters if she didn't have a carriage.

Michael stared at her over his shoulder for a long moment, shook his head, and stood, bracing his hands against his knees. "I've got carriages for rent if you need one."

"Yes, that should work."

"Follow me inside, and we can get the paperwork started. I'll hitch up a buggy, but I'm not sure your horses should pull it. They're both still pretty agitated."

She glanced over at them and had to smother another sigh of frustration. "Yes, they are. Do you have others?"

"Yes, ma'am." He smirked. "I do own a livery and have a few around. I'll hitch up one and tie yours to the rear. Is your husband--"

"I don't have a husband," she snapped, jutting her jaw. Of course, he'd ask if she had a husband.

He looked at her for a moment, the beginnings of another charming smile turning up his lips. "Sorry to hear that. Is there someone I should send for? To make sure you get home safely, that is?"

"No, I'll be perfectly fine on my own." She marched inside the smithy.

As she walked away, she heard him murmur, "Oh, I'm sure you will."

Two

Michael secured the lock. Looking up at the sign, he smiled. *Thundering Sunset Smithy and Livery, proprietor Michael Seymour.* He was carrying on the tradition of naming his place after their family ranch, Thundering Mountain. Their mother had started it, and he and his siblings were all following suit.

Slapping the door, he turned and headed toward the diner. The unexpected carriage accident had made him late. When he discovered it was Marie, Walter's sister, he'd been gobsmacked. She'd been forced to tell him her name before he let her rent one of his buggies. Irritation had lined her lips until he explained she was like any other customer. If she wanted what he offered, then her name and where she lived were required before he let any horses or carriages out of his sight.

As soon as she repeated her name through pursed lips, he'd immediately realized who she was. He thought he'd recognized her, but the last time he'd seen her was when she'd stood next to Louisa as she pledged to marry his brother almost a year ago. He'd been reeling from everything that had happened and had been unlike himself that day and for months after.

Marie's brother had been invaluable in helping to end the

woman who had ruined their family, and they were indebted to him. Without Walter's aid, Connie would have escaped, and things could have turned out much differently. Seeing Luke helpless with Connie holding a gun aimed straight at him was something Michael would never forget.

Hurrying down the dirt road, he dodged men and women alike, murmuring apologies when he might've brushed past them too abruptly. Ben wouldn't mind that he was late, but he hated making him wait on account of him. His smithy was only a few blocks from Mimi's Diner, and he would get there in a few minutes.

Jogging up the path to the diner, he grinned when he saw Ben sitting casually on a wooden chair as though he had nothing better to do. His brother was the head of their family and worked hard to keep them intact. They'd had a rough few years, but they were growing stronger as a family unit, and for that, he was appreciative.

"Ben. Sorry I'm late. Took longer than I expected."

Ben stood, holding his hat in his hand. "That's all right. I just got here, as a matter of fact. No harm done."

"I'm mighty hungry." Michael's belly grumbled at that exact moment. He'd built up an appetite after the afternoon's excitement.

"If you can wait a bit longer, we might have a better time somewhere else."

"Oh, and where's that?" Michael raised an eyebrow.

"I ran into Walter. Ever since Luke and Louisa left, he's been itching to hear how they've been doing. He's having friends over and thought we might care to join them."

Michael grinned. "Will his sister be there?" He avoided looking at Ben. He was astute enough to wonder why Michael was asking, and if he saw Michael's face, he'd be even more curious.

"I'd imagine so," Ben said. "Why are you asking?"

"No reason." He was lying through his teeth, as he wasn't sure

Marie would be pleased to see him, but he wanted to see her again, especially after she had left in such a huff.

Ten minutes later, they arrived at Walter's place. Lights blazed in every room, and loud music and laughter boomed. While the windows were closed tightly to keep out the cold winter air, the occupants inside were having a good time, and joyful sounds oozed from the cracks in the walls.

They knocked, and Walter ushered them in. A rush of warm air enveloped them as they stepped into the foyer.

"Ben, Michael. I'm glad you're here. Come in, come in." Walter's cheeks were red, and there was a merry twinkle in his eyes. He was a tall man with black hair, almost as dark as Marie's. He held a glass of whiskey in his hand and appeared to have had a few drinks already. "We need to get you both a drink right quick."

Michael chuckled under his breath. Clearly, Walter was having a good time, and as evidenced by the people loudly singing, it appeared others were having an equally good time.

They followed Walter to his large parlor on the right, where he wove through the throngs of people inside and to a high table laden with decanters of liquors and tasty treats. The sweet smell of sugar mixed with warm savory bacon made Michael's mouth water, but first, he wanted to find Marie. He hadn't seen his buggy and horse, but they could've been in the barn behind the house.

He wished she would've let him get a doctor to look her over, but she'd insisted she was fine and had been bristly when he suggested it. Michael would've followed her home, but because he'd continued to call her ma'am, he might have angered her far more than he realized. He was the jokester in his family, and getting her riled up had tickled something deep within him. He normally wouldn't have joked with someone he didn't know, but he couldn't stop.

"I expected you earlier." Walter handed them each a glass of amber whiskey.

"It was my fault. There was a snag at the livery and…"

Marie had walked into the room. She had changed and didn't look as though she'd been in a serious accident. She was in a white blouse and a dark blue skirt that hugged her hips and shimmered when she moved. Her cheeks were pink, and she'd pinned her black hair off her neck, showcasing her long neck.

Heat crawled up his neck. He was unsettled. She was perhaps the prettiest woman he had ever laid eyes on. He vaguely remembered her from Luke's wedding, but he'd been distracted. He wished he had noticed.

Marie was a spitfire, full of energy and gumption. She intrigued him far more than anyone else he'd ever met. Probably more than she should have after meeting with her only a few times, but watching her stirred his blood.

She raised her eyes, and their gazes met. She frowned, sending him an evil glare as though he shouldn't be there, but he couldn't take his eyes off her. While he teased her earlier that day, he had been distracted by the accident, and she hadn't given him much of a chance to observe her. Now, he had an unobstructed view, and he was shell-shocked and fascinated.

"And what?" Walter asked.

Michael swung his gaze back to Walter and stared at him, stupefied. He couldn't recall what Walter had said. He wasn't typically distracted, but clearly, he was more discomfited than normal, especially standing in front of Marie's brother.

He swallowed hard, hoping Walter hadn't noticed his reaction to Marie. "Not sure I understand."

"Whatever happened earlier must've addled your brain. Might want to take a sip or two of that whiskey"--Walter nodded toward the glass of whiskey in Michael's hand--"and then get yourself something to eat if you can't remember."

Michael chuckled to hide his confusion. It was as though every coherent thought he'd ever had had disappeared in the blink of an eye. Marie's gaze had undone him, and he didn't know why. She hadn't done a thing but walk into the room, but she stripped him bare with one look from her silvery blue eyes.

Ben nudged him, and the glass of whiskey slipped from his fingers and shattered on the wooden floor.

"Shit!" He stared in dismay at the mess he'd made.

The sounds in the room stilled. The laughter and music ground to a halt, and all eyes swung to him. Embarrassed, he dropped to his haunches to pick up the broken pieces of glass, muttering to himself. He'd just compounded his foolishness, and staring at her like a lovesick calf would not impress her.

The rustle of dark blue silk appeared in his peripheral view. Marie came to his rescue, which further humiliated him. Avoiding her gaze, he continued to pick up the broken pieces of glass, trying not to cut his fingers but was unsuccessful. Blood oozed from a long gash across his palm, but he'd ignore it. The last thing he needed was for anyone to notice that he'd hurt himself like a child.

A white handkerchief fluttered next to him. A moment later, the glass was removed from his fingers, placed into a wicker basket, and long, soft fingers wrapped the cloth around his palm.

"If you wanted to hurt yourself, Michael," Marie murmured, "I could recommend a few other ways that are less dramatic... Like a carriage accident, for example."

He coughed to hide the sheepish chuckles that bubbled inside him. She'd been adamant earlier that she didn't want her brother to know what had occurred, so he was surprised she'd mentioned it.

"Let's get that tended to." She held his hand with the handkerchief pressed closed and pulled him to stand.

He followed her lead and noticed Walter had disappeared. The guests in the room returned to their revelry as though nothing had occurred. To him, though, the air had been sucked out of the room. He was flabbergasted, and his tongue was stuck to the roof of his mouth.

Ben stood to the side, a smirk on his lips. He raised his glass and winked at him. Before Michael could tell his brother there was nothing to be smirking about, Marie led him to the kitchen. Her gait was strong and determined, which was remarkable considering how the skirt of her dress hugged her hips and legs. Before he had any other amorous thoughts, she released his hand, burst through the kitchen door, yanked out a chair, and pointed to it.

"Sit." Her tone brokered no argument.

He didn't think his tongue would work properly enough to argue with her, so he did as she bid and dropped heavily into the chair. He looked at his hand and muttered a curse. The once-white handkerchief was coated in dark red blood. He was bleeding profusely, which might explain why he was dizzy.

Michael leaned up against the table, trying to clear the fuzziness from his vision. *What's happening to me?* He watched the blood drip from his palm to the table, the spot growing with alarming speed. He couldn't possibly have cut himself that badly with the glass.

He swayed in the chair.

"Whoa, there, big boy." Marie grasped him by the shoulders and held him steady against the back of the chair. She then reached for his hand, pulled it up high, and wrapped another cloth around it tightly. "I think we need to stop that blood flow. You must've cut yourself worse than it appeared."

He tried to loosen his tongue, but it seemed permanently rooted to the top of his mouth.

"Cat got your tongue there?" She scooted around, still holding his hand up high.

Michael fought to keep his eyes open. He wanted to close them and take a nap, but if he did that, he wouldn't be able to gaze into her lovely eyes. He could get lost and stare into them all day, every day if she let him.

Marie clucked, narrowing her eyebrows. "Let's get you something to eat and drink. Maybe that'll help, as I'm gonna venture that you haven't eaten, and the blood loss is affecting you more than it should."

He finally unstuck his tongue. "I think maybe you're right."

"Can you hold your hand in the air while I grab you something to eat?"

He nodded. "Yes, I can manage it." He sure hoped he could, as he didn't want to look like a complete fool in front of the woman he was determined to marry.

Wait, what am I thinking? Have I completely lost all leave of my senses?

Marie looked at him carefully and then moved away, brushing her skirts against his leg as she released his hand. He held it up high, which likely gave her the assurances that he wouldn't collapse at her feet, at least not yet.

He did as she bade, keeping his throbbing hand high. Blood wasn't dripping any longer. Michael didn't know if that was because she had put another piece of cloth around it or if holding it above his head was staunching the blood flow. Either way, he didn't feel quite as woozy as he had just minutes before.

Michael listened carefully as she worked behind him. He wanted to turn and stare at her but feared she believed he was an imbecile of the first degree who couldn't handle blood loss. A moment later, she slapped a plate full of food and a tall glass of water in front of him.

She stood next to him with her hands on her hips. "Well, are you going to stare at it, or are you going to eat it?" He dropped his hand, but she snatched it back and held it in place. "No, stop! You can't drop your hand until the bleeding has stopped."

He looked at the food and then at his hand, his right hand, the one he used to eat. "Well, ma'am--"

"Stop calling me ma'am," she snapped. "My name is Marie. If you're going to call me something, then use my given name."

"Yes, ma"--" He swallowed back the rest of the word when he saw her eyes narrowed further. "I mean, yes, Marie."

She nodded, softening her gaze. "Now, eat."

"I would," he said, "but I eat with my right hand."

"Then use your right hand."

"Marie, I would, except that's the one that's bleeding."

"Oh!" Her eyes widened, and a soft smile lined her lips, lessening the glare she'd been sending his way. "I guess that would be a problem."

She pulled his hand to her chest. Carefully unwrapping the cloth that had been keeping the blood from dripping all over her table and floors, she examined it. She furrowed her eyebrows as she concentrated before pushing at the wound. He winced. While it wasn't the worst injury, it did sting when she poked at it.

"The bleeding appears to have stopped, but you're going to need a couple of stitches if I were to hazard a guess."

"All right," he said. "I kind of figured as much from how I was feeling, or rather how I *am* feeling." Another wave of dizziness surged through him, and with his good hand, he gripped the table hard to get his bearings. He lifted his head a moment later and caught the look of concern on Marie's face. "I'll be fine."

When Michael pushed to stand, she muttered something under her breath and stopped him by placing her hand on his shoulder. "I don't think so, big boy. You're not going anywhere."

"I ain't gonna get those stitches sitting here. I need a doctor, you said so yourself."

She bristled with consternation. "I didn't say you needed a doctor. I *said*"--she dragged out the word as if he were a toddler who needed instruction--"you needed stitches."

"And that usually entails getting myself a doctor unless you think I'm capable of sewing it up myself?" Dizziness threatened to overwhelm him once again, but he pushed through, shook his head, and looked back at Marie.

"You're dizzy, aren't you?"

"Why would you ask me that?" He smiled like a besotted fool.

"Because you're gripping the table like it's the only thing

holding you up. If you aren't careful, I'm afraid you might rip the table in half as hard as your fingers are digging into it."

He slowly released his fingers, although he was sure that if he did, he'd likely fall over. The dizziness had only intensified.

"Why don't you drink this?" She held a cup of steaming coffee.

He took a whiff and smiled. "That smells like more than just coffee." He took the cup with his left hand, as awkward as it was, and took a drink. It wasn't too hot and tasted good, especially with the extra kick of whiskey Marie had added.

"Not so fast, big boy." Marie removed the cup from his hand and replaced it with a piece of buttered bread. "Why don't you take a bite of this?"

The bread was warm, and the butter was soft and creamy. His mouth watered, and he eagerly took it. He chewed softly, not wanting to choke, even though he wanted to devour it. Michael knew better than to eat too quickly, especially as unsteady as he was.

After he'd eaten the piece of bread, he used his good hand to wipe his face. His injured one was still held fast in Marie's arms.

"Are you going to continue to examine my hand?"

"What?" She raised her head.

"My hand," he said. "You're peering at it as though it's going to fall off or something."

She blushed and dropped it. Not expecting her to let go, he immediately missed her touch. Placing his injured hand on the table, he looked at it and grimaced. It was a nasty cut, which he shouldn't be surprised considering he had bled like a butchered pig. One piece of glass must've had quite a sharp edge.

"So about those stitches," he said. "I guess I should find myself a doctor."

Marie brushed a stray black hair behind her ear. "You don't need to do that."

"And why not?" He tilted his head to the side. "You said I needed stitches."

"And you do, big boy." A smirk lined her lips.

"Big boy?" He had heard her say it a few times, but it seemed she was saying it on purpose, as though to irritate him. She was doing to him what he'd done to her, and he quivered with anticipation. She was trying not to like him, but he was pushing past her defenses.

"Don't go anywhere. I'll be right back." She opened the kitchen door and disappeared, leaving him wondering what she was up to but excited to see what she'd return with.

Three

An hour later, Marie had sewn a couple of stitches into Michael's palm. She wasn't a doctor or a seamstress, but she could put a few rudimentary stitches in an open wound. She had sewn a few of Walter's injuries over the years, especially when he got himself mixed up in a few scrapes with his endless investigations for his newspaper. He was like a bear after a juicy fish. He didn't stop until he satisfied his appetite.

Michael had been stoic and hadn't moved a muscle as she pushed the needle through his skin. It had to hurt, as the palm was sensitive, but he didn't utter a sound. Once she finished, she rubbed a balm she kept for wounds on it, wrapped it in a clean strip of cotton, and tied it off.

"There, that should do it, big boy."

Laughing irritation flashed in his eyes, something akin to earlier when he kept calling her ma'am. She hadn't planned on teasing him or giving him the same treatment, but when it slipped off her tongue, she decided it fit. He deserved it after not stopping after she had asked not once but many times.

"Thank you for taking care of my hand." He wiped the sweat

from his forehead. That was the only sign that her ministrations had bothered him.

"It was the least I could do, considering you kept quiet about the accident and didn't tell Walter."

"Oh, you haven't told him?" Michael said.

"No." She picked up her medical supplies and placed them next to the water pump. She would store them later. "And I'd like to keep it that way."

"Why?" Michael leaned back in his chair, almost relaxing now that his medical emergency had eased, although to call it an emergency was likely an exaggeration. The man had lost quite a bit of blood, but once he had something to eat, his energy seemed to return.

"I'd just rather Walter didn't know about all my exploits."

"And what exploit have you gotten yourself into now?" Walter said, stepping into the kitchen.

Marie abruptly turned toward the door and groaned. "Do you always have to sneak up on me like that?"

Walter held up his hands in mock surrender. "Don't try to deflect, sister dear. Care to tell me what happened?"

"Not particularly." Marie swung back to the counter, effectively dismissing her brother. She picked up the medical supplies and decided they should be returned now instead of later. Perhaps if she disappeared fast enough, Walter wouldn't question her.

"Marie, I know about the accident."

She braced her fingers against the counter and counted to ten before she faced her brother. Depending on what he'd heard would decide whether or not he would let her continue with her suffragist cause. He'd wanted her to stop months ago, but she'd been adamant that she wouldn't.

She placed her hand on Walter's arm. "Nothing you need to worry about."

"When you say something like that, then I need to worry. Mind telling me what happened?" He placed his hip against the kitchen counter. His eyes were red-rimmed, and sweat beaded along his brow. It was clear he'd had a lot to drink, but he was coherent enough to question her.

"Just a minor mishap with the carriage this afternoon." She waved to Michael sitting at the table, whose smirk was enough to irk her to no end. With any luck, he'd keep his mouth shut with whatever story she decided to tell Walter. "Well, he was kind enough to offer to repair the carriage."

"What kind of mishap?" Walter asked again, but Marie ignored him and turned back to Michael.

"I do appreciate Michael's willingness to take on the necessary repairs from that minor accident."

Michael arched his brow and then carefully eyed her as though searching for what she was really up to. She'd likely have to do a bunch of explaining once her brother was appeased.

"Of course, ma'am. It was my pleasure," Michael drawled, an undertone to his voice that sent shivers up her spine.

He'd called her ma'am once again, and the urge to strangle him filled her, but if she wanted him to keep quiet, she had to keep her hands to her sides.

"Walter, can you check on our guests and take out this plate of cookies?" Maybe if she deflected and convinced Walter to attend to his guests, he'd quit questioning her. "I've been busy helping him with his injured hand, and I'm afraid we might've run out of food." Marie handed him a platter of cookies from the counter before he could answer and gently pushed his arm in encouragement.

Startled, he looked at the plate and nodded. He clearly wanted to say more, but good manners dictated that he do as his sister bid and not argue with her in front of their injured guest.

After Walter left the kitchen, Marie grabbed Michael's good arm and not so gently yanked him out of his chair and pulled him into the servants' hallway. Not that they had servants, but the house had been built by a family with servants, so there were hallways that most never saw. They'd come in handy on occasion, and she'd be able to speak to Michael in relative privacy.

Once they were hidden in a dark hallway, a lone gas lamp lent the only light. "What happened this morning stays between us. Do you understand?"

Michael startled at her tone. "We hardly know one another, so it isn't right for me to keep your secrets."

"It is if I tell you to do so." She poked him in the chest and regretted it when she knocked his hand on accident.

He grimaced but didn't remark on her hurting him, even if it was a relative accident. "I don't know about that. We don't know each other well enough."

"You don't have to in order to keep quiet."

Was he really going to be this difficult?

"I certainly would like to get to know you better." He lifted an eyebrow and had a serious and thoughtful gaze.

She was shocked. "I..." This was not what she expected him to say.

"In fact, would you accompany me on a carriage ride tomorrow afternoon? We can become friends, and then it would be appropriate for me to keep your secrets."

Heat crawled up her neck. "I don't have any secrets."

"Oh, you do. If you didn't, you wouldn't have stopped me from telling your brother what really happened this morning."

"Nothing happened this morning." She tried to scoff away his words, but she was only proving his point instead.

"You had a carriage accident, so something *did* happen." He ran his good hand through his thick brown hair, the curls having fallen across his brows.

"A minor accident. Nothing to be concerned with."

"If it was nothing to be concerned with, then why did you drag me into this dark hallway?" He waved his good hand in the air.

"Arghh." If only he hadn't come to Walter's party tonight, she could have likely come up with a good story that her brother would've believed, and he would have never looked for the truth. She muttered obscenities under her breath. She was likely kidding herself. Walter sniffed out stories daily. If he caught any whiff of something amiss, he would've endlessly questioned her until he got the answers he sought.

"Michael." She dropped the *big boy* and tried to be serious. He appeared to be astute, but maybe she could play on his sympathies, although she wasn't completely sure he would fall for it. "I don't want to worry my brother. Can you understand that?" She brushed her fingers against his arm. She was never good at flirting with men, but desperate times called for desperate measures.

He raised his gaze. "Yes, I can."

"Then you have to understand that he doesn't need to worry."

"No," he said.

She yanked her hand away and stomped her foot in frustration. He chuckled.

"This isn't funny," she muttered.

Michael frowned. "You're right, it isn't, but since you're trying to hide what happened from your brother, I wonder if something more serious is going on. That's what concerns me."

"You don't need to be concerned." She appreciated his sentiment, but she didn't know him, she didn't trust him, and she didn't need his help.

"Maybe you do."

"I don't."

He rubbed his chin. "Then what are you suggesting?"

She breathed a sigh of relief. Perhaps he would be reasonable. "Let me tell Walter what he needs to know. He believes I should stay home, get married, and have a passel of children. I want something more."

Michael looked around the small hallway and walked a few steps away before slowly turning around to face her. "No, this won't work for me. If something were to happen to you, then I'd be responsible. I already have the weight of death on my shoulders, and I'm not going to add to that."

She started to respond, to tell him he wouldn't be responsible, but she caught the tortured look in his eyes. The look disappeared almost as quickly as it appeared. Marie wasn't completely sure she saw it, but she couldn't in good conscience make light of it. She wasn't that insensitive, no matter how much Walter thought she was.

"How about we get to know one another?" Michael said.

His change in subject made her head spin. "And what would that accomplish exactly?"

He grinned, a twinkle in his dark brown eyes. "Well, it would satisfy my curiosity and"--the twinkle diminished and was replaced by something more serious and somber--"since you're refusing to tell your brother what you know about your accident, then I feel it's only right that I protect you."

"I do not need you to protect me." Marie's eyes flashed with anger and irritation.

Michael was likely jumping into a pile of horse manure, but he felt a duty toward this woman. He wasn't willing to walk away. "I already did it once today, seems only right that I continue to do it."

"You did not save me."

"Oh, I most certainly did. The way your legs were flapping there in the wind for all the world to see, you definitely needed rescuing."

Her mouth dropped open. "I was not flapping in the wind."

"Oh, you were, and then you couldn't get out, which is to be expected. You, of course, being a woman of delicate sensibilities." He was exaggerating, but he enjoyed watching her flush. It brightened her cheeks and made her even more becoming.

"Delicate sensibilities." Her voice grew loud, and she pounded her fist into her palm. "How dare you say――"

"It appears you're getting flushed. Perhaps you need to sit." He reached for her elbow, but she slapped him away.

"I don't know what you're thinking or doing, but I am not a delicate woman. I certainly don't need a man to help me sit."

In her haste and frustration, she tripped. Michael immediately saw what was happening, and before she could do or say anything, he grabbed her around the waist and stopped her fall. Her screech was muffled when her face hit his chest.

He had never tried to antagonize a woman as much as he was antagonizing her, but it was so much fun seeing her frustrated. It was obvious she was one of those independent women who didn't think she needed help and probably thought she could do everything on her own. While he appreciated their independence, sometimes having a man around wasn't exactly awful.

She pushed at him. "Let me go this instant."

"I think you're traumatized by today's activities. It's pretty obvious you've lost your balance. Stumbling around, confused. I'd hate for you to fall and conk your head on something."

"I didn't stumble. I tripped. There is a big difference." She glared at him.

Eager to see what more she would say, he said, "Tripped on what?"

"There was a…" She stopped as if trying to remember what she might have tripped over.

"See, it's clear you're confused. You're not even sure what you might or might not have tripped over."

"I'm not confused."

"And you're awfully flushed. Do you feel faint?" He brushed his good hand against her forehead, but she swatted it away.

"Faint," she said. "What in the world are you blathering on about?"

He looked down into her brilliant blue eyes. "Yes, I can see you're about to faint. I should get you a glass of water. Oh, no, I can't do that. I need to stay to catch you if you were to fall again."

"I..."

"Yes, ma'am."

"Quit calling me ma'am," she snarled.

"Now, now. Getting upset won't help. You need to rest. Perhaps I should take you up to your bedroom." As soon as he said the words, he cringed. He sounded like a reprobate, but he couldn't seem to stop himself, especially since she had quit fighting him and was nestled in his arms. He hadn't even noticed the pain in his hand when he held such a spitfire.

"You won't take me up to my bedroom."

"You're absolutely correct. That is completely inappropriate. You shouldn't be left alone with a man. We need a chaperone." He looked over his shoulder as though looking for one.

"I don't need to be chaperoned."

"Clearly confused. Of course, you need a chaperone. A young lady such as yourself should never be left alone with a man unless he is her husband."

"I decide who and where I can be left alone with a man. If I want to be alone with you, then I could do so."

Michael tilted his head, a grin threatening to cross his lips. Did she realize what she had just said?

He had the sudden urge to kiss her. Shock or anticipation was written all over her face, but before he could kiss her, she smacked him across his cheek. Her jaw was clenched, but a sparkle lit up her blue eyes.

Then, before he could stop her, she shoved him away and fell to the ground. Her skirts tangled around her legs.

"Are you all right?" He reached to help her, but she slapped his hands away.

"Do not touch me. How dare you! I should scream. Walter will have your head for this."

He had gone too far. The game he was playing was too much.

It was one he shouldn't have started. He could have hurt her, and that wasn't the man he wanted to be.

Marie was furious. She rolled over and scrambled to stand.

"Never touch me again." She swatted at her skirts, anything to hide her frustration. He pushed her buttons, made her say things in anger, and had caused her to humiliate herself. She moved a few steps away, but he grabbed her arm. She wrenched away and glared at him. "I said, do not touch me!"

"Marie--"

"Oh, so now you can call me by my name."

"I'm sorry. I didn't mean for things to escalate this far." He rubbed the back of his neck and leaned against the wall.

"Right," she drawled, anger dripping from her tone. "Because men never--"

"I'm not most men," he spat.

"I certainly don't know that, and after that, I..." She shook her head. "If you don't mind, I need to return to the party before Walter realizes I've been gone too long."

Walter already had an inkling she wasn't telling him everything, and if she disappeared for a long period, there was no telling what he would do in the light of day. She had miscalculated and never should have brought him into the darkened servants' hallway.

"You don't want to do that."

Aggravated, she glowered at him. "And why don't I want to?"

"Because you look as though you've been ravished. If you don't want to return to the party looking like you've had a romp in the woods, you might want to stop and let me help you."

Startled, she stopped. Her blouse had come untucked from her skirt, and her hair hung in clumps, having fallen from its pins. She was mortified. Her nervous hands went to her hair, then to her waistband, then to her skirt. She couldn't go back looking like this. Walter would definitely lock her up and throw away the key if her honor had been besmirched, as antiquated as that thought might be. She still had to live with him and didn't want to upset him unnecessarily.

Michael's hands reached for hers and held them. She tried to pull away, but he held tight. Why was he being this way?

"Let me go!" she growled.

"I will, but you need to take a deep breath."

"Don't tell me what to do." She tried to rip away, but he held firm. Anger pulsated inside of her like a drum, growing with intensity each passing second.

"I'm not telling you what to do, but you're flustered. Since most of this is my fault, I'm going to help."

"I don't need your help." His chivalry was beyond frustrating.

"You do."

"But--"

"Let me help, Marie, please." His voice was contrite.

Perhaps he had realized he had gone too far, but before she could protest, he released her hands, grasped her around the waist, lifted her off the ground, and flipped her around. He gently took her hair, pulled out the remaining hairpins, and deftly twisted it, tucked it, and pinned it up in moments. He seemed a little too comfortable fixing a woman's hair, and that sent a feeling through her body that she didn't recognize.

She glanced over her shoulder to look at him, and he gently turned it back as he finished pushing in the last of her hairpins.

"There," he said. "That looks better. It isn't as nice as you had it before, but I'm sure no one will notice."

He tried once again to reach for her waist and tried to tuck in her shirt, but she pulled away. He had done enough.

"No, I can do that." His touch evoked feelings she wasn't prepared for.

She quickly tucked in her blouse and smoothed down invisible wrinkles in her skirt.

"You look presentable. No one'll be the wiser." His voice was soft and full of remorse.

She opened her mouth but snapped it shut. Saying thank you didn't seem appropriate, as she wasn't thankful, but at the same time, he had tried to help her maintain her dignity.

Instead, she nodded and then fled down the hallway to find her brother. He was safe, secure, and familiar.

Four

Marie stormed down the hall. Walter was being unreasonable again. She had dissuaded him from inquiring about the carriage accident, spinning it as a minor mishap, but someone had seen what had happened and had inquired after her safety, claiming the accident had been quite horrific. Walter had been furious when he came home for dinner, roaring with disbelief that she hadn't told him what had truly happened just two days before.

"Get back here, Marie!" he bellowed, the sounds reverberating off the walls.

Done listening to his troublesome demands, she yelled, "No!"

"We're not finished."

She bent over the railing, dug her fingers into the soft wood, and glared down at him. "Yes, we are. You're being unreasonable. When you can talk to me like an adult and not like a blazing idiot, then I'll talk to you. Until then, I'm going to bed."

Marie spun around and marched to her room. She slipped inside and closed the door behind her before leaning against it, breathing heavily. She hated it when she and Walter fought, but he shouldn't issue ultimatums to her. Marie was not a child, and no matter what he thought, she would do and say whatever she wanted, whenever she wanted, wherever she wanted.

Marie had been independent too long to let any man tell her what to do. She wasn't some young girl with no experience and no knowledge of the world. Working with the suffragists had exposed her to the darker parts of marriages and how women were treated with no one to advocate for them. She would do everything in her power to change that dynamic.

Walter had gone too far tonight, insisting she would never find a husband if she didn't change her ways––as though she lived for finding a husband. Finding one of those was the last thing she was looking for, and he didn't understand why she wasn't trying to tie herself to a man.

He was worried about her, and while she didn't fault him for that, he didn't have the right to stop her. He was her older brother, and she respected him, but she didn't obey him. There were plenty of times when she acquiesced to his wishes, but this was one time she would not. He was misguided to think that if she stopped attending the suffragist meetings, she would be safe from harm. She could be trampled by a herd of buffalo if she were in the right place at the right time.

It had been an accident, pure and simple, but Walter was too stubborn to admit it while they'd been arguing in his study earlier that evening.

Unfortunately, in her anger, she had reminded him that she didn't have to live with him, and that had been the wrong thing to say if she'd wanted him to listen to her.

"I don't need to stay here, Walter. I'm happy to find a new place to live."

"You wouldn't dare." He slammed his desk drawer shut. He ripped off his spectacles and threw them on the desk. "We agreed when our parents passed that we would live here until..."

She stared at him silently, waiting for him to finish his thought. She could be patient even when he was being an obstinate pain in her backside. He hated it when she did this, which was why she did it. He used his loud booming voice and clout to get his reporters to do as he wished, but it didn't work with her.

"Dammit, Marie. Don't play that game with me." His face was red and his cheeks were puffy. "We agreed years ago that we'd never sell this place."

"I never said I wanted to sell it. I said I could move out. I have enough put away to find a place and could live comfortably for some time."

"That's a ridiculous notion. There's no reason you should waste your inheritance when you could stay here. That's always been the plan." He jabbed his finger into his desk as though that was going to make her stay. But if he didn't stop his authoritarian actions, she would have to do something drastic.

"Then quit trying to dictate what I do."

"I'm not dictating anything––"

"Yes, you are."

He looked like a blowfish, or at least how she imagined one, with his bulging, splotchy red cheeks. She had to hide her smirk. He was already incensed, and that would only infuriate him further.

"Your threats won't intimidate me." She squared her shoulders, determined not to let him get his way.

"I'm trying to protect you."

She stood, stalked to his desk, placed her palms against the cold wood, and stared hard at her brother. "Let me make one thing clear. I do *not* need protection. I'm tired of you and every man thinking that women can't take care of themselves." She took a breath. "It was an accident. Nothing more, nothing less. Keeping me locked up won't change what happened."

With that, she whirled around and stalked out of his study. Walter's blistering words echoed behind her. She'd ignored him until she yelled at him over the stairwell. Normally, she wouldn't have done that, but when he told her to return to his study like he was her father, she had finally lost her composure.

She needed to talk to Michael first thing in the morning. With any luck, he would agree to tell Walter it'd been a minor accident, and her brother would stop with his threats. The problem was, she didn't want to be anywhere near Michael. He was the most annoying man. She could only imagine what his future wife would go through. He thought he was so funny, but he wasn't. He was rude and inconsiderate, but if she wanted to calm Walter's nerves, she had to get someone to convince him that everything was fine.

Shaking her head, she stalked toward her wardrobe, ripped open the doors, and snatched up her nightgown. There were days she wondered about all the possibilities of a future where women were as equal as men, and then there were days she wondered if her efforts were fruitless. Too many obstacles stood in her way, and not having the support of her only blood relative made it hard to push past the naysayers in town.

A part of her wanted what Walter did––a family and a home of her own––but she wasn't willing to give up everything to have a husband. They controlled too much and had too much to say in what a woman did. If only she could get the women's vote in the state of Montana. Wyoming had allowed women the right to vote for years. She didn't understand why Montana was so far behind. At the rate they were going, she wasn't sure when or if it was going to happen. She was frustrated. No matter what she did or how much she cajoled, she couldn't get women or men, for that matter, to understand how important it was.

She had to quit dwelling on the negatives. She was determined to gain equality for women, and she would. It just might take longer than she'd anticipated. One thing was for certain: she wouldn't let Walter's overbearing attitude stop her. There was too much to gain and too much to lose. It was up to her to continue.

If she didn't have that, what else did she have?

The next morning, Marie entered the kitchen once Walter left for his newspaper office. She had no wish to confront him, and with time, maybe he'd cool down. She had stayed up most of the night thinking about what she could say to Michael and wasn't convinced he would agree, but she had to try.

She hitched the horse to the buggy, climbed inside, and urged the horse forward. The movement jerked her forward in her seat, but unlike a few days ago, the horse didn't take off like the pits of hell were chasing after it. The loaned buggy wasn't as nice as Walter's, but it had two wheels and was better than walking. With any luck, she would catch Michael before his day became busy.

She would approach Michael with a calm and rational explanation. He had an older brother, so he was bound to understand that being dictated to by an older brother was stifling, difficult. He just needed to tell Walter it was a minor accident, assure him she was capable, and then Walter would settle his nerves and get off his high horse about her attending the suffragist meetings. The only thing that stuck in her craw was what Michael was going to require for his cooperation. She didn't believe he would help her out of the goodness of his heart. Men always wanted something in return.

Once she reached Michael's livery, she set the brake and jumped to the ground. Bundled up from the crisp air as she was, the heat from the forge billowed out the wide-open doors and caused her to sweat. Snow hadn't fallen in days, but there was no shortage of it and more was bound to fall soon. With Christmas just a few days away, she hoped it would be a white one. It wouldn't be the same without it.

Marie tied the horse to the hitching post and hurried toward the door labeled Office. She didn't see Michael, but considering the doors were open and flames rose from the forge, he was bound to be around there somewhere. She couldn't imagine a blacksmith leaving a fire burning without being close by. There was too much fire danger these days, and although it was cold, buildings could easily go up in smoke.

She briskly knocked on the door, her misty breath crystallizing in the frigid air, and impatiently stomped her feet when no one answered the office door. Where was he? She knocked again, her patience wearing thin. This was ridiculous. As she reached for the door handle, it flew open, causing her to gasp with alarm.

"I'm coming," Michael said, his voice irritated. "Oh, it's you. I was in the back."

"Can we talk?"

"Um, sure."

He stepped aside to let her pass by him, and she smelled sweat and honey. Honey? She wasn't sure why that intrigued her, but it certainly did.

Shaking off thoughts that were better left somewhere else, she went inside his office and turned to look at him as he snapped the door shut to keep in the warm air.

Suddenly, the room seemed overly warm, and her heart hammered. *What is wrong with me?* His office wasn't that warm. Maybe she was coming down with a fever. That certainly sounded reasonable. Anything else was not rational.

"So what can I do for you, ma'am?" His broad, teasing grin told her he enjoyed taunting her.

She rolled her eyes. "Are we really back to you calling me ma'am?"

"What do you mean?" He turned his back to her and removed his thick leather coat. She swore he shook with laughter, but she brushed it off. He couldn't possibly be this infuriating. Marie didn't want to believe he was making fun of her, and she didn't see the purpose of arguing with him again over his insistence on calling her ma'am. While it bristled her to no end, she had to remember her reason for being there, and it wasn't to start an argument.

"Never mind." She removed a wayward hair from her cheek, pushing it behind her ear. "It isn't worth it."

He stared at her for a long moment. "I shouldn't be giving you a hard time, ma'... I mean Marie." He gestured to the chair in front of his messy desk. "If I haven't completely ruined your impression of me, would you care to have a seat?"

She looked at him for a moment, trying to decide how much of what he said was sincere or if he was continuing to give her a hard time. Deciding to give him the benefit of the doubt, she sat in the wooden chair and gazed at him thoughtfully. He was a contradiction, and she didn't know what to make of him.

"I was an ass yesterday, and I'm right sorry about that. I rarely act like that around ladies. My ma would've likely yanked on my ear and made me apologize for the way I was behaving." He rubbed the back of his neck. "I hope I haven't offended you in any way, but I fear I have without meaning to. Could we start over? I'd like to be your friend, if you'd let me?"

She was shocked silent. He appeared contrite, and his apology was the last thing she'd expected. His sincerity threw off her composure. She wasn't used to men being anything but rude toward her when she didn't succumb to their charms, especially those she was trying to convince to vote for women's rights.

"I––"

"Please, Marie. I won't tease you like that again, especially if it makes you uncomfortable."

Since she couldn't mutter a word, she nodded instead.

His shoulders slumped in relief as though he were expecting a different reaction from her, but he smiled widely when she didn't protest. His smile and endearing dimples brightened his face. She hadn't noticed them the other day. She'd been irate at both him and herself for finding herself in that predicament that she hadn't been paying attention to anything but her frustration.

"Good!" He slapped his desk, the force of his blow fluttering the papers. "So, what can I help you with today? Is the loaner buggy giving you any problems?"

"No, it's fine. Thank you." She sounded so prim and proper, which was definitely unlike her. She just couldn't seem to let down her guard around him. He brought out the worst in her.

"I won't be done with yours for a few more days, if that's what you're wondering about." He tilted his head, his gaze seeming to examine her more fully than she was comfortable with.

What was it about this man that made her unsure of herself? "No, I'm not here to check on that." She lowered her eyes, shifting her feet under her chair, as his intensity was too much. "Although I do appreciate you looking at it. But if you wouldn't mind, could you... could you convince Walter that the accident wasn't as bad as it looked?"

"I don't like to lie."

"I'm not asking you to lie." She avoided his gaze. His stare was too intense, too personal.

"Aren't you?"

"Walter is a tad overbearing. He just doesn't trust that I can take care of myself."

"Your accident could've been worse."

"But it wasn't, and that is what I need you to tell Walter," she snapped.

"So you sought me out this morning to ask me to tell Walter that the accident that could have killed you was a minor inconvenience?" He lifted an eyebrow, pursed his lips, leaned forward, and rested his elbows on his desk. "I'm not sure I can do that."

Irritation climbed up her spine. She just wanted him to agree to her demands. "Why not?"

"Because it wouldn't be the truth."

"Oh, for heaven's sake. I wasn't even hurt when the carriage crashed."

"I'm not so sure about that. You've seemed a bit addled. Maybe you hit your head harder than you think."

"Addled? Isn't that a bit presumptuous?" Her back was stiff as a board. How dare he?

"I wouldn't call myself presumptuous," he said. "How about I take you out to dinner?"

Her head reeled from the sudden change in conversation, and it took her a moment to form coherent words. "No, I'm not here to get a dinner date."

"Well, darn it. Then why are you here?"

The twinkle in his eyes made her want to throw a wet snowball straight into his smirking lips. "Oh, you're infuriating. Are you always this difficult?"

"Didn't think I was being difficult, but I'll apologize if you believe that's how I've been behaving."

His sudden change in attitude toward her, almost condescending and placating, was wearing on her nerves.

"If Walter had come in here with the same questions, would you be asking him?" As soon as she said it, she wished she hadn't.

His eyes widened, and he leaned back, crossing his arms over his chest.

She muttered, "I don't want him to worry unnecessarily."

"Then tell him it was an accident. You don't need me to do that."

"He believes someone must have tampered with it for the axle to have snapped like it did."

"Do you believe that was what happened?"

His gaze had grown even more serious, and that infuriated her even more. She didn't want him to be empathetic or concerned. He was just the local blacksmith, nothing more.

"Of course, I don't. It was a stupid accident. The horses spooked, and something broke. These things happen."

"Do they?" He leaned back in his chair and stroked his chin.

"Arghh. You are one troublesome man." Her anger toward him was unlike her, and she didn't like it.

"I didn't realize that, but thank you for sharing that kind observation with me." His tone was mocking.

"I wasn't sharing a thing with you." She wasn't sure how to convince him to help her, but he just looked at her, waiting for her to tell him why she had sought him out. "Please, I need your help."

"And I'd like to help, but telling Walter it was a minor accident is a lie."

"He doesn't need to worry unnecessarily."

"Worrying about your family is not unnecessary. It comes with the territory. I'd think it'd be more cause for concern if he didn't worry or care for you." He leaned farther back in his chair. "Unless you disagree with me, of course. I wouldn't want to presume how your brother feels."

Marie stared at him for a long moment. He was right, but she wouldn't admit it to him. She didn't need her convictions questioned, and he was doing that. She frankly didn't have time for this.

"Can you please just keep quiet if he asks you about the accident?"

"I'm not comfortable with that."

"Please." She hated the pleading sound in her voice. The suffragist meetings were important to her. It was her duty and her moral obligation to see this fight through to the bitter end. If Walter took them away from her, she would have nothing left.

He muttered something unintelligible under his breath. "I don't know."

"You're like a dog with a bone."

His mouth opened wide, and he laughed, the mirth crinkling his eyes. "I haven't been compared to a dog before, but I guess I can't disagree with you. I won't lie for you." His voice shifted from amused to serious.

Marie clenched her fists in her lap. She would have to convince Walter and pray her progress with the suffragists wouldn't be for naught.

Michael pushed away from his desk and knelt in front of her. He looked at her for a long moment, as though measuring her response. She was surprised he seemed hesitant, whereas the day before, he hadn't had any problems touching her without her permission. Perhaps he had realized he had gone too far and was trying to make amends.

Michael finally reached for her tightly clenched fists, rubbing his thumbs across her knuckles until she relaxed her fingers. The tension eased in her hands and her shoulders with his gentle touch. No one had ever affected her like this.

"Can I have some water?" Her mouth had suddenly gone dry, and it was difficult to lift her tongue.

He nodded and released her hands. Losing his touch affected her more than she wanted to acknowledge.

"I'll be right back. Please, relax and don't go anywhere." He turned and left the room, leaving the door to his smithy open. She could hear him talking to someone, but he was back moments later with a pitcher of liquid in one hand and two glasses in the other. "Lemonade, all right? The water isn't fresh, and I don't think you're gonna wanna drink the water I've been using to cool the horseshoes I've been workin' on this morning."

She smiled. "Yes, that would be most appreciated."

He poured them each a glass before handing her one and sitting back in his chair. "Telling Walter the truth isn't as awful as you might think."

"Walter is insistent that I give up my causes. I refuse to do that. If I can't convince him the accident wasn't serious, then I'll have to move out of our home, and I'd rather not do that."

He sighed and shook his head. "As much as I'd like to help you, I won't do what you're asking."

"Fine," she grumbled. "If you won't lie, even though I'm not asking you to, then could you just not say a word?"

Five

Michael examined Marie closely. She was trying hard to show a strong front, but there was a tremor to her hands and a shakiness to her voice that he'd likely venture to say she didn't realize was there. Something had rattled her far more than she had likely admitted to herself. Was it truly just her not wanting Walter to know much about the accident, or was there something more nefarious?

"What's going on?"

"Nothing!" she squeaked.

Realizing he was pushing her too far, he gave her a moment to decide what, if anything, she was willing to tell him. When he thought it was a lost cause and he was about to offer to take her home, she finally spoke.

"I've been working with the National American Woman Suffrage Association to gain the women's vote here in Montana and to gain our freedom." She looked at him for a moment as though waiting for him to proclaim that women's rights weren't wanted.

Michael had heard it often enough from plenty of his customers, but he saw nothing wrong with women having the vote. The women in his life were strong, independent, knew their minds, and could definitely fend for themselves. He wasn't of the mindset that women were helpless, but he kept silent and waited for her to continue. She likely wouldn't believe him, regardless of how sincere he may be. Too many men were naysayers and didn't appreciate all that women offered, and she'd likely been demonized by her participation in the women's movement.

She fiddled with a button on her thick coat. "You're not going to tell me it's a fool's mission, that I should know my place as a woman, and it isn't to have the vote or equality?"

He grinned. "Well, I suppose I could say that, but I won't, 'cause that ain't how I feel."

Her eyes widened with disbelief. "Really?" She shook her head and pursed her lips. "I'm not sure I believe you."

He kept quiet. It would take time before she would trust him. Trying to convince her otherwise wouldn't change a thing. Only actions would do that, and he was determined to show her he was a man she could trust.

"Most men in this town are against any talk of women's equality."

"I'm not most men." He'd have to show her he was more than she'd thought.

"I don't know about that."

He wanted to laugh at her consternation, but that would only antagonize her, so he swallowed back his laughter. "I think I have to be offended."

"You *think* you have to be offended? What kind of statement is that?" she asked, a growl in her tone.

"It's one where you're assuming something about me."

"Oh." Her cheeks turned bright red. "I shouldn't assume anything, as I don't know you, and you don't know me." She pointed to her chest.

Instead of responding to her ire, he said, "Why don't you keep on explaining?"

He took a sip of the lemonade. It was entirely too sweet for him, but his neighbor was constantly bringing him sugary drinks and sweets. She was after a husband and had set her sights on him, but he wasn't interested. She was a nice enough lady, but she was old enough to be his mother, and that just didn't sit quite right. Not to mention he just wasn't plain attracted to her. She wasn't an ugly woman, but no sparks flew when he talked with her. He wanted more than just a companionable relationship with a woman if and when he decided to take that plunge.

He turned his attention back to Marie and watched the slew of emotions crossing her face. She took a deep breath, as though she had to brace herself for his response. The words raced out of her mouth so fast he wondered if she'd faint dead away without taking a breath in between them.

"Women have been suffering under antiquated laws and old-fashioned thinking that needs to change. In order for women to get reform, we need to have the vote." She pounded her fist on his desk. "There needs to be changes to divorce laws and an end to treating women like cattle. The only way that is going to happen is if women can partake in legislation, which requires us to have the vote."

Her eyes sparkled with excitement, and the enthusiasm in her tone was unmistakable. Marie was very passionate, and he'd do well to give her the time and consideration she deserved.

"I've been helping organize rallies and events to get women mobilized to help the fight. Nothing will change if we don't work together."

"I definitely support your movement."

"You do?"

"You seem surprised." It was going to take a miracle for her to believe what he said, but he was willing to do the work.

"I am." She blew out a breath, a curl low across her forehead.

"You shouldn't be," he said.

"But most men—-"

"I'm not most men," Michael interrupted her. He could only take so much before he'd be forced to say his piece. "Listen, Marie, plenty of strong women exist in my family, and I was raised by one of the strongest." His ma had truly been a remarkable woman and likely would've loved Marie and her cause. "The one thing I've learned is that it works better if men'll work with women instead of fighting and trying to suppress them. If I could give you the right to vote, I would, and I look forward to the day you can."

He pointed a finger at her. "Women need independence, should have the right to own property outside the will of their husbands, should be able to control their money, and more than likely could do the same job as any man. I've seen firsthand from Elizabeth, my sister-in-law, how I shouldn't try to tell a woman what she can or cannot do. Elizabeth can ride and shoot better than my brother. Although, I don't think Ben would admit that to anyone but her."

He chuckled at the memory of the two of them going head to head when Ben realized how stubborn Elizabeth was, but she'd always won, and Ben was the better for it.

"I have to admit, I didn't expect you to say that."

"Sometimes people can surprise you." He didn't want to press her, but there had to be a reason why she was determined to garner his silence. "You still haven't explained your true reason for asking me to keep silent about how dangerous your accident was. Does it have anything to do with your involvement with the suffragists?"

She sighed and lifted a hand to her forehead before dropping it to her lap. "I don't know, but I can't take the chance that Walter will think it does."

"Have there been other accidents?"

"I wouldn't call them accidents, exactly." She avoided his gaze.

There was more going on here than he had at first realized. Was she willing to tell him everything? "Go on."

She fidgeted with her skirt. "It started with small things. Flyers going missing, signs being removed, our meetings getting canceled without notice, venues being vandalized."

"Vandalized?"

"Nothing serious. Just chairs and tables being knocked over. Nothing we couldn't fix within a few minutes."

"Still..."

"At first, I wasn't that concerned. Suffragists have been dealing with these types of issues for years in the fight for equality."

"But?"

"But then it got worse."

"How so?"

"It feels, well... It feels like I'm being specifically targeted."

Unease crept up his spine. "Targeted how?"

"You ask a lot of questions." Marie was growing more and more agitated, but he couldn't seem to help himself.

He just looked at her, waiting for her to continue.

She shifted in her seat. "I shouldn't have said a word. It's not important. I should get going." She bent to grab the reticule she'd dropped by her feet, but he jumped from his seat and was by her side before she could leave.

He rested his hand on her shoulder. "You can't leave it like this. You started this, so don't you think you should finish it?"

She tried to brush his hand away, but he kept it firmly where it was. "Let go of me."

"No." He wasn't proud of trying to keep her in place, but if he let her go, he was afraid of what might happen. "If you want me to keep quiet, I would highly suggest you tell me what else happened."

"You have plenty of nerve." She glared at him.

He lifted an eyebrow. "Perhaps I do, but you came to my office and asked me to minimize the seriousness of your accident to your brother. A man, I might add, that I admire and who helped keep my brother Luke from harm."

Fire leapt from her eyes. If he were a stick of wood, he would've gone up in flames.

"You are the most infuriating man--"

"Why don't you tell me what else happened instead of listing off my virtues?"

"Virtues." She crossed her arms across her chest. "Arghh! Fine. I found a dead rat on my doorstep with the word *stop* written in blood. I've received numerous threatening letters. Someone broke into our house--"

"Does Walter have any idea what's going on?"

"No, I cleaned up the blood, and I'm usually home before him most nights, so I intercepted the letters. I'm fully capable of handling this mess."

She was in a heap of trouble and likely didn't realize it, given her cavalier attitude and her determination to keep her brother in the dark.

"What about when your house was broken into? What was taken? Did you call the sheriff?"

"Nothing was taken as far as I could tell. They just ransacked the parlor and the kitchen. I got it cleaned up before Walter came home, and no, I didn't call the sheriff."

"Why not?"

"There was no point. Nothing was stolen." She scooted the chair from his reach, likely to make a point that he shouldn't touch her.

"What if you had walked in on them?" He didn't like where this was going.

"Well, the thing is..."

"What?" he said.

"You're maddening."

"And you're avoiding the question."

She glared at him and gripped the edges of the chair. "There might've been someone inside when I came home." She held up her hand to stop him as anger for what could've happened to her burned through him. "But he ran out the back when I came inside. He didn't come near me, and I wasn't in any danger."

"Of course, you were in danger," he snapped. "There was an intruder in your home. Your brother should absolutely know that happened."

She waved her hand in the air as though pushing away an annoying fly. "Don't be ridiculous. I was *perfectly* fine. I can defend myself, and besides, he ran away. I wasn't hurt, so there's no reason to worry Walter. Besides, he couldn't have done anything."

"There's something I can do."

"Ha, and what would that be, Mr. Seymour?"

If things weren't so serious, he'd laugh at her switch to his formal name. "It seems as though you need a bodyguard."

"I don't need a bodyguard."

"You could've been killed by the intruder and by your carriage accident. Now that I know someone's been targeting you, it makes me more inclined to examine the carriage a bit closer to see what, if any, damage was induced by someone trying to harm you."

"It wasn't that serious." She was trying to downplay how grave it was, but she was doing a horrible job of it.

He wasn't convinced. He sat back in his chair and ran his fingers through his hair. "Your nonchalance about what's happening changes things for me considerably."

"It doesn't change a thing, especially for you. I'm fine. It doesn't matter what these... these fools try to do to me. I won't stop. Women deserve equality."

"You don't have to convince me of that. I agree that women deserve equality. The problem I have is you"––he pointed at her–– "putting yourself in danger."

"I'm not putting myself in danger... On purpose." She lifted her lips into a soft smile.

She was trying to tease him. He recognized it for what it was. He wouldn't be swayed by her charming smile, however, and it slowly slipped away when she caught the look in his eyes.

"What are we going to do?" He immediately regretted asking because he could see her pulling away.

"*We* aren't going to do a thing. I'm not sure why I told you any of this."

"Because I'm a skilled listener, that's why." He cracked a smile, but it didn't ease the look of regret on her face.

"I don't believe that's accurate, but whatever the reason, I shouldn't have told you any of this. You're going to tell my brother, aren't you?"

He studied her carefully. Michael wanted to wrap her in his arms and hold her close. The instinct to do it was almost overwhelming, but he'd keep his distance for now.

Michael had this undeniable urge to protect this woman with everything in him. He had never felt that way about a woman before, but he was savvy enough to recognize it for what it was and dumb enough to throw himself at her feet. However, he didn't think she'd appreciate it either.

"How about we make a deal?" His mind scrambled for a way to get her to accept his protection.

"What type of deal?"

"You don't need to look at me like that," he said. "I don't bite."

"Something tells me you do."

He chuckled. "Not unless you want me to."

She jumped to her feet and clenched her fists tightly. "I thought you were different?"

He had miscalculated again. *What is it about this woman that makes me say the wrong things?* "I apologize, Marie. I didn't mean that the way it sounded."

"I think you meant exactly what you said." Her face was bright red with anger. "I have to deal with men every day who think that with a cute word or a sly look, I'll fall down at their feet. I'm not that type of woman, and I don't appreciate you treating me like that, especially since I just confided in you."

He was ashamed of his behavior. "No, I didn't. I was trying to lighten the mood but failed miserably. I'm accustomed to making jokes or playing around, and it... it wasn't the right time for that. I should've known better."

After a long moment, she nodded as though taking his measure. He hoped he lived up to her expectations.

"What kind of deal were you referring to?" she asked.

He might have gotten her to listen, but he'd best be careful he didn't blow it a second time. "Well"--he scratched his chin--"it's clear you want to keep this from Walter."

"I do." She held her reticule to her chest as though preparing for an attack.

"But it's also clear that you're in danger."

"I think that's extreme. I haven't been hurt," she snarled.

"I'm not too sure about that, considering how careful you're moving." She had tried to hide it but had grimaced a few times when she moved too quickly. She opened her mouth, but he held up his hand to stop her. "I'm not saying you were hurt enough to worry but definitely bruised if I'm not mistaken."

Marie nodded reluctantly.

"It appears the incidents are escalating if the mishap with your carriage is any sign."

"What are you suggesting then, Michael?"

He surely loved the way his name sounded across her lips. "You need someone to keep an eye on you. A bodyguard, if you will."

"I already told you I'm not hiring a bodyguard."

"I'm not suggesting that you hire one," he said.

"Then what are you suggesting?" She rapidly breathed as though her heart were beating erratically in her chest.

"I'll watch over you."

"You're surely not serious." An incredulous expression crossed her beautiful face.

"Serious as a snowflake," he said with a smile.

She giggled. "A snowflake?"

"All right, maybe that isn't the best analogy, but my point is, this gives you what you want and gives me peace of mind. Besides, it'll give me a chance to learn more about you."

She furrowed her brow. "What if I don't want you to?"

"I guess that *is* your prerogative. But I either do it or I'll need to tell your brother. Your safety is paramount. Whoever is behind these attacks is increasing their onslaught, and I could never forgive myself if something were to happen to you." Michael watched the wheels turn in her brain. He wondered if she realized how much her thoughts were reflected in her expressions.

"I told you, I can defend myself," she drawled.

He had to contain his grin. "I'm sure you can, but I don't think it'd hurt to have a second set of hands and eyes, don't you?"

"Your idea's unconventional. You have work to do, a business to run. You don't have time to be with me during the day."

"Don't worry. There's always men looking for work."

She bit her plump bottom lip. "I'm still not sure this is a good idea."

"How about we give it a run for a few days? Maybe just having an extra presence will deter whoever is doing this. Besides, I'm not asking for your permission. Whether or not you want it, I'm going to watch out for you."

"Why would you do this?"

"Why shouldn't I?" He was looking forward to it. He just had to keep her from realizing that. It was going to be hard enough keeping himself from grinning wildly and clapping his hands in glee.

"Fine, but you"--she pointed at him--"will not interfere in any of my activities."

"I can't promise that, but I will try to be respectful."

$\sim$

What have I just gotten myself into?

Marie was outside his livery waiting for Michael, although he was confident she'd rather have lunch with a snake than allow him to be with her. His suggestion was unconventional, and it wasn't even clear to him why he'd encouraged it.

It would've been easier to inform Walter and let him deal with whatever was transpiring, but as she explained, Walter became more and more agitated over her safety. So, Michael did what any Seymour man would do--he'd offered to protect her. It was reasonable and yet unconventional. It wasn't going to end well if he didn't mind his manners.

Her beauty and fierce independence drew him like a moth to a flame. He wanted to know all about her, wanted to know her innermost thoughts, and if he were completely honest, he wanted her in his bed. But she was a lady, and that would never happen unless they were man and wife.

Shit! What am I thinking?

He wasn't in the market for a wife, or at least he didn't think he was, but from the moment he pulled her out of the carriage, he hadn't been able to stop thinking about her. Maybe it *was* time for him to settle down. Getting married to Marie would definitely keep him on his toes and entertained for the rest of his life.

"Are you coming or not?" Marie stepped into his office and glared at him. "I don't have all day."

Sheepishly, he prayed his thoughts weren't written all over his face. "I'm coming. I got distracted. Let me speak with Tony--"

"Who's that?" She tilted her head.

"He's my new assistant." He'd hired Tony just that morning. The boy had come looking for work, and it had been divine intervention. He was eager to learn and wasn't afraid of hard work.

"Oh." Marie blushed. "I shouldn't have asked. It certainly isn't any of my business." She fiddled with a string dangling from her coat.

"It's not as though I told you I had an assistant. We don't

know each other well enough for that yet." He was being contrary, but he couldn't help but get her all riled up.

She glared at him. "We'll never know one another as well as you seem to think we're going to."

"And what makes you think we won't?"

"Ugh, I don't have time for this." She pinched the area between her eyes and then slapped her hand against her waist.

He grinned, but she had averted her gaze and likely missed it. "Let me tell him I'll be gone for a few hours."

She nodded and then turned away, her voice carrying over her shoulder. "Well, hurry it up then. It's cold outside, and I need to be downtown by nine."

Michael had a backlog of work that Tony wouldn't be able to handle on his own, but he'd made a commitment to Marie and wouldn't leave her to fend for herself.

"Tony." Michael walked into the dark livery. The days were shorter, so the sun hadn't risen yet. "You back here?"

"Yeah, boss." Tony stepped out of a horse stall, a rake in his hands. His ears stuck out from his head, and his scrawny frame seemed out of proportion. He was young and barely had whiskers, but he'd eventually grow into his body.

"I need to leave for a couple of hours."

"All right, but what about the work?" He pointed the rake at the area behind him. "You said it was going to be a busy day and weren't sure if you were going to get it done. I ain't equipped to run the smithy on my own." A frown lined his thin lips.

"You'll be fine. I need to take care of something."

"With her?" Tony pointed the rake toward the wide-open doors, his frown turning up into a cocky grin.

"Something like that."

"She's a beauty," Tony said.

Michael glared at him. "Probably should keep that to yourself."

Tony's smile dropped. "Sorry, boss. Didn't mean no disrespect."

Michael shouldn't be too harsh. The boy was young but eager to learn. "I was planning on hiring another smithy in the next couple of weeks, but I'm gonna have to move up my timeline."

"You have someone in mind?"

"No, I'll put a notice in the newspaper and hang a sign out front when I get back."

"Whatever you think best," Tony said.

"Glad I have your approval." Michael smiled at the young man. He might be impertinent, but he was a hard worker. Tony reminded Michael of himself at times. "I'll be back in a couple of hours. Nothing's real urgent, so I'll handle what's left when I return later today."

Tony scratched at his chest. "How late do you need me to stay tonight?"

"How about 'til three?"

Tony bobbed his head. "If you need me to stay longer, just send word. I need the money, so I'm willing to work as late as you need."

"Thanks. I'll send word if I can't make it back by then."

He lifted an eyebrow. "Well, I suspect you better get before she marches back in here and drags you away by your hair. Wouldn't want to make that lady mad again if I were you."

Michael laughed. "You're right about that."

Walking outside, he found Marie pacing back and forth in front of the open doors of the smithy. Her face was flushed, and her posture was ramrod straight. A fiery shot of heat soared through Michael, and it wasn't from the forge. It was something more primal. He would have to work hard to control his interest if he didn't want her running off or telling him to go straight to hell. Considering how forthright she was, he figured it would be the *go straight to hell* variety coming from her mouth. He chuckled at the thought.

"What?" She stopped and glared at him. "What is so funny?"

"Oh, nothing. I was just thinking about something."

"Hmph," she muttered. "Are you finally ready? I'm going to be late if we don't leave soon."

"Yes, my lady." He bowed with flourish.

She bristled with that but just shot him another glaringly disgusted look that only made him grin more.

"That took longer than I'd expected." He pulled on his gloves. "Let's go. Can I help you inside the carriage?"

"No," she muttered, slapping her reticule against her skirt. "I can climb into a carriage by myself. I would think you would recognize that."

"Sorry, didn't mean no disrespect. It's one of my disreputable habits." He quickly checked the harnesses to make sure all was snug and that they wouldn't have any issues. Considering she'd had problems with her carriage, he didn't want to take any chances.

"Maybe it's a habit you should break."

"I don't think so. My sisters would hang me alive if I didn't act the gentleman."

She shook her head. "Fine, let's go."

Marie jumped inside the carriage, lifting her skirts and giving him another glimpse of her white stockings. They were utilitarian, nothing special, but the memory of her legs was firmly stuck in his mind, and he would never forget.

He followed her inside and reached for the reins, but she snatched them from his fingertips.

"I can certainly drive the carriage," she said.

"Didn't think you couldn't. I just thought you might prefer to sit back and relax. You've had quite the morning."

She looked at him hard, as if searching for something. After a long moment, she slapped the reins into his hands. "Fine, but don't think I couldn't do it myself."

"Nope, would never presume that. You've certainly shown me how capable you are."

Six

"Marie," Walter hollered, "are you home?"

"Yes, I'm in the kitchen," she yelled. Marie pulled the roast out of the oven, closed the oven with her hip, and placed it on the table. Dropping the mittens on the table, she used her apron to wipe away the sweat dripping from her forehead. The kitchen was stuffy from the heat blowing from the hot stove, and while it'd be nice to have a cool breeze, it was way too frigid outside to open a window.

"Dinner's about ready," she said when Walter strode into the room.

"Dinner?" He braced his hands against one of the kitchen chairs. "This isn't like you."

She scowled. "I can cook. You know that."

"I know you can cook. You just don't do it very often." He laughed.

"Often enough." She ignored his laughter, pointing to the meat on the table. "Do you want to cut the roast while I put everything else on the table in the dining room?"

"We're eating in the dining room?" He looked shocked.

"Yes, we're having company tonight, so I thought it would be nicer if we ate there." She plucked hot yeast rolls from a pan into a serving bowl and had to stop herself from ripping one open, slathering some apple butter on it, and shoving it into her mouth. The warm yeasty scent made her stomach rumble with anticipation.

"Company?"

"Don't act so surprised. I do invite people over occasionally." She put a spoon in the thick cream gravy and lifted it to her lips, blowing on it before taking a lick to make sure she had seasoned it correctly. No one would appreciate gravy that didn't have enough salt and pepper in it.

"It isn't some of your suffragist friends, is it?" He rolled his eyes as he popped a piece of roast in his mouth.

"And what if it were?" She reached for the cooked carrots and carefully spooned them into a ceramic bowl before glaring at him.

"No need to get all riled up." He held up his hands as though to fend off her wrath.

"I'm not, and what's wrong with my friends?" Marie rested her hands on her hips, just begging him to say something.

"Nothin'. Nothin' at all. They just get a little heated and are always asking me to print something about their opinions." He continued to slice the roast, the thick pieces looking delicious.

"I ask you for the same thing." She lifted the hair off the back of her neck, hoping it would cool but no such luck.

"Yes, but you"––he pointed the knife at her––"aren't quite so insistent."

"Well, maybe I should start."

"Oh, please no. Don't do that." He waved his hand without the knife in the air. "Stay the way you are. Who did you invite to dinner?"

"It's––"

Shattering glass and pounding at the front door startled her. She jumped, and Walter cursed. Then, a moment later, an explosion ripped through the front of the house.

"Get down," Walter yelled, dropping the knife on the table, the sound in sharp contrast to what was happening out front.

She had already dropped to the floor after pulling the cord on the electric lamp, blanketing the room in darkness.

"Stay here," he ordered.

Her eyes slowly adjusted to the darkness, and when they did, Marie saw the kitchen door swinging. Walter had left her to fend for herself. He was nothing if not impetuous at times, thinking only of the potential story, although he had told her to stay in the kitchen so she supposed he had considered her safety for a brief moment. Not that she needed him to protect her, but it was kind of irritating that he thought he should.

Logically, she should stay in the kitchen, but she wouldn't cower like a frightened child. There was no telling what would happen to Walter if she left him to search on his own. She stood and almost tripped over her skirts. Dammit, they were always getting in the way. Marie gripped them in one hand, kicked off her fancy slippers, and looked for a weapon. She grabbed a heavy cast-iron skillet from a shelf near the door and crept slowly in her stocking feet to the kitchen door. She cautiously pushed it open and peered around the corner.

"Walter," she whispered, trying not to breathe in the smoke billowing around her.

Their house was on fire.

Her pulse increased. She crouched low, trying to see or hear her brother, but she could only hear the beating of her heart. Where was he? Holding the skillet above her shoulder, she would smack anyone who came near her.

Marie stopped at the entrance to the parlor and stared in horror. The fire had spread and grew with intensity. She needed to find her brother soon, but fear competed with the smoke choking her. This was bad, really bad. The smoke grew thicker with each passing second, and she struggled to see even mere inches in front of her when suddenly the smoke cleared, and she saw his brown boots on the floor behind the sofa.

"Walter!" she screamed, holding her arm across her nose and mouth.

Marie hit something with her knee, and the skillet fell to the ground unheeded. She was more concerned with getting to her brother, and with strength she didn't know she had, she pushed the sofa out of her way. He was out cold, blood trickling across his forehead.

"Walter, wake up." She grabbed his shoulders and shook him.

He didn't stir. She leaned forward, and short puffs of air lifted from his lips. Marie sighed with relief, but the thick gray smoke was filling up the room, and she couldn't sit there. She had to do something. She grabbed his boots and tried to drag him, but his dead weight was too much. Marie couldn't take a deep breath. She shook her head as though trying to clear the ever-growing smoke, but then dropped his feet and coughed uncontrollably. Her head started to swim, and her vision grew blurry.

Bending low, she tried to grab a lungful of clean air. There wasn't much to be had, but she couldn't let that stop her. She needed to get her brother to safety. Marie once again grabbed his boots, taking small, short breaths in between fits of coughing as she pulled him slowly, painstakingly as the fire licked up the walls, burning the drapes, the furniture, and the paintings on the walls.

The fire had moved from the parlor and was working its way down the hall and up the stairs. Whatever had been thrown into their home had been strong and potent and was going to overtake everything soon. She had little time left before they both perished.

The front door slammed open, and sweet voices sounded behind her.

"Marie, Walter, where are you?"

"Help." She tried to scream, but it came out as a croak instead. What should have been a scream was nothing more than a gurgle in her swollen throat. The smoke was dense, and flames crackled around her. There was no way she was getting out. Tears filled her eyes.

No! She wouldn't give in. She couldn't. Marie tried to move again, but it was too much. The smoke was unbearable. She gasped for breath, and her energy disappeared.

"I'm sorry, Walter," she whispered before darkness overtook what was left of the light.

"Are you sure she won't mind me tagging along?" Ben asked as their footsteps crunched through the icy snow-covered road. "I don't want to impose."

Michael ran his hand across his cheeks. "Honestly, I'm not sure, but I doubt she'll be nothing but kind. Besides, I'll just distract her with my good looks and charm."

"Your good looks and charm, huh?" Ben nudged him in the shoulder.

"Yep. I am quite irresistible."

Ben chuckled. "At least you haven't lost your humor."

"Nope." Michael ignored the reference to the dreadful things that had happened to their family over the past few years. "Besides, I want to invite her and Walter to the ranch for Christmas dinner. I'm banking on her not refusin' if you're there with me."

"You seem pretty confident of that." Ben gave him a look across his shoulder, as though trying to measure what he was thinking.

"Oh, I'm not confident. She's one confounding woman, but..." Michael stopped and looked up at the broken streetlight. That was odd, but he turned to his brother and caught the concerned look in Ben's eye. He had said more than he wanted to. He could tell Ben wanted to ask more but held his tongue, which was surprising, as Ben was completely invested in his siblings' lives.

"But what?" Ben asked.

"I've met plenty of pleasant women over the years, but none have..."

Ben tried to hide his smirk, but Michael caught the look and grimaced.

"Look, Michael." Ben reached for his shoulder and stopped him. "If there's something special about her, then you owe it to yourself to see if there's something there."

Michael wasn't sure what else to say. He didn't want to assume anything about what might or might not happen between him and Marie. He had a sinking feeling that if he were to win her heart, it would be a long and enjoyable road, and she'd give him hell throughout it all.

"What's that?" Ben pointed to billowing gray smoke in the distance.

Michael looked where Ben pointed. "I'm not sure. Fire, maybe?"

They shared a glance and ran toward it. Fire couldn't be ignored even in the dead of winter. It didn't take long to realize that it *was* a fire.

"That's Marie's place." Michael picked up his pace toward the burning house.

"Michael! Wait! Stop!" Ben called.

Michael ignored him. He couldn't stop. He wouldn't stop. Marie was inside that house, and he needed to get to her. He wasn't about to lose the one woman who made his heart sing.

Just as Michael reached the front stoop, Ben caught up with him and yanked him to a stop.

"Let me go!" Michael tried to pull away, but Ben's grip was strong.

"Wait a minute. You can't just go rushing inside. That fire is raging out of control."

"I have to. She's inside." The thought of anything awful happening to her made him sick.

"You don't know that. She could've made it out."

"If she had, she and Walter would be somewhere close."

Ben's grip relaxed. "Shit, you're going in whether I want you to or not, aren't you?"

"Yes." Michael ripped his arm away. "And I can't stand out here having a conversation with you. Every second counts."

"I'm fully aware, but before you run in half-cocked, you need to think about this logically." Ben looked around the area in front and pointed. "There's a pump. Hopefully, it's not frozen. Let's wet our coats so we can breathe and give us a fighting chance against those flames."

Agreeing, Michael followed Ben as he ran to the water pump. Ben grabbed the handle and started pumping. It took a moment, but before long, frigid water spewed from the spigot. They removed their coats and held them under the water until they were sopping wet. This was not the time to wear a wet coat, but better to be cold than burnt from the fire.

"Ready?" Ben asked.

Michael nodded, and they headed toward the front door. By then, a crowd had gathered in the road at the front of the house.

A neighbor yelled, "Don't go inside! That place is a firestorm."

"Has anyone contacted the fire brigade?" Ben yelled as men ran past them to the pump with buckets in their hands and started filling them. A water line formed to help keep the fire from spreading to nearby houses.

A man said, "Yes, they should be here soon."

"Not soon enough." Michael pushed open the door. Thick black smoke billowed out. Coughing, he covered his mouth and yelled, "Marie, Walter, where are you?"

Seven

ﾒﾟ

Michael rushed inside, the flames snapping, licking, drawing him inside like a newborn kitten to its mother. The heat scorched his skin and singed the hairs on his arms within seconds of entering. It was an inferno, but he wasn't leaving without her. He prayed she was already safe, but his gut told him she was inside. Whoever had done this was going to pay.

"Marie!"

The fire roared and crackled as it consumed everything within its path, taking no mercy. Michael peered into the parlor, but the heat was unbearable. Just as he began to turn away, movement caught his eye, and he saw her, bent over a prone form.

Right behind him, Ben grabbed his arm and pointed. They both rushed forward. Michael reached Marie first and pulled her into her arms. Her body was limp, and she barely breathed.

"Get her out of here!" Ben yelled. "I've got Walter."

Michael nodded and stood, Marie firmly in his grasp. The smoke was thick. He struggled to breathe, but he wouldn't let it stop him. Michael stumbled out of the room and down the hall. He burst through the front door and tripped down the stairs but stayed on his feet. Someone tried to help by taking Marie from his arms, but he refused. Blankets were thrown over his shoulder, and he was pushed onto a wooden bench in a neighboring yard.

"Did my brother make it out?" Michael asked the man in front of him.

"If he was the man that went in with you, then yeah, he did. He's got Mr. Owens, and the doc's working on him." Soot covered the man's face, and he coughed into his elbow.

"Are they all right?" Michael asked.

The man leaned against the edge of the bench, trying to take a breath. "It appears so. They're both breathing, if that's what you're asking."

"It is. Thanks for your help." He could breathe a little easier knowing that Ben and Walter had made it out alive.

"How's Miss Owens?" the neighbor asked.

Michael looked at Marie. She hadn't stirred. "I think she's all right, but I want the doc to look her over."

"Do you need any help?"

Michael shook his head. "Nah, I'm fine. Can you point me in his direction?"

As Michael stood, the roof on the house crumbled and sparks flew, showering those around it. Yells and curses could be heard from those who'd been trying to keep the fire from spreading any farther, but luckily, it appeared no one had been caught in its aftermath. Moments later, the fire wagon arrived, and the fire brigade began pumping water onto the flames to keep them from consuming any other structure. Lucky for them, a fresh snowfall had fallen earlier in the day, and the fire couldn't lick the frozen ground.

Michael followed the neighbor across the dirt road and found Ben and an older gentleman crouched next to Walter. He had a head full of white hair sticking straight up, but he seemed intent on caring for Walter.

"Ben, is he all right?"

"Not sure." Ben looked at the man with him. "Doc?"

The doc sat back and winced. "He's inhaled quite a bit of smoke, but he's still breathing, so that's a good sign. I'm more worried about the gash on the back of his head."

"Did he fall?" Ben asked.

"I don't believe so. It appears someone hit him. If he doesn't wake soon, there could be permanent damage."

"What should we do?"

"Need to get him inside someplace warm and where we can keep an eye on him. With any luck, he'll be fine, but we won't know for sure until he wakes." The doc stood and looked at Michael. "What have we got here?

"Doc," Michael said, "can you look at Marie?"

The doc walked to Michael's side. Pulling out his stethoscope, he placed it against her chest and took a listen. "She's inhaled a mouthful of smoke as well. If we get her cleaned up and inside someplace warm, the both of them should recover soon. I'm just more worried about her brother and that nasty bump on his head."

"You can take him inside here, doc," a kind older woman said. She stood on the front porch of the house of the yard they were sprawled on.

"Thank you, Mrs. Moses, awfully kind of you, but I don't want to make things hard on you," the doc said.

"Mr. Owens here"––she waved to Walter––"has always been neighborly. It's the least I could do. You need to bring Marie inside as well. I'm sure she's chilled to the bone. She don't have a coat on, and it's mighty cold out here."

Michael looked at the prone woman in his arms and grimaced. He hadn't even thought to grab her a blanket. What type of man was he that he hadn't taken more care of her? If he were going to convince her that she was for him, he had to do a better job of showing he was the man who'd protect her at all costs, against all enemies, and he'd start by figuring out who had attacked Walter and burned their house down.

Eight

Marie's gut-wrenching coughs yanked her awake. She pried open her eyes, and an unfamiliar ceiling greeted her. She pushed up and looked around her, the coughs making her gasp.

Where am I?

White lace curtains hung from two windows, which were clearly only for decoration because they didn't block any of the bright light. Her aching lungs, dry mouth, and deep coughs made her wish she'd never woken.

A tall glass of water beckoned from the table next to the bed. Grabbing it, she drank gratefully. The cool water soothed her dry throat for a moment, but the smoke from the night before had done more damage than she could've possibly realized.

The door opened, and her neighbor, Mrs. Moses, peered around the corner. "Marie, my dear. You're awake." A beaming smile lifted her plump cheeks.

Before Marie could say a word, she started coughing again, but she had drained the water from the glass that had been left for her.

"Oh, my dear, that cough." Mrs. Moses clucked. "Let me get you more water." Mrs. Moses bustled inside, picked up a ceramic white pitcher from beside the bed, and refilled the glass. "Do you need my help?"

Marie shook her head, the water sloshing over the rim as she held it with shaky fingers. The all-consuming cough made it difficult, but she needed to drink. Water would be the only thing to help her scratchy throat.

After a few moments, the cough subsided, and she put her thoughts to words. "How long have I been asleep? Oh no, Walter. Where is he? Is he all right? I tried to get him out, but the smoke was so thick. Is the fire out? How bad is it?"

Mrs. Moses's eyes crinkled with concern. She lifted her hand. "Young lady, take a deep breath before you work yourself up into a pure frenzy." She tugged on the blankets around Marie's waist, straightening them like a mother would for a young child. "First, Walter's fine. He's a little banged up and is having a hard time breathing, but the doc's optimistic he'll recover in a few days."

"Oh, thank heavens." Marie dropped her tense shoulders, and they sagged with relief.

"Yes, definitely. A pure miracle indeed that the two of you made it out of there alive."

"How did we get out? I tried dragging him, but I don't recall leaving the house. I must have blacked out at some point." She remembered picking up Walter's boots and trying to pull him out, but it had become too difficult, and her energy had dwindled far faster than she could have ever anticipated.

"Yes, you did, my dear. The Seymour brothers pulled both of you to safety. They got there just in time." Mrs. Moses rested her hands on her hips.

"Just in time?"

Mrs. Moses looked at Marie for a long moment, and Marie was afraid the news was dreadful. Her next words confirmed Marie's fears.

"Yes, I'm afraid to tell you that the fire completely consumed your home."

"No, no, no." Marie shook her head, tears falling down her cheeks. "This is all my fault." She hit her hand on the mattress under her.

"My dear, this was absolutely not your fault."

"I should've stopped this from happening." All her bluster about helping women get the vote had brought this to their front door.

"And what makes you think you could have stopped it, young lady?" Mrs. Moses's tone was firm, unwavering. "The fire brigade said you were lucky. If you'd been in there much longer, there's no telling what might've happened."

Marie swallowed painfully. Her suffragist's actions had caused this, no matter what Mrs. Moses said.

"Whatever you're thinking, you need to stop. You are *not* to blame. You tried to save your brother and for that, you should be proud." Mrs. Moses patted her hand, trying to comfort her, but it didn't help.

Marie fought against the instinct to give in and do what Walter wanted her to do if it kept him safe, but she couldn't give up. If she didn't fight for women's rights, who would?

"But––"

"No buts." Mrs. Moses clucked her tongue. "Now, let me fluff those pillows for you to make you more comfortable. Then I'll go to the kitchen and get you some beef broth, if you're up to it?"

Marie nodded when her rumbling stomach startled them both. Mrs. Moses tried to contain her chuckle, but Marie laughed, the giggles interspersed with her raucous coughing.

"I shouldn't laugh," Mrs. Moses said after their chuckles died away. "It's only making your cough worse."

Before Marie could say a word, a loud knock interrupted her, and Mrs. Moses jumped in fright.

"Oh my, I certainly wasn't expecting anyone." Mrs. Moses looked toward the door. "Yes?"

"Sorry, Mother," a woman's voice said, "but Mr. Seymour's here to see Marie. He wants to see how she's doing."

"Oh, that young man is so concerned with your well-being, Marie."

Marie blushed. He wasn't her young man, but another fit of coughing stopped her from speaking.

"Mother?" Sally said.

"What? Oh yes, Sally, tell him I'll be down in just a moment to talk with him." Mrs. Moses leaned heavily against the wooden post of the bed and gazed at Marie. "I'll go down right quick and tell Mr. Seymour you're awake. Do you want to see him?"

Marie wasn't sure she did, but she had to thank him for coming to her rescue, even though it was against her nature to let a man save her, but he had come when she needed someone the most.

"I'll get dressed and come down. Do you have something I could change into?" Someone had put her in a thick cotton nightgown, and while it was soft and warm, it certainly wouldn't be appropriate to prance around a handsome, unmarried man in nightclothes.

"Oh yes, my dear. Are you sure you have the energy, though? That cough sounds downright horrible."

"Yes, I'm much better now that I've had some water." Marie coughed again and grinned sheepishly. Her hacking was in sharp contrast to her words.

"I don't know about that, but I won't argue with you." She wagged a finger at Marie.

Marie grinned widely. Mrs. Moses knew her well. She had grown up playing with Sally and had been in her home just as much, if not more, than she had been in the one she and Walter grew up in.

"If you're sure, young lady. I don't want you to overdo it. Your brother would have my head if he thought for one moment you were in any danger."

Marie nodded. Mrs. Moses was right, which was a good reason to get dressed and show Walter and Michael that she was none the worse for wear.

"There are a few old skirts and blouses of Sally's in the wardrobe. I'm sure something'll fit."

"I certainly don't want to impose. Would Sally mind?"

Mrs. Moses wrinkled her forehead. "Young lady, you should know better than that. Take whatever you would like. I'll let Mr. Seymour know you'll be down momentarily."

Properly chastised, she said, "Thank you, Mrs. Moses, for everything." Marie had to swallow back another round of coughing. Perhaps it'd be best to stay quiet, as talking seemed to only aggravate it more.

Mrs. Moses shuffled out of the room. Her gray hair peeked out from under her white cap. She tugged her green shawl tightly around her shoulders. She was getting older, but was still as spry as ever. Marie would have to repay Mrs. Moses and Sally. They'd been a second mother and sister to her and had played a significant part in her life, especially when her and Walter's parents had passed away.

She had wrapped Marie in her arms the day Walter broke the news of their parents' passing. She hadn't let Marie wallow in her pity, had reminded her that her parents had loved both her and Walter with everything they had, and that they wouldn't have wanted Marie and Walter to change their lives. It had been a difficult lesson to learn, but Mrs. Moses was one reason why Marie was determined to change the plight of women in Montana. A strong woman who loved fiercely and protected proudly, but had paid the price when her husband drunk almost everything they had before he'd fallen in the street and had been trampled to death by a herd of cattle. Luckily, he hadn't sold the house out from under her, and she'd been able to rebuild by renting out rooms, doing laundry, and catering events. If he hadn't died, there was no telling where Mrs. Moses would be today.

She had watched firsthand what Mrs. Moses and Sally had been through. The tears, the struggles, the heartache, the worry over where their next meal would come from, and the chance that his fist would connect with either Mrs. Moses or Sally. Marie had decided that there was no way she would ever let what happened to Mrs. Moses happen to her. It would be easier to stay single than to take the chance that a man could take everything that was precious. That was why her determination to get women the right to vote was her number one priority and nothing would dissuade her from that purpose.

As soon as the door closed behind Mrs. Moses, Marie's shoulders sagged. Michael was likely going to tell her brother everything, and Walter would become even more insufferable. The fire had been aimed at her, and if Walter discovered that, there would be hell to pay.

Michael paced back and forth in Mrs. Moses's parlor, waiting for Marie. He had an uncontrollable urge to run up the stairs and check on her himself, but Mrs. Moses's daughter had pointed him to the parlor and told him to wait. Her tone had brokered no argument, and while he'd wanted to protest, he wasn't about to make a scene. He kept reminding himself that the doc said she would be fine, but he needed to see her himself.

After what seemed like hours but was likely only a few minutes, Mrs. Moses stepped inside the parlor. "Mr. Seymour, how good it is to see you."

"Ma'am," Michael said. "How is she?" He should've been more polite, but he was desperate.

She chuckled. "You *are* in love with her, aren't you, young man?"

"What? No. I... I just met her. No... Absolutely not." Although he hadn't just met her.

Mrs. Moses laughed again, a twinkle in her green eyes. "You haven't realized it yet, but you will."

"I'm just concerned. She's a friend of the family."

"Of course she is." Her white hair bobbed under her cap as she shuffled across the room. "And yes, she's fine. She just woke."

"Does she remember what happened?"

Mrs. Moses sat in a chair and picked up the teapot her daughter had brought for him. "I believe so. She was coughing quite a bit, but the doc said that was to be expected, considering how much smoke she inhaled. She'll cough for a few days and have little energy, but with plenty of rest, the doc expects her to have a full recovery."

He ran a hand through his hair before resting it against the back of his neck. "That's right good news. Can I see her? Talk to her?"

"Yes, yes, young man. She'll be down momentarily."

"Is that wise? Shouldn't she stay in bed?" He was pacing like a caged animal and surely looked like a fool in front of the woman.

"Perhaps, but it isn't proper for you to go upstairs." Mrs. Moses thinned her lips. "She seemed determined to come down-stairs. So you sit right there"--she pointed to the sofa--"and have some tea."

Michael sat on the fancy rose sofa, feeling like he might dirty it as Mrs. Moses poured him some of the steaming tea. She handed him the tiny cup. If he wasn't careful, he would either drop it or crush it. He should be used to handling small things, considering his line of work, but he was shaky as a newborn foal.

Deciding he'd be better served if he took a sip, he did so to appease Mrs. Moses and then placed the cup on the table so he wouldn't drop it, or worse, spill on himself.

"Now, young man, why don't you tell me about yourself?" Mrs. Moses picked up a cookie and nibbled on it.

Michael swallowed his frustration. He didn't want to make

small talk, but it appeared he had no choice if he wanted to see Marie. "Not much to tell, ma'am."

She clucked her tongue and waggled her eyebrows. "Now don't be so shy. Don't you own that smithy on Liberty Avenue?"

"Yes." He stared at her in shock. "How did you know that?"

She tittered softly. "Young man, I've lived in Helena for over thirty-five years and know more than you young folks give me credit for."

"Did you know my parents, by chance?"

"It's funny that you ask me that. I did." Her smile was sweet, as though a memory of a time gone by had crossed her mind. "Your momma was quite the woman. I was dismayed to hear they'd passed. It's a shame, really. Your ma was quite the talk of the town when she arrived with your pa."

"And why's that?"

"She was a woman who knew her mind and didn't take guff from no one. Reminds me of that girl of yours up there." She pointed toward the ceiling and winked at him.

"She ain't my girl," Michael mumbled as heat crept up his chest.

Mrs. Moses smiled, but instead of commenting on the glaring lie, she took another sip of her tea. "I can remember the day you were born. Your mama was so proud of you boys."

Michael felt a tug of something deep in his gut. Even though it had been over ten years since they had passed, some moments hit harder than he'd expected.

"Mrs. Moses." Marie's voice was gruff, likely from inhaling all that smoke.

Michael jumped up and drank in the sight of her. She moved slowly, and while she'd be beautiful in his eyes no matter what she looked like, it was clear she was hurting, and he shouldn't have insisted on seeing her.

"Marie, please sit." He moved away from the sofa and pointed to the seat. "I shouldn't have made you come downstairs. You look pale, tired."

"Why, thank you, Michael, for being so brutally honest about how rough I might look."

He cringed at her sharp tone as she looked down her nose at him.

"I realize I had a hard night last night, but you don't have to critique my appearance so harshly," she snapped.

"No. I mean, yes. I mean... I shouldn't have said that," Michael stuttered and then proceeded to trip over the thick wool rug and fall flat on his face.

Nine

Marie gasped as Michael fell to the floor, then had to suppress her giggles at the look of frustrated consternation on his face. He likely was embarrassed to have fallen in front of her, but he jumped up quickly and brushed off his trousers as though nothing had happened.

Instead of embarrassing him further, she let him lead her to the sofa, only because another coughing fit prevented her from stopping him. Some women might appreciate his efforts, but they just irritated her. She wasn't a defenseless woman who needed a man to take care of her, but because she was in her neighbor's home and had been raised with some propriety and dignity, she kept her comments to herself. There was a time and place, and it wasn't that time, even if it was quite difficult to suppress the words.

"How are you feeling?" he asked.

"Good." Then she was made a liar with another hacking cough.

Mrs. Moses poured a tall glass of water and handed it to her. Taking the cool liquid, Marie drank slowly in between each cough until the scratchiness eased, and she could take a breath without barking like a seal in distress.

"You should be in bed resting," Michael said.

"I'm fine, but I couldn't sit in bed all day." She fiddled with a wrinkle on her skirt and caught the look of concern on his face. "Would you quit hovering?"

Michael's face paled, and he shifted uncomfortably next to her.

She was being rude and tried to soften her tone. "I'm sure the cough will ease soon."

He cleared his throat. "Is there anything I can do?"

She wished he'd quit being so honorable, but she swallowed back an angry retort. She had no business being impolite because things had not gone her way. "No." She took a breath. "But I appreciate everything you and Ben did to help my brother."

"It was the least we could do. When we saw the fire, well, I... I mean, we couldn't get there fast enough." He blinked furiously.

"I'm sure if I hadn't blacked out, I would've gotten Walter out myself." As soon as she said the words, she realized how ridiculous she sounded. Would he call her on those facts?

The creases at the corners of his eyes deepened. "I'm not too sure about that."

"And why would you say that? I had Walter by his feet and was working my way to the door when you got to us."

"Do you even remember me carrying you out?"

Marie thought for a moment. The last thing she remembered was trying to drag Walter and then nothing. "I... I don't remember."

He shook his head. "It doesn't matter. The important thing is that you and your brother are all right. It's a shame we didn't get there sooner. Perhaps we could have prevented what happened."

The thought that they'd lost everything was something Marie was trying to avoid thinking about. All of their memories and possessions had been inside that house. Nothing could replace them, but she and Walter were alive, and that was what should matter.

"What makes you think you could've prevented it?" she snapped. "You aren't the savior of me or my brother."

He sat in stunned silence for a moment, and shame crept up her spine. She was being unforgivably rude, but he brought out the worst in her.

He sat back and crossed his arms. "You're right. I was presuming too much. I certainly didn't mean to offend you."

She caught the concerned look in his eye and swallowed hard. "Please thank your brother for me."

"No need for thanks," Michael said. "Anyone would've helped if they'd been there."

"Perhaps," Marie murmured. "Well, thank you for coming by, but I'd imagine you have plenty to do today. Don't let me keep you."

She started to stand to encourage him to leave, but he seemed determined to stay from the way he leaned back into the sofa.

"The thing is," he said, "I was wondering, well... We were wondering, that is... If you'd like to come to the ranch for Christmas, with your house, well..."

She ignored his invitation to come to the ranch. Marie couldn't think about Christmas right now. Too many other things were going to take up her time.

"It was a miracle the two of you got out of there alive," Mrs. Moses said. "If it hadn't been for the Seymours, I hate to think what could have happened."

Marie swallowed back the lump in her throat and stared at a spot on the wall above Mrs. Moses's head. She had to think about something else, concentrate on anything but what he was telling her, or she would break down in tears. He couldn't see her lose her composure. She couldn't let him have that type of control over her.

"I'm sorry, Marie. I wish we could have saved it."

She slapped her knees and stood. "Well, I should check in on Walter, and then I need to find a place for us to stay." She couldn't sit there and talk about it. It was too much.

"My dear, you're more than welcome to stay here," Mrs. Moses said.

"I appreciate that, more than I can say, but I need to find us a new home. Walter would want that."

"I understand." Mrs. Moses's face fell. "You're welcome to stay here as long as you need."

"Thank you." Marie would need to talk to her later and apologize for being so curt. She hadn't meant to hurt her, but Walter wouldn't want to impose on anyone.

"I need to step outside for just a moment." Mrs. Moses grimaced when she stood. Michael went to her to help, but she waved him off. "Go. Go sit with Marie. I'm perfectly fine, young man."

"Yes, ma'am," he said.

Marie looked at Michael after Mrs. Moses left them. "Thank you again, but I should go look in on Walter."

"Could we talk for a minute first?" he asked.

"Talk about what?" She concentrated on the paintings on the wall. It was all she could do to hold in the fear and frustration that bubbled inside of her. What were they going to do? Christmas was in a few days, and they had no place to go. Granted, Mrs. Moses had offered them a place to stay, which would be good in the short term, but they couldn't stay there forever. Would they rebuild? Would they look for something else? Where would they stay? It could be days or even weeks before she could start looking, as no one would want to help them hunt for a place during the holidays.

"Marie? Marie?" Michael said.

"What? Oh, my mind wandered there for a minute." She didn't like how she reacted around him. He flustered her, made her uncomfortable in her skin, and even made her jealous and hysterical. She didn't want to be the example of why men refused to let women have the vote if she couldn't even handle a traumatic situation. She was made of stronger stuff, and she had to show it.

"I'm sure you have a lot of thoughts coursing through your pretty little brain," he said.

"Pretty little brain?" She stood, fisted her hands as she rounded the table in front of the sofa, and glared at him. "Of all the insensitive, brutish comments you could make. I am more than a pretty little brain."

He crossed his arms, stuck his feet out in front of him, and grinned.

He grinned.

"Why are you grinning?" Pulsating anger rushed through her veins.

"I'm not." He appeared to try to suppress his smile but failed miserably.

Her hackles grew even more. "I find nothing funny about this, Michael."

"I'm sorry. I'm not laughing about the fire."

"Then why are you laughing?"

His smile disappeared, and he slowly stood. "I'm just happy you don't look like you're going to cry any longer."

"I wasn't going to cry!" she roared.

He held out his hands as though to show he posed no threat. "Never said you were going to. Just said you looked like it, but now you don't."

She slapped her hands together and held them tight against her chest. "Arghh, you *are* the most frustrating man."

"Why do you have to tell me that in almost every conversation we have?" he said.

"Maybe you should take heed of my words and quit doing it. Then, I wouldn't have to repeat myself."

He leaned up against the fireplace and loosely wrapped his arms around his waist. "Good point. I'll have to work on it... One day."

She plopped back into her chair and glared at him. He didn't take her seriously.

"So--"

"So what?" She wasn't sure she wanted to hear anything he had to say. It was easier to be mad than to think about tomorrow.

"Ben was wondering if you and Walter would like to come to the ranch for a few days... Until you can figure out what you'd like to do next."

"We couldn't." She didn't want to be around him any longer. Michael confused her.

"And why couldn't you?" He cocked an eyebrow.

"Christmas is in a few days, and it should be spent with family. You don't need us there to ruin it for you."

"First"--he pushed away from the fireplace--"you wouldn't ruin it for us, and second, you're right, Christmas is for family, and you're a part of ours."

"No, we aren't." She didn't understand what type of game he was playing, but she wouldn't have any part of it.

"In a way, you are. Luke worked for Walter for years and thinks of him as an older brother. I consider you a friend, so in our minds and hearts, that makes you part of our family."

"That doesn't make any sense. Just because you think I'm your friend doesn't make me part of your family."

"I don't just think you're my friend. I *know* you're my friend. And I'm hurt"--he clutched his chest--"that you would say otherwise." He ruined the moment by smirking.

She wouldn't fall for his act. "No, I need to look for a place for us to live, and we can't do that if we're at your family's ranch."

"Please, Marie. We'd like you to stay with us. It'll give you both a chance to recuperate. Nothing or no one will work for the next couple of days, so you won't be able to find a new place, anyway."

"We could just stay here with Mrs. Moses. You heard her. She offered and has been awfully kind to us." Mrs. Moses was going to think Marie had lost her mind if she accepted her invitation now, even though it had been clear she wanted them to stay. It just made more sense for her and Walter to do that. Going to the Thundering Mountain Ranch wouldn't serve any purpose.

"You're right, you could. But, and I only say this with respect... she is much older. I'm afraid of the burden it would put on her."

Was he trying to make her feel guilty about staying with Mrs. Moses? "We wouldn't be a burden." She would make sure they weren't.

"You wouldn't try to be, but consider this." He sat, leaned forward, and rested his elbows on his knees. "You'd be living right across the road from what's left of your home. I'd hate for you to be reminded of that every day, every hour."

"I--"

"Please," he said. "We'd be honored to have you at the ranch. Elizabeth would've undoubtedly told Ben in no uncertain terms that we weren't to take no for an answer, especially if she knew what happened last night. Trust me, you don't want to fight my sister-in-law. She's a force to be reckoned with."

Ten

The next day, Marie and Walter were bundled into a lavish carriage and headed to Michael's family ranch.

Before leaving, Marie took Mrs. Moses's hands and squeezed affectionately. "Mrs. Moses, I can't thank you enough for everything you've done for me and Walter. I'm extremely grateful. If there's anything I could do to repay you, please let me know."

"Oh, my dear. It was my pleasure. I'm just sorry you had to suffer such losses, but I'm glad you and your brother escaped with your lives. Things can be replaced, but people cannot. Treasure these moments with your brother."

"Thank you, I will. Have a very Merry Christmas."

"I will. I plan on visiting my son's house for the day and will get to love on my grandchildren."

"Please tell your family how grateful we are. They have a wonderful matriarch in their family."

"Oh, phish." Mrs. Moses blushed. "I'm no one special. I just believe in helpin' my neighbors."

"You are my hero. If I can ever--"

"Oh, stop, young lady." Mrs. Moses blinked furiously. Her eyes were wet with unshed tears. "You go with your young man and enjoy your Christmas. Let him bring a sparkle to your cheeks and a twinkle to your eyes. He sure is handsome, don't you think?"

Marie opened her mouth and then snapped it shut. It was easier to smile than try and come up with a response to that question. To hide her reddening cheeks, she gave Mrs. Moses a hug. "Thank you. You are a sweetheart."

Mrs. Moses sniffled and gently pulled away. She dabbed at her eyes with her handkerchief. "Now, you get, young lady, and enjoy your Christmas."

Marie gave her one more quick hug and then hurried outside to where the men waited. She was worried about Walter. He'd been pale earlier but was insistent that he was fine and just needed to rest. Not wanting to aggravate him any further, she'd acquiesced and let the matter drop. With any luck, she wasn't making a mistake.

An hour later, the carriage arrived at an impressive ranch where the opening was marked by rows of pine trees. It was a majestic entrance, even in the dead of winter. The pine needles were heavy with snow, but the foliage was thick. Older trees were mixed with young ones as though the family were continually replanting. She'd have to ask Ben later when she was in a better state of mind. She was too irritated with Michael at the moment to ask him anything.

On the way to the ranch, he prattled on and on about how comfortable they would be, how they could stay for as long as they wanted, and how he would finally get the chance to learn more about her. He just presumed they needed to become close friends. He didn't even consider what she wanted.

His presumptive attitude regarding their relationship had struck a nerve. He was turning their *friendship* into something more, and she needed to set him straight. There would be no future between them. She had no interest and never would. She could be casual friends with him, but that was it. Nothing more. Ever.

The carriage rolled to a stop in front of a massive three-story ranch house with a wraparound porch. Green wreaths with red bows decorated the porch, the windows, and the door. It was quite festive. If she'd been in a better frame of mind, she would've been excited to spend Christmas on a beautiful ranch.

The front door opened, and Elizabeth, Ben's wife, stepped outside. She was wearing trousers. Marie had seen women in trousers before, but she hadn't expected it of Elizabeth. Michael had described her as sophisticated and strong, and it was almost shocking but yet liberating. Marie had wanted to wear trousers for years, but the men in town wouldn't take her seriously if she did. They looked comfortable, freeing.

"You're here," Elizabeth said. "Come in, come in. Let's get you out of the cold."

Ben had mentioned that he'd sent a message to the ranch warning them of their arrival, and it appeared the message had arrived. Elizabeth didn't seem surprised to have a bunch of unwanted guests days before Christmas.

Ben and Michael both helped Walter out of the carriage. Walter could walk, but he appeared exhausted and had little energy. All the smoke he'd inhaled had done significant damage, and the doc was worried about his lungs.

Following the men, she stopped at the top of the steps where Elizabeth stood, waiting to greet her. "Thank you for having us, Mrs. Seymour."

Elizabeth reached for her hands. "Oh, please call me Elizabeth. Mrs. Seymour is too formal. Let's go inside where it's warm." Elizabeth ushered her inside, where the heat from the many fireplaces thawed Marie's chilled skin. "Would you care to lie down for a while? Or perhaps I can get something for you to eat? Ben's message said he wasn't sure when you would arrive, so I had Sophia prepare a few things."

"I wouldn't mind something to eat, if that's all right?" Marie hated to be a burden.

"Of course. And we have a big dinner planned for later

tonight. I hope you'll join us?" The concern in her eyes warmed Marie's heart. Elizabeth was someone with whom Marie could see a deep and comfortable friendship forming.

Marie just hoped she didn't ruin it if Michael pushed her too far with whatever he had planned for the two of them, especially if she didn't agree to what he wanted and insisted on what she wanted, which was not a romantic relationship.

"Walter and I can stay in our rooms so your family can be together without us intruding."

"Nonsense." Elizabeth clucked her tongue. "It's Christmas. The more, the merrier. We love having our friends and family over, and you're family. Didn't Michael tell you that? Sometimes, that boy--"

"Oh no, he did. I just don't want to be presumptuous and impose. You're doing so much for us already."

"Not hardly enough with everything you have been through. But let's not dwell on that. We'll have time enough to figure out your future after Christmas." Elizabeth gently grabbed Marie's arm and pulled her close to her side as though she were a close friend. "Let's just get you settled and something in your belly. I'm sure you're still weak from the smoke you inhaled."

"I'm all right," she said, just as another coughing fit overcame her. It progressed quickly into a full-blown hacking cough that racked her entire body. Bending over, she coughed uncontrollably. She was shaky, sweaty, and afraid she'd had an accident in her drawers. She was mortified, and tears filled her eyes.

When she could finally take a breath without coughing every other second, Elizabeth took her arm. "Oh, my dear. Come with me." Elizabeth led her into a large bathing room. "You sit right here, and I'll be right back."

Marie continued to cough, her undergarments soaked with urine. She couldn't believe she had lost control of herself. *How am I going to explain this?* They wouldn't want someone like her in their home.

The door opened, and Elizabeth stepped back inside. Her arms were full of clothes, and another young lady was right behind her holding a tray with a pot of tea. They shut the door behind them.

Elizabeth placed the clothes on a table next to her. "Marie, this is Anne, Ben's sister. Do you remember her from Luke and Louisa's wedding?"

"It's been some time, and I know we didn't talk much then, but it's great to see you," Marie said.

Anne smiled. "It's good to see you as well. I'm so sorry to hear about the fire."

"Thank you," Marie said, and then another bout of coughing overtook her.

"Oh my dear," Elizabeth said once the coughing finally settled. "Let's get you some of this tea. Anne, can you pour Marie a cup, please? It has ginger and honey in it."

Marie gratefully took it. She could taste the sweetness of honey and the tangy spice of the ginger and prayed it would soothe her aching throat. After a few moments, she controlled the cough to minimal hacks that slowed with each passing second.

"Please tell me if you need anything while you are here," Anne said and then slipped out of the room.

While Marie sipped the hot tea, Elizabeth had stepped behind a curtain and turned on a faucet of water. Hot steam billowed above the curtain and filled the room.

Coming back into view, Elizabeth said, "Now, let's get you into that tub. I'm sure you'll want to make use of it."

"But... how...?"

Elizabeth smiled. "I may overstep, and if I am, please tell me, but something tells me that the coughing fits are causing parts of you not to be as well controlled as we would like."

"I... Thank you." Marie was sure a bright, fiery blush had crept up her neck and into her cheeks. She was vexed and out of sorts.

"Of course. Do you need any help?"

"I don't think so." She didn't need anyone else to know of her indignity.

"There are towels behind the curtain, and here are some clean clothes." Elizabeth pointed to the clothes she had brought with her. "Michael said you lost everything, so I hope it fits. If it doesn't, we'll find you something else."

"I... I'm not sure how to thank you." She blinked furiously, trying to keep the tears at bay. She was made of stronger stuff than this, but she was tired, and her belly and chest ached from the coughs.

"No thanks are needed. Let's just get you taken care of." Elizabeth picked up a bell on a table next to the window. "Just ring this if you need anything, anything at all." Elizabeth stopped at the door. She rested her hand on the doorframe before she turned back to her. "Marie, if I'm overstepping, please stop me. But you and your brother are welcome here for as long as you need." She drummed her fingers on the wood as though considering her next words. "What happened here will never leave our lips. No one will ever be the wiser. It isn't your fault, and you shouldn't be embarrassed. Things have been very stressful for you, and no one would fault you for anything that may have happened."

With those last words, Elizabeth left Marie alone, closing the door softly behind her.

Marie sank onto the bench, her humiliation complete. She didn't know how she could face Elizabeth after this. What a sight she must be. First, nothing to her name, and then she made a mess of her undergarments, the only clothes she had left.

She wanted to crawl into a hole and never exit. Elizabeth had been kind, but Marie didn't want to emerge ever again. She was supposed to be stronger than this, and instead she had reacted like a schoolgirl who'd been frightened by a common rodent.

What type of suffragist will I be if I continue to respond like this?

Marie left the bathing room feeling much better than she had an hour earlier. She didn't want to see anyone, but she wasn't one to hide, so she might as well get it over with. She wandered down the hall, not sure where everyone was, but she finally heard voices and followed the murmurs. With any luck, no one would notice her return, and she could slip inside and pretend as though she had been there the whole time and not in the bathing room cleaning up after herself.

But she wasn't that lucky. As she stepped inside the room, Michael looked up from the card game he was playing with Ben and smiled broadly.

"Marie." Michael placed his cards on the table.

Ben stood. "I'll leave the two of you alone."

Before Marie could tell him she didn't want to be left alone with Michael, Ben slipped out the door and closed it softly behind him.

Michael took her arm and led her to a plush blue sofa. "Sit. Elizabeth left some cookies for you." He gestured toward a plate on the small coffee table in front of him. "Sophia's a splendid cook, and I'm sure she'll whip you up something lickety-split if you'd like something more substantial."

"Lickety-split?" She laughed. "I don't think I've ever heard words like that before."

"Hey, at least I made you laugh. I haven't seen a smile on your face in quite some time." He sat next to her and picked up a gingersnap cookie.

Her smile faded as she was yanked back to reality. "I shouldn't be laughing. My life's a mess. I haven't even asked how Walter is doing. Where is he? Is he all right?" She swiveled her head like a top on a child's toy. It was a wonder it didn't fly off and land square in his lap.

When she couldn't see a sign of her brother, she started to stand, but Michael placed his hand on her knee and, with slight pressure, kept her where she was.

"Let me go," she said.

He yanked his hand back as though he'd been burned. "Marie, he's fine. Walter's upstairs sleeping. He had something to eat and then went to take a nap." He took a bite of the cookie and closed his eyes for a moment, as though savoring the tasty treat. Seeing the look of delight on his face sent a warm feeling to the pit of her belly. He opened his eyes and smiled, brushing the crumbs away from his lips. "I sure do love Sophia's cookies. You should have one."

Not wanting to cause a scene and to quell the hunger in her belly, she grabbed one and took a small bite. It was good, and she couldn't help but finish it in a few bites. She wanted another, but she wouldn't look like a glutton.

"The doc was just here, looked him over to make sure the carriage ride didn't do any added harm, and said with plenty of rest, he'll recover," Michael said.

"Oh." She slumped forward. "Thank you. I--"

"You just want to make sure he is all right. I'll take you up to his room in a few minutes, so you can check in on him, if you'd like?"

"Yes, yes, I would. Thank you."

"Of course. Why don't you get something more substantial than a cookie to eat?"

She nodded, although she wouldn't mind having more of the cookies.

"What would you like?"

"I can get it myself." She stood, but the cookie hadn't been enough as she swayed from dizziness.

Michael was by her side at once and gripped her elbow to keep her from falling. "How about I get it for you instead?"

Marie didn't want to, but she was smart enough not to push it when she was feeling weak. She carefully sat. Her head swam. It had been a rough twenty-four hours, and she wasn't sure when she had last eaten a generous meal. "Thank you."

"All right. I'll be right back."

"Michael?"

"Yes." He turned back to her.

"Can I have some water too?"

"Yes, absolutely." He quirked an eyebrow. "Don't go anywhere."

She smothered a grin. He was determined to make her smile. "No worries on that front. I'll be right here waiting." She patted the sofa.

"Just the way I like it." With that, he sauntered off.

Marie should have stopped him and read him the riot act for that comment, but she didn't have the energy to spar with him. Maybe after she ate and her throat didn't feel as though it had been scratched with a hot poker, then she'd tell him what she really thought.

A few minutes later, he returned, balancing two full plates and a tall glass of water. She reached for the glass and placed it on the table next to her before taking a plate from his hands.

"How much do you think I can eat?" She looked at the mountain of beans, potato salad, roasted chicken, brisket, ham, carrots, green beans, and bread he'd piled on the plate.

"I wasn't sure what you'd like, so"––he paused dramatically, a sparkle in his eye––"I got you a little bit of everything."

"If I eat half of this, I won't be hungry for dinner, and I'd hate to be rude."

"Oh, don't worry about that. The table will be so full of people, no one'll notice." He pointed to the food. "Now eat."

Eleven

Sunlight poured through the windows, the glare bright. Michael rolled over and rubbed his eyes. It was Christmas. The evening before had been a night he wouldn't forget, and he had a crazy wish to repeat it over. He was falling for Marie hard and fast and couldn't stop it. She was everything he could have ever wanted in a partner.

It was fast, but he had never felt this way about another woman. He had enjoyed the company of women over the years, but none of them had ever struck such a chord. Marie was elegant, independent, fiercely loyal to her brother, and she fit within his arms. Holding her after the fire had produced such a primal need in him to comfort and protect her, he was almost fearful of the depth of his feelings, and she didn't seem inclined to reciprocate.

Today was a day for celebrating and for spending time with those he loved. Not everyone was home for Christmas this year, but for those who were, it was a special time. There was an abundance of children running around, all excited for presents and plenty of sweet and savory foods. He was surprised he didn't hear the squeal of children yet. There must've been a few well-intentioned threats last night from their loving parents.

He jumped out of bed, threw on his clothes, and hurried down the hall. As he bounced down the stairs, he heard whispers and giggles. There were children likely prowling in front of the large room that housed the Christmas tree and gifts. His nieces and nephews had been told the night before that they couldn't enter the room until the adults were awake. He could guess the children were waiting not so patiently, wishing for any adult to arrive. He wasn't sure if he qualified as an adult, but he could at least end their whispers and let them have some fun. Besides, he always enjoyed being with the little ones. Their excitement was contagious, and he wanted to be the first to enjoy it.

"What do I have here?" Michael found the children camped out with blankets and pillows in front of the double doors. They jumped up and hollered.

"Uncle Mikey."

"Uncle Michael."

"Merry Christmas."

They all scrambled over him, hugging and pulling on his arms and his legs toward the double doors.

"Can we go in?"

"Can we open our presents?"

"Hurry, Uncle Mike, we've been waiting *forever* for someone to wake up."

The questions came at him hard and fast, but he smiled. He loved each and every one of them and hoped that one day he would have children as sweet and rambunctious to call his own. With any luck, he might even have a beautiful woman named Marie by his side.

"I'm not sure if we should go inside yet." A wide grin was on his face. He loved to tease them, and they knew it.

"But, Uncle Mike."

"Please, Uncle Michael."

"We'll be good, we promise."

"Yes!"

"Yes!"

"Oh, all right. Let's go in." He reached for the doors and pushed them open. The children ran inside, screaming and screeching with joy at the piles of gifts strewn under the Christmas tree and against the wall. Mounds of presents were everywhere.

Michael watched as the children exploded with enthusiasm. They clearly wanted to tear into the gifts to see what they had received, but they weren't to open anything until their parents arrived. That didn't stop them from shaking the gifts that contained their names, however. They pointed and helped one another find their gifts.

Within minutes, the adults started arriving, tying their robes and wraps, pushing back tangled hair, and rubbing at sleepy eyes, but smiles lit their faces from the children's joy. It was contagious, and soon laughter and jovial conversation filled the room as the adults became just as enthusiastic as the children.

When everyone had gathered, sitting on the sofas, chairs, lounging against the wall, or on the floor on pillows, Ben stood, held out his hand, and quieted the room. He commanded the attention of everyone as the patriarch of the family.

"I just want to say Elizabeth and I are thrilled to have you here to celebrate our lord's birthday, and the children are dying to open presents." Ben smiled at the young children as they nodded and probably hoped he'd be quick with his words. "But I think we should take a moment and express what this day means to us."

A few groans came from the youngest children, with shushing coming from the parents. Chuckles followed, but that didn't stop Ben from proceeding. He nodded to Elizabeth.

"I echo Ben's sentiments." Elizabeth stood, tightening the sash around her waist, and reached for Ben's hand. "I, too, am thankful you're here today. It's so nice to have our friends and family share this special day, and I'm blessed to have found such a wonderful family to call my own."

Ben pulled her close and gave her a quick hug, whispering

something in her ear. Michael felt a tug of emotion. With Marie close, he'd like to have the same love and closeness that Ben and Elizabeth shared, and perhaps one day he would.

The sentiments continued around the room, each adult expressing their love and appreciation, with a few calling out moments they wanted to highlight.

When it was his turn, Michael stood, and suddenly, the words he wanted to say were stuck firmly in his throat. He looked at his brothers, their wives, their children, and he wanted to have the same thing. He gazed at Marie. It was difficult for him to speak without thinking he would embarrass himself immensely.

"I..." He swallowed and grabbed at his collar, suddenly feeling like he couldn't breathe.

"Are you all right, Michael?" Ben asked.

"Umm... Yes..."

"I think he's smitten." Stanley laughed.

Michael glared at him. Ever since Stanley had married Charlotte and returned to Montana, he'd been disgustingly happy all the time. Michael shouldn't be angry with him, as Stanley was pleasant now that he and Charlotte were together, but it was times like these where Michael wished Stanley was still his sullen self. Then he wouldn't deem it necessary to embarrass his younger brother.

Swallowing, he pushed the words out. "Merry Christmas, everyone. I'm grateful for my family, including my annoying older brothers."

He sat and cursed silently. He had wanted to say so much more, but perhaps it would be better to wait to talk to Marie when they were alone, with no prying eyes.

Marie watched as Michael stood and received playful ribbing from his brother, but it was clear Michael was not comfortable with it. It confused her because he seemed to enjoy laughing and making jokes, but something had made him uncomfortable this morning. She wondered if he'd wanted to say more, but he'd blushed after Stanley's comments and then muttered out a "Merry Christmas, everyone." He'd avoided looking at her after that, and considering she had felt his eyes on her all morning, she wasn't sure what to make of it. Was he embarrassed that his brother had said he was smitten, or was it something else?

She, on the other hand, was just as embarrassed. As soon as Stanley said it, heat had bloomed up her chest. Everyone's attention had been on Michael and not her, even though she kind of wondered if Elizabeth had glanced her way. Luckily, Elizabeth hadn't said anything, and Marie had taken a breath to calm her pounding heart. If no one had noticed, she wanted to keep it that way.

The well-wishes continued, and even Walter stood, leaning against his cane while sweat glistened across his face. He was determined to thank them for their help, even if he should be resting.

Walter was insisting they stay at Thundering Mountain Ranch until after the first of the year, but Marie wasn't sure it was a good idea. He was asking too many questions, and her anxiety had increased for fear that her brother was going to think the fire had been caused by her involvement with the suffragists. She was in a trifle of a mess, and she might ruin her relationship with her brother if she didn't stop, but she couldn't. Getting women the right to vote was the most important thing.

When everyone had spoken, Ben looked around the room, a devious twinkle in his eye. "I think we've made the children wait long enough. Shall we let them open their gifts?"

A resounding "Yes!" could be heard, and the squeals of pleasure and pounding of children's feet as they pounced on their gifts were a pleasing sound. Ripped paper and anticipation permeated the room as each child found toys they'd wished for and games they weren't expecting. The adults smiled with contentment, holding each other, smiling, and whispering as their little ones expressed their joy.

Marie wished she and Walter had the means to contribute to the gift-giving, but it was fun to watch. She sat quietly next to Walter and was thankful her brother was alive.

Elizabeth handed her a gift with a brightly colored red-and-green bow wrapped around it.

"Oh no, Elizabeth, you shouldn't have." Marie was horrified. She had nothing to give any of them and couldn't accept.

"Nonsense, it's Christmas," Elizabeth said.

"But... I... We have nothing for you."

Elizabeth covered Marie's hand with hers. "Shh, you being here is gift enough. Now, please take this."

Marie begrudgingly took the gift. She didn't want to call any further attention to herself. "Thank you."

"You're certainly welcome."

Moments later, a pile of small gifts appeared in front of both Walter and Marie from different members of Michael's family.

Marie was honored that they were so kind, and she felt painfully inadequate. She didn't want to appear ungrateful, so she said little and quietly opened the gifts that were laid out in front of her.

She received a delicate music box, a satin scarf, a pair of soft kid leather gloves, hair ribbons, and a woolen shawl. Walter had a few gifts himself--a knife with an intricately carved handle, a thick woolen knit cap, a shiny belt buckle, and a pair of leather gloves.

The roar in the room dimmed as the children gathered their gifts and took them to the playroom on the second floor to share and play. Before long, the only children left were the babies still in their mothers' arms. The couples whispered to one another as they exchanged their gifts.

Marie watched Stanley and Michael talking. Stanley was laughing, while Michael grimaced at whatever his brother had said to him. Stanley then reached and slapped him affectionately on the back before escaping out the back of the room, his wife, Charlotte, by his side.

Walter patted her arm and pushed to stand, shaking as he leaned on his wooden cane. "I'm going to go to my room for a rest." Marie started to follow, but he placed his hand on her shoulder and stopped her. "No, stay here. Enjoy the morning."

"Do you need help?"

"Marie, I might need this cane, but I'm not an invalid." He smiled to soften his words. "I can go up the stairs without any help."

"Are you feeling all right?"

"I'm perfectly fine. I just want to lie down for a bit."

He didn't look fine. His skin was ashy, and he was not steady on his feet. "But--"

"No buts. I'm fine. I'll see you in a few hours."

She couldn't stop him, so she nodded and watched him shuffle out of the room. Her heart was heavy. She had likely been the cause of his pain, but she didn't want to make a fuss, so she sat fiddling with her gifts.

As the minutes ticked by, each person left the room until she was alone. She was settled comfortably on a sofa near a window, a thick afghan across her lap. She'd curled her feet under her and watched the lazy snow fall. It was overcast, but as the flakes fell, they covered the ground, creating a winter wonderland.

It was peaceful, and she was content to sit and enjoy the silence, amazed at how kind the Seymours had been to them. She picked up the music box, lifted the lid, and let the soft music surround her.

The door behind her opened and shut quietly, and she pushed around to see who had come inside. It was Michael.

"May I join you?" he asked.

She nodded. "This is your home. Of course you can."

"I don't want to disturb you. You look mighty peaceful sitting there." He appeared nervous, fidgety as he shuffled his feet back and forth.

"I was just marveling at how beautiful it is outside."

He took his hat off and brushed the snow off it. "I was in the corral with the horses and saw you through the windows."

"Oh, I didn't realize anyone was out there." She fingered the buttons at her neck. Her nightgown covered her from head to toe, and she was in a thick wrap, but she was still not properly clothed for being in the presence of a man who was not family. Everyone had been in their nightclothes while they opened presents, but she hadn't made it upstairs to change. She probably should have, but she hadn't wanted to move from her comfortable cocoon.

"A ranch never shuts down, even on Christmas."

Heat crawled up her neck. "I didn't mean to imply––"

"I know you didn't." He laughed quietly. "I'm just having fun with you."

"You sure enjoy doing that, don't you?"

"Doing what?" He grinned.

"I don't have to tell you. You're fully aware of what you are doing."

She relaxed back against the sofa and turned away from him. Suddenly hot, she feared she was blushing and didn't want him to notice. This was becoming an unwelcome pattern and was annoying. She was not like the girls in town who simpered whenever a handsome cowboy came their way. Perhaps if she didn't look at him and pretended to ignore him, he would go away, and her heart would stop racing a mile a minute.

But he didn't. Instead, he rustled behind her. She pretended to stare out the window, but out of the corner of her eye, she saw him kneel in front of the fireplace, his thick sheepskin coat covered in a dusting of snow that quickly melted from the heat. Dark brown curls nestled at the base of his neck, and she itched to run her fingers through them. He straightened, extending to his full height, and rubbed his hands to warm them.

After a moment, he shrugged out of his coat and placed it on the chair next to the fireplace. He then turned to look at her. She averted her gaze, but she could sense his smile. Blast him. He always caught her in awkward positions, and staring at him like a lovesick calf was not the look she was going for.

"Did you have a nice Christmas?" he asked after a long moment.

"Yes, thank you," she said.

"I'm glad. Did you get everything you wanted for Christmas?"

"Your family was very generous, more than generous. I just wish I could have given you each something in return."

"Ah, no worries on that front. We're just glad you are safe and could spend Christmas with us." He sat in the armchair next to the window, giving her no choice but to look at him.

"Elizabeth is very kind to open her home to strangers," she said, feeling suddenly awkward and unsure of herself.

"You and your brother aren't strangers."

"Maybe not to you, but I'm not familiar with many members of your family outside of Luke and Ben."

"Well, at any rate, we're glad you're here." His eyes twinkled, the brown orbs reminding her of some of the cliffs next to Helena.

"Thank you," she whispered.

They sat quietly for the next few minutes. The fire crackled, and the snow continued to fall. She examined the satin scarf and hair ribbons. Anything to keep her eyes away from his.

"Are you going to continue to avoid looking at me?"

She stiffened and, without looking at him, said, "I certainly have no idea what you're talking about."

He laughed, a deep laugh that curled her toes. "Oh, you do, Marie, and it's quite the game we're playing, isn't it?"

"I'm not playing a game."

"Oh, you are."

"No, I'm not!" she snapped, raising her head to glare at him and instantly wished she hadn't.

He'd leaned forward in his chair, a thick lock of hair having fallen across his wide forehead, and his mouth was slightly open as if he wanted to devour her.

What am I thinking? He is not about to devour me, but I almost wish he would.

"So adamant in your refusal. Makes me wonder why." He pulled on his earlobe.

"I'm not playing a game with you. I'm sitting here enjoying Christmas morning, or at least, I was until you returned. You're ruining it by accusing me of playing a game."

He once again went silent, so she turned to look out the window, but as the minutes ticked by and he stayed quiet, her nerves got the best of her, and she looked back at him. He had relaxed in his chair, his long legs extended in front of him. He bent his left arm and placed one finger against his cheek. He didn't move and continued to stare at her, not smiling, not frowning-- just staring.

"What?" she muttered.

He nonchalantly placed his hand in his lap. "I didn't say a word."

"But you're looking at me."

"Is it a crime to look at a gorgeous woman?" A serious smile lined his lips.

"I'm not... I mean..." She stopped speaking. She was speechless.

"What? You don't have a smart retort for that one?" His eyes twinkled merrily.

"You are the most infuriating man." A tingle of awareness clenched inside her belly.

"It seems we continue to have this discussion anytime I compliment you. Do you not like compliments?" His gaze had grown serious, intent, perhaps containing a bit of desire that she refused to acknowledge.

"Of course I enjoy compliments *if* they're said with sincerity."

"Are you saying my compliments aren't sincere?" His charming smile slipped a bit.

"Yes... I mean no... I mean yes... Oh, bother."

He flustered her, and she didn't like it one bit.

"Is it yes or no?"

"It's... I'm not dignifying that with a response."

"Would you care to go for a walk?" he asked.

"What?"

He went from one topic to another, not giving her a moment to catch her breath. She couldn't keep up with him.

"I said, would you like to go for a walk?" He lifted an eyebrow as if daring her to refuse.

"It's snowing outside." Her excuse sounded lame. She lived in Montana, where snow was a part of everyday life.

"Are you afraid of a little snow?"

"Of course not." Irritation prickled the back of her neck. She didn't understand this man.

"Well, then, let's go."

"I can't. I'm still in my nightgown and wrapper. Besides, I don't have any boots or a coat or--"

"That's easy enough to fix. Elizabeth keeps a wardrobe with all kinds of outerwear for guests who might've forgotten something."

He stood and held out his hand. If she refused, she would look weak, yet she was afraid of what would happen if she didn't.

She glared at him for a moment, swung her legs down, and found her slippers. "I need to change."

"Don't worry, I won't ravish you." He looked like he wouldn't mind doing just that if she gave him even a bit of encouragement.

"What?" Why did she suddenly want him to do just that?

"You heard me." A knowing smirk lined his lips. "You can wear what you're wearing. There's plenty of winter gear in the mudroom you can pull on over your nightclothes. Come on, let's go."

Twelve

⌒⌒

Twenty minutes later, Marie was dressed in a very strange concoction of clothing––the bottom half of a man's union suit, leather trousers, heavy boots, and a thick woolen coat with a knit cap over her head. She might look mighty peculiar, but at least she'd be warm.

Marie then stepped outside, with Michael following close behind her. The snow was still falling, but the sun peeked out from behind the clouds. If he hadn't been so close, where she could feel his heat, she might've enjoyed being outside on this crisp Christmas morning.

"Shall we?" He held out his arm.

But being the stubborn woman she was, she refused his gesture and instead stomped on the snow-covered porch when she suddenly slipped on an icy patch and her legs went out from under her. For a moment, it felt as if she were floating in the snow, like a lazy snowflake, but just when she should have hit the ground, powerful arms grabbed her from behind and stopped her descent.

Michael pulled her and dragged her against him until her feet were back under her. He wrapped his arms tightly around her waist, bent his head, and whispered, "Careful, my dear. I wouldn't want you to fall."

"Let go of me," she muttered.

He released his grip and stepped away. "Now, now. No need to get angry. I was just trying to save you from breaking your backside."

"I wasn't falling," she hissed.

"No? It must've been my imagination that your hips were about to hit the ground."

She whirled around, and her feet again went out from under her.

He caught her, but this time, he swept her into his arms. "Wow, Marie, you're having a hard time today staying on your feet." He strode forward with her clasped in his arms.

"Unhand me, you brute." She pushed at his muscular chest. "I won't say it again."

"I listened to you, and you fell... *Again*."

She sighed with frustration. "Only because you angered me with your impudence."

"Oh, it's *my* arrogance we're talking about then?" He gave her a smug smile.

She was going to ignore that blasted charming grin that curled her toes. "Yes. So if you would kindly put me down, this time I will be prepared, and I *won't* fall." She struggled to get out of his arms, but he had a steady grip and continued to stride forward, ignoring her attempts. "Dammit, Michael." She hit his chest, but only an occasional grunt emitted from him.

He finally stopped near the fence and murmured something under his breath that she couldn't quite understand.

"What did you say?"

"Nothing of importance." His eyes had darkened, and his breath had grown quick and heavy. "I'll only put you down--if you hold on to my arm."

"Of all the insufferable, infuriating--"

"Now, now. No need to get all riled up," he said.

"I'm not riled up." She was most definitely riled up, not to mention hot and sweaty. She suddenly wanted him to do things to her that she never thought possible.

"You are, my dear, and what a sight you are. I'm concerned. Your cheeks are flushed, your eyes are flashing, and you're breathing quite heavily." There was laughter, but at the same time, his voice had a sensuous undertone that felt deliciously sinful. But she wouldn't let him distract her.

"Oh, shut up, you mongrel. Put me down. Right... this... instant."

He laughed and then carefully lowered her legs, but he didn't let go until she gained her footing. He was forever the gentleman, and that stuck in her craw even more.

"Ready for our walk?" he asked.

Ugh, she wanted to smack him. She nodded and stepped forward, but he placed his large, warm hand on her shoulder, sending a chill through her. "Wait."

"What?" She glanced over her shoulder.

He held out his arm, and his eyes looked to it and back again to her.

"Oh, heavens. Are you always this stubborn?"

He grinned that heavenly dazzling smile of his that, if she weren't careful, would sweep her off her feet and that would not do. Shaking her head, she did as he wanted. Otherwise, he was likely going to drive her to distraction with his insistence.

He wrapped her hand around his arm and pulled her close. "Now, that is much better." He strode forward. "This way, I can make sure you won't fall again."

"Oh... bother," she muttered.

His body shook with what she assumed was suppressed laughter. It was a good thing he hadn't laughed aloud because that would have probably knocked her over the edge, and she might've pushed him into the snow. She still might do that, too, if he nudged her far enough.

He walked with her around the yard, around the multiple barns, through the corrals, not saying much but occasionally pointing out something he found interesting. Items such as the horses and their silent communication with one another, the rare bald eagle that soared above them, the rooster who flapped in irritation, the ranch hands who participated in a quick snowball fight, and several small inconsequential things she would've never noticed if he hadn't pointed them out.

As they walked, her anger and frustration at his impertinence waned, and before long, she began to enjoy herself. It was cold outside, but he kept her from freezing. She didn't want to take pleasure from this outing, but she did, nonetheless.

"Would you care to sit?" he asked.

They stopped outside of a wooden swing with a covered awning set away from the house. It was secluded, yet open, with tall pine trees surrounding it.

"This ranch is unbelievably majestic." Marie gazed around in awe. She could see why his family had picked this place to live. It was truly magnificent.

"It is, isn't it? My pa created it for my ma. She liked to have time alone but didn't want to be too far away from us. I never understood why, but I wonder..." He stopped and didn't say more.

She looked up at him but couldn't read his thoughts.

"Let's sit." He let go of her arm and swept away the snow that rested on the seat.

She sat, and the swing swayed.

"All good?" he said. "Are you warm enough?"

"Yes." And then she promptly shivered, but he'd looked over his shoulder and had missed it.

"I can run up to the house and get you a blanket."

"No, I'm fine."

"May I?" He gestured toward the space next to her.

Marie nodded. She should send him on his way, but it'd be rude considering he had taken the time to show her around his family's ranch.

Michael settled next to her and rested his arm on the back of the seat. He lightly brushed his fingers against her shoulder and bent his legs to push the swing forward. "Are you all right if we sway?"

She chuckled. "I think it's too late to ask me that, don't you think?"

He stopped the swing and then kicked it off again. Laughter shook his shoulders.

"I can see why your ma liked it here."

"Yes, she sure did. She used to come out here at least once a day. We knew better than to disturb her when she did. Pa said this was her special place, and when she was here, we weren't to bother her."

"Would she stay out here for long?" She could imagine his ma coming out here to breathe in the fresh air in the winter, to smell the flowers in the spring when they bloomed, and even bask in the sultry heat of summer.

"No. Usually for only twenty or thirty minutes. I used to wonder what she did out here, but I never knew."

"Based on how serene it is, I imagine it was to get away from the chaos of having four sons and two daughters. You were likely pretty wild."

He laughed. "Point taken. I always wondered, though, if it was something more than that. There was a time or two I ventured near the circle of the pine trees, and I could've sworn I heard her crying."

"Oh." She turned to gaze at him.

"Yes." He smiled and brushed snow off her cheek. "But I never knew for sure, and when she would come out of the circle of trees, she'd smile at us as if nothing had happened. I probably was hearing things, but sometimes I wondered."

"As you got older, did you ever ask?"

"No, I wish I had, but I never did." A sad smile lined his lips.

"How old were you when she passed?" She immediately realized she had no right to ask that question. "I'm sorry. That was insensitive."

"It's all right. I don't mind talking about it." He ran his fingers across his thigh, almost in a nervous gesture. "I was nineteen. She was taken from us too soon. Both of 'em were."

"I'm sorry, it had to have been hard to lose them at such a young age." She also felt the pain of losing parents who loved you dearly.

"Yeah, and they weren't exactly taken from us the way they should've been."

"What do you mean?"

"You don't know?" He stopped the sway of the swing with his feet. His arm came out from behind her, and he leaned forward and braced his elbows on his knees with his hands clasped tight.

"Don't know what?"

He sighed. "I'm surprised you didn't after everything that happened with Luke two years ago."

"Luke and Walter were after an evil brothel madam, but Walter never told me the details. He said I was too delicate to hear such things." She snorted. Her brother didn't realize how much she saw and heard while working with the women in the suffragist league. If he did, he'd for sure ban her for life.

Michael chuckled.

Her back stiffened. "It's not funny."

He choked back his laughter. "No, it's not, and I shouldn't make light of it. Your brother doesn't understand you too well, does he?"

"Not as much as he'd like to believe." Marie might regret telling him this, but perhaps it would help him understand why she needed Walter to stay in the dark. "What he doesn't realize is that I know more about the world than he thinks. I don't know what happened with your family, but I am privy to more than he'd like to admit."

"I have no doubt," he said.

She shifted on the swing and turned to face him. "You don't have to tell me what happened to your folks. We lost my parents years ago in a cliff accident. The officials said they jumped to their death, but I never believed it, so I understand the pain of losing them is something no one can fully understand unless they've been through it themselves." She had never told anyone that much about their death, but for some reason, it was easy to tell him.

"I'm so sorry to hear that," he said. "How horrible for you and your brother."

"I think one of them slipped, and the other tried to save them, but something went very wrong. It took a long time for me to accept that people will believe what they want." The vicious comments and looks she had gotten after their death was something she didn't like to remember. People had been brutal with their heartless gossip. "They loved each other, and they loved Walter and me. They would've never left us intentionally."

Michael squeezed her hand before letting go. "Ma died of the influenza, and we thought Pa had died that way too, but it turned out, he was murdered by Stanley's first wife. She was after our pa's money, and luckily, her schemes failed, but our pa was taken from us way too soon."

Marie sat stunned. Her parents, while not murdered, had a stigma attached to their deaths that she didn't like to discuss. "How horrible for you and your family. And Stanley, what did he... No, I shouldn't ask. That is none of my business." Her inquisitive nature could be detrimental. She didn't mean to be nosy, but sometimes she couldn't help herself.

"It isn't a secret. It's been eleven years, so the pain lessens each day."

"Did you catch the woman who did this to your family?"

"She's dead." Michael's voice had lost its luster and instead was filled with a heavy pain.

"How?" As soon as she asked, she could've slapped herself. "No, don't answer that. I'm sorry. I'm being insensitive."

Michael stared into the distance and ran his fingers across his upper lip. "You aren't, and it's a perfectly normal question to ask." He turned to face her, dropping his lips into a frown that marred his handsome face. "I killed her."

"Oh." She was surprised. Of all the things she expected him to say, that was not it. "I'm sure..."

He abruptly stood, the swing swaying enough that she had to grab the wooden armrest to keep from falling.

Michael faced away from her, an unbearable weight crushing his shoulders. "I didn't intend to, but she was about to kill Luke, and I couldn't let that happen. I'd never killed anyone before and... and I hope I never have to do it again."

She grabbed his hand and pulled him next to her. Marie held his large hand in hers. His palm was rough but smooth at the same time. "I'm sure you had no choice, and killing shouldn't be easy. If it were, I'd be more concerned for your soul than I am right now."

"You're far too kind."

"I'm not kind," she said. "I'm realistic. We have to make choices, and sometimes they're hard."

"It wasn't hard to kill her." His eyes narrowed. "I'd protect my family over anything. She terrorized our family, and I couldn't let her take someone else. Now, we just have to figure out what her sister Pauline is up to, but she refuses to tell us anything."

"Are you talking about Pauline Chandler?"

Michael pulled his hand away. "Do you know who she is?" Disbelief was in his gaze.

"Um, well, yeah, I guess you could say I do." She was in a pickle now. If Walter discovered she was in cahoots with a parlor house madam, all hell would break loose.

"If you don't mind me asking, why would you be talking with a harlot?"

"Don't look at me like that," she muttered.

"Look at you like what?" He tried unsuccessfully to hide his smirk.

"Like that." She pointed at him. "You're laughing at me."

"No, I'm not. I'm just surprised you would."

"Would you quit calling her a harlot?" she growled. "In my line of work, I run into all kinds of women. Pauline and I have an understanding. She tells me when she hears of any women needing help."

"Why would she be involved in such things?"

"Well... Um... Her... Well." A blush crept up her cheeks. While she wasn't ashamed of her association with Pauline, she didn't exactly understand everything that happened in the brothel, either. Taking a breath, she continued. "Her clientele or customers... Um, the men... You know."

He laughed. "No, please explain. I'm not sure I understand."

She glared at him. "You shouldn't be laughing."

"I shouldn't, but it sure is fun to watch you squirm. Anyway, what were you saying?"

"Arghh. Her... Well, her customers sometimes mention things about their wives, and she passes that information on to me."

"Why would she do that?"

"We have the same goal."

His mouth fell open before he formed his next question. "What possible goal could you have with a harlot, especially her?"

She slapped her hand on the swing. "Would you quit saying that?"

"Saying what?"

"Har... Harlot," she muttered.

"Isn't that what she is?"

She sighed. "Maybe, but I prefer to look at her differently. She knows of women who are hurt, and I help her."

"How do you help?"

"That doesn't matter." She wasn't going to tell him everything. If he discovered she'd hidden the women in the cellar of her house until her network could smuggle them out of town, Walter would definitely prohibit her from continuing.

"Don't trust the woman, Marie. She's dangerous." Michael's voice was strained.

"I don't believe that. She's––"

"Pauline was involved with the woman who killed my pa and almost killed Luke. She's not innocent and knew far more than she would admit. Don't trust her."

Marie swallowed. His tone brooked no argument, but Pauline had been an invaluable asset in saving many women. Marie didn't understand Pauline's involvement in Michael's family loss, but she was having a hard time reconciling that with the woman who seemed determined to help women in trouble.

Thirteen

Michael had been looking for Marie all evening, but he hadn't found her. The house was full of people, more so than at Christmas. Elizabeth and Ben always threw a New Year's Eve party and invited many friends and neighbors. If the weather was nice enough, they'd have fires in the yard, and the party would venture outside for the fire show that was set off at midnight.

He wanted to make sure he was near Marie when the clock struck midnight, as it was tradition to kiss the ones near you, and Michael was determined to continue that tradition––if she let him. He had tried on numerous occasions to get her under the mistletoe but had been unsuccessful. It was like she had a sixth sense for avoiding any chance of being near him after their walk on Christmas Day.

They had talked about things he hadn't expected. He'd shared more about his parents than he had with any other woman before. He was moving too fast, but Michael wanted her for his wife and intended to propose to her tonight after he kissed her at the stroke of midnight. They barely knew one another, but he wanted to learn more about her and figured marriage was a start to make that happen.

Moving through the crush of people, he saw Walter and headed toward him. Maybe he knew where his sister was hiding.

Michael gripped Walter's shoulder. "Walter, how you feeling?"

Walter grinned. "Good. Better than good. I can't wait to get rid of this"--he pounded his cane on the floor--"and get back to Helena."

"When you planning on heading back?"

"Tomorrow." He took a sip of his drink.

"Is Marie going with you?"

"Yes." Walter saluted. "She's eager to find us a new home."

Michael's heart sank. He didn't want her to leave, but she was purely independent and would want to get them back on their feet.

"Honestly, Michael, she's more interested in getting back to her blasted meetings and protests." Walter's smile had slipped a bit. "I think she can't breathe without a sign in her hand and fighting someone about what she believes women in Montana deserve."

Her suffragist actions made Michael proud. He couldn't help but take pleasure in her working hard to achieve her goals. "That certainly sounds like your sister. Where are you going to stay?"

"I'll get us rooms at the hotel."

"You don't need to do that. Let me talk with Ben, but I'd think you both could stay at Luke's. It's plenty big enough."

"I thought it was being rented by that family from New York."

"It was, but they moved out right before Christmas. Ben was doing repairs before we tried to find someone else to rent it."

"We couldn't do that," Walter said. "That's a lot to ask, especially with everything your family has done for us over the last week."

"I'm sure it won't be a problem. We don't care to leave it empty, so you'll be doing us a favor." While that was true, Michael couldn't help but hope that Marie would see that he had good intentions and was on her side in her fight for women's rights. Changing her mind that he was an honorable man would be difficult, but it would be a step in the right direction.

"I don't think this is a good idea."

"Nonsense," Michael said. "We'd be offended if you didn't stay. Luke would be happy to help you out. You did plenty for him, remember?" Walter had been instrumental in helping end Connie's terror, and their family would always be indebted to him.

Walter nodded. "If you put it like that, then, yes, thank you. We would be honored to stay at least until I can find us a place to rent permanently or until I can build a new house."

"Great. Then it's settled."

"Shouldn't you talk with Ben first?"

Michael chuckled. "That's fair. I'll find him and confirm, but I'm sure it won't be a problem."

"All right. It'll be nice to get back to Helena."

"I need to return to town myself, so we can travel together." Marie wouldn't be pleased with that, but it made sense for them to go together. He'd left the smithy long enough, and Tony would be eager for his return.

"Perfect. I'm going to acquire a fresh drink." Walter held up his empty whiskey glass.

"Could we talk later?" Michael asked.

"Sure." Walter lifted an eyebrow. "Do you want to do it now?"

Michael couldn't talk to Walter until he talked to Marie first. He owed her that much because he couldn't imagine her being impressed if he were to ask her brother's permission to marry her without first asking her. "No. I'll come and find you soon. I need to do something else first."

"Well, I'm off. Come find me when you want to talk. I'll be around here somewhere." Walter winked at him and moved to a table filled with decanters of liquor and platters of food.

Michael scanned the crowd again, looking for Marie's signature black hair. When he didn't see her, he walked the perimeter of each room, stopping to say hello to friends from neighboring ranches. After an hour of searching, he moved into the quiet hallway and sat on the bottom step of the back staircase. Most everyone was in the front of the house, and he could sit in peace.

Where was she?

"Michael?"

He looked over his shoulder and scrambled to stand. Stunned, he stared at a woman he'd never expected to see again. Suzette. He hadn't seen her since she'd spurned Ben years before when they were living in Spring Creek. He and Luke had joined Ben there after Stanley believed he had inherited the family's ranch and thrown his brothers off the ranch because of his ex-wife's machinations.

While living in Spring Creek, the three of them had worked for Elizabeth's brother, James, before he'd been sent to prison for robbing stagecoaches. Suzette had pursued Ben, leading him on a merry chase before abruptly running away with another man. Lucky for Ben, Suzette's abrupt departure had allowed him to step in and help Elizabeth when her father's threats had grown dangerous. If things hadn't turned out the way they had, Ben would've never married Elizabeth.

Shaking his head from the memories, he said, "Suzette, you're the last person I expected to see."

Suzette smiled. She was just as beautiful as she'd been eleven years before. If he hadn't already seen how conniving and manipulative she could be, he might've chased after her all those years ago, but she'd set her cap on Ben, and for that, he was glad.

"I never expected to be back in Montana, but it's home, and I'm glad I've returned." She pranced down the stairs, almost as though she were floating instead.

"Does Ben know you're here?"

She frowned slightly before replacing it with a beaming smile. "Not yet. I came with Janie and Tom. I've moved back to Spring Creek with my children."

"And your husband?"

Her eyes filled with tears, but she blinked them back. "I'm sorry. I didn't mean to lose my composure."

"No need to apologize. I shouldn't have asked..."

"No." Her hand rested on his arm. "It's all right. It's still just so hard. My husband... He... he passed away last year. I still have days where I think he's still here, and seeing the pain on my children's faces is difficult to bear."

While he wasn't fond of the woman, he hated to see anyone lose their family. "Is there anything I can do?"

She trembled. "No, but I do appreciate your kindness. I'd expect you to hate me." She dropped her hand and clasped her hands together in front of her waist. Her eyes were contrite, a look far different from what he'd expect of her.

"We don't hate you." They didn't much like her, but hate was a wasted emotion, as they'd all learned.

She tilted her head. "Even after what I did to Ben?"

He stared at her. "Well, that was hard to watch, but ultimately, he ended up with Elizabeth, so all's forgiven, I'm sure."

"And how is the happy couple?" Her smile showed one thing, and her eyes said something else, but what it was, he couldn't name.

This was why he wouldn't trust the woman.

"They are doing well." He didn't think Suzette cared. She'd never cared about anything besides herself, even though she could have changed. It had been almost ten years since he had last seen her. She could have matured––anything was possible.

"I heard they have two children, a boy and a girl." She shifted, posing against the railing, clearly to her best advantage.

"Yes, Jimmy and Vicky. They are a blessing."

"I'm surprised they haven't had more," she said.

He wondered if there was a bit of maliciousness to her tone, but he wasn't sure. "No, they haven't been blessed with any more."

"Are you married? Any children?" Her gaze became coquettish. She fluttered her eyelashes as though he would fall for that simpering act. There was only one woman for him, and it definitely wasn't Suzette.

"No, not yet."

"Well"--she grinned broadly--"I'm sure someone will snatch you up before too long."

"Mama, Mama," yelled a young girl with bright yellow hair. She skidded around the corner and slammed into Suzette's legs.

"Natalie, my dear. What is wrong?" Suzette bent, her pale pink gown collapsing in a mound beneath her as she peered into Natalie's blue eyes.

"It's Todd," Natalie said with disgust. "He's being mean again and was callin' me names."

Suzette shook her head. "That wasn't nice of him. I told your brother to treat you with kindness tonight."

"He didn't listen, Mama. You should punish him." Natalie pulled at her pigtails, pouting.

"Why don't I talk to him first and then I'll decide what his punishment should be?"

The girl nodded reluctantly. Suzette stood, and the girl placed her hand trustingly in her mother's hand.

"Michael, this is my daughter, Natalie. Natalie, this"--she pointed to Michael--"is someone I met a long time ago."

"Hello," Natalie said with a shy smile.

"Hello, young lady," Michael said. "Aren't you a pretty little girl? I bet you're going to be as beautiful as your mama."

Natalie shuffled behind Suzette's skirts and peeked at Michael. "Thank you."

"Michael, it has been good to see you, but I need to find my oldest. It sounds as though he's been into a bit of mischief."

He nodded, and then, to his surprise, Suzette hugged and kissed him on the cheek. "You've certainly grown into a handsome man. Next time I'm in Helena, we should have supper."

Reaching the parlor door, she stopped and looked over her shoulder. If he wasn't already aware of what she was truly like and wasn't infatuated with Marie, he might've taken the open invitation Suzette was offering. But he knew how she operated, and he wouldn't get ensnared in her web like his brother had all those years ago.

Fourteen

Marie retreated into the kitchen after witnessing Michael's embrace with the beautiful blonde. She had never met the woman, but Michael's smile was enough to tell Marie that she was somebody important to him. Marie didn't want to believe that Michael was the type of man to string multiple women along, but most men had no qualms about having their cake and eating it, too. Perhaps Marie had misjudged him, and he had no issue with having them at his beck and call.

She had been a fool to let Michael break down the confines of her heart. A serious jolt of jealousy surged through her as she watched him hold that woman. Marie thought she had guarded her heart, but clearly, she hadn't. She would just stay away from him tonight, and then she would return to Helena tomorrow. There she could get on with her life and never see him again.

"Marie... Marie..." a questioning voice called from behind her.

"What...?" Marie found Elizabeth behind her, holding a decadent chocolate cake, with swirls of frosting and pieces of shaved chocolate. "I'm sorry, Elizabeth. Did you ask me something?" She cradled her hand against her chest, praying she didn't look like she'd just had her heart ripped out, which was an unfortunate response on her part. Marie didn't know Michael well enough to be upset by what she saw, but she was.

Elizabeth smiled. "I was just curious if you needed anything. Your mind was somewhere else just now."

"You could say that." Marie raised shaking fingers to her cheek.

"Wouldn't have anything to do with Michael, would it?"

Marie swallowed. From the look in Elizabeth's eyes, she likely had observed Michael's interest in her over the past few days.

"Um, no..." The heat climbing up her neck and into her cheeks was at odds with her words. Marie had been thinking of him, but after what she just saw, she wasn't sure he was as honorable as she had thought. But she wouldn't tell Elizabeth that.

Elizabeth chuckled. "I'm sorry if I'm teasing you. I certainly don't mean to. It's just Michael hasn't shown interest in anyone in years, and I believe he's infatuated with you."

"I can't say if that is true." Marie couldn't get the image of Michael's tender embrace with that woman out of her mind.

"I do, and if I may"––Elizabeth put the cake down and lightly placed her hands on Marie's upper arms––"I'd be thrilled to see something develop between the two of you."

"I don't have time for a man."

"Oh." Elizabeth's eyes widened over Marie's words.

"No disrespect, but having a man could derail my mission."

"Your mission?" Elizabeth looked perplexed, scrunching her forehead in confusion.

"Yes, I'm determined to gain women the vote here in Montana."

"Oh, that mission. A very noble mission, if I do say so myself, but can't you still have a husband even while accomplishing your goals?"

"No." Marie shook her head. "Men only get in the way. Once I marry, I'll be forced to do and be whatever my husband tells me. You should understand that." Marie gestured toward the cake resting on the table. "Here you are stuck on this ranch, running your husband's household, taking care of his children, and not being able to lead your own life."

Elizabeth carefully untied the apron around her waist, her lips in a straight line. "Would you come with me, please?"

Marie nodded, confused by Elizabeth's request, but she wasn't about to insult her and refuse, although she might have done just that with what she had just said. As Elizabeth walked toward the back staircase that led upstairs, Marie touched her arm. "Elizabeth, I'm sorry. I think I might have offended you. I get carried away sometimes and don't realize that my opinions aren't always appreciated."

"I'm not offended, Marie." She smiled. "Now come."

Marie followed Elizabeth up the stairs and down the hall until Elizabeth stopped at the large double doors that led to what Marie presumed was her bedroom. Elizabeth opened the door and gestured her inside, closing the door behind them.

"You don't need to look so timid. I'm not going to bite."

Marie laughed. "I'm sorry. I just didn't expect to be taken to your room. I'm invading your personal space."

"Oh, nonsense. It's just a bedroom, albeit a very nice one, I'll have to admit. Now, come, sit." Elizabeth moved to a pair of chairs that sat against a large window and settled into one of them. She turned on the lamp, as the light outside was dimming with the fast-setting sun. "So, you think that marrying a man will stifle your future?" Elizabeth got right to the point. She was nothing but direct.

"Yes... Well, no... Not exactly... But yes."

Elizabeth giggled. "I see you aren't entirely convinced."

"Yes, I am." Marie sat stiffly in her chair, her hackles growing at her indecision. "I admit... I'm nervous, as I'm not sure what you would like to tell me."

"Let's straighten out a few things." Elizabeth held up a finger. "First, I'm a bit concerned you have the wrong opinion of me, but I'll forgive you for that, as we haven't had the chance to talk while you've been here, and that is entirely my fault. I haven't been a very good hostess."

Marie was ashamed. She hadn't wanted Elizabeth to feel that way. "No. You've been wonderful. Your whole family has welcomed us, letting us spend the holidays with you. I'm not sure what Walter and I would've done if we hadn't been invited. We would've survived, but it would have been hard."

"I'm glad then that you and Walter have enjoyed your stay and that you have felt welcome."

"We have, and from the bottom of my heart, we thank you for that."

Elizabeth squeezed Marie's hand. "How much have you heard about my relationship with Ben?"

Marie sat in stunned silence at the sudden turn of the conversation. "Not much, other than you two appear to be very happy and very much in love."

"Yes, we are, but we definitely didn't start that way." Elizabeth's gaze was sad.

"You didn't?" Marie was surprised. She would've never thought that their relationship was anything less than a love match with how affectionate they were with one another.

"No, far from it. I despised Ben. I thought he was arrogant and had unrealistic opinions about what women should do and say. And at first, I was right, but then again, I didn't give him half a chance either."

"What changed your mind? Or I'm assuming he did something to change it?"

"I wouldn't say it was that, but more of a matter of us understanding one another." Elizabeth's gaze settled somewhere past Marie's shoulder as though she were remembering something far in the past. "When I first met Ben, I was, how shall I say this"––a smirk crossed her lips––"I was unsophisticated, and as he saw it, *if* you asked him, that is, very unladylike." Elizabeth laughed, the chuckle filled with joy, not anger.

Marie sat back in her chair and waited for Elizabeth to continue.

"We clashed from the very start. He was looking for work and arrived at my brother's ranch. At the time, my brother was hiding from the law."

"What?" Marie leaned forward, shocked. "I had no idea. But wait, do you have another brother besides James?"

"Oh, no, James is my only brother."

"But if he is your brother, then..."

"Then, yes, he was the one running from the law. My father betrayed him, and he served his time. I admit, I shouldn't have protected him, but he meant everything to me, still does. I'd just found him after we'd been separated for years." Elizabeth rubbed the back of her neck. "I didn't want to lose him, and I was afraid of what my father would do if he found us, but in the end, it didn't matter. My father found us and did what I feared."

"What was that?" Marie cringed as soon as she asked the question. She was too curious and sometimes didn't think things through. "I'm sorry, Elizabeth. You certainly don't have to answer my question. I'm being unnecessarily nosy."

Elizabeth shook her head. "No, it's an honest and fair question. Besides, I invited you up here and shared my story."

"But--"

Elizabeth held up her hand. "It's all right, I promise. My pa made an agreement with Ben and forced me to marry him."

"You and Ben married against your will?"

"I wouldn't say we married against our will. Ben agreed to marry me to protect my brother's secret. He didn't know what secret he was protecting, though. James had offered him employment when he needed it most, and James had a secret he was hiding. So he offered to marry me, albeit with a financial obligation attached." Elizabeth stood and walked around the chair before leaning against it. "And boy, was I furious when I discovered that. I accused Ben of buying me, and I suppose in a way he did, but Ben didn't see it that way. He was trying to protect both of us. If he hadn't offered to marry me, I would've been married to a truly awful person."

"What do you mean? It sounds awful that Ben paid your father for you."

Elizabeth laughed, a beaming grin indicating she wasn't angry at Marie's impertinence. "The alternative would've been far worse. My father was looking for money. It didn't matter what he put me through as long as he got what he thought he deserved." Elizabeth's fingers dug into the wood, her knuckles growing white with the pressure. "He had a friend who'd lost a few wives and needed a nursemaid for his children. It didn't help that I was young and passably pretty."

"You are more than passably pretty, Elizabeth."

"Thank you, my dear. That is kind of you to say, but at the time, I didn't care too much for my looks and had no desire to dress or act like a proper lady. If my father hadn't come to an agreement with Ben, I would've been married to a man who liked to hurt women. At one point, he found me and badly beat me up in the streets of Spring Creek. If the grocer's son hadn't come outside, it's hard to say how much worse it could've been."

Marie was shocked. "I'm so sorry. That is horrible."

"Thank you for saying that. But enough on that sorry part of the story." She waved her hand in the air. "Ben offered to marry me, *and* he offered a high enough price that my pa was satisfied. Or so he thought. Eventually, he still told the marshal what James had done. But outside of that, Ben and I were forced to make it work. We were a very unlikely match. I was very unladylike, wore trousers, and used cuss words, although I still do all of that." Elizabeth laughed again. "And Ben was very traditional. Believed that women were to wear dresses at all times, would never use a cuss word, and were perfectly content to stay in the home. He didn't believe I should ride a horse astride with trousers." Elizabeth caught the look in Marie's eye and chuckled. "It doesn't bother him as much now as it did then, though."

Marie shook her head. "You're proving my point. Men do what they can to change us. Just look at you, you're very sophisticated, I haven't heard a cuss word, and you are the very epitome of a lady."

"My dear, I definitely have you fooled if you believe that." Elizabeth sat back in her chair. "Yes, I can comport myself, and it took a lot of work to get here, but I chose to do it."

"Why?"

"Because my husband respected those qualities, and *I* wanted to make him happy. You have to understand. His mother was very much the lady, and he compared every woman to her. I don't think he realized he was doing it, still not sure he does, but what did happen was he began to respect who *I* was, and I began to respect who he was. In the end, he compromised, and so did I. As a result, we've had a very happy relationship for the last eleven years."

"But you gave up what made *you* to make him happy--"

"Oh, I didn't do any of that. I still do the things he isn't particularly fond of, although I try to do it sparingly."

"But not all relationships end like yours," Marie said.

"You're right, they don't, but with hard work, a lot of love, and a whole lot of compromise, you can have the same type of relationship. One where you both come out ahead."

"I'm at a loss for words," Marie said after a long moment of silence.

"I wanted to give you insight into my experience, which isn't much, but the Seymour men are very loyal, kind, and very, *very* stubborn, but they will give you their whole hearts if you only let them."

Marie swallowed. She wanted to believe Elizabeth, but she'd seen Michael hug another woman tonight, so he may be a Seymour man, but he obviously didn't want her and her alone.

And she wasn't sure why she cared. She didn't want a husband. She never had.

It was five minutes to midnight, and everyone was gathering in the big room at the back of the house. Michael had been searching for Marie for the past thirty minutes and still hadn't found her. Instead, he had found his friends and family with glasses of champagne, whiskey, rum, bourbon, or glasses of cider for those too young to imbibe, and they were waiting to ring in the New Year.

He skirted through the throngs of people making their way to celebrate together, and he glanced in each room as he passed. He couldn't see her striking black hair, but she had to be here somewhere. Elizabeth told him they'd spoken an hour before, and Marie hadn't said she was going up to bed, so he just had to find her.

After looking in the kitchen, he glanced at the back door and wondered if she had stepped outside. It was freezing, and he doubted she was there, but best to take a quick look just in case. Grabbing a thick coat hanging on the wall next to the door, he slipped it on and stepped outside.

The moon was full and cast a glow across the snow-covered ground. A fresh batch had fallen earlier that afternoon. They'd cleared the porch earlier of snow and ice in case anyone wanted to get a breath of fresh air. They didn't want anyone to slip and fall.

The night was quiet outside of cattle snorting as they huddled together near the fence lines. They were likely looking for feed or water. He'd find a ranch hand in the morning to make sure they'd been fed. Ben didn't need his help on the ranch, but some things were ingrained deep inside of him, and he'd never be free of them.

Michael didn't want to own a spread as big as Ben's. He enjoyed his smithy and livery and would be content with that for the rest of his life, as long as his future wife was as well. He'd never be rich, but he'd be comfortable. At some point in the future, he would need to decide what to do with the parcel of land his pa had left him, but it wasn't something that he needed to do now. It was on the south side of the ranch, and Ben used it for grazing as he rotated the cattle from pasture to pasture. It had a nice source of water, and it didn't hurt him to let Ben use it for the family's cattle.

"One more minute, everyone!" someone yelled from inside the house.

Laughter and the murmur of voices could be heard as his family and friends gathered to celebrate.

"You should get inside. You'll miss the celebration being out here," Marie said, her voice barely heard above the noise coming from inside.

He'd found her, but from her tone, she wasn't excited to see him as much as he was to see her.

"What are you doing out here?" he asked. "It's pretty cold."

She had a stocking cap on her head, and a thick woolen blanket was wrapped around her frame, but there was no way she was warm.

"It's not that bad," she said. "I haven't been out here that long, and I'll go inside in a few minutes."

He pointed to the chair next to her. "Do you mind if I sit?"

"It's your home." Her tone wasn't pleasant. Something had upset her, but he wasn't sure what he could've possibly done.

"It's my brother's if we're going to be perfectly frank. If you were out here to seek solace and wanted to be left alone, I wouldn't presume to intrude."

She sighed, and while he couldn't see her face in the dark, he thought she might've rolled her eyes. "Oh, just sit."

He bent his head to hide his grin. With any luck, she wouldn't see it, but he didn't want to antagonize her any further.

Michael should have grabbed a blanket as well, but he wasn't about to complain, not if Marie had been outside for any length of time. He wasn't about to show any weakness in front of her.

"If you're chilled, go back inside." A twinge of laughter was in her voice.

Marie had picked up on his thoughts. She was quite in tune with things around her, and she was aware he had powerful feelings for her, although to admit that seemed laughable. He hadn't known her long enough to profess such things, but she was the one for him. He was completely and utterly in love with this woman.

"I'm fine," he said. "If you can be out here, then so can I."

"That's why you were shivering just a moment ago."

"I didn't shiver." He didn't even believe his lie, so he couldn't expect Marie to, but he didn't want her to think he was weak.

"Hmm," she murmured. "It must've been a figment of my imagination."

"Maybe. Or maybe I'm just not willing to show all of my cards to you... Just yet."

She laughed, and then the house burst with happy yells, clapping, and loud music from the fiddlers. It was 1903.

"Happy New Year, Marie," he murmured.

Marie turned to face him. "Why are you out here?"

She was quite frank, and that was one of the many things he admired about her, but her question silenced him. He'd wanted to slowly build up to what he had to say since he wasn't quite sure what to say.

Finally, he swallowed and pushed out some words, his voice croaking as he did it. "I just wanted to get a breath of fresh air."

"Don't lie to me," she growled. "I'm not a simpering young woman who'll tell you what you want to hear and accept anything that comes from your lips."

Her divisive tone gave him pause.

"Fine, Marie." He turned to fully face her and reached to take her hand, but she snaked it under the blanket, not giving him a chance to touch her. She wouldn't make this easy on him. "I was hoping I could speak with you."

Lights exploded in the sky, and he could hear everyone out front cheering, clapping, and elated with joy.

But she stared at him, not blinking. She wasn't giving him any sign that she'd be open to this conversation.

"Are you going to say anything?" he asked.

"You wished to speak to me. I'm just waiting for you to say your piece."

His heart hammered. She was angry with him. "Did I do something to upset you?"

"No, of course not."

Michael *had* upset her, but she clearly wouldn't be forthcoming with that information. "Well, Marie, I was thinking--"

"Are you sure that's wise?"

"Do you like to interrupt when someone is speaking to you?" As soon as he said the words, he regretted them. He was going to start a fight with her if he wasn't careful, and then she'd never consider his proposal. "That was rude of me. Please forgive me."

"Nothing wrong with stating the facts," she said. "I do have a tendency to do that, but I don't enjoy wasting time either. You clearly have something to say to me, and I wish you'd just get on with it."

"All right then." He pushed out of his chair and dropped to one knee. The icy wood seeped through his trousers.

"What in heaven's name are you doing?" She scooted back.

Michael wouldn't be deterred. He snatched her hand when it emerged from behind the blanket. She tried to pull away, but he held strong.

"Please, Marie. Let me say this."

She kept quiet and relaxed as though resigned to whatever he had to say, which wasn't necessarily a good sign. He couldn't read what she was thinking, but he'd best get on with it, as she had so eloquently just told him.

Michael ran his thumb across her smooth palm and marveled

at how different it was from his. He would do everything in his power to make her happy if she let him.

His mouth grew dry now that the moment was at hand, and he wasn't sure how to begin. The frigid air caused his cheeks to sting. He couldn't make her sit out here indefinitely while he tried to work up the courage to tell her how he felt.

"Ma..." He cleared his throat. "Marie, from the first moment I saw you, I was intrigued."

She cocked an eyebrow, a smirk lining her lips.

He sounded like a complete imbecile, but it was the truth, so he wouldn't let her smirk stop him. Michael had a mission tonight, and he was going to do it, no matter what.

"Yes, I realize I sound like a lovesick fool right now, and perhaps I am."

Her smirk faltered.

Is it because she sees that I'm serious?

"But I didn't know what I was missing in my life until you *literally* ran straight into it."

"I didn't run into you," she said.

He chuckled. "Perhaps not directly, but as soon as I pulled you from that carriage—"

Her lips pulled into a thin line. "You didn't pull me from that carriage."

He ran his free hand across his thigh and scratched the rough threads. She wouldn't make this easy on him, and he certainly didn't expect her to. If she did, then she wouldn't be the woman for him. He wanted someone who would banter with him daily, and there was no question she would do that. It wasn't in her nature to be subservient, and she'd state her mind without reservation. But she would match him, encourage him, fight him, and motivate him, and he would hope he could do the same for her if she were willing.

"Regardless of who pulled whom from the wrecked carriage, I

fell for you hard, and I fell quickly." Sweat lined the back of his neck.

"Michael, we should go inside where it's warm. Let's get you something to eat, perhaps something to drink, and you can... Well, you can forget whatever this is." She flitted her free hand in the air.

He ignored her and didn't move when she tried to scoot from the chair. He had to say this now––for if she walked away, he wasn't sure he'd have the courage to do this again.

"Marie, I'd be honored if you'd consider becoming my wife."

Marie yanked her hand away. "No, no, no!" She shoved the chair away and scrambled to stand, the chair ricocheting against the wall. "This has to be one of your jokes, which I do not appreciate."

He fell back on his haunches, shocked at her vehement response, but at the same time, he fell even harder for her at that moment. Her cheeks were pink, irritation flashed in her eyes, and he was even more certain he had to convince her that his proposal was real and he meant every word.

He had to stop her. If she disappeared into the throng of people, he'd never be able to tell her how he felt. He stood and blocked her from leaving. "Marie, please, wait."

"No, Michael." Her head shook furiously, the blanket having fallen forgotten to the ground. "We don't know one another, so why would you even suggest this?"

"It shouldn't be that surprising," he said.

"Of course it is." She visibly trembled.

He tried to show he wasn't a threat. "I appreciate your passion for your cause, your determination not to let anything stop you. Not to mention, you are the most beautiful woman I have ever laid eyes on."

"Why is it that men always bring up how a woman looks?"

"I also said I appreciated your passion and determination." This was going south fast, and he had a sinking feeling she wouldn't listen to him, no matter what he said.

"But you ended with me being beautiful. I'm not the most beautiful woman here. I can name a few others, and yet you are claiming I am. That is not accurate and completely insincere."

"Beauty is in the eye of the beholder, and I'm the beholder." He was saying and acting like a fool, but he couldn't seem to help himself. His good intentions had completely blown up in his face. "You're not going to even consider my proposal, are you?"

"No." Her face contorted into what he wanted to believe was regret, but it wasn't.

"Would you at least consider letting us become friends before you say no?" He was pleading because the future he had envisioned was slipping away.

"I don't think that's wise."

"May I ask why?"

"Because we *don't* know one another." She stomped in frustration.

His heart might as well have been on the ground with the vehemence in her tone. "Then let us get to know one another."

"I don't want to." Marie had furrowed her eyebrows and a scowl lined her lips.

"Am I that abhorrent to you?"

"This isn't about you, Michael. I have never desired to get married and have no intention of hitching myself to a man." She lifted a shaking hand to her lips before abruptly hiding it behind her back.

Is she nervous around me?

He had no idea how to combat her misconceptions about men. He wasn't like the ones she was desperate to fight against. "What is so awful about getting married? Having a companion for the rest of your life, so you aren't lonely in your old age?"

She laughed, although it was far from happy. "I could list a million reasons why marriage is awful and having a husband doesn't guarantee that I won't be lonely."

"That is a harsh and sad viewpoint."

"You call it sad, I call it realistic. Now, if you'll excuse me, I'm going back inside the house." Marie brushed past him, and a moment later, she disappeared.

He plopped into the chair she had just vacated and snatched the blanket from the floor, putting it around his hips.

"That could've gone better," he muttered, running a hand across his eyes. His head was pounding, and his heart was empty.

"Yep, it could've."

Michael swung around to the voice at the end of the porch. It was Ben, a cigar clamped between his lips.

"How much of that did you hear?" Michael was humiliated and didn't need his brothers giving him a hard time about having his heart stomped on like a cattle herd rushing toward a lake full of fresh water on a hot summer day.

Ben removed the cigar and sat in the chair next to him. "Enough."

"I made a colossal mess of that."

"Yes, you did."

"Thanks, big brother, for the vote of confidence." Michael grunted with disgust at what had just happened.

"I have confidence in you, but you didn't show it to her."

Michael avoided looking at him. Ben was right. He had appeared weak and not someone she could lean on.

"How do I fix this?" The words were heavy on his lips.

"I think the better question is, why do you want to marry her? And they aren't the reasons you gave her. They didn't sound like you and wouldn't convince a squirrel, let alone a woman as strong and independent as Marie is. She doesn't need a man who will grovel. She needs something more, and it's up to you to figure out what that is."

Fifteen

Marie picked up the carpetbag Elizabeth had let her borrow. It contained everything she owned in this world, which had all been given by the Seymour family. It held the Christmas presents as well as two dresses Elizabeth had given her. She'd insisted Marie could keep them. Marie didn't feel right about taking them, but she didn't argue with Elizabeth's hospitality. She didn't have a reason to argue or reject the gift, and she was grateful Elizabeth had been so kind.

She grimaced as she looked around the room that had been her home for the past ten days. Her time at the ranch had been pleasant, but the night before had been too much. She hadn't anticipated Michael's proposal. It had come out of nowhere and was not appreciated. He appeared to have good intentions, but if he had truly known her, he would've never proposed. It showed she was right in refusing his proposal. She wasn't heartless, but Michael deserved someone who would cook and clean and give him children. She couldn't give that to him.

Sighing, she picked up her cloak and threw it over her shoulders. She would miss the ranch, but it wasn't her home, and it was time for her and Walter to get back to their lives. Walter needed to return to his newspaper, and Marie had her mission of gaining the vote for women. There were several events after the first of the year that she needed to organize. She had committed herself to helping, and she wouldn't back out of those promises regardless of her temporary depressing situation. Plenty of women had it far worse, and she had to do what she could to improve the lot of those who didn't have the resources she did. She had her health, her brother, and the means to rebuild. She had no reason to complain or be depressed.

Marie had removed the linens from the bed and had taken them to the washroom. Elizabeth had shaken her head but hadn't argued with Marie's attempt to help alleviate the load she and Walter had put on their family. No matter Elizabeth's protestations, Marie wouldn't let Elizabeth and Sophia clean up after them. It wasn't much, but it was the least she could do for their kindness.

Leaving the room, she closed the door softly behind her, and a few moments later, she arrived in the foyer before the front door. It was quiet. She looked at her lapel watch to see if she was late, but it was just a few minutes after seven. It was still dark outside, but she'd expected to find Walter waiting for her. She dropped her bag near the front door and headed toward the dining room. He had said nothing about having breakfast, but maybe he'd changed his mind.

Sophia likely had a full spread ready for the guests who had stayed the night. She had one every morning since she'd been there. Many of the party revelers had left the ranch in the wee hours of the morning wanting to spend the night in their beds, but there were plenty who had stayed the night in the house, in the barn's loft, or in covered wagons around the ranch house.

The low hum of voices could be heard when she reached the dining room doors. Pushing it open, she found Michael, Ben, and Stanley.

As soon as Marie stepped into the room, their conversation

ground to a screeching halt. The three men looked guilty, as though they'd been doing something they shouldn't have. If she were to take a gander, they were likely talking about her, but she wouldn't ask what they had been discussing. It truly was none of her business.

"Am I interrupting?" she asked.

Ben placed the plate full of food he was holding on the table and pulled out the chair. "No. Why don't you join us? I'm sure you'd like something to eat before Michael takes you back to town."

Her spine stiffened. "*You're* taking us back to Helena?"

Michael lifted an eyebrow and held out the spatula in his hand. "Yep." He had a mischievous grin.

"Oh." Between his proposal and his tête-à-tête with that blonde woman, she had no desire to be around him. She wasn't the jealous type, or she hadn't believed she was, but when she thought of Michael with another woman, she wanted to rip out the woman's eyeballs. Which told her she needed to get away from him. If she were getting jealous, then that meant she was getting attached, which would not do. She had plans, and they didn't include Michael. She had a sinking feeling he would try to propose again, and she couldn't have that either.

Michael turned back to the food on the sideboard. He scooped up eggs and a couple of pancakes before setting the plate on the table next to Ben. "Can I get you a plate of food?"

"No," she said. "I can get it myself." She was belligerent, and Michael's smile faltered. She should be kind, but irritation crawled up her spine. She didn't want or need his help.

Stalking to the sideboard, she nudged him out of the way, scooped random food onto her plate, and then plopped into a chair on the opposite side of the table. Her movements were abrupt and out of sorts. She was acting like a petulant child, but she hadn't expected him to be the one taking her back to Helena. Marie didn't want to spend any more time with him.

She looked up and then cursed under her breath. In trying to avoid Michael, she'd sat directly in his line of sight. Not to mention, when she looked at her plate, she had to stifle a groan. Oatmeal was a nasty concoction she never ate and would've never chosen if she'd been in the right frame of mind.

This was his fault. If he'd just quit looking at her like she was a piece of cake that he wanted to devour, all would be right in the world, but it wasn't and wouldn't be for as long as she had to be in his presence. With any luck, the ride to Helena would be quick and painless, and then she would never see the man again.

He caught her eye and lifted a fork in salute. Muttering under her breath, she picked up the napkin, dropped it onto her lap, and then tried to muster up the courage to eat the disgusting-looking oatmeal in front of her. She couldn't do it, she couldn't eat the stuff, but she couldn't push it away without looking like a first-rate fool.

"Something wrong with your food?" Michael asked.

Of course, he would ask. Michael couldn't leave well enough alone. All eyes at the table were on her and her lack of excitement over the oatmeal.

"Um, no... Not exactly." She shoved the fork inside the disgusting glop and lifted it to her mouth, but she couldn't do it. She would either gag or lose what was in her belly all over the table. Neither scenario was welcome.

"You don't have to eat that if you don't want to," Michael drawled, raising an eyebrow.

She lifted her gaze and glared at him. Then, to prove him wrong, she shoved it into her mouth and immediately regretted it. The texture made her taste buds revolt, and she couldn't swallow it. She snatched her napkin and tried to spit it out, but it'd been thick and stuck to her teeth and the roof of her mouth. Marie tried to breathe through her nose, but it was useless. She could still smell and taste the nasty concoction.

Her gag reflexes were in full force, and she was going to embarrass herself. She shoved away from the table and abruptly ran out of the room and down the hall, pushing out the doors to the outside, where she promptly threw up in the snow. Tears streamed down her face.

Marie was completely and utterly embarrassed, and there was no way she was going back inside the house. She had never liked oatmeal, couldn't eat it. The smell of it alone was enough to make her gag, but she'd been stubborn and out of sorts, and she had paid the price.

Suddenly, a white handkerchief fluttered in front of her face, and brown boots came into view. It was Michael. She snatched the handkerchief and used it to wipe her mouth. While she was completely and utterly humiliated, she wasn't too stubborn to refuse the handkerchief that was sorely needed. When her belly had finally settled, she slowly stood and looked at him.

There was no censure or laughter in his gaze, only concern. She wasn't sure if she should be angry over that or be grateful he wasn't laughing at her. Laughter might've been worse.

"Thank you," she murmured.

"You're welcome," he said. "Can I get you a glass of water to rinse your mouth?"

"Yes, that would be most appreciated." She hated to be beholden to him, but she had to get rid of the taste or she'd likely throw up again.

He nodded, and a few minutes later, he returned holding a glass of water and a woolen blanket. Humiliating herself in front of Michael was bad enough, but Ben and Stanley had seen her acting like a petulant child. Then running out of the room because she couldn't eat oatmeal was something she'd never live down.

It was a good thing she was leaving the ranch and would never return. She could then avoid the laughter in their eyes, although a part of her had to believe the Seymour men weren't like that if what Elizabeth had told her the night before was true. Her experience told her otherwise, but she'd reserve judgment considering how kind and welcoming the family had been.

She took the glass of water, swished her mouth out, and bent over the railing to spit out the nasty taste. After doing that twice more, she felt immensely better and settled back into the chair.

Not saying a word, Michael gently placed the blanket around her shoulders. He then sat in the chair next to her, letting the silence of the morning wrap around them. The sun was rising over the mountains, and the view was magnificent. Elizabeth had told her that the sunrises were something special, but Marie hadn't viewed one until today.

It took her losing the contents of her belly to see something so beautiful, and blast it, she had to enjoy it with the man who caused her toes to curl, her belly to tighten, and her spine to straighten with irritation daily. She had to get away from him before she jumped into his arms, as she suspected that was exactly what he wanted, and that was exactly what she wouldn't do.

"Feeling better?" Michael finally asked.

Not looking at him, she said, "Yes, thank you for the water. I'm––" She gulped. Apologizing was not something she liked to do, as it only showed weakness, but it appeared she needed to. "I'm sorry."

"Nothing to apologize for. I think I likely antagonized you to eat something you clearly don't care for, or at least I'm assuming you don't like oatmeal."

Even hearing the word made her belly revolt. "Yes. I mean, no, I don't like it, but it was my stubbornness that got me into the mess. I wasn't paying attention to what I was putting on my plate. I should've just admitted that I can't stand the stuff and gotten something else."

"I'll have to remember to never serve you oatmeal."

"Yes, please never do that." A smile threatened. "I can't promise that I won't throw up again."

"I don't think I've ever seen anyone have such a reaction to the stuff," he murmured.

"Not one of my finer moments. I'll apologize to your brothers--"

"No need to do that. I think they'll understand. It isn't my favorite meal myself, but I'll eat it in a pinch."

"I won't eat it in a pinch," she said. "I'd rather starve."

"We don't want you to starve, so when we're old and gray and don't have our teeth, I'll make sure you never get it." His tone was light and teasing.

Her belly tingled with an unfamiliar feeling. "Who says you'll know me when we're old and gray?"

"Who says I won't?" he smarted back.

Marie had to cut this off now. She hadn't wanted to have this conversation, but she was an adult, and if she wanted to be treated equally in the law, it was only fair that she not play games and tell Michael that there would be nothing between them, especially after their conversation from the night before. Shifting in her seat, she took a breath and turned to look at him and had to swallow back the saliva that pooled in her mouth.

He stared at her. His brown eyes were dark with need, a need she'd never before seen in a man. A dark brown curl hung across his brow, his cheeks were pink, and a tentative smile hung across his lips. This was going to be harder than she thought, but she had to make sure he understood there could be nothing between them.

"Michael, I--"

"Please, Marie. Can you let me say something first before you... well, before you crush my dreams once again?" His voice was full of sadness.

Shocked, she stared at him in silence. *Am I that transparent? Can he read me that easily?* She nodded, and he relaxed.

"Thank you." He ran his fingers through his hair. "I wanted to apologize for what happened last night. I realize I've been unfair and caught you off guard. It won't happen again."

Marie's throat tightened. She didn't want to hurt him, but she feared she was going to. He wouldn't understand or make this easy on her. She thought she'd made herself clear the night before, but he was going to try again. She just knew it, but she couldn't say anything, not yet.

"I've enjoyed being in your life, as much as you've let me, of course." He smiled, his pearly white teeth gleaming under the rising sun. "And I'd like to get to know you more, but I believe you're against it for reasons I likely don't understand. I'd venture to guess it has something to do with your goals of getting women the right to vote."

Maybe he understood more than she gave him credit for.

"I'll admit my knowledge of the suffragist movement is lacking, but I'd like to learn more. I'd love to support you in your dreams and your endeavors, and I'd like to"--his Adam's apple bobbed furiously in his throat, and sweat glistened across his brow--"I'd like to be your friend."

His last words were said in such a rush, it was as though he was afraid that if he didn't blurt it out, she wouldn't listen. She was going to hurt him without meaning to, and that was the last thing she wanted. It would've been so much easier if he'd just chased after that blonde woman and let her be, but after his proposal last night, she wasn't sure even being his friend was a good idea.

"Michael, I--"

"Please don't tell me that there isn't a chance without taking a day or two to think on it." His brown eyes were earnest with hope.

She was going to dash it away.

"I don't need a day or two to think about it," she said. "I don't want to disappoint you. You're a kind man, even if you have irritated me beyond measure at times, so I don't think it's fair to you to give you hope for something that just won't happen."

"Please, can't you just consider what I said?" His voice pleaded with her. "I only want to be your friend."

He wanted more than that, and they both knew it. It was time to end it once and for all.

"What is there to think about?" She pushed out of the chair, the blanket held firmly in her hands. She suddenly had a chill. The air between them was frigid, as though an icy wind had wrapped around them. "I told you last night I'd never planned on getting married, and I don't plan on changing my mind."

"I'm not asking you to marry me now. I'm just asking if we can be friends." Michael's voice had grown hollow.

"I'm not sure I believe that." She wrapped her arms around her waist and faced away from him. "You're hoping if we become friends, we'll eventually become something more."

"Things change, Marie," he said.

"Not for me. It isn't right for me and never will be. I can't achieve my dreams if I'm married." She pushed against the railing.

"Who says you can't do that?"

She turned to look at him. "Be honest with yourself. Do you want a wife who'll cook and clean and give you children?"

He leaned back in the chair, resting it on its back two legs. "Of course. Who wouldn't want that?"

"And if I didn't want to cook, clean, or have children, then would you still want to pursue a relationship with me?"

The chair fell forward, and he stood to his full height. "Do you not want children?"

His intense stare made her almost want to give him the answer he was seeking, but she couldn't change course. Too much was at stake. "I haven't thought much about having children."

"Well, then there's hope." He smiled and shoved his hands into his coat pockets as though he had just solved the world's problems with those simple words.

Michael was incorrigible.

"I don't want to stay in the home taking care of a husband, cooking and cleaning and giving up on the things that are important to me."

"I'd never stop you from chasing your dreams or your goals." He brushed a knuckle against her cheek.

Her breath hitched, and she took a step back. She couldn't let him distract her. Not now, not ever. He had the power to break down her defenses, and she wasn't about to let him try.

"Maybe not at first, but there'd come a time when you'd expect your wife to do the things wives do."

"You're assuming an awful lot about me." He scrunched his forehead in anger or confusion. She wasn't sure which.

"You're a man. You want a wife. You want children, so naturally you'd want her to stay at home."

He ran a hand against the back of his neck. "Yes, I'm a man, and yes, I want a wife and children, but I wouldn't expect you or any woman to do something she doesn't want to do. Look at my brother as an example. Elizabeth doesn't cook or clean, and Ben hasn't expected her to do that."

She scoffed at his words. While she heard what Elizabeth had said, she couldn't take that chance just because he said he wouldn't now. There was no telling what he would want or demand in the future.

"You don't believe me about Elizabeth?" Michael looked at her incredulously.

"No. Elizabeth mentioned how she is and what Ben expected."

"And Ben gave up those expectations to keep the woman he loved."

Sixteen

Michael watched Marie walk back inside the house, and it was as though his insides had been ripped out. He barely knew the woman, yet the dream he had developed over the past week was eviscerated again.

After his proposal failure, he'd sat in his bedroom last night and convinced himself that she would be open to being friends. Then, with time, he'd be able to convince her to marry him, but she was adamant that she wasn't interested in pursuing a relationship. She had a misguided idea that if they married, he would make her do things she didn't want to do. No matter how much he protested and told her he'd never force her to do anything against her will, she'd been adamant that having a husband was a rotten idea. What he'd hoped would've been a happy evening had been disappointing and strange.

Running into Suzette had been unexpected. Then this morning, he and his brother had been discussing Suzette's arrival when Marie had walked into the room, and it had grown quite uncomfortable, and Marie had felt it. He could see it in her eyes, but he didn't know how to explain it.

Ben had been shocked that Suzette had arrived at the ranch

with her sister, Janie, and Janie's husband, Tom. Ben had said that she'd been remarkably contrite and conciliatory to both him and Elizabeth. According to Ben, she had apologized profusely for her actions years before and had wanted to make amends. Ben, of course, didn't trust her as far as he could throw her, but he was willing to let bygones be bygones. Michael wasn't sure he'd be so accommodating, but Suzette had never done him any harm, so it wasn't his place to judge her.

The door opened, and the woman he'd just been thinking about stepped outside onto the porch.

"Oh, hello, Michael," Suzette drawled, a woolen pink shawl draped around her shoulders. "I hope I'm not disturbing you."

"No." He was growing increasingly uncomfortable with the way she gazed at him. There was an unmistakable appreciation in her eyes. It was a look he'd seen on plenty of women's faces over the years, but he'd never acted on it and wouldn't when the woman he truly wanted had just gone inside the house.

"It sure is a beautiful morning, isn't it?" Suzette brushed past him to lean against the railing of the porch.

"Yes, it is," he said.

"I appreciate your family being so kind to my sudden arrival. I surprised Ben and Elizabeth, but I wanted to apologize, and they were kind enough to accept it." Suzette tightened her shawl. "Truth be told, if I were them, I wouldn't have forgiven me. I was purely awful back then." She chuckled to hide her embarrassment.

His apprehension eased with her confession. "We all do things we aren't proud of."

"Yes, we do." She beamed. Her smile was a spark of joy, and he couldn't help but be touched by it. While she was a superficially pretty woman, she wasn't near as beautiful as Marie.

"What are you planning on doing today?" she asked.

"I'm headed back to Helena this morning. I need to get back to my smithy."

Her smile dropped a bit. "Oh, that is unfortunate. I would've liked to catch up. Perhaps we could do that another time?"

"You planning on staying on the ranch for very long?"

Suzette raised a hand to her forehead, brushing away the blonde strands with her delicate fingers. "Oh, no. We definitely don't want to overstay our welcome." She chuckled wryly. "Tom and Janie are heading home to Spring Creek tomorrow, but I'm taking my children and spending a few days in Helena. It's been a rough year, so I thought it would be nice for them to experience something different."

He leaned against the porch railing and crossed his arms. "It's the middle of winter."

She giggled. "Yes, I realize that, and it wouldn't be my first choice, but Spring Creek just doesn't have the same amenities that Helena offers."

"That is true. Helena is a far cry from Spring Creek. I'll have to take you and your children to dinner one night, if you'll let me, that is?"

"Oh, Michael." She placed a hand on his arm and gently squeezed. "That would be lovely. We would enjoy that very much."

He pulled away slightly, and she dropped her hand. "What hotel are you staying at?"

"The Hotel Helena on Grand Street," Suzette said.

It was one of the nicest, if not the nicest, hotels in Helena. "You'll surely be comfortable there."

"Yes, that is what Tom and Janie said. I'm looking forward to it." Suzette shivered.

"It's mighty cold out here," he said. "We should go inside. Have you had anything to eat this morning?"

"No, not yet. I wanted to see the sunrise first. I knew it would be something to behold."

He grinned and held out his arm. "Let me accompany you to the dining room, then. We wouldn't want you to starve."

She chuckled. He led her inside and down the hall to the

dining room. From the cacophony of voices coming from the room, it sounded as though several people had arrived.

He led her inside and caught Marie's gaze. She was sitting at the table, a plate in front of her. It contained bacon and pancakes, and there wasn't a bowl of oatmeal in sight. Marie looked at him before her gaze moved to the woman on his arm. A frown marred her lovely face.

Suzette moved closer to him, emitting a small shriek.

"Is everything all right, Suzette?"

"No, yes... I mean, yes, it is. I just wasn't expecting so many people to be in here this morning. Large crowds make me uncomfortable."

"I'm sorry to hear that. Do you want me to help you get settled in a quieter room of the house?"

"If you wouldn't mind, that would be most kind." She lowered her gaze as though embarrassed she had to admit that.

"Of course." He glanced over his shoulder and saw a look of disgust on Marie's face. Michael wondered what had put it there, but he didn't have the luxury of asking her, at least not now. He should have the opportunity to talk to her more on the ride back to Helena.

Marie's belly revolted once again, but not from the piece of bacon she had just put into her mouth. Michael had proposed last night that he wanted to get to know her, and yet he was with the blonde woman *again*. Considering the way the woman was draped all over him, as though he were her prize, there was no way Marie was going to compete with a woman like her. Not that she wanted to compete for Michael's attentions, but it aggravated her to no end that he had claimed to want her, but then, not five minutes later, he was with the blonde.

"Arghh," she muttered.

"I'm sorry. What did you say?" Ben asked.

Startled, Marie dropped the fork she had been holding, and it clattered against the side of the white ceramic plate.

Ben pulled out the chair next to her and sat. "Is everything all right?"

Marie forced a smile to her lips but was afraid Ben would see right through it. "Yes, I'm just right clumsy today." She tried to chuckle, but it came out like a croak instead.

"You don't need to worry about Suzette," he said.

She tilted her head and saw his concerned gaze. "I'm sorry. I don't know who Suzette is."

A thin smile lined Ben's lips. "Suzette was the woman holding on to Michael's arm like she owned him."

"Oh." Marie turned her gaze back to her plate, afraid she blushed at being caught like a jealous schoolgirl over another woman. She picked up her fork and pushed the pieces of pancake around her plate. "I'm not worried about that."

"I'm glad to hear that. Suzette is a woman from my past. Never expected her to show up to one of our New Year's parties, but her sister and brother-in-law are good friends of ours, and I suppose it was bound to happen at some point."

She shifted to look at him more fully. "I don't understand."

Ben held a coffee mug and leaned back carefully in his chair. "I met her the same time I met Elizabeth and James."

Marie released her fork and picked up her napkin to wipe her face. Ben had a story to tell, but she wasn't sure she wanted to hear it.

"I thought I was infatuated with her. She had a talent, and still does, of getting men to fall for her."

"Is your brother one of those?" As soon as the words fell from her lips, she hated herself for asking the question. It made her look weak, as though she cared whether Michael had feelings for Suzette.

Ben lifted an eyebrow before taking a sip of his coffee.

"Forget I asked that question. I have no interest in who Michael might or might not be infatuated with."

Ben leaned forward, placed his coffee mug on the table, and ran his fingers along the rim. "Michael has always been the kind one in the family, not to mention the jokester. He wants to make sure there's laughter and smiles with everyone he comes in contact with. Michael doesn't have the heart to hurt anyone, and when he had to eliminate Stanley's ex-wife, it tore him apart. He won't admit it, and if you ask him, he'll tell you he's fine, but... but he's not."

"Why are you telling me this?"

Ben sighed and clasped his hands in front of him. "Lots of reasons, but the one that sticks out the most is that whether or not you've intended to, Michael has smiled more since he met you than he has in quite some time."

"I can't... I don't want to hurt him, but I'm afraid you both have expectations I might not live up to."

Ben smiled. "I don't have expectations, Marie. Suzette is not who you think she is——"

"I don't have any opinions about Suzette." Her tone said otherwise. She was lying through her teeth. She cared more than she wanted to admit, even to herself.

Ben smirked, then whisked it away a second later. "Perhaps." He tapped his finger on the table. "Maybe keep this in mind. Michael has always had a soft spot in his heart for those who need his help."

"I don't need his help."

"You certainly do not. I can see that probably more than you realize. You remind me of my Elizabeth."

Ben had just given her quite the compliment. "I do?"

He smiled broadly. "You do. Elizabeth said she told you how we met."

"She did."

"I was bullheaded and didn't see what was right in front of

me." He rubbed his thumb against his chin. "Actually, I think I did, but I had a different idea of what I thought I wanted. I didn't understand what a gem she was until it was almost too late." His voice broke, but he took a breath. "I guess what I'm trying to say is that sometimes things aren't always what they seem. Suzette is not what he wants, but he'll never hurt her or *you* intentionally."

Marie stared at him for a long moment. She was at a loss for words again, which was not like her. Michael was bringing out a side of her she didn't recognize.

"I've kept you long enough. I hope you're feeling better and have a safe trip back to Helena. Please visit us again soon."

Before she could say anything, Ben pushed away from the table, nodded, and then promptly left to speak with someone on the other side of the room.

She was shocked by what Ben had told her, but it changed nothing. Marie wasn't interested in Michael. If he wanted to pursue Suzette, then he was free to do so.

Seventeen

"No. I'm not staying in his brother's house," Marie hissed. "You told me we were going to get a room at the hotel."

Walter frowned, reached for her elbow, and led her away from Michael. The grin on Michael's face sent an irritated pulse through her skin. Michael had been plumb tickled when he set the brake on the carriage in front of Luke's house. The name *Thundering Ridge* was on the sign above the fence. It was similar to his livery, Thundering Sunset, and his family ranch, Thundering Mountain. There was a story there, but she wasn't about to ask anything. She was too irritated to do anything but scowl at Michael's hidden agenda.

"Don't embarrass me," Walter said when they were far enough away that presumably Michael wouldn't hear their conversation.

Marie ripped her arm from his grasp, although it wasn't as though his grip was that tight. She was making a scene, but she could not stay there because Michael would visit with any number of reasons, and she'd get no peace. "I'm not embarrassing you, Walter. I think you've embarrassed me by lying."

"I didn't lie to you, sister dear."

"Don't you *sister dear* me." She placed her hands on her hips. "I can't stay here. He is not our friend."

"That is rude, even for you. The Seymours not only offered us a place to stay when we lost our home, but they also rescued both of us from that inferno, let us recuperate in a warm, safe, and loving home during Christmas, gave us gifts, and are offering us a place to live until I can rebuild. Money doesn't grow on trees, and he isn't expecting us to pay rent."

"You will pay him rent!" she snapped, then immediately regretted the words because that meant she had agreed to Walter and Michael's cockamamie plan.

The grin lining Walter's face told her he'd led her straight into the trap. He knew her better than anyone, or at least as much as anyone really knew her. Walter was aware she didn't like to be beholden to anyone, and by saying that they wouldn't have to pay, he pushed her over the edge.

"Of course, I'm gonna pay him." Walter pushed back his coat, rested his hands on his hips, and rocked back on his heels. "I have every intention of making sure their family is compensated for letting us stay here, but I also don't want to insult them. Which means you need not to be so cantankerous and maybe crack a smile occasionally when he talks to you."

"I smile." Her lips turned into a frown, a direct contrast to what she had just said.

"Maybe you should try doing it now." Walter eyed her carefully.

"I'm not talking to him now, so why should I smile?"

"Because you likely need to practice."

"I'm not a child, Walter, so quit treating me like one."

He quit rocking back and forth. "Then maybe you should quit acting like one and appreciate that we have kind friends and neighbors who are helping us."

Shame poured through her like a waterfall after a winter snowstorm. "I'm sorry. I've been petulant and ungrateful. I can't be around him."

Walter's eyes narrowed. "And why's that? Did he do something to you? If he did, I'll..." He stiffened his shoulders and balled his hands into fists. Walter had a temper he controlled most of the time, unless he thought something or someone had hurt his baby sister.

She placed her hand on his arm to stop him from ripping Michael's arms from his chest. "He did nothing to me. He just irritates me, that's all."

Walter took a good look at her, and then his eyes crinkled with mirth. "He irritates you? And how is that?"

Marie recognized the look. It was the one he gave when he was sniffing out a good story. He was like a porcupine facing off against a predator, knowing his spikes would hurt worse than any damage the predator could do to him. Walter wouldn't back away until he was good and ready.

"Enough, Walter. I just would prefer to be in my own space. The Seymours have done a lot for us, and I don't want to make a nuisance of myself."

Walter rocked back on his heels and grinned. "You always make a nuisance of yourself. It's what you do best."

She scowled, but if she said anything, she'd only make things worse, and he'd continue to dig into why she was adamant about not being around Michael.

"Fine," she snapped and tugged on her mittens as though they were hanging on by a thread. Instead, it just gave her a moment to gather her thoughts. "How long will we stay here?"

"I wish I knew, but it might take longer than I'd like. I can't rebuild until the weather improves."

"We could always live above the newspaper office. Put up a few cots." She warmed to the idea. "It would be cozy."

Walter shook his head. "No, it's a bad idea. I don't want my sister living in a bunch of old offices above the printing press. We'll be staying here."

Eighteen

"Remember what Susan B Anthony said, 'Women must not depend upon the protection of man, but must be taught to protect herself. No man is good enough to govern any woman without her consent.[1]'"

Loud applause burst through the auditorium. Stomping, whistles, and clapping echoed and grew with each passing second.

Marie stood off to the side of the stage, watching as the last speaker, Gail, emboldened the crowd of women and a few men in the fight for women's rights. The Helena Suffrage Club had been working hard trying to get supporters, but it hadn't been easy. The state convention was being held this September in Butte, and they were working hard to get a woman's suffrage amendment to the Montana State constitution. With any luck, it would pass, but they still had months until the state houses voted on it.

Gail walked off the stage with a satisfied grin. The cheers continued, as the crowd was clearly pleased by her speech. Marie had goosebumps running up and down her skin. Listening to these strong women speak was both an honor and a pleasure. She

---

1. https://www.history.com/articles/susan-b-anthony

was lucky to have been in the position to welcome them and be able to talk to them in person. She was on the committee that organized the speeches at the labor unions and had been thrilled when Gail had agreed to speak to the crowds. Gail was speaking at numerous locations throughout the state, and this was one of her many stops.

As soon as Gail stepped behind the curtain, Marie grabbed her hands and squeezed. "That was amazing."

Gail grinned. "Definitely an enthusiastic crowd. I just wish more men had come."

"There were a few out there." Marie had seen a fair number arrive with their wives and mothers.

"Yes, but not as many as we need." Gail let go of Marie's hands and grabbed her elbow, walking with her through the darkened stage and toward the backstage doors. "We still have plenty of work to do in the next eight months, and the more men we can align to our cause, the better."

"We have events and fundraisers scheduled. With any luck, we'll garner additional funds." Gail wasn't wrong, but it had been difficult to garner the same enthusiasm that Gail managed to get from just a few words. Marie didn't have the same charisma as Gail, which was fine, but it didn't help to get more men on their side.

Gail patted Marie's arm as they snaked through the hallway. Dim lighting led their way. It was an old building that hadn't been remodeled, so only kerosene lanterns provided the light. "That's well and good, but we need to do more."

"What would you suggest?" Marie asked. She would do anything Gail required. This was what she was meant to do and was in her element.

"We need more women to join the cause."

Marie's heart sank. "I wish we could, but we've scoured the area and are still running into those who think we're asking too much. They still believe that their husbands, brothers, and fathers have good intentions and will always care for them."

"The problem is there are plenty of men who believe a woman should be seen but not heard and are not willing to let them have a say," Gail said. "It's dark back here. Are we going in the right direction?" Gail pulled Marie to a stop.

Marie looked up and down the hallway. She'd been distracted and hadn't been paying attention to where they'd been going. She didn't recognize the hallway, and it had grown quiet the farther away from the stage they had wandered.

"I'm not sure." Marie pulled from Gail and walked toward a doorway on her left. She pushed open the door and muttered a curse. It was a storage room holding old props. They had taken a wrong turn, and she was lost. The building had been used in different ways over the years, and she wasn't quite sure where they had ended up. "I think we need to head back the way we came."

Gail nodded. "I hate these old buildings. You would think I'd be used to them by now with all the places I've been giving speeches, but there's just something about them that gives me the chills."

Marie grinned. "Sometimes I think there might be ghosts inside of them."

Gail shivered but laughed low. "I'm glad I'm not the only one who thinks that."

"Let's head back that way." Marie pointed behind Gail.

Gail looked over her shoulder. "Are you sure?"

"No, but we won't find our way out of here if we continue to stay here."

The two of them turned and walked carefully back the way they came. Skirting around old broken furniture, racks of clothing, and numerous other odds and ends, neither said a word as they worked their way back to what Marie hoped was the right direction. Eventually, they would find their way out, but it was getting late, and the last thing they wanted was to get locked in the old building.

They turned another corner and sighed with relief. Gail's entourage was waiting and gasped when they saw them.

"Gail, Marie," Ida said, walking toward them. "We were getting worried. Where did you go?"

"We got turned around," Gail said. "But Marie kept her composure and helped us find our way back."

"What composure you have," Suzette said. It was the blonde woman from Ben's past––the one who'd staked a clear claim on Michael.

"Suzette." Of all the people to meet, it had to be her.

Suzette stepped forward, her eyes appearing wide and innocent, but Marie had a distinct feeling she was anything but. "Have we met before?" Suzette tilted her head and eyed Marie carefully.

"We weren't formally introduced, but I believe you were at the Seymours' New Year's party," Marie said.

"Why yes, I was." Suzette smiled, but it was insincere and gave Marie pause. "Were you there?" Suzette had seen her at the party, but she was pretending as though she hadn't.

"Yes. They were kind enough to let us stay there after a fire took my home."

"Oh, yes," Suzette said. "Michael told me they had let a poor family stay with them. I didn't realize who you were." Her words were neutral, but there was an undertone to her voice that gave Marie chills. This was a woman not to be trifled with.

"Marie, Suzette," Ida said. "I hate to interrupt, but we need to leave. We will surely miss our train. It's scheduled to leave in twenty minutes."

"We don't want you to miss your train," Suzette said. "Marie, it was a pleasure. I'm sure we *will* see one another again."

Another woman handed over Gail's coat. Gail slipped it over her shoulders. "Thank you, Marie, for everything you have done for us. I believe we are supposed to be back next month. Isn't that right, Ida?"

Pulling on her gloves, Ida nodded. "Yes, we should be back on the twentieth, and we will be here for a week. There are several events scheduled, including a fundraiser."

"Yes," Marie said. "We are looking forward to having you back here for that."

"Remember what I said, Marie," Gail said. "We need more men involved." She slapped her gloves into her palm.

Marie nodded. "I'll do my best."

"We need to leave." Ida glanced at her lapel watch while holding open the door.

"Yes, yes," Gail said. "We will see you next month."

Gail swept out of the building with the women who'd come with her, including Suzette, who followed in her wake. Before Marie could take a breath, they had disappeared, leaving her alone. She raised a hand to her eyes and rubbed them. Gail's message was simple. Marie was to get more men involved in their cause, but she was unsure how to do it.

She had tried everything. The women in the suffrage club had been trying for months to get more women and men involved, but they hadn't filled their ranks as quickly as they would have liked. Between knocking on doors, holding rallies, and practically accosting people on the street, it had been difficult to get more to join.

It didn't help that a group of men was staunchly against their cause and was doing everything in their power to stop them. A part of her wondered if it wasn't someone in that group who had set fire to their house, but she had no proof, and there was no reason to raise an alarm when she had nothing but her gut telling her they were involved.

She was surprised protesters hadn't shown up to tonight's speech. In the past few months, at every speech, fundraiser, or rally, ten to fifteen men would show up and cause a scene, interrupting the speeches, throwing decayed vegetables at the speakers, and even accosting the speakers when they left the events. It had been a battle, but one that was well worth the fight *if* they could get the Montana legislature to change the state constitution.

A door slammed in the hallway behind her. It was time to leave. Grabbing the coat she had left hanging on the wall earlier that evening, she pulled it over her shoulders. They were closing the building, and she'd do best to leave as soon as possible. Looking at her lapel watch, she cringed. It was much later than she'd thought. Walter was going to be displeased that she'd be walking the streets late without an escort, but it wouldn't be the first time, nor likely the last.

Suddenly, the lights disappeared, and the room went dark. Marie emitted a small shriek but calmed herself. It was likely just the janitors shutting things down. The door to the outside was in front of her. She would find it, leave the building, and all would be good.

Holding her hands out, she shuffled forward when she crashed into a chair and muttered obscenities under her breath. Heaven help her. *Will I make it out of this building alive?*

She chuckled at her dramatics. It wasn't as though the room she was in was that large. Her eyes would adjust to the darkness.

Moving the chair out of the way, she continued forward, taking small steps, when a chair crashed behind her. She halted abruptly. Marie hadn't touched a chair, had touched nothing.

She was not alone.

Nineteen

Marie groaned. Her head ached like a sledgehammer had smashed into it multiple times. She pried open her eyes and encountered nothing but a darkness so thick it reminded her of black roof tar. Nothing or no one could peer through it.

Where am I?

She forced herself to sit, pushing against what she presumed was a wooden floor from the rough slivers that grazed her palm. She blinked, trying to adjust to the darkness, but no light penetrated the room.

Did someone move me? Or am I still in the theater?

Marie remembered nothing after Gail, Ida, and Suzette had left. Maybe she had tripped and fallen, and that was why she couldn't remember. But that made no sense. She hadn't tripped and fallen.

Her fingers brushed against the wound at the back of her head, and she immediately regretted doing so. Whatever had happened had left a big old nasty bruise, and it hurt something fierce, but she wouldn't get anywhere sitting on the floor of wherever she was. Time to get up and find her way out.

She kept her head as still as possible as she stood because every time she moved it even an inch, it ached even more. Marie was going to have a horrible headache for days, she was sure.

Once she was upright, she held her hand out, trying to find anything to tell her where she was. She brushed her fingers against a wooden table or perhaps a desk. She followed along its side until she reached the edge, moving slowly so she wouldn't trip. She didn't think her head could take another hard hit.

After what seemed like hours but was only a few minutes, she finally found the wall. Running her hands against it, she continued until she found the casing of a door. Sighing with relief, she found the doorknob a moment later, twisted it, pulled it open, and found a full moon and stars twinkling in the night sky, giving her much-needed light from the darkness she'd found herself in.

Being careful not to jar her head even further, she looked around. She was still in the theater. Marie hadn't wanted to admit it to herself, but someone had hit her. She didn't know if they'd intended to just stun her, permanently do damage, or kill her, but she had to keep this to herself.

Marie couldn't tell Walter or Michael, as they'd both be upset. Michael would insist on accompanying her more than he already was. He hadn't escorted her to the theater tonight because she'd convinced both him and Walter that she would be safe from harm surrounded by other women. What she hadn't counted on was everyone disappearing as fast as they had and leaving her alone, but she wouldn't mention it. Better for the men to be unaware.

With the light from the moon shining brightly, she could see a bit and found her coat on the floor where she had dropped it. Snatching it, she pulled it over her shoulders and buttoned it. She'd stuffed her scarf and gloves into the pockets earlier, and she pulled them on.

Her head spun like crazy, but she'd be home soon, where she could put on a pot of tea, grab a bite to eat, and head to bed. The roads were mostly clear of people, but occasionally a horse or carriage would pass her by. Snow had fallen that morning, but between the horses, carriages, wagons, buggies, people, and dogs, the snow was trampled to either a muddy mess or a sheet of ice.

Taking care not to fall, she walked home much slower than she normally would've, but the knot on the back of her head hurt something fierce. Marie finally turned the corner to her temporary home. All the lights blazed from inside, and several horses were tethered in front. Her plans for a nice, quiet evening where she could sneak inside with no one aware had been derailed. She'd have to sneak inside, get upstairs, and hope no one saw her.

She pulled open the gate and closed it behind her, trying to stay quiet. She skirted around to the back of the house, where, with any luck, she could get inside with no one the wiser. Walking up the porch stairs, she cringed when she stepped on a loose board, the creaking loud in the quiet air. Holding still, she listened, and when no one came to the door, she continued up the stairs and went inside.

The kitchen was empty, but with the scattered dirty dishes on the table and counter and a pot of stew still simmering on the stove, there had been people in there. Not wanting to dawdle, she slipped off her boots so she could creep up the stairs on her bare feet.

She pushed open the swinging door and held it so it wouldn't swish closed and alert those in the house that she was there. She ran her hand along the banister railing when Michael's voice stopped her.

"You're home." Amusement was in his tone.

She whipped around and immediately regretted it. It was a good thing she hadn't let go of the banister. If she had, she'd have likely fallen to the ground, and that would have only made the pounding worse.

Marie raised a hand to her chest to calm her breathing. She wasn't sure it would work, but it gave her a moment to think of what she would say.

"Michael, I didn't expect to see you here."

"And why wouldn't you? It is my brother's house." A cocksure smile lined his lips.

He was arrogant and charming. She was having a hard time keeping herself from fawning over him like the other women in town, but underneath that swagger was a man who would break past her defenses if she gave him an opening. Which was why she wouldn't let him.

"Yes, it is. Are you and Walter having a party?"

"I wouldn't call it a party, but we have been worried about you. You're home much later than you said."

"Hmm, well, as you can see, I've made it back home alive and well." She was lying through her teeth, but she would not let him see that. When he said nothing, she said, "Well, as much as I've enjoyed this tête-à-tête"—she flicked her fingers—"it's late, and I'm right tired. I'm going to head up to bed." She turned to head up the stairs.

"Did everything go well at the rally?" he said.

She slowly turned her head and eyed him over her shoulder. "Yes."

Her tongue was thick in her mouth, her headache had grown with intensity, and her vision had blurred. If she could just lie down, she'd feel much better. She tried to focus on him, but he'd disappeared. Suddenly, he was by her side and had his hand on her elbow.

She lifted her head to look at him, and it was a mistake. The spinning intensified, and everything darkened right before her eyes.

Michael watched helplessly as Marie's eyes rolled back in her head and she went limp. If he hadn't noticed that she'd appeared out of sorts, he might not have been close enough to catch her before she collapsed.

He swept her up into his arms and climbed the stairs. She

weighed next to nothing and fit perfectly within his grasp. He didn't know why she had fainted, but he'd get her upstairs and send for the doc at once. While he was concerned for her well-being, he wanted to hold this moment in his heart. It would give him a chance to gaze at her unfettered, without her scowls or scolding words.

When he reached the second-floor landing, Marie's eyes flitted open.

"What are you doing?" She slurred her words, and her lids were heavy.

"Carrying you to your room."

Marie tried half-heartedly to push at him, but she was sluggish, and there wasn't much strength behind her wrists. Dread circled him. Something was wrong with her. He'd best get her into her room and get the doc to the house soon.

"You can..." She closed her eyes.

"Marie," he said.

She didn't respond.

Increasing the length of his strides, he pushed open the door to the room she had been sleeping in and carefully placed her on the four-poster bed. The blankets and sheets were a rumpled mess. She hadn't made the bed that morning, and as he looked around the room, he shook his head in disbelief. There were clothes, books, dirty dishes, shoes, and sundry other items scattered across the room, on the floor, on the chairs, on the windowsill and fireplace mantel, and even items strung across the dressing screen in the far corner of the room. No one could call her a meticulous housekeeper.

He pushed back a lock of her black hair and grazed his fingers against her smooth pink cheek. She'd scrunched her eyebrows together, and harsh lines marred her forehead. She looked as though she might be in pain, and Michael worried she had injuries he couldn't see.

Giving her one more glance, he strode out of the room and

down the stairs to find her brother. Walter had invited him and a few of his reporters over for dinner. Someone should be able to find the doctor.

He stepped into the parlor and found Walter making numerous toasts, a glass of whiskey in his hands. The men were laughing and enjoying their liquor.

Michael had been playing cards when he'd left to grab something to eat from the kitchen, and that was when he'd found Marie. If he hadn't gone when he had, he'd hate to think what would've happened to her.

Catching Walter's eye, he gestured for him to come into the hall.

"Something wrong?" Walter asked.

Michael nodded. "Marie collapsed––"

"Where is she?" Walter tried to push past him, scanning the hallway.

Michael stopped him. "She's in her room, but we need to send for the doctor. Her eyes were unfocused, and she didn't wake when I put her on her bed."

"You were in her room?" Walter pursed his lips.

"Walter, you know me better than that. I'd never take advantage of her. Hell, I'd marry her if she let me."

Walter's mouth opened in shock. "You'd what?"

Michael smothered a groan. He hadn't meant to say that to her brother, at least in this way, but he had nothing to hide. "I'd marry her, but she wants nothing to do with me or any other man, for that matter. But that isn't what we need to focus on. She needs a doctor."

Walter nodded. "Frank!"

A man stumbled out of the parlor. "Yeah, boss."

Frank's face was bright red, and his hair stuck straight off his head as if lightning had struck him, but his eyes were clear, and instead of a glass of whiskey in his hand, he held a biscuit. He was likely the only man not deep in his cups.

"Can you find the doc? Something's wrong with my sister, and I'm not sure I could sit a horse."

Frank nodded, shoved the rest of the biscuit into his mouth, snatched a coat off the coat rack, and bustled out of the house a moment later.

"I'm gonna head upstairs. Would you watch for the doc?" Walter didn't wait for Michael's response and disappeared up the stairs.

Michael desperately wanted to follow, but after his slipup about saying he wanted to marry Marie, he wasn't sure he'd be welcomed into her room. He'd have to wait for the doc and see what he said.

An hour later, the doc finally arrived. If he'd been much longer, Michael might've worn a hole in the wood from all the pacing he'd been doing back and forth in the hallway.

"Seymour," he said. "What's wrong now?"

"It's Marie Owens. She'd fainted, but something doesn't look right. She couldn't focus and was unaware of where she was. I'm concerned."

"You should be. Why didn't you call for me sooner?" He poked a finger in Michael's chest.

Michael blew out a frustrated breath. "We did."

His words fell on deaf ears as the doc pushed past him, muttering something under his breath about cowboys never getting him to patients in a timely fashion and waiting until it was too late. Michael followed, feeling a big sheepish even though they'd sent for him as soon as possible. It wasn't his fault that it'd taken Frank as long as it had to find the man.

The doc headed upstairs, and Michael followed, pointing to her room when they reached the second landing. The doc opened the door and disappeared. Michael's heart hurt knowing he couldn't be in there with her, but the doc would look her over, and everything would be all right.

It had to be.

Besides, Michael didn't want her to think he was intruding, even if he wanted to be near her side. Walter wouldn't let him in there either, not after his confession. He'd be surprised if Walter let him anywhere near her in the future after that. Patience was the only thing he had left.

Twenty

"I won't continue to sit inside that room and act like an obedient little sister." Marie pointed to the ceiling and her bedroom above it. "I've been stuck inside for over a week while you clucked around me like a mother hen."

"Someone attacked you!" Walter's face had grown red with anger. He slapped his hand against the doorframe. "How can I live with myself knowing you're in danger and that I didn't do everything in my power to protect you?"

"I've been in danger for months, and I never told you," she snapped and immediately regretted it. She hadn't meant to reveal that much information, but he had pushed her too far.

"What?" Anger reverberated off the walls.

Marie took a step back, not liking the look in her brother's eyes. His overprotectiveness in thinking she couldn't take care of herself was too much.

"What do you mean, you've been in danger for months? What have you been hiding from me?"

"Nothing. Otherwise, I would've told you." She actually wouldn't have told him a thing, but she had to try to deescalate the tension in the room.

"Is this why Michael's been taking you to your events?"

Marie blushed but refused to admit that Michael was.

He stalked back and forth in front of the fireplace. "Marie Evelyn Owens, I am so angry right now. You've given me even more of a reason to insist that you not leave this house. Your participation in those rallies and events is dangerous. I will *not* have my sister taking part in this any further."

Her spine stiffened, anger pulsating through her skin. This was exactly why she had kept her brother in the dark. "I will not sit here and do nothing." She stomped her foot. "It's *absolutely* imperative I continue my work. Do you think women will get the vote if I sit around here and do nothing... every... single... day?"

Walter closed his eyes and leaned against the wall, tightening and releasing his hands as though he were trying to decide what to do with himself. "There are other women who––"

"No!" she yelled. "If I give up and do as you ask, then I'm no better than the men who are trying to stop us. I don't care if I'm in danger. I have nothing else to live for except this. This is my passion, this is my mission, and I won't give it up, even for you." She heaved with exertion and fury.

"Yes, you will." He pushed away from the wall and stalked toward her.

She didn't appreciate the look in his eyes, but she would not bow down, not over this. She held her ground and glared at him. "What are you going to do to me, Walter?" she drawled. "Tie me up, lock me in my room, keep food and water from me until I do as you bid? If I wanted that, I would've married a man who believes women should do as they are told every time he utters a command."

"Marie, I didn't mean––"

"No." She held up a hand to stop him. "You did mean it. You're just like the rest, thinking we can't take care of ourselves, that we can't think on our own, that we can't vote on our own." She dropped her trembling hand to her waist. "Do you think I want to end up like the women I'm trying to help? Marry a man, believe I'd be happy, and the next thing I know, I'm trembling in fear, bruises on my arms, my face, and no one to turn to. Do you want me to end up like that?"

Walter's eyes grew sad. "Do you really believe all men want to control their wives, want to beat them into submission? Is that what you think I would do if I had a wife? What Michael would do? What his brothers would do?"

"No, you wouldn't do that, but I don't know Michael, and I don't know his brothers."

"Even after spending a week in their home, watching them with their wives and sisters, you still believe they might harm you?"

"Not exactly." Shame billowed through her like smoke from a chimney. The Seymours had been nothing but kind, but she was trying to prove a point and wouldn't back down.

"Then why are you so determined to put yourself in danger?"

"I'm not. I've seen too many women harmed, and I refuse to end up like them. Why shouldn't I fight to keep myself from that kind of fate?"

"That is such a harsh reaction to a small set of marriages in this world."

"How can you say it is small? Just because you wouldn't harm your future wife doesn't mean that plenty of men don't. Besides, you're trying to control me, well-intentioned as it might be."

"I'm not trying to control you!" he snapped.

"Yes, you are. You want me to quit participating in the suffragist movement. If that isn't control, then what is it?"

"It's keeping you safe from a madman."

"Phish, we don't know it's a madman. It's likely a husband of a woman I've helped or a group of misinformed miscreants. I refuse to quit helping women because of it."

"You don't know who it is."

"Maybe it's just a series of unfortunate events." She didn't believe that, but she'd do or say whatever she could to get Walter to leave her alone.

Walter threw up his hands. "You'll never stop, will you?"

"No, I won't," she said with a devious smile. This was too important.

Twenty-One

"Tony!" Michael yelled over his shoulder. "Where's my farrier knife?"

Michael had been distracted all morning and was paying the price by being unprepared when he started working on the stallion.

Tony burst through the door behind him and slammed it against the wall. Knives, hammers, wrenches, and nails clattered to the floor. The horse snorted, air exploding from his nostrils as he pulled on the bridle and backed up from the unexpected and unwelcome noise.

"Shit, Tony, I've got a horse in here."

Tony scrambled to pick the tools from the floor. "Sorry, boss." He tripped over himself, dropping the tools as quickly as he picked them up.

Michael turned his attention to calming the high-strung stallion. Between him trying to keep an eye on Walter and Marie while they lived at Luke's place and following Marie to her various suffragists' meetings and rallies, his concentration had been diverted from the work that'd been waiting. If he wasn't careful, he'd lose what he'd worked hard to cultivate. He was proud of what he'd accomplished, although he wondered if horses and carriages would soon be replaced by automobiles. He'd been considering buying one and having it shipped to Helena, but that'd be something to think about another day. The ranchers and farmers in the area would be fit to be tied having one of those loud contraptions busting through town, but he'd sure like to get his hands on one and tinker with it.

Michael was at his wit's end. Tony was a great assistant, but he had much to learn and wasn't able to do many of the tasks on his own. Michael would need to find more experienced help, and soon. The work wasn't slowin', and he needed another experienced blacksmith to keep up with everything with the way people were moving into town.

"Just get me my knife, please." Michael held the bridle, whispered in the horse's ear, and rubbed at his muzzle. With patience and time, the horse settled, and Michael was able to go back to trimming and shoeing his hooves.

As the day wore on, the smithy grew hot while the temperatures outside continued to fall. A snowstorm was blowing in, which wasn't that unusual in January, but it would've been nice to have a slightly warmer day instead of a brisk one.

Michael's muscles burned under the weight of trying to keep up with the work, and by the time the sun disappeared, he was plumb worn out, but he'd gotten through several jobs he'd been putting off for days. He pulled out his watch and checked the time.

He'd promised Marie he'd meet her at the assembly hall by six. She wasn't thrilled he was coming, but it had been a way to appease Walter, and she had begrudgingly agreed to the supervision. Her brother had been quite adamant that she was not to attend any event alone and that either he, Michael, or one of his reporters would be with her at every event. Michael wasn't convinced that sending his reporters wasn't a bigger motivator, as the suffragist movement was headlining the front page of many of the local and national newspapers, and Walter was taking advantage of the hype.

Michael had just over an hour to clean up and be there in time to watch her speak. An hour later, he arrived at the assembly hall. It was only a few blocks from his smithy and livery. The place buzzed with people, including a bunch of angry men shouting obscenities in protest. He eyed the angry crowd, but they stayed on the other side of the road and didn't interfere with those attending the event. A few of the sheriff's deputies were scattered about, standing with their hands behind their backs, and their expressions stern as though to say, *You can protest as long as you don't interfere.*

Marie had warned him that there would be protesters, but Michael hadn't truly anticipated the anger on the men's faces. A few had clubs in their hands, raised above their heads, but they kept their distance. Michael worried that they'd get out of control, but Marie had insisted it was normal. There were always protesters, she said, but they were harmless.

He wasn't sure he believed it was as safe as she claimed, but the sheriff was there, so he would trust her for now, even though he'd still be on his guard. He straightened the tie around his neck and bounded up the stairs. He scanned the crowd, looking for Walter, and finally, Michael saw him standing just inside the glass doors. Michael's sister, Anne, was with him. She had come to Helena to do a bit of shopping, and she wanted to get away from the ranch for a few days. He didn't have the room at his place, and Walter and Marie had offered up a guest room to let her stay.

Walter caught his eye and raised a hand to wave him over. Michael maneuvered through the crowds until he reached their side. Pulling Anne into a quick hug, he kissed her on the cheek and then shook Walter's hand.

"I was getting a mite worried you weren't going to make it." Laughter crinkled the corners of Walter's eyes.

"There's no way I'd miss tonight. It's too important for Marie."

Walter waggled his eyebrows. "I wonder why."

Michael grinned. "I ain't afraid to admit I'd like to get to know your sister more, as you well know. If you'd let me, that is."

"Oh, I'm aware, but it isn't me"––he pointed at his chest–– "that you'll have to convince. If you haven't figured it out by now, she has a mind of her own."

Michael tipped back the brim of his hat. "I'm figuring that out, but I'm patient."

"You'll have to be more than patient to get her to want more than her causes."

"I'll keep on a-tryin' until she can't help but fall in love with me."

Anne smiled. "I had no idea you had such powerful feelings for Marie. She'd be lucky to have you."

"I agree," Michael said, a wide grin splitting his cheeks.

"Oh, you." Anne tapped him on the shoulder in jest. "I'm glad to see the jovial one in the family is still here. For a minute there, I was afraid you'd gotten all serious and stern after... well, after everything with Connie."

Michael's smile faltered. It wasn't a time he liked to think about.

"I'm sorry, Michael." Anne caught the look in his eyes. "I didn't mean––"

"It's all right. No harm done."

Anne touched his arm. "I shouldn't have brought up terrible memories. You seem happy, and I imagine we have Marie to thank for that."

"Well, she brings a smile to my lips and a spring to my step. If only I could convince her to have the same feelings toward me, then all would be right grand."

"Give her time," Anne said. "Sometimes it's hard to see what's been in front of us. Just don't give up, for it's much harder knowing you didn't give it your all when it's taken from you."

There was more to what she was saying, but before he could ask questions, a loud bell rang twice.

"I think we'd better find our seats," Walter said. "We don't want Marie scolding us for being late."

"No, we certainly don't." Michael held out his arm, and Anne took it.

Two hours later, the final speaker, a suffragist from England, Emmeline Pankhurst, held up her hand. "Men make the moral code, and they expect women to accept it. They have decided that it is entirely right and proper for men to fight for their liberties and their rights, but that is not right and proper for women to fight for theirs.[1]"

The room erupted into thunderous applause. The assembly hall was filled to the brim with hundreds of women and a fair number of men. Far more than Michael had expected to see. He believed in what Marie was fighting for, and his brothers felt the same, but he also felt they were a far different breed than most of the men in Helena. As shown by those in attendance, he'd greatly underestimated the suffragists' appeal. Perhaps with any luck, the women would get the vote and get the measure passed to be on the state's constitution this September.

As the crowd made its way out of the auditorium, the three of them stayed in their seats until most of the attendees had left. They had agreed to meet Marie at the stairs on the left side of the stage, but instead of trying to fight the crowd leaving, they sat talking about the speakers and their message.

Finally, once the crowd had dispersed, they stood and walked down the aisle toward the stage. Several speakers had gathered, congratulating each other for a job well done. Michael hated to interrupt, but it was getting late, and they still needed to walk to his livery to get the carriage and horses to take Walter, Marie, and Anne back to Luke's house.

---

1. *My Own Story* by Emmeline Pankhurst

"Michael," a high-pitched voice called.

He looked around and groaned internally. It was Suzette.

"What is she doing here?" Anne whispered.

Suzette flounced toward them, holding her hands out in welcome. She took his free hand in hers and held it close to her chest. "It is *so* good to see you. We *really* need to make plans to meet for dinner."

He gently pulled away. Suzette's simpering was too much. "Suzette, I didn't expect to see you here."

"Oh yes. I've gotten so involved with the movement. It's exhilarating seeing women come together to fight for more rights, don't you believe?" Her eyes were wide and almost innocent.

"Yes," he murmured.

Suzette's gaze trailed to Anne, a question in her eyes. They likely had never met. Anne and Katie had only been in Spring Creek once, and from what he understood, when they'd seen her with Ben, it had been from a distance, and no proper introductions had been made.

"Let me introduce my sister Anne," Michael said.

Suzette grinned broadly. "How nice to meet you. I'm surprised I didn't see you at Ben's New Year's party. I thought his whole family was in attendance."

"Not everyone," Michael said.

"I was under the weather that night," Anne said, "And spent most of the night in my room."

"I'm so sorry to hear that. I hope you have recovered?"

"Yes," Anne murmured. "Thank you for inquiring."

"Did you enjoy the speakers?" Suzette turned her gaze back to Michael, clearly trying to catch and hold his attention. Attention he did not want.

"Yes." Michael didn't want to prolong the conversation with Suzette much longer than he had to. "Have you seen Marie Owens?"

The light dimmed in her eyes. He shouldn't be so quick to

dismiss her, as she had been nothing but kind since coming back into their lives, but he wasn't interested in her as much as she seemed to be in him. He wasn't oblivious to the way she practically undressed him with her eyes. It was disconcerting when he only had eyes for one woman.

"Yes." Suzette raised a hand to the gold chain around her neck. "She's over there." She turned and pointed to the edge of the stage where Marie stood conversing with one of the first speakers of the night.

"Thank you kindly, miss," Walter said.

"I apologize. I should have introduced my friend," Michael said. "Suzette, this is Walter Owens, Marie's brother." He looked at Walter. "Walter, please meet Suzette..." He paused. "I'm sorry, Suzette. I don't think I ever learned your surname."

She giggled. "It's perfectly all right. My married name is Suzette Cole, but please, just call me Suzette."

"Suzette, it certainly is a pleasure," Walter said, bending his head in acknowledgment. "We should have you over for dinner. Make a party of it."

That was the last thing Michael wanted, but if he said as much, it'd be rude, so he only nodded in acquiescence. With any luck, she'd head back to Spring Creek soon, and he could avoid the invitation.

"Don't let me stop you from going to your sister. I'm sure you'd care to speak with her. Have a nice evening." Suzette flitted her hand and waved goodbye, skirting past them and going up the aisle. Her pale blue skirt fluttered behind her.

Marie stopped in her tracks when she saw Suzette next to Michael, Anne, and Walter. That woman had started showing up at her suffragists' meetings and had somehow become a close confidant to Eloisa and Greta, but there was something about her that put Marie on guard. Marie didn't think it was because Suzette was interested in Michael. It was more than that. It was as though Suzette's motives were carefully calculated, as though she had a hidden agenda. Marie didn't want to sound paranoid, so she said nothing, but she had no desire to trust Suzette, no matter how much she simpered and praised the speakers and leaders of the movement.

It had been a long day. Marie longed to go home and rest her feet, but she wasn't about to go near Suzette. She'd rather stay late than go there. Besides, she found it abhorrent the way Suzette was draped across Michael, as if he were her prize bull. Of course, Michael wasn't exactly pushing her away and even seemed to enjoy the attention Suzette paid him.

"Marie," a woman said, interrupting her woolgathering. "How do you think the crowd received us? Do you think we made any progress?"

Marie turned to the woman. Watching Michael with Suzette was too much after the long day she'd had. It had been one catastrophe after another, but luckily, the speakers had been none the wiser and had no idea how close they'd come to canceling the event.

Marie raised a hand to her forehead. "I think it went well. None of the protesters interrupted, which is a blessing, and the crowd"—Marie smiled, closing her eyes briefly, remembering the swell of applause after each speaker—"the crowd was amazing. We will keep pushing hard until September, when the vote's taken at the state legislature. With any luck, the women here will convince their husbands, brothers, fathers, and friends that our cause is just and worthwhile."

"It seems like such a long battle," the woman murmured, fingering the collar of her blue blouse.

"But long battles can be hard fought and won," Marie said.

A moment later, the woman skittered away, another woman calling to her from across the auditorium. The room had emptied, the speakers having long gone. She went up the stairs to the stage and went behind the curtains, where she had left her cloak and reticule.

A thud sounded behind her. Turning, she called, "Who's there?"

No one answered. She shivered. Maybe she was hearing things. No one was there. She couldn't worry over every sound, as though it were someone coming after her.

A hard body slammed into her, pushing her into the wall. Her face smacked the cold wood, and something was pushed hard into her back. She froze.

It was the barrel of a gun.

"What--"

"Don't say a word," the man hissed.

Fear clogged her throat, and her hands and legs trembled. She couldn't speak even if she wanted to.

"What's it gonna take for you to learn your place? Ain't fittin' for a woman to have the vote. She's beholden to her husband. Nothin' more."

The barrel dug into her spine. This man would kill her if she made the wrong move.

She gulped. "What do you want from me?"

He slammed his fist against the wall near her face. "I want you and your kind to stop with these infernal speeches"--his voice dropped--"and learn your place."

She tried to turn her head to look at him, but he shoved his other hand against the base of her neck and pushed her head forward, digging his fingers into her scalp. Splinters scratched her cheek.

"Don't move," he said. "Gotta teach you a lesson."

Marie's blood ran cold, and she couldn't utter another word, fear pulsating through her.

"Stay away from all this, and stay away from--"

"Marie?" Michael yelled. "Are you back there?"

The man threw her to the ground and ran away. She fell hard, her wrists and knees smarting against the impact, leaving her with a bruised ego and a pounding heart.

"Yes." She tried to stand, but her legs were shaky and wouldn't seem to work the way she needed them to.

"Marie!" Michael grabbed her elbow. "Did you fall?"

"Not exactly." She pulled from his touch, brushing at her skirt and grimacing at her stinging palms.

"What happened?"

"An angry man grabbed me, and--"

"What? Where?" Michael pulled his revolver from his holster, swiveling his head in all directions, and stepped in front of her as though he could protect her from danger. The danger that had already disappeared.

"He's gone." She rubbed the back of her neck, a headache blooming. This was not how she'd expected the day to end. It should have been a celebration. Instead, it would just worsen with Michael and Walter hovering as though she couldn't care for herself. They were already driving her nuts and would continue after this.

"Did he hurt you?" Michael asked after determining the man had disappeared. He shoved his revolver back into his holster and stepped close, but she retreated. She didn't want him to comfort her, not when he'd been enamored with another woman just moments before.

"Not really," she said. "He pushed me to the ground when he heard you call my name, but I'm all right. More of a bruised ego than anything else."

"I'm going to kill him," he said.

"No, you're not," Marie said. "He's a coward and will likely disappear once again. You don't need another death on your hands."

Michael stilled, a look of shock crossing his face.

What did I say?

And then she realized she had inadvertently referenced him killing the woman who had harmed their family.

He spoke before she could apologize. "You really need a keeper, don't you?"

"I don't need anything of the sort," she growled. "I can take care of myself."

"Like you did tonight?"

"I am perfectly fine."

"Are you?" He reached for her arm, but she wrenched it away.

"He was all bluster and just wanted to say his piece. Men like that hide in the shadows and only come out when they think they'll be able to beat someone more defenseless. What he doesn't understand is that I'm not defenseless."

"You're still a woman, Marie."

She laughed. "Of course, I'm a woman, but I've survived every single time."

"But how many more times are you going to be attacked?"

She snatched her cloak and threw it across her shoulders. "If only I had a way to look into the future."

"You don't need to be glib about this." Frustration lined his face, but she wouldn't let his concern stop her.

"I'm not," she said. "But I can't live my life in fear over what *might* happen."

He ran his fingers through his hair and pursed his lips. "But you can be more aware, more careful, take precautions."

"And what precautions am I supposed to take? Sit in the house with the doors locked and the drapes drawn?"

"That's not a bad idea." He grinned mockingly at her.

"I don't find you amusing, Michael Seymour."

"None of this is amusing."

"Dammit," she muttered. "I have a headache. It's been a long day, and I just want to go home."

"Well, don't let me stop you from that," he drawled, waving his arm, but anger flashed in his eyes.

This was far from over, but she'd fight with him in the morning after she had a good night's sleep. Right now, she wasn't in the mood and stalked past him, determined to get home.

Twenty-Two

Marie gathered her cloak and snuck down the back stairs. She'd never hear the end of it, but she needed time alone, away from their protective glances and their blustering attitudes that she was only going to stay safe if she was in their presence.

While she agreed that someone was trying to hurt her, she'd come away from every accident without permanent damage. Preferably, she didn't want anything bad to happen, but she also couldn't live her life in fear.

Slipping out the kitchen door, she tightened her scarf around her neck. She had a pamphlet she needed to get to the printer, and it couldn't wait any longer. She should have delivered it a few days ago, but she'd been distracted by Michael's incessant helpfulness.

After his proposal at the ranch on New Year's Eve, she had been trying to avoid him, with no success. She had told him no, but his determination to convince her to change her mind was clear. He engaged her in multiple conversations, asking questions about the suffragists, offering to help carry and distribute pamphlets, setting up chairs and tables for their meetings, and performing numerous other considerate actions that made it hard to resist him, but she couldn't forget her goals. She was smarter than that.

No matter how much lust tightened her belly, she would ignore his advances. No matter how dry her mouth grew when he gave her that charming smile, she would look away. No matter how kind he was in helping the women she worked with, she would remember he was still a man who could take away her rights if she were to even consider a marriage proposal.

"Marie!"

She stopped and scanned the crowds clogging the streets. She didn't see who was calling her, but the voice was familiar.

"Marie, over here."

As she followed the sound of the voice, the crowd split to reveal Suzette. She was with two young children, a boy and a girl. The boy stood tall, trying to look older than he was, and the young girl bounced on her heels, clearly excited.

Marie groaned inwardly. Suzette was the last person she wanted to talk to, but she'd be polite, even if it killed her.

Suzette pulled her children with her across the dirt road to where Marie stood. She waited patiently, even though she needed to get to the printer. Hopefully, whatever Suzette wanted would be quick.

"Brrr," Suzette said. "It's cold out here."

Marie hadn't noticed, but she murmured something in reply.

"Mother," the young boy said. "Who is she?" He pointed to Marie.

A scowl crossed Suzette's face briefly before she turned on a beaming smile. If Marie hadn't been watching her closely, she might have missed it as fast as it came and went. "Todd, may I present Miss Marie Owens? Marie, these are my children, Todd and Natalie."

Marie nodded to them. "It's nice to meet you, Todd, Natalie.

Todd straightened his shoulders. "Likewise, ma'am."

Natalie didn't say anything, but she shyly pushed her face into Suzette's skirts.

"Are you having an enjoyable time in Helena?" Marie asked.

Suzette preened as though she were the queen of the ball, but based on the interactions Marie had had with her, it was part of her personality. Suzette enjoyed being the center of attention, almost craved it. Many insecure women acted this way, and Marie had wondered on more than one occasion if there was more to Suzette than what she appeared.

"We were on our way to see Mr. Seymour," Suzette said.

"Oh," Marie said, trying to hide her shock, but she shouldn't be surprised. Suzette's intention to get Michael in her snare was obvious. Marie had no interest in Michael, but the thought of him having anything to do with Suzette sent a surge of jealousy straight to her gut. Michael was a good man and deserved someone far more to his liking than Suzette, who would run him dry.

"Yes," Suzette murmured, pushing back the brim of her hat. "We discussed taking the children on a picnic, so I thought I'd see when he'd like to do that."

Marie wasn't sure what to say to the preposterous statement. It was January in Montana, and the woman wanted to take her children on a picnic. Was she delusional? The ground was covered in snow, the temperatures were low, and the blustery winds stung as they blew through the valley. Who would want to spend any length of time outside?

Not to mention, her children weren't appropriately clothed. It was a wonder they weren't complaining about the cold. Marie's thick gloves didn't prevent her fingers from stinging, and she was dressed much more warmly than Suzette and the two young ones.

"It's a bit cold for that, isn't it?"

Suzette tittered. "The sun is shining. The sky is blue. Why shouldn't we take advantage of it?"

Marie stared, flabbergasted. Yes, the sky was blue, and the sun was shining, but it *wasn't* weather for a picnic. She shrugged. It wasn't her business, and Michael wasn't careless enough to take two young children out in this weather for any length of time, no matter how much Suzette would simper and preen.

"Is he at home?"

"I don't keep track of Michael's whereabouts," Marie said.

"You don't? I thought you and your brother were living with him since your house burned to the ground." A malicious grin lined Suzette's lips.

Irritation climbed up her spine. Suzette had no tact, but then she wasn't trying to impress Marie. She was more interested in getting Michael in her clutches. A part of her was sad that Michael might be interested in this woman.

"Marie?" Suzette asked.

"We're living in his brother's house, but yes, I've been distracted with losing everything in the fire." Her tone was sarcastic.

Suzette released Todd's hand and patted Marie's arm. "You poor thing. It has to be difficult depending on such a thoughtful friend as Michael."

Marie wanted to yank her arm away from the insincere woman, but she kept her composure. "Thank you," she murmured. "I would imagine he'd be working at his livery."

"Hmm." Suzette's smile faltered, but then she brightened enthusiastically. "We'll just meander over there and see."

"You do that. But I must be going," Marie said.

"Of course, of course," Suzette said. "It was *so* delightful to see you this morning."

Marie nodded and then headed toward the printer, very glad to get away from Suzette. She was already late, and if she didn't hurry, she wouldn't make it in time.

Two hours later, Marie returned to Luke's house. She was sure Walter had discovered she'd snuck out, and she wasn't looking forward to seeing his reaction. But nothing untoward had happened, so their overprotectiveness had been for naught.

Pulling open the gate, she closed it carefully behind her and briskly walked up the path when the front door pushed open. Michael stepped outside, crossed his arms over his chest, and spread his legs in a stance that should have made her cower, but instead, it made her insides quiver with excitement.

What is wrong with me?

"Nice of you to finally arrive," he drawled.

"I didn't realize I had a schedule to keep." She scooted past him and went inside the house. Tingles erupted across her skin where he touched her, but she wasn't about to acknowledge that. She'd barely gotten the information to the printer. Then there had been an issue with the printing press, the first few pamphlets being a complete mess. Luckily, the printer had straightened out the mess, but it had been a few moments of panic.

"Marie," he said, following her.

"You can stop with that authoritative tone," she said. "What are you doing here? Did Walter send for you?"

She pulled off her gloves, placed them on the foyer table, and went to shrug off her cloak when Michael's hands brushed across her shoulders. He helped her remove it. She bristled at his touch and assumptions, but she'd pick her battles. Fighting with him over her cloak was not worth the effort when he was about to give her a piece of his mind. That was the fight she would do, not one over her cloak.

Marie murmured her thanks and then headed into the parlor. She was chilled and could use a glass of whiskey. That would surely warm her quicker than anything. She could feel his presence behind her, but she was going to ignore him until she had that drink in her hand. Even then, Marie wasn't sure how she was going to respond to his reprimand.

A moment later, she poured herself a glass and turned to face him. Michael had a stern look on his face. His arms were crossed around his chest, and he leaned against the wall. If he was trying to be intimidating, it wasn't working. He could growl at her all he liked, but it wouldn't change her mind.

She lifted the whiskey to her lips and took a small sip, eyeing him carefully over the rim. He cocked an eyebrow. If he were trying to disarm her, it wouldn't work.

Marie slowly placed the glass on the fireplace mantle. Her hands would need to be free for this. "Are you going to continue to glower at me like that?"

"I'm not glowering." He relaxed his arms around his chest.

He was completely glowering at her, but if he wanted to deny it, who was she to stop him? "Then what would you call it?"

"I'm just waiting for you to explain where the hell you've been." He narrowed his eyes.

"Don't speak to me like that, Michael Seymour. You're not my father, my brother, or my husband--"

"And whose fault is that?" He pushed away from the wall and stalked abruptly toward her.

"Don't you dare try to intimidate me." She stepped forward, planted her feet, and pointed a finger at him.

He stopped in his tracks and softened his expression.

That only antagonized her further. "Don't you get kind now, especially after acting like you had any right to ask me where I've been or interrogate me in any fashion."

A smile crept up his lips.

"Are you laughing at me?" she choked, tears clogging her throat.

What is wrong with me? Why do I let him get under my skin?

"Marie, I'm sorry. Please don't cry."

She swiped at her eyes. "I'm not crying," she snarled, but the tears running down her cheeks said otherwise.

His voice lowered. "I've been worried sick."

"I don't need you to be worried about me."

"Whether you want me to be worried doesn't change the fact that I was."

"You are not responsible for me. Why can't you realize that?"

"Dammit, Marie." He scratched at his scalp and crinkled his eyes. "I want to be responsible for you. Why can't *you* realize that?"

"I don't want you to be."

"And why not? What have I done that is so horrible for you to even consider that I might want to be there for you, to care for you?" He raised a hand as though to touch her.

"I don't need a man to care for me."

"Well, then how about a man to support you, love you, prop you up when you are sad?"

Marie saw the anguish in his eyes, but she couldn't be swayed. "I've never said I wanted that."

"I never said you did. I'm asking––why don't you?"

She stared at him, confused and angry. He took a few steps toward her, and while she wanted to retreat out of his reach, she couldn't show any weakness. Weakness gave men power, and she wouldn't give any man that.

Michael's fingers grazed her cheek, wiping away a tear. Her breath hitched.

"What are you so afraid of?" he whispered. His breath wafted across her skin, and goosebumps prickled.

"I'm not afraid of anything." Her voice lacked conviction. She was losing control of her emotions and sliding down a snow-covered hill straight toward an icy lake.

"You are." He leaned his forehead against hers.

He was clearly trying to break down her defenses, but she was smarter than that. She couldn't let him be kind to her or love her, as he so desperately tried to do.

"No." She tried to deny what was very obvious to him and to her. If she were completely honest with herself, she would admit she was scared. Scared of the unknown. Scared if she gave in to what Michael wanted, she would give up her independence and be forever beholden to what he wanted.

"Yes," he said, and then he did what she should have anticipated but didn't.

Michael brushed his lips against hers. Awareness surged through her like a church bell ringing––loud, thundering, yet the lingering resonance was a calming boom to her soul. Only his lips touched hers.

She grabbed his lapel and pulled him closer, but he twisted away, the memory of his kiss remaining on her lips.

"No." Eyes wide, she touched her lips.

His soft, tender smile made her want to slap him, but was it because she wanted him to go away or was it because she wanted him to continue? Either way, she regretted saying no because it only bolstered his spirits.

Michael's chest puffed out with pride, and she was instantly irritated. He wouldn't stop. Michael was going to continue to pursue her now that she wanted more. And more *was* what she wanted, and she didn't understand why. It went against everything she had always believed.

Something had shifted, and there was no telling what she might do next.

Twenty-Three

"Marie." Anne walked into the kitchen. "You've been hiding for days."

Marie's hand hesitated as she was about to take a bite of the piece of bread she had just slathered with warm apple butter. She slowly dropped it onto her plate.

"I..." Marie swallowed. While she'd been avoiding Walter and Michael, she hadn't meant to ignore Anne. "I'm sorry. I *have* been avoiding Walter and Michael. I've been a coward, not wanting to see or talk with them after the fight I had with Michael."

"My brother is pigheaded, but..." Anne hesitated. "He has good intentions and is a good man. He's been placed in a few situations that have been hard on him, and he has demons he still hasn't worked through, but if you're afraid he'll hurt you, then you don't know him very well."

"I don't think he would hurt me intentionally," Marie said. "I just don't want to give him or any man that much power over me."

"Why would you think men would hurt you?" Anne pulled a plate from a shelf and picked up the knife. The blade gleamed in the sunlight pouring in through the windows.

"Aren't you afraid your future husband will hurt you?"

Anne laughed, though her expression spoke of something not of laughter. "I'd have to have a husband to worry about that, wouldn't I?"

"I'm so sorry, Anne. I didn't mean to be cruel."

"You aren't being cruel." She placed the knife against the loaf of bread and cut herself a piece. "You just have a very strong opinion about what you want and"—she pointed the knife at Marie—"what you don't."

Marie chuckled. "You aren't wrong about that, but I realize some women want husbands, and while it isn't in my future, I shouldn't be so heartless to think it isn't something you would want."

Anne took a bite of the bread and chewed thoughtfully before swallowing. "I would like to marry, have a home, children to care for." Her soft gaze looked off into the distance, as though she remembered something from her past.

"Do you have a beau?" Marie asked.

Anne coughed and shook her head wildly. "No... Although, there was this man I met a few years ago who made my heart go pitter-pat."

"Pitter-pat?" Marie tried to keep from laughing.

"Go ahead and laugh. I was head over heels for him, but at the time, he couldn't commit." She rubbed her forehead. "I couldn't stay, and that was the end of that."

"It sounds as though there's a story there."

Anne smiled tenderly, playing with the piece of bread, picking it apart as though she wasn't aware she was doing it. "There is. Maybe one day I'll tell you all about it."

Realizing this was a subject Anne didn't want to continue discussing, Marie left it alone. Some things were best left private. She knew that now.

"Do you ever think you'll change your mind about marrying?" Anne asked.

Marie looked at Anne sharply. She thought she had made that

quite clear on numerous occasions.

"I'm not asking because I question your goals or mission, Marie," Anne said. "I'm just asking because life can be long and hard, especially in Montana. Without someone to share it with, won't it become lonely?" She looked down and grimaced. "I sure made a mess of things, didn't I?" Anne swept the crumbs into a pile, stood, and dumped them into the waste container next to the door.

Marie considered her next words and the innocence Anne still had. She wished she still had that innocence at times, but she had seen too much in her fight to help those in need. Women beaten down, bruises lining their arms and legs, and despair in their eyes. Children hungry because their pa was too drunk to work and provided nothing for them to eat. Children too scared because they'd seen their pa beat their ma. Prostitutes filled with any number of diseases, their bodies beaten, their spirits squashed because they'd been left with no choices after men had taken everything they offered. Women thrown out of their homes because their husbands failed to pay the rent. Women struggling to protect their children from their pa's wrath.

"I have thought about it, but I also believe it'll be a long and difficult road to get women the vote. But once we have that, then maybe, just maybe, we can stop the beatings, the control, the despair. It has to start somewhere, and this is the first step. I have to fight because if I don't, then who will?"

"There are plenty of women and men who will fight the fight. It can't just be you alone. Will there come a time when you can't?"

"I won't ever stop." She slapped her hand on the table to force her point.

"And you want to do it alone?"

"I..." Marie paused. "It's not that I necessarily want to do it alone, but what other choice do I have?"

"Oh, Marie." Anne placed her hand on her arm and squeezed

gently. "There are a lot of choices we can make, and you've made a noble one, but be careful that you haven't made one you'll regret."

"Men can't be trusted, Anne."

"I can understand why you can't trust men who are cruel, who fight against women having equal rights, or who hurt their wives, but not all men are like that. Men, like my father and my brothers, are ones you can trust."

"You're only saying that because they *are* your brothers." Marie pulled away and placed her hands in her lap.

Anne sighed, releasing a heavy breath. "Yes, they are my brothers, and I love them dearly. I also know their faults, their weaknesses, and their strengths. They aren't perfect, but they aren't like the ones you're fighting against. In fact, they're willing to help you with the fight. They want women to have the same equal rights, to have the right to vote, to own their property––just like you do."

Marie studied Anne for a long moment. She didn't want to hurt Anne's feelings, but no matter what Anne said, it wouldn't change her mind. Michael might be a good man in his sister's eyes, but there was no telling what he could do.

Marie wanted to explain her reasoning as best she could without hurting Anne's feelings. "The law doesn't give women any recourse when the men in their lives have control. If I were to marry, my husband could take everything from me. I wouldn't be able to own property. Everything becomes his. He could even lock me up in his house and keep me from friends and family."

"Maybe," Anne spoke slowly, as though weighing her words. "But you've seen how Elizabeth is treated by Ben. He has never laid a hand on her and lets her do as she pleases. Trust me, there are things she has done that he completely disagrees with, but he loves her and would never take away her freedom. In fact, he saved her from her despicable father and the horrible man he was trying to sell her to."

"But if I don't put myself in that position to begin with, then no one would have to step in to save me."

"And if you never give someone a chance, you'll be alone for the rest of your life." Anne picked up the coffee pot and poured herself a cup. "Would you care for a refill?"

"No, thank you," Marie murmured.

Anne sat and blew on the lip of the cup before taking a sip. "Mmm, that is good. Marie, do you want to go to bed every night alone? Do you want no one to spend time with, no one to share your hopes and dreams with? No one to hold you, to kiss you, to make you feel like you are the most beautiful woman in the world, even when you've been dragged through hell trying to save two little children? When your face, hands, and body were so filthy, your hair hanging down your back in a tangled mess, hungry and desperate to save them, but he carried you and them to safety without a care for his health? Then one day he holds you in his arms and tells you that you were his moon, his star, his everything? And then the next, he is gone forever, and you never see him again?"

Marie's mouth had dropped in shock. Anne's eyes had glazed over as though she were somewhere else. Marie wasn't even sure Anne realized what she had said. Anne's past contained a moment that was both beautiful and painful. But no matter what Anne said, Marie didn't see what good it would do to trust someone if she was only going to get hurt in the end.

Anne looked at the bread on the table and pushed it around the plate. When Marie considered leaving Anne alone with her thoughts, Anne raised her head, her lashes wet with unshed tears. "I'm sorry. I think I gave you a bad idea of what trusting someone special could do for you. I forgot where I was for a moment." She fingered the buttons of her blouse. "I would take one more moment with someone special than not to have tried again. I lost someone, and I would give up everything to see him again."

"But trusting someone only gave you pain."

Anne reached across the table and took Marie's hand. "No, it gave me a few months of a love so wonderful and perfect that I'm thankful I had it. I think the memory of Nathaniel is what gives me the strength to go on."

"But--"

"No," Anne said. "There are no buts. You have two choices. Continue to live without love when someone offers it to you, or take a chance and see how splendid it can be."

Twenty-Four

꩜

Tony ran up to Michael's side, breathing heavily. "That was something, boss."

Michael was standing outside his livery, watching as the sheriff and the county coroner left with the bodies. It had been an exciting afternoon, at least from Tony's viewpoint. There weren't as many shootouts in Helena anymore, but two men had decided they were gonna fight it out the old-fashioned way. Neither one of them had come out of the altercation alive, and it had taken place right outside his place of business. It was a good thing most of the horses were used to shots being fired since many of them were raised by the cowboys on local ranches. Otherwise, he might've had a more dangerous situation on his hands.

"It could've been a lot worse." Michael slapped him on the shoulder. "Thank the stars we weren't close enough to get caught in the crossfire."

"I thought for sure one of 'em would come out of it alive." Tony's eyes bugged out of his head. His enthusiasm likely came from the dime novels he liked to read about the Wild West. While they were in the west, things were a bit more civilized these days, or Michael liked to think they were.

"Let's go clean up. It's getting late." Michael looked up at the sky. The shorter days were difficult. Between that and the vicious weather, it made for long winters. While winters were hard, they were a small price to pay for warm springs and hot summers, not to mention the views when standing on the front porch of his family's ranch. He had no reason to leave and every reason to stay. After all that had occurred over the past ten years, he wouldn't leave Montana for anything or anyone.

An hour later, he and Tony wrapped up the remaining work, closed down the fire, made quick work of feeding the horses, and locked the barn doors.

As he tightened the cinch on his saddle, he patted Tony on the shoulder. "Have you got any plans for the night?"

Tony beamed. "Yes. Fern invited me over for dinner. I gots to get spiffed up."

"Are you giving her a small token of appreciation?"

Tony gasped and then swallowed. "A token." He grabbed Michael's coat sleeve. "What am I gonna do? What should I get her? I'm gonna mess this up, and then she ain't gonna want nothing to do with me."

Michael had to hold back his grin. The poor boy was sweating up a storm and was as nervous as a newborn kitten. Michael hadn't meant to make things worse for the boy and had just asked the question without thinking.

"Now, Tony. No need to get yourself all riled up. A batch of flowers, a box of chocolates, or perhaps a ribbon for her hair is all you need."

"But where am I gonna get something like that at this hour?"

"Try the A.P. Curtin's on Grand Street. I'm sure they'll have something that'll work."

"That's a good idea." Tony's head bobbed up and down enthusiastically. "Thank ya kindly, Michael. I appreciate the tip."

"Don't douse yourself with cologne and mind your manners." He squeezed the boy's shoulder affectionately.

"Yes, sir," Tony said. "I'll see you tomorrow morning."

"I expect a full report, Tony," Michael called and chuckled as Tony ran down the street, his head going up and down as he skirted the horses, dogs, and people lining the dirt road. Michael hoped the boy would have a good time. Tony surely was infatuated with his girl, Fern, so with any luck, he'd make a good impression on the young woman. Otherwise, Michael would likely get no work out of him for days.

Leading his horse out of the corral, he dropped the latch and started to mount when a voice stopped him in his tracks. He had to hold back a groan. Suzette was relentless. She consistently dropped by unannounced and dragged her poor children with her. The other day, she'd suggested he take them on a picnic. It was January, cold as sin on a good day, and she wanted to sit on the cold snow with children who weren't dressed for Montana weather and eat grapes and drink wine.

The children needed a responsible adult in their lives because their mother was far from that. Suzette was still the flighty, irresponsible woman Ben had thought he loved all those years ago. Ben had come to his senses, although the real saving grace was Suzette running off with another man before Ben could propose. If she hadn't done that, Suzette might be his sister-in-law today. He shuddered at the thought. He couldn't imagine spending every holiday with her.

Unfortunately, he believed Suzette had a mission to make him her next husband. She kept mentioning that she needed a father figure for her poor, poor children. It irritated him to no end when she gushed compliments and batted her eyelashes, although she must've thought it was endearing, considering how often she did it. With any luck, she'd lose interest and eventually leave him be.

"Good evening, Suzette." He wrapped the reins around the fence and turned. He had to keep himself from groaning in frustration. Once again, she had her children next to her side, wearing clothing that was more appropriate for a brisk autumn day, not a cold January winter. Not a hat or glove in sight. If she wasn't care-ful, those children of hers would have frostbite and likely lose a finger or a toe.

"It's so nice to see you, Michael." She preened like a china doll on display. "Where are you off to?"

"Headed to Luke's place." His tone was curt. "It's been a long day."

Her smile faltered a bit at his less-than-welcoming tone, but it had been a long day, and he wasn't in the mood to entertain her.

"Oh," she murmured and then grinned as though she had just thought of a great idea. "We can walk with you then."

"Suzette, I appreciate--"

She didn't let him finish, interrupting him like a bullheaded cow. "We've had such a wonderful day, but Todd and Natalie have asked if they could come and see you again. Todd"--she pulled her son forward--"has mentioned how much he'd love to see your horses."

Michael looked at the boy who was grinning broadly, and it tugged at his heartstrings. The boy was clearly excited and had asked him numerous questions the last time Suzette had shown up unannounced, wanting him to drop everything to entertain them. He couldn't in good conscience not show the boy his horses.

"It's late, Suzette."

Todd's hopeful expression fell. Clearly, Suzette had promised him more than she should have.

"But how about next Saturday morning? With any luck, the weather will be good, and maybe I can take Todd out for a horse ride."

"Why, that would be quite considerate of you. Don't you agree, Todd?"

When Todd didn't say anything, Suzette nudged his shoulder. Todd tried to smile, but he avoided looking at Michael and reluc-tantly mumbled, "Yes."

"We could make a day of it. I'll have the hotel prepare us a picnic basket and––"

"Suzette, it's far too cold to have a picnic. And we'll only do a quick ride if there isn't any new snow and no ice on the ground. I can't take the chance that any of my horses will go lame."

Suzette bristled a bit. "Of course, Michael. We wouldn't want anything to happen to your horses, do we, Todd?"

Todd stayed quiet, a sullen expression on his face.

Natalie pulled away from Suzette and ran to Michael's side. "Are you gonna be my new papa?"

Michael's eyes shot to Suzette, and she looked mighty uncomfortable, though a hint of a smirk played on her lips that she quickly wiped away. She snatched Natalie back and crouched to her level, whispering something in her ear. The girl's eyes filled with tears, and she bit on one of her tiny fists.

Worry filled Michael's soul. He didn't like Suzette's expression. It had turned to one of malice and greed.

A moment later, Suzette smiled and patted Natalie on the head. "My poor dear, misses her father and doesn't understand that good men all can't be her papa."

Michael nodded, but there was more afoot here. It only confirmed his suspicions that Suzette was looking for a new husband and father to her children. While he appreciated her dedication to them, he wasn't the one who was going to fill that role.

Not now, not ever.

～

The front door opened, and voices filled the hallway. Marie put down her cup of coffee and Anne followed suit. They had moved to the parlor and had been visiting after Anne had confronted her in the kitchen. Anne had been frank with her, but Marie didn't begrudge Anne for stating her opinion. Every woman should be able to be honest without fear of repercussions, and Marie appreciated Anne's honesty.

It had just been difficult to hear, and it would take her some time to work through it all. She wanted to run up to her room and avoid speaking with Michael or Walter for at least a few hours, but she couldn't hide now or appear as a coward. She was made of stronger stuff.

"Who would that be?" Anne raised an eyebrow. "It sounds like children."

Suzette had come to the house with Michael. Marie hadn't heard Michael yet, but he was likely here as well. If Marie could hide from them, she would have, but she was trapped in the parlor and couldn't disappear.

"It sounds like Suzette," Marie said.

"Suzette," Anne said. "She keeps popping up unexpectedly, doesn't she? First at the ranch for the New Year's Eve party, then at the event last week, and again tonight."

"Yes. She does appear to be quite enamored with your brother."

Anne laughed humorously. "I can't see Michael having any feelings for her. Besides, he has only got eyes for you."

She wiggled her eyebrows, and Marie had to keep a groan from emitting past her lips. No matter what she said, everyone had an opinion.

"I wonder why she's here with Michael," Anne said when Marie didn't respond.

Marie shrugged, even though she was completely aware of why Suzette was here. Suzette was on the hunt for a husband, and she had set her sights on Michael.

A laughing Suzette stepped inside the parlor. She'd wrapped her hand around Michael's right arm, holding on for dear life. "You are such a tease, my dear. I haven't laughed like this in years." Suzette glanced around the room and caught Marie's eye. "Oh!" she exclaimed. "I didn't realize *she* would be here."

Marie had to refrain from rolling her eyes at Suzette's obvious lie. She was fully aware that Marie and her brother were living at Luke's home. It wasn't a secret.

Michael, being the consummate gentleman, patted Suzette's hand. "You remember Marie and my sister Anne?"

"Oh, of course." Suzette skipped to Anne's side and pulled her into a quick hug. When she released her, she gripped Anne's forearms. "It's so great to see you, Anne."

Anne smiled and then gently extracted herself from Suzette's grasp. "Suzette, I didn't realize you were still here in Helena. Are you visiting or...?"

Suzette smiled and looked coyly over her shoulder toward Michael. "I'm just visiting, but you never know what the future might hold."

Marie wanted to gag at the obvious manipulative flirtation, but it was Michael's life. If he wanted to become ensnared by Suzette, then that was his choice, even if disgust rolled through her gut. A part of her wondered if she had made a mistake and should have accepted Michael's proposal, if nothing else than to save him from this woman. But it wasn't her responsibility to save him from himself and any mistakes he might make.

This just reinforced her decision to never let a man have any control in her life. For they could change their mind on a whim and throw one woman over for another. She wasn't necessarily thinking that Michael was doing this, but it was awfully suspect that he had proposed to her and then brought Suzette to his home when he claimed Marie was the only woman for him.

Suzette's two children ran inside the room, yelling and screaming playfully. Marie smiled. They were exuberant and happy children right up until the moment they laid eyes on their mother. Suzette glared at them, her congenial expression being replaced by one so mean and heinous, it sent chills down Marie's back, but Michael missed the look, as he had knelt to talk with them. They were suddenly fidgety, and frowns had replaced their once-happy smiles.

They backed away from Michael and carefully eyed their mother.

"I'm sorry, Mother." Todd's eyes were downcast. "We shouldn't have run in here. We... We will go outside and wait like good children." Todd grabbed his sister's hand and started to drag her out of the room.

"Now, now," Michael said. "It's mighty cold outside. I'm sure your mother understands that you were excited. Why don't you come with me to the kitchen and we'll get you a cookie, if your mother approves?" Michael stood and looked at Suzette to gain her approval.

Suzette's scowl had been replaced by a wide smile. The emotions Suzette expressed ranged extensively and were insincere, but Michael seemed oblivious to the changes. Men usually were from Marie's observations over the past few years. She'd seen all manner of women entice and reject plenty of men using their wiles and sometimes their fists.

Suzette clapped her hands before placing them on her hips. "That's very generous. Children, would you like a cookie?"

Todd and Natalie shared a glance that spoke of uncertainty, but finally, Natalie said, "Yes, Mother."

"Well, that settles it." Michael took each of the children's hands. "Let's go get you a cookie and perhaps a big glass of cold milk."

A moment later, the three of them disappeared down the hall. The excited chatter of both Todd and Natalie faded as they reached the kitchen.

"You have beautiful children, Suzette," Anne said.

Suzette pulled off her coat, dropped it across the back of the sofa, and plopped onto it. "I do, don't I?" She slipped off her gloves and dropped them forgotten on the cushions next to her.

Marie was surprised at her holier-than-thou tone but kept her opinions to herself. She shared a glance with Anne before sitting in the chair she had vacated upon their arrival. Her coffee had cooled somewhat but was still a bit warm. She picked it up and lifted it when Suzette spoke.

"Is that coffee?"

Marie slowly lowered the cup. "Yes."

"I'd surely love a cup." She gave Marie a pointed look.

Marie glanced at Anne, who only shrugged. What she wanted to do was tell Suzette she could get it herself, but Marie was a guest in a Seymour family home and had been raised to be polite.

She held back her ire. "I'll head to the kitchen and get you a mug."

Marie stood and walked toward the hallway when Suzette called, "Two cubes of sugar and a dollop of cream. Oh, and a cookie or two as well. I'm right hungry."

No thank-you. No please. Just an assumption that Marie would be pleased as punch to get the woman everything she asked. It took everything in her not to turn around and tell Suzette she could get it herself. Instead, Marie dug her fingernails into her palms and marched down the hall toward the kitchen.

Perhaps it was a good thing she had left the parlor. She might've wrapped her fingers around Suzette's neck if she had to talk to her for any length of time. The woman was not as she seemed and had put on a facade, acting one way when she was in front of Michael and a completely different way when she wasn't. Marie could only hope Michael was smart enough not to fall for her. He deserved someone better.

She abruptly stopped. *Why do I care if Michael likes Suzette?* She scratched at her scalp and leaned against the wall. She was very agitated with what was happening between Michael and Suzette when she shouldn't be. She had told Michael she wasn't interested in a relationship, and yet she was jealous that Michael was entertaining another woman. She couldn't have it both ways. It was time to get her emotions under control.

Marie had thought she wanted to stay unmarried for the rest of her life, but she was now questioning her intentions and hated that about herself. She was growing weak, uncertain, and that wouldn't do.

Muttering to herself, she pushed away from the wall. She wouldn't be able to solve this now. Suzette was waiting for her coffee.

Marie pushed into the kitchen and had to contain her laughter. Michael was standing near the pantry door, covered in flour. A cloud of white was drifting to the floor. Todd and Natalie were sitting at the table, a pile of cookies in front of each of them, and they were giggling incessantly.

Michael blinked furiously and went to wipe his eyes.

"No." Marie stopped him. "You don't want to do that."

He grinned. "And why not?"

"You'll only make it worse."

He jumped, and flour flew up from the floor. "Like this."

Todd and Natalie giggled more, and Marie had to cover her mouth to hide her laughter. Michael smirked as though he could read her mind.

"No," she said, smiling. "Let me grab a wet cloth and wash that flour from your face."

"Not sure that'll help."

She cocked her hip against the end of the table. "You may be right. It'd probably be easier if you headed outside and jumped in a lake."

"Except the lakes are frozen over," Todd yelled.

"And you'd surely freeze to death," Marie said.

Michael nodded, and flour flew off his head. The man had made a mess but didn't seem bothered by it a bit.

"Let me put on some water to heat." Marie scooted around the flour, trying to keep her feet out of it, even though from the flour floating in the air, it was everywhere. Michael jumping in it hadn't helped the situation in the least.

"No need to do that." Michael walked toward the back door. "I'll just head outside and brush myself off there."

"But what about your face?" She eyed him carefully.

"I'll be fine, I promise." He slipped out the door, his charming smile sending a warm tingle straight to her toes. The man was surely adorable when he wanted to be.

Grabbing a broom, she tried to keep the flour from floating onto more surfaces, but the white substance had a mind of its own. However, she was determined and managed to get most of what was on the flour into a dustpan and had just dumped it into the trash bin when Michael came back inside.

"Brrr," he said, rubbing his hands together. He still had flour in his hair and across his cheeks, but for the most part, he'd managed to get the bulk of it off while outside. "It's mighty cold out there."

"Let me get you a hot cup of coffee," she said. "It'll warm you up."

She quickly poured him a steaming cup of coffee and turned to hand it to him, but he had stepped closer, a twinkle in his eyes.

"Thank you," he murmured.

Before she could stop herself, she brushed flour off his cheek. His breath hitched, and he stared deep into her as though he were reading all the tumultuous thoughts tumbling through her mind. His gaze always seemed to disarm her and make her feel vulnerable. She had to consider if giving in to his proposal would be as bad as she'd thought.

"Marie," Suzette called. "Did you get lost?"

The door to the kitchen burst open, and Suzette sauntered inside.

Marie stumbled back away from Michael, a blush blooming up her neck and into her cheeks. They had done nothing wrong, but she felt as though she'd just been caught putting her hand in the cookie jar.

"What in heaven's name happened in here?" Suzette drawled,

taking in the flour across the countertops, on the stove, and still in places on the floor.

Michael leaned his hip against the counter, lifted the cup of coffee, and took a sip before he replied. "Just a little mishap, that's all."

Todd and Natalie giggled like they were all sharing a conspiratorial secret, and in some ways, they had. They hadn't even told Marie what had happened, but she wasn't necessarily as concerned as Suzette appeared to be.

Suzette wrinkled her nose. "Well, I suppose we should be leaving." She lifted her skirts and stepped carefully across the floor toward her children. She glanced down at them and grimaced. "You are both filthy. We will have to get you into the bath straight away when we get back to the hotel. It will not do at all to have you in such disarray."

Todd shoved the last of his cookie into his mouth and nodded. Suzette bit her lip, snatched a cloth, and tried to wipe Natalie's face clear of chocolate, but she only seemed to smear it further. She muttered something under her breath but helped Natalie from her chair.

"Watch where you are going. You don't need to have more of what I presume is flour on your new shoes."

"Yes, Mother," Natalie said and then proceeded to stomp straight through a pile that Marie had missed when she swept. The flour coated Natalie's shoes, and Suzette's smile dropped into a menacing frown.

"This will surely not do, Michael. I sure hope this isn't normal behavior, for it will certainly change when we..." She abruptly stopped whatever she was going to say.

Michael's brow rose as though he couldn't believe what Suzette had almost said.

"Say your goodbyes, children. Michael, we will see you next Saturday." Suzette grabbed the children's coats from the hook on the wall, shoved them onto her children's arms, and a moment later, she stomped down the hall and out the front door.

"Well, ain't she something," Marie muttered as she picked up the dirty plates on the table and placed them in the kitchen sink.

"Her children sure are a delight," Michael said. "We had plenty of fun back here before she arrived."

Marie smiled. "I can see that from the flour all over the place."

"Oh, that was just a bit of an accident. One I didn't anticipate but one both the children thought was hilarious."

"You do seem to have a knack for entertaining them," Marie said.

"Oh, children are always a delight."

"Do you want some of your own?"

"Children?" He pushed away from the counter. He dropped his mug into the sink and began helping her clean. He never seemed to have a problem stepping up and helping when the need arose.

"Yes." She avoided looking him in the eye for fear he'd think she wanted some with him.

"I'd love to have a few. I always expected to have a passel by now, truth be told." He lifted the chairs and placed them out on the back porch. "But I hadn't found the right woman until…"

Marie looked up and saw the look in his eye. She didn't respond to his unanswered statement. There didn't seem a point in rehashing what they had already done on numerous occasions. He knew what her answer would be and would always be, even if he continued to look at her like he'd give her the moon, the stars, and everything else she could've possibly dreamed of and more.

Twenty-Five

M ichael looked out the frost-covered window and sighed.
There was no new snow on the ground, so he'd have to
keep his promise. He'd hoped to have a valid reason not to take
Suzette out that morning, but he'd agreed to take Todd for a ride.
While he didn't mind disappointing Suzette, Todd was just a child
and deserved much more than he'd received in his short life.
Besides, Todd was a precocious boy who was inquisitive and
sought acceptance from the adults in his life.

From what Suzette had told him, Todd had been close to his
father before he'd passed away and had been devastated. It had
taken months before he finally started speaking, but staying in
California had been too difficult. When Suzette's sister suggested
they come for a visit, she had packed up her children and headed to
Montana. And now Michael was left entertaining her.

Michael made quick work of getting dressed. Suzette and the
children were to meet him outside his livery doors at nine a.m., and
with him staying at Luke's place, he had to leave soon. It had been
a challenge convincing Suzette that having a picnic was a bad idea
when it was as cold as it was. She'd come by the livery the night

before to confirm their plans and had been quite put out when he'd told her there wouldn't be one.

She'd insisted the children would be fine outside, and they loved the snow, but he knew better. He'd remember to grab a couple of pairs of gloves and see if he had any thicker coats he could bring for them. Todd would surely need warmer gear if he were to ride a horse for any length of time.

An hour later, he'd eaten a cold biscuit and a piece of ham. Ever since he and Walter had decided that Michael would stay at Luke's house with them, Marie had been avoiding him like the plague. She'd been furious, but she'd pulled her lips into a thin line and made no effort to speak to him cordially whenever they were in the same room.

He'd seen the look on Marie's face when he'd brought Suzette by the week before, and ever since then, her tone with him had been curt. He was afraid Marie believed he wanted to pursue Suzette, but she hadn't given him a chance to explain that he wanted nothing to do with the woman. Michael wasn't interested in Suzette, but until he could talk with Marie, her perception was incorrect and likely wouldn't change.

He rummaged through some old coats and gloves that Luke had left behind and found a few that would undoubtedly be too big for Todd and Natalie, but they would at least offer protection against the frigid temperatures.

A knock sounded at the front door, and he glanced at his pocket watch. He still had time to get to his livery, but it would be close. Down the hallway, he pulled open the door. It was Suzette. She was alone, her blonde hair was disheveled, she had no coat, and tears streamed down her bright red cheeks.

"Suzette, are you all right?"

She fell into his arms, gripping the front of his shirt between her hands, sobbing uncontrollably. "Please help me. I can't believe this is happening. What am I going to do?"

Michael awkwardly patted her back. He hadn't thought they

knew one another well enough for her to come to him, but he wasn't heartless and couldn't stand seeing a woman in tears.

He pulled her inside and led her to the parlor. She clung to him like a spider gripping its web. Her sobs grew in pitch. Whatever had gotten her this way appeared to be quite upsetting and likely would take a bit of soothing to get her tears under control. He'd seen his sisters upset before, but nothing like this. He couldn't even imagine Marie losing her composure this way. She was too strong of a woman to become inconsolable like a child who'd lost her favorite toy.

Suzette collapsed onto his sofa, pulled out a handkerchief, and bent her neck to hide her face in her hands. She bawled, the sound growing louder with each second. He tried to speak, but that almost seemed to intensify her distress. There was no way he was going to find out anything until she calmed, but something about her tears felt forced.

Michael sat across from her, relaxing into his chair, and shook his head when she lifted her face just slightly to look over her handkerchief. It was as though she were checking for his reaction. When she caught him eyeing her, she dropped her head again and wailed even louder.

There appeared to be something calculating in her gaze, but he'd wait until she was ready to talk. He didn't know how he had gotten involved with this woman, but here he was. His patience was wearing thin.

After a few long moments of her bawling like a calf who'd lost its mother to wolves, she finally hiccuped and slowed the onslaught of her tears.

She sighed heavily, dabbing under her eyes with the handkerchief. "You must think horribly of me."

He wasn't sure what to think. "No, but I'd sure like to help. Can you tell me what's wrong?"

Suzette shook her head, her blonde curls bouncing across her shoulders. If he didn't quite believe she might be playacting, he might've been swayed by her tears.

"I can't help if you don't tell me, Suzette." He kept his tone low and calm.

"Todd ran away."

"What?" He sat forward in his chair, gripping the edge. "What happened? Why didn't you tell me that to begin with? That boy can't be out in this weather. He could surely be in danger."

"I know," she cried and burst into tears once again.

He mumbled a few curse words under his breath. The blasted woman seemed so intent on gaining his attention that she'd failed to tell him that her son was in danger.

"Did something happen to––"

"Yes, something happened," she snapped, dropping the handkerchief. All pretense disappeared in a flash. Her eyes filled with anger, the sadness gone like a lightning bolt––out of nowhere, sharp and loud. "You don't seem to care about how I'm feeling." She pounded her fist against her chest.

He stared and waited. If her son were in danger, she didn't seem to be overly concerned with telling him what had happened. Instead, she seemed more upset that he wasn't consoling her than giving him the information he needed to help Todd.

Suddenly, she released more tears, and he had to contain the groan of disgust bubbling inside of him. She was putting on an act.

Finally, she sniffled. "I shouldn't have lost my composure, but you've been so kind in my time of need."

When he said nothing, she sat back and wiped at her face. "My poor Todd. He needs a strong father figure in his life. He was so despondent this morning when he realized he'd never have his father take him for a ride again or anything that a father would do for his son. Todd got so angry with me and told me it was my fault his father was gone. Then he slapped me and ran out of the room."

"Did you follow him? See where he went?"

"No." She sniffled. "I was so shocked by him hitting me that by the time I realized what had happened, he had disappeared."

"Where's Natalie?"

A scowl briefly crossed her lips, but he wasn't positive he'd seen it. "A hotel maid came by just as I ran out of the room to look for him. She offered to look after my darling girl while I came to find you."

"Do you know where he would go?"

She shook her head and burst into tears again. "Oh, Michael. What am I going to do? I can't make my boy happy. I've tried so hard to be a good mother, but when he hit me, it just near broke my heart."

"Does he have a place he likes to visit, a fun place he enjoys going to play, perhaps?"

Suzette's gaze was focused on her hands. "I pulled him into my lap. He wrapped his arms around my neck as he cried out for his father. What do I do to make his heart heal?" She raised her head, the tears having left streak marks across her cheeks. "Perhaps if he spent time with you?"

Unease crept up his spine. "Shouldn't we find him first?"

She slammed her fist on the sofa pillow. "My poor children are without a father. I've been trying to be there for them, but they cry into their pillows every night." She picked up the pillow and shook it. "I can't continue to listen to that every single night."

It was as though she had lost all sense of reason. Her focus was entirely somewhere else, which was concerning if her son were truly outside in this weather.

"What are you suggesting?" He crossed his arms.

"A little father-son time."

"I'm not his father, Suzette." He stood and went to grab a glass of whiskey. He needed a drink. It was way too early, but he was going to need it to get through this day. Her true intentions were becoming clearer, and he wasn't about to fall into her snare.

Suzette bowed her head, tears once again falling down her

cheeks. She produced them at a disturbingly rapid rate, but he would not be swayed.

"I think it's time you return to Natalie. I'm sure she needs her mother's care." He tried to make his tone kind, but it had a hint of harshness to it.

Suzette stiffened and angrily swiped at her tears. "Why, I never thought you... of all people, would be so rude and insensitive."

"I should be out looking for Todd, don't you think?"

She threw the pillow on the floor and swept past him. "I'll trouble you no more."

"Let me..." He reached to touch her, but she swatted at him.

"Don't touch me. I thought you were different from Ben. Someone more considerate and kind toward young children who have no choice in this cruel world."

"I didn't mean to upset you," he said, although the lie that pushed through his lips sounded false even to him.

Suzette glared at him, her tears of pretense having all but disappeared. "Humph," she muttered. "I'll show myself out."

"What about Todd?"

"Don't you worry about my son," she muttered. "I'll find him myself."

She stalked out of the parlor, and a moment later, the front door slammed. He sighed. While he wasn't disappointed she'd left, he worried Todd had gotten himself into a bit of a pickle by running away from her and out into the cold weather.

Michael worried that both her children would suffer at whatever machinations she was plotting. He figured it had to be his family name and the wealth she might perceive that came with it. But he wasn't taking from the Seymour coffers. His father had set aside land for him, but he had done nothing with it other than encourage Ben to use it for the cattle as he saw fit.

He wasn't interested in ranching and had instead focused on his smithy and livery and found joy and satisfaction from that endeavor. What Suzette didn't realize was that he wasn't living in the lap of luxury but instead had many months where it'd been difficult to cover his debts, but he wouldn't have it any other way. He'd paid a hefty price for the smithy and livery, not to mention a piece of land at the far edge of town that he planned to build a house on one day. If Suzette wanted a rich husband, she had set her sights on the wrong man.

He snatched his coat from the hallway and grabbed his wool cap, gloves, and scarf. While he had no intention of falling for Suzette's scheme, he wouldn't rest easy until he found Todd. With any luck, the boy had gone back to the hotel, so he'd check there first, even if it meant dealing with Suzette again. If the boy hadn't returned, then he'd search for Todd himself.

Twenty-Six

M arie walked slowly up to the house and stopped at the gate, staring at the two-story home Luke Seymour had built. Luke and Louisa would turn it into a home in a few years, and she was sure the Seymour family would be thrilled to have them home when Louisa finished medical school. Knowing Louisa was fulfilling her dream gave Marie hope she'd be able to achieve her dream as well. If Louisa could become a doctor in a world that tried to keep women in the home, then there was no reason she couldn't get women the vote.

Her emotions had been in turmoil for days, and then seeing Suzette in Michael's arms that very morning just made her skin crawl. That blasted woman would ruin Michael's life if he wasn't careful, but it was his life, and she had no right to hold an opinion. She had returned to the house to grab a packet of pamphlets she had left behind in her rush to leave and had seen Suzette fall into his arms, sobbing like a peevish child.

Marie couldn't stay in the same house with Michael any longer. She had to convince Walter to leave. Michael's charming smile was too much of a temptation, and she didn't know if her heart could take any more turmoil.

She wasn't generally jealous of other women, but seeing Michael with Suzette time and time again had made her lose focus. Marie had actually considered for one moment what the future might hold if she were to have a relationship with him. And that would not do. She had made a choice years ago to never, ever let a man become her husband. By never marrying, she would be the only one to decide her future.

She grasped the edge of the gate, the worn wood smooth against her palm as she pulled it open. Standing outside wouldn't fix anything. She wasn't looking forward to interacting with Suzette, but she couldn't continue to stand out in the cold. In some ways, she lacked the courage to approach them, but if she believed what she stood for, then she would go inside and face the happy couple.

Pushing open the front door, she found nothing but silence. A dim light came from the parlor, but nothing else. No sounds of children running, no hum of voices, no clinking of dishes, not even the crackle of wood in the fireplace. In fact, the house was chilled, as though all the fires had been banked and it'd been empty for days.

Goosebumps prickled across her skin, and she didn't know if it was because it was almost as icy inside as it was outside or if because something sinister filled the space. Either scenario left her with too many unanswered questions and nervous energy nagged at the base of her spine. *Am I walking into something I'll regret?* A part of her wanted to run and hide.

"Michael?" She dropped her reticule on the table in the foyer and hung her cloak on the hooks next to the front door. She rubbed her hands together to warm them and proceeded farther into the house. A part of her wondered if she should enter with a bit more caution, but she wasn't timid and wouldn't start now.

"Michael? Anne?" Marie looked in the parlor and found no one. A single gas lamp was the only source light. She glanced at the fireplace. The fire had dimmed, although a few embers burned red.

A pot of coffee and a plate of cookies lay forgotten on the table next to what had become Michael's favorite chair. He hadn't wasted any time becoming comfortable once he and Walter had decided they would be better served to have Michael move in with them. With Anne staying in the house as well, it had become quite full, but at times it had actually been pleasant, except of course when Suzette showed up. She managed to suck the life out of any fun that might have been had.

Marie thought Michael would have been home by now, although not finding him was a blessing in disguise, or so she tried to convince herself.

Picking up a few of the split logs resting next to the hearth, Marie placed them inside the fireplace, careful not to touch the hot embers. Using the black metal poker, she poked and prodded until they caught and a fire burned. It would take a few minutes, but it wouldn't be long before the room was warmer and her fingers would thaw. She rubbed her hands together and held them to her lips, blowing warm air onto them. After a moment, the cold ebbed, and she wasn't as chilled.

A floorboard creaked. Marie turned and screeched in alarm.

"Oh, I didn't mean to startle you," Anne said. "I thought you heard me come down the stairs."

Marie waved a hand in front of her face, trying to calm her breathing. She'd thought she was alone, and when she'd seen Anne's shadow, it'd taken her by surprise.

Once Marie had caught her breath, she said, "It's all right. I'm just a bit jumpy. I didn't think anyone was home with the fire burning low and no one responding when I called out."

Anne shuffled inside, a thick shawl around her shoulders, her face pale and drawn. "I was taking a nap and only woke a few minutes ago. I didn't realize the fire had burned low. Otherwise, I would have put more wood on the grate."

"Are you all right, Anne?" Marie asked.

She smiled tremulously, raising her hand to her forehead. "Yes. I'm just tired. I didn't sleep well last night."

"Should I call for a doctor?"

"Oh, no," Anne murmured. "I'll be right as rain tomorrow. No need to worry."

Realizing whatever was bothering Anne was none of her business, Marie changed the subject. "It's getting late. Have you seen my brother or yours?"

"No. I think Michael must still be out with Suzette and her children."

Anne eyed her carefully, as though trying to judge her reaction, but it wasn't anything Marie hadn't expected. Seeing Michael hold Suzette that morning had told her all she needed. Michael had given up and moved on. This should be good news, as Michael would finally leave her alone, but considering the pit in her belly was growing, she didn't know for sure anymore.

"It's getting late," Marie murmured.

Anne glanced toward the window and sat. "I'm sure he's perfectly fine. He knows better than to stay outside. He's probably taken Suzette and her children back to the hotel. She's likely convinced him to stay for dinner or something. She is nothing but creative in her manipulations." Anne smirked.

Marie grabbed the blue afghan that sat folded on the chair and dropped it around her waist. "She is quite the woman."

Anne scowled. "She almost ruined Ben and Elizabeth's relationship. Why Michael has given her the time of day, I do not understand." Anne fiddled with a loose yellow strand dangling from her shawl.

"He's a gentleman and likely can't tell her to leave him alone."

"Yes, he is, but he also saw firsthand what she's capable of."

"Perhaps he's just being kind." Marie didn't know why she was suddenly defending Michael's behavior.

"Michael is always kind. He's the good-hearted one in our family and has paid the price on numerous occasions."

"What do you mean?"

"He sees the good in people even when they don't deserve it. He's been like that since he was a young boy."

"Do you think he sees the good in Suzette?"

"I can't speak to that, but I believe he's more interested in helping her children than he is in helping *her*."

"Why would you say that?"

"Michael loves children and is the favorite uncle in the family and with our friends. Each time he comes to the ranch, the little ones always seek him out. He plays with them, tells them fantastical stories, and constantly makes them laugh. There's always disappointment on their faces if he doesn't come home."

"I had no idea." Marie's heart warmed at the thought.

"I'm surprised you hadn't noticed."

"I'll be honest, I've been distracted, and for that, I'm ashamed of myself."

"Oh, no. I hadn't intended to make you feel that way," Anne murmured. "I just thought... Well, I guess I thought there was something brewing between you and Michael."

Marie choked back a cough of laughter. "Nothing is brewing between me and your brother."

"And why not? He's quite taken with you."

"He might've been, or so he claimed, but after what I saw this morning, I'm sure he's moved on to Suzette."

Anne's eyes widened. "What did you see this morning?"

Marie blanched. She hadn't meant to tell Anne that, as it made her sound jealous. "Um, nothing to speak of. Are you hungry? Would you like me to get you something to eat?"

"No, I ate earlier, and I think you're trying to distract me." Anne smiled.

Jumping up, Marie paced back and forth behind the sofa. "I'm not trying to distract you." She ran her hand across the back of her neck and halted. "That's not true. I am."

"I don't mean to pry." Anne tugged on her shawl and pushed back into the sofa cushions.

"You aren't," Marie said. "When I left this morning for my meeting, I realized I'd forgotten the new pamphlets. When I returned, I saw Suzette in Michael's arms. He was holding her as though she were the only woman for him."

"I'm sure it wasn't as it seemed––"

"It was, and that's perfectly fine. I have no hold on Michael, nor do I want to have one. He's free to do as he wishes, including ensnaring himself with that spiteful woman."

Twenty-Seven

Michael closed the door to Suzette's hotel room behind him. Todd was safe with his mother. Suzette had glared at him for the past hour, but she'd seemed happy he'd found Todd, and that was all that mattered.

It hadn't taken Michael long to find the boy. He'd been sitting in front of Michael's livery. Todd's tear-streaked cheeks had been obvious to anyone who looked at him closely, even if he'd tried to swipe them away. Michael had ambled up to him and draped the coat he had brought over his shaking, thin shoulders. He was glad he'd thought to grab one before he'd left to look for him.

Todd had glanced at him, his eyes filled with a pain that no young boy should have. It was a look Michael recognized when he'd looked in the mirror after his pa's death. Todd had pulled the coat tight around him, his shivering slowing as the coat gave him the warmth he'd been missing in the frigid air.

Michael had sat next to him, giving the boy time to regain his composure. He pulled a couple of pieces of jerky from his coat pocket and held one out to Todd. A moment later, Todd took it from his fingers and played with it a moment before putting it to his mouth. From the way he devoured it, Michael was glad he had some in his pocket.

"Thank you," Todd mumbled.

"You're most welcome. Are you warm enough?"

"Yeah, I'm fine," he grumbled.

"Do you want to go back to the hotel?"

"No," he said. "I don't want to see my mother."

"Oh," Michael said. "Anythin' I can do to help?"

"No," Todd said. "Nobody can fix this." His tone was belligerent, but there was an underlying level of agony behind his words. The pain in the boy's voice was heartbreaking and brought back the misery Michael felt, but he was an adult and could help Todd regardless of his loss.

Michael rested his elbows against his knees, clasping his hands. He didn't want to spook the boy and instead thought maybe he could share some of his pain, to share that he wasn't alone.

"I lost my pa about ten years ago," Michael said.

Todd stiffened next to him but didn't say anything.

"He was taken from us way too soon. I remember thinking that I had so much to say to him, but never got a chance to do it."

"What happened?" Todd whispered.

Michael swallowed back the lump in his throat. Even now, after all these years, it was hard to say the words. "He was murdered."

"Really?" Todd swiveled his head toward Michael. Shock was written across his innocent features.

"Yes." Michael's throat became thick with emotion.

"I'm sorry, Michael."

He coughed to clear his throat, placed his hand on the boy's shoulder, and squeezed reassuringly. "No reason for you to apologize, young man. It wasn't easy. My ma passed a few days before. She got the influenza, and we originally thought Pa died of that too. Come to find out, he'd been murdered instead. It took me years to come to terms with it."

"It ain't fair," Todd mumbled.

"You're sure right about that. It wasn't, but there was nothing I could've done to stop it."

"Humph."

Michael rubbed his hand across his chin. "I tried to hide my sadness by laughing and making jokes all the time. I didn't want to talk about how I felt."

"Do you talk about it now?"

Michael froze. The question was a fair one but a hard one to answer. He'd started this conversation, so he had to continue it, especially because this boy needed his help.

"Not as much as I probably should. It hurts too much knowing I couldn't stop it from happening."

"Why does it hurt so much?"

Why did it hurt so much? "I don't know, Todd. All I can tell you is that the hurt does fade. It's not as sharp as it was when it first happened."

"Will it ever go away?" Todd whispered.

"Probably not, but it does get easier. I'll never forget losing my pa, but I don't wake up every day wishing I could've done more. I've realized that my pa will always be here"--Michael pounded his chest--"and I choose to think of the good times. That's what's most important. Knowing he loved all of us. If he'd had a choice, he would've never gone the way he had."

"How did you know he loved you?"

The poor boy was in so much turmoil, it rolled off him in waves. Suzette had been right about one thing--her son was hurting.

"Lots of ways," Michael said, smiling. "He'd always tell us, but he'd show it by giving us big hugs, by encouraging us in our dreams, by disciplining us when we did wrong but explaining why he was doing it. He loved us, which has made it easier for me to remember him with fondness instead of remembering how horrible the end was."

"My pa didn't love me." Todd swiped at the tears streaming down his face.

"I'm not sure--"

"No, it's true," Todd yelled. "He didn't love me. He never showed it, he never said it, and I hate him. I hate him." Todd's fist hit the edge of the steps. He cried out in agony and leaned forward, sobs pouring from his tiny frame.

Michael sat stunned, but Todd was angry and wouldn't want Michael to comfort him. He wasn't his father. He wasn't a replacement for his father. He was just a man who had been a brief part of his mother's life almost ten years ago.

Todd's eyes were red-rimmed from crying, and snot ran across his upper lip, which he smeared away with the sleeve of his shirt. "Why didn't he love me?"

Michael gazed at the boy. Todd desperately wanted to hear that his father had loved him, and while Michael wanted to tell him that, he couldn't tell the boy half-truths. "It's unfortunate you feel this way. Can I help?"

"No." Todd forcefully shook his head. "No one can help."

"What about your ma?"

Todd muttered something under his breath. "She don't care about us either. She's only looking for another husband, as though that'll fix everythin' that's gone wrong."

Michael was startled by the vehemence in the boy's tone. Losing his father and then seeing his mother exhibit that kind of behavior had to be gut-wrenching.

"How old are you, Todd?"

"Seven," he mumbled.

"You seem much older than that."

Todd grinned a toothy smile.

"You've carried quite the weight on your shoulders, young man." Michael pulled a handkerchief from his pocket and handed it to him.

Todd took it and blew his nose.

"You don't know me, but I'd like to think that if you need someone to talk to, you're welcome to seek me out. We could take the horses out for a ride——"

"We were supposed to do that today, and I ruined that, didn't I?"

"No. You didn't. You're a young man who's been dealing with plenty, it sounds like, and it just got to be too much."

"No man would do that," Todd muttered.

"That's not quite true. I've done it plenty of times. What's most important is learning from those choices and doing better the next time."

"My ma is gonna be plenty mad at me." He twisted the handkerchief between his small hands.

"I think she's just worried."

"She's worried that I've messed things up for her. She just wants a new husband."

Michael was afraid Todd was right, but that was neither here nor there. "I can't speak to your mother's intentions, but she's right worried about you."

Todd hmphed and blew his nose again.

"Do you want to get something to eat before we head back to the hotel?"

A pleading look was in his eyes. "Do I have to go back?"

Michael shifted to face him fully. "What do you think you should do?"

Todd's shoulders collapsed under the weight he was carrying. "Go back to my mother." His tone was resigned.

"I'm proud of you, young man. There's a lot happening in your life. Being a man is sometimes doing the things we don't want to do but are the right thing to do."

Todd's shoulders straightened, and a tenuous smile brightened his face. It seemed all the boy needed was a bit of encouragement.

Michael stood and held out his hand. "Let's go get something to eat and then I'll take you back to the hotel."

Michael led him down the road a bit when Todd pulled him to a stop. "Did you *really* mean I could talk to you whenever I want to?"

Michael put a finger under Todd's chin and looked him dead in the eye. "Absolutely. Anytime, anywhere, I'll always be available."

Two hours later, Michael returned Todd to the hotel, and Suzette barely spoke to him. She hadn't said much to Todd, and her indifference in his return left a sick hole in Michael's belly.

Twenty-Eight

Marie sat in the parlor, the only light coming from the fireplace. A worn afghan rested around her shoulders as she gazed out the frost-covered window into the night sky. She'd been so busy planning the next rally that she'd barely had time to ruminate over everything Anne had said to her that fateful morning, just one month ago, but things had finally slowed enough for her to take a breath. The big event was happening in two nights, and they didn't need her this evening. She had said good night to Eloisa and Greta and told them she would meet them in the morning to greet Gail and Ida at the train depot.

She'd fixed a pot of coffee and a plate of cookies, and she'd been nibbling on them after she dragged an armchair near the window. Marie was torn between what she wanted in life and what Michael had to offer. She still wasn't sure if she would ever give Michael a piece of her heart, but she had to admit her perception of him and how he would treat her had been altered by Anne's words. The problem was, she might've waited too late to come to that conclusion. Michael had been spending a lot of time with Suzette's children, and because of her hesitation, Marie had likely pushed him straight into that woman's arms. But it had been what she'd wanted, so she had no one but herself to blame.

She fingered the afghan and smiled, looking down at the soft wool. It was one of the few things they'd salvaged from the fire. Her mother had made it for her when she was just a young girl. Her mother had liked to crochet and had made plenty of items for friends and family. Her father had wanted her mother to sell them, but her mother had said the smile on their faces was all the payment she needed.

Most days, she'd not remember the pain from her parents' passing, but it'd sneak up on her when it was quiet and she was alone. Concentrating on the good things made her heart hum with comfort instead of trying to reconcile the tragic accident and how it should've never happened. The smiles her mother had for Marie every afternoon after school, the notes she would leave in her lunch pail, the songs she would sing as they danced in the kitchen before dinner, the tight hugs, and the way she would comb Marie's hair--her fingers gentle and soothing. Her father's booming laugh, much like Walter's, his warm, comforting hugs, and his ability to listen and offer advice when she needed it most.

She would never accept the sheriff's explanation that they'd jumped off the cliff to their death. She would watch them when they were alone and see the smiles, the looks, and the subtle touches that told her how much they loved one another. Some claimed it was an accident, but her parents had been experienced hikers. The only explanation that made sense was that one of them had slipped and the other had tried to save them, and instead of coming home safely, they had both fallen to their death.

Marie brushed back a strand of her hair, and her fingers came away wet with her tears. She hadn't even realized she'd been crying, and she wouldn't even call it crying. They were more tears of sadness and regret for the things she had lost, the pain she was causing, and her uncertain future.

She had believed she had everything figured out. Her whole

life was mapped out--fighting for women's rights, seeking justice for her parents' deaths, and fighting for women who didn't have someone to fight for them. But now, everything was a jumbled mess. She still wanted to fight for women's rights, but she wasn't sure that being alone was what she thought it might be.

A door opened and closed, pulling her from her melancholy thoughts. Snatching her handkerchief from her pocket, she wiped away the tears and blew her nose. She didn't want to be caught crying, regardless of who'd come inside.

"Marie?"

She turned toward the voice she heard in her dreams. It was Michael. He was a dark shadow against the doorway.

"Yes," she murmured.

"Why are you sitting here in the dark?" He moved inside the room, shadows shifting as he stepped into the light of the fire.

"There was no reason to turn on a gas lamp." She pulled her legs up under her and tightened the afghan around her shoulders. With any luck, he wouldn't feel inclined to turn it on.

He struck a match and lit his cigar, the red tip glowing in the dark. "You don't mind if I smoke, do you?"

It was too late to ask her that question, considering he'd already lit one, but it was his brother's house, so who was she to complain? "No."

He chuckled low in his throat.

"Did I say something funny?" Her tone was irritated, but he always brought out the worst in her.

"No, but you would rather I didn't smoke?"

She wasn't in the mood for his antics tonight. "My opinion on you lighting or not lighting your cigar has no bearing."

"You don't care for me at all, do you?" His voice was low, with a touch of something she couldn't identify.

"I never said that." She liked him way too much, and that was the real problem.

"Your constant irritation and your denial of my marriage proposals might say otherwise."

She opened her mouth to send a scathing rebuke but stopped herself just in time. She was too tired to argue with him. He had proposed again to her last week, and she had told him no then, too.

Dropping her feet to the ground, she pushed to stand. It was late. She should go to bed and leave him to his cigar. "I'm going up to my room."

"Don't leave on my account." The red ember of his cigar highlighted his mischievous grin.

"I'm not." Although, both of them knew that was exactly why she was leaving.

"I didn't take you as someone who could be scared so easily."

Her fingers itched to smack him, but she had more composure than that. "I'm not *scared*, Michael Seymour."

"Oh, using my entire name. I didn't think you had it in you."

Before she could stop herself, she stalked toward him until she stood mere inches from him. She poked him in the chest. "Didn't have *what* in me?"

He lifted his chin, took a long drag of his cigar, and blew the white smoke above her head. He was taunting her, and angst prickled her skin.

"Why are you trying to argue with me?" she said.

"Never said I was trying to do that." He lifted his eyebrow.

"Then you're trying to make me say something I'll regret."

"I don't think any man has much control over you."

"No man controls me," she snapped, burning anger pulsating through her skin.

"Then why are you worried about what I'm supposedly trying to do?" He stuck the cigar back in his mouth and wrapped his full lips around it.

Is he trying to entice me? These were the types of thoughts she couldn't let take hold for they would derail everything she thought possible.

"I'm not worried about you," she spat.

"Quit trying to fool yourself."

"I'm not fooling myself. I know what I want, when I want it, and who I want it with." She was lying to him and to herself, but she didn't know how to stop.

"Do you?" He took another drag of his cigar, the scent of sandalwood and smoke filling her nostrils.

"I don't need or want to explain myself to you." She gripped the afghan tightly and dug her fingernails into her palms.

"Then don't let me stop you." His mocking tone was irritating. "Unless you want to *actually* talk to me instead of running and hiding every time you see me."

She narrowed her eyes. "I don't run or hide. I just don't want to talk to you."

"And why is that, exactly?"

It took all of her composure not to pound her fists into him. Instead, she acted like a bratty child, stomped her foot, twirled around, and stalked back to the chair she'd been sitting in.

"So let's talk," she snarled. If he wanted to talk, she could talk.

"So much anger."

"I'm not angry," she said, but she was. He irked her like no one else.

Michael sighed, the sound competing with the wood snapping in the fireplace. He snuffed out his cigar before pulling on the chain for the gas lamp.

Her eyes smarted from the sudden light, even though it wasn't that bright, but considering she'd been sitting in the dark for hours, it took a moment for her eyes to adjust. When they did, she found him perched on the chair across from her. He was like a wolf, chasing his prey until he got it between his teeth.

"I don't want to fight with you, Marie," he whispered, leaning forward on his elbows. "But I can't get you out of my head."

"I never wanted to be there!"

Hurt flashed in his eyes.

She ran her hand across her forehead and rubbed the spot between her brows. A headache was brewing, and they never stopped when she was around him. But she'd been raised better than this, and being rude was not something her parents would've approved of.

"I'm sorry," she murmured.

"Don't apologize for something you're not sorry for."

His words were far too true. Most times when she argued with him, she *really* wasn't sorry, but today she was. She caught his gaze. "No, I am. When I'm around you, I can't help myself."

"It must be my charm."

Did he ever stop? Instead of responding, she just glared at him.

His smile dimmed. "I guess you don't find me charming?" When she still didn't respond, he sat, a sad frown on his lips and regret burning in his eyes. "I can't do anything right with you, can I?"

She wasn't prepared for his soulful eyes or the disappearance of his jovial attitude. That let her keep him at an arm's distance. The serious man sitting in front of her was not who she recognized, and it disarmed her.

"I can be overexuberant, and I have a tendency to laugh more than others, but I do have feelings, Marie."

A pang shot straight through her heart. "I don't want to hurt you."

"Do you think you have the power to do that?"

She stared at him in shock. She had no idea how to answer that question.

He abruptly stood and paced in front of her, one hand against the back of his neck. "I'm in love with you. Why can't you see that?"

"I never asked you to be."

"I know you didn't," he bit out. "No one asks someone to love them. It just happens."

"It doesn't just happen. Love is fickle, and it can be snuffed out like that." She snapped her fingers. "Why give yourself over to someone who might have the power to hurt you?"

Michael stood, shocked, his mouth agape.

"I want nothing to do with it, which is why I chose this path. I don't want to hurt you. I've been avoiding this conversation with you, which I realize is unfair to you, but you can't take *no* for an answer."

"You've never given me half a chance or sat down and talked with me. You avoid talking to anyone who isn't part of your cause. You've thrown me into the same bucket of men who you're fighting against. I'm not like that. I would never lay a hand on a woman. I never have, and I never would."

"I'm not willing to take that chance."

"It will be a long and lonely existence."

"Then it will be my long and lonely existence." She couldn't continue to sit here while he mocked her. "You don't understand and never will."

"That isn't fair. You haven't given me a chance to prove that I'm nothing like those men you're fighting so hard. No man in my family has ever touched a woman in anger or ever without her consent. Didn't Elizabeth tell you that?"

She narrowed her eyes. "Have you been talking to your sister-in-law about me?"

"Yes," he said. "I needed advice."

"Advice about what?"

"You!" he shouted. "I've been waiting for you to give me a chance, trying to be honorable, trying to become your friend, trying to make you understand that I'm not what you think I am, but no matter what I do, you have decided something about me that isn't even true."

"That isn't--"

"It is true. You've made judgments about me based on something I had nothing to do with. You're putting all men in this box based on preconceived notions. While I understand your hesitation, it isn't fair that you're labeling me the same."

"Nothing in life is fair, Michael. Maybe you've been coddled your whole life and don't know what it's like to lose someone who means the world to you."

His pupils grew in size, the black overtaking the amber brown of his eyes, and his face turned a bright red. "You have no idea what I've lost, and just because my parents didn't kill themselves doesn't mean I don't know the pain of that loss. Not to mention, I took the life of the woman who killed my pa. So don't you dare presume to lecture me on what it feels like." Barely suppressed rage rolled off him in waves.

She had gone too far in her anger and had hurt him unintentionally, but he was being just as cruel. "How dare you. My parents didn't kill themselves. I don't care what the newspapers or people say. I told you that in confidence."

"And I told you how my parents died, so it looks like we are at an impasse. I won't bother you again. I'll leave Helena. This will be the last time I ever tell you how much I love you. Until you grow up and realize that everyone experiences pain, then you'll experience nothing more than that."

He scooted around her and walked out of the room, leaving her all alone and empty of everything. Just as she demanded.

Twenty-Nine

M arie should have been behind the stage, ensuring all the speakers were present and accounted for. Women filled the large hall, and the noise level was increased with each minute. She should have been ensuring the speakers had everything they needed.

Instead, she stood in a corner, shedding tears she shouldn't be shedding. Her heart was torn. She couldn't stop thinking about the night before and what Michael had said. She should be happy he was finally leaving her alone, but she wasn't.

Marie needed to greet Ida and Gail and welcome them, but she hadn't moved from this spot. Michael had shattered everything she thought she understood. She'd been selfish and inconsiderate with her words, and he had reacted in kind. She had no one besides herself to blame for her foolhardy words and actions.

"Marie," Eloisa said. "What are you doing? Ida and Gail are here. You're needed."

Marie wiped the moisture from her cheeks and took a deep breath. She had to gain control of her emotions. She was like a fish gasping for air after being pulled from the safety of the water. No air to breathe and no reason to keep on moving.

"Were you crying?" Eloisa looked at her closely.

She didn't want to explain her turbulent emotions. "My eyes are watering from the dust. It's quite dirty in here."

"Oh, it is." Eloisa patted her skirt. "Mr. Fields said it would be cleaned, but obviously, his idea of clean is not mine. If I had gotten here earlier, I would've discussed the lack of preparation with him, but the roads were jammed with horses, carriages, and women. I was worried I wouldn't get here in time." Her excited movements caused her elaborate white hat to bob precariously on her head. She was quite animated at times. "Have you seen all the women? This is going to be an amazing event. So many want to hear Ida and Gail speak. They are such inspirations."

Eloisa continued prattling as she led Marie around the various props, chairs, and miscellaneous items scattered throughout to the back of the stage. If they didn't watch where they were going, they'd likely trip and fall flat on their faces. She'd best pay attention and think about what Michael had said when she had more time, and it wasn't now.

Marie had to have misunderstood his intentions. He wouldn't leave Helena or his smithy business just because they had different opinions. She would find him later, tell him she and Walter would leave Luke's as soon as she could make it possible, and then they would be out of his hair. They could go back to being acquaintances. He could continue his life as he saw fit, and she could continue her fight for women's rights. Then all would be right in both of their worlds. She could make this better. She would.

The next morning, Marie stood in front of Michael's smithy. The harsh words on the sign below Thundering Sunset Livery and Smithy left a gap so deep and personal in her heart, she realized she had made the biggest mistake of her life.

CLOSED INDEFINITELY

～

"Marie!"

The pounding on the front door, combined with the incessant yelling of her name, made Marie groan. Her head ached, and she just wanted to take a nap. All of the meetings, speeches, rallies, and protests had finally caught up with her. She was exhausted.

The event the night before had been a resounding success. After the speeches, she'd been bombarded with questions from numerous women and even a few men who wanted to help and be part of the movement. She should have been excited, but instead, all she could think about was talking to Michael.

Then, when she found his smithy closed, it had torn her heart sideways as she realized it was done. She had finally pushed him away so she could concentrate on what was important. The problem was, she wasn't sure if it was as important as she had first believed.

The loud hammering knocks hadn't stopped. They just seemed to grow in intensity.

She pushed to stand, sweeping her tangled hair away from her face. She had pulled out the pins earlier when she returned to the house and hadn't bothered to pin it back. Reaching behind her, she quickly braided it as she made her way down the hall to find out who was so anxious to have her open the door.

"Marie, are you in there? Marie."

"What?" She wrenched the door open and startled Eloisa, who stood on the front stoop, her hand raised in mid-knock.

"I'm sorry to bother you, Marie, but we need to talk." Eloisa pushed past Marie and marched inside.

"What is it? I'm not feeling well, and..."

Eloisa whirled around and glared at her. "You don't have time not to feel well. Where have you been? Everyone was looking for you at the train station when Ida and Gail left this afternoon. They were waiting for your speech, to wish her well, but you were nowhere to be found."

Marie's heart sank. She couldn't believe she had missed Ida and Gail's departure. She'd been wallowing in her self-pity and missed the exit of two of the most important women in the country, all because she couldn't stop thinking about Michael.

"I'm sorry, Eloisa."

"Get your hat. You need to come with me now." She impatiently tapped her foot on the wooden floor.

"What? Why? She's already left."

"It isn't her I'm worried about, but there's a gathering of women who need your leadership, who want to help, and they want you."

"Me... Why?"

"Why do you think? You *are* the face of this movement."

Marie's neck snapped up. "I'm not. Ida and Gail are."

"They're the face of the national movement, but you"––she pointed to Marie––"have risen to be the face of the movement here in Helena. We have an opportunity to rally the women and men here in Helena, and the momentum is high."

"No, I'm not, and I look a fright." It was a ridiculous reason, but she wasn't in the best position to be what the women of Helena needed. How could she gather her thoughts when the only thing she was thinking about was a man?

Eloisa grabbed Marie by the forearms and shook her. "What is wrong with you? Where was the woman last night who stood on that podium encouraging women to join? It's almost as though you've lost your way. Is it Michael? Has he changed your mind about what you want?"

She curled her fingers into tight fists. "Of course not. No man could ever change my mind about how I feel." But Michael had changed her mind. She'd just been too stubborn to realize what had been happening.

"Then what is it?"

Marie pulled away. "It's... nothing. Let me throw water on my face and put on a clean blouse. Give me a minute." She ran up the stairs to her room and quickly freshened up. Eloisa was right. She had to see this through. This was what she had been working for. She couldn't let the momentum collapse just because her friendship with Michael had disintegrated into a million pieces right before her eyes.

Thirty

Michael followed Suzette off the train, Natalie in his arms and Todd right behind him. The trip from Helena to Spring Creek had been uneventful, but the children were tired and hungry. He needed to get them fed and into bed soon. It was late, and the temperatures in Spring Creek were just as frigid, if not worse than what they'd been in Helena. And they still weren't dressed appropriately. The first thing he was doing in the morning was outfitting them in clothing more suited to a life in Montana. If he was going to be their pa, then they were going to be treated with an abundance of care.

"I'm hungry, Michael," Natalie mumbled around the thumb stuck firmly in her mouth.

Michael shifted her in his arms. "I know, little one. We'll get you something to eat soon, I promise."

She nodded and snuggled in close. She was a sweet thing, and he was tickled pink that he was to become her and Todd's pa. He'd always wanted a family, and while it wasn't with the woman he'd fallen in love with, he'd make it work if he could give these two children a family.

"Michael," Suzette murmured. "It's late, and I need sleep." She raised the back of her hand to her forehead, fluttering her eyelashes.

She was still trying to impress him. He'd already proposed, and she'd accepted. In fact, she'd been quite giddy and pleased with herself when he suggested they get married. Michael had shocked himself when he offered her marriage. But, if he couldn't have Marie, then he didn't want anyone else.

It would be a marriage in name only. Suzette had seemed content with that, although she had stipulations to the match. He was to act the loving husband when they were around their families, and he would never step out on her, regardless of the fact that they wouldn't be sharing the marriage bed.

He was to provide her with a new home built to her specifications. She had wanted it to be in Helena, but he'd put his foot down on that one. He didn't want to be anywhere near Marie. The temptation was too great, and he had his sanity to protect, so he'd suggested Spring Creek. She'd be close to her sister, and he'd be in a familiar place. Suzette hadn't been excited about moving to Spring Creek, but he'd told her she'd be the envy of everyone in town, and that had been enough to satisfy her.

Michael had agreed to the rest of her demands, and they'd solidified their relationship with a handshake and a glass of whiskey. It had seemed odd, but considering they were far from a love match, it'd made sense in a strange way.

He wasn't sure how he was going to build her the house of her dreams, but he'd figure it out. If he had to, he'd sell the livery and smithy in Helen and use those funds. In the meantime, he'd find work on a ranch and would just slowly work on building her what she wanted. The sacrifice would be worth it if he could make those two children happy.

He'd be content with them, as Suzette didn't want any more children. The two she had were too many, she'd said in a moment of true honesty, and considering how she treated them, it seemed only prudent that he step in to protect them. The only way he could save them from a life of misery was to become their father. His family would offer a stable environment and all the love the children needed. She wanted to be in the Seymour family, and he wanted children. A win-win.

"I'd sent a telegram to the doc," Michael said. "He should be waiting outside the depot with a wagon to take us back to their place."

"I don't want to stay with them," Suzette said, a scowl lining her lips. "Why can't we stay at the hotel?"

"We could do that, but then it will take me longer to get the funds together for your new house and the wedding." He didn't understand why Suzette was so against staying with her sister and her husband, the local doctor. They were far more pleasant than Suzette was and would be happy to have them stay on for a few days until he could make arrangements elsewhere.

"If I'd known we wouldn't stay in the hotel, then I might have––"

"Might have what?" He glared at her. She had done nothing but complain since they stepped on the train. If this were to be his future, he'd have to get thicker skin or a whole lot more patience.

"Never mind," she muttered. "You just better keep your promises."

"I always keep my promises." He saw that the porter was pulling out their bags and trunks and was stacking them, waiting for them to grab them. "Our bags are over there."

He started to hand Natalie to Suzette, but she backed away, waving her hands.

"No, she's filthy, and I'll not have my new dress smeared with her grubby hands."

Michael had to suppress the irritation building inside him. This was one of many comments she had made about her children that disgusted him, but they gave more power to his determination to keep them safe from her hurtful ways.

Looking at Todd, he bent and placed Natalie on the ground in front of him. "Take your sister's hand, Todd, and keep an eye on her while I take care of our bags."

Todd nodded and took Natalie's hand. He desperately wanted to please and would do as Michael said.

"I'll be right back."

"Please hurry, Michael. I'm not sure how much longer I'll be able to stand here without fainting."

"I'm sure you'll be fine."

Her lips pulled into an ugly scowl, but he ignored it. She was nothing but peevishly sulky at the best of times. The only time she was pleasant was when she was surrounded by powerful men and women, especially those in Helena's premier society. She wouldn't find that in Spring Creek, and he'd likely pay the price.

Michael reached the porter and made arrangements to have their luggage brought out front to make it easier to get the bags into the wagon. He'd been surprised by how much Suzette had when he met her at the train station in Helena. The number of trunks and bags was outrageous. He'd spent a pretty penny getting the luggage on the train, so he hoped the doc had brought a large wagon. Otherwise, they would be making a few trips to get everything back to the doc's place.

When that was done, he turned and cursed under his breath. Suzette was flirting outrageously with a group of local cowhands, and Todd and Natalie were huddling against a bench. Natalie was sniffling, and Todd's face was bright red as he rubbed a spot on his cheek. Suzette had likely slapped her son. Touching her children in anger was one of her many cruel qualities, and she had likely done so again.

While he'd love to tell her exactly what he thought, he had to tread carefully. He wanted to be the children's father, and she was going to hold that over his head until he put a ring on her finger and the preacher declared them man and wife. If he tried to stop her nasty behavior with too heavy a hand before that date, there was no telling what she would do. She had made it clear that the children were hers, not his, and until their arrangement was legally binding, he had to be mindful not to anger her to the point where she'd leave and take the children with her.

She was using the children as a bargaining chip, and he hated that he was following her around like a puppy on a leash, but some things were worth the effort.

Over the next few days, Michael explored Spring Creek, catching up with old friends and seeing what had changed and what had stayed the same. There was a smithy, and the poor man had more than enough work to do and not enough help. After negotiating, Michael convinced the smithy to give him a job, and he was going to start work there next week. It wasn't much money, but it was a start and would keep Suzette from whining more than she already was.

With a jaunt in his step, he headed back to the house where Suzette was staying. Within two days of arriving, she had found a place to rent. He was still staying with her brother-in-law and would move in with her after they were married. Then, once he had built her the house she desired, they would move there. It wasn't optimal and was costing him a fortune, but she had done signed the lease before he could stop her. There was no stopping the woman. All he could do was mitigate the damage as best he could.

There was a town dance that evening, and every hotel, boardinghouse, and empty room in the saloons was bursting with men, women, and children who'd come for the festivities. They'd been in town for only a week, and Suzette had created enough havoc to ward off an army. The only bright spot was the smiles Todd and Natalie had brought into his life.

Michael pushed open the white picket gate when a terrified scream tore through the air. He ran to the back and found Todd under the limb of the big oak tree, holding his arm, tears streaming down his face.

Michael ran to his side, bent, and lightly touched Todd's shoulder. "Todd, what happened?"

Todd continued to cry and whimper, not answering. His forehead was bleeding, and from the way he held his arm, it appeared to be broken. A snapped branch was next to him.

Michael scooped him up and held him carefully so as not to jostle his arm. He strode to the back of the house, through the screen porch, and into the kitchen. Setting him carefully onto the table, he tried to touch Todd's arm, but the boy pulled away in fright.

"Son, I need to look at your arm. Can I do that?"

Todd whimpered. "No, it hurts."

"I'm sure it does, but I can't fix your arm unless I look at it."

"No!"

Pulling back, Michael scratched his head. Todd needed a doctor. "Where's your ma?"

"I don't know," he cried. "Mother! I want my mother!"

"I know, but I don't know where she is."

"Mother!" He shook with pain and agony.

Michael kept his voice low and calm. "I'll find her, but first we're going to find your uncle, so he can look at your arm."

"Mother!" Todd's cries intensified, but Michael had no idea where Suzette was. Considering her behavior, she was likely somewhere that only benefited her.

"I'm sorry, buddy, but I'll find her after the doc looks at your arm. I promise."

Todd looked at him through suffering-filled eyes and reluctantly nodded.

"I'm going to pick you up. I'll try to be as careful as I can, but I need you to help me and hold it near your chest."

Todd sobbed as Michael swept him into his arms, carried him down the hall, and out the front door. The doc lived close, so it wouldn't take him long to get there. Michael's pace was quick, but he tried not to jolt the boy's arm unnecessarily. Todd rested his head against Michael's chest and cradled his hurt arm tightly against his tiny body.

An hour later, Todd lay sleeping on one of his uncle's beds after being given something to sleep. The doc set his arm and cleaned the cuts on his forehead and back. He had taken quite the fall and had broken his arm in two places, from what the doc could tell. Wrapping it securely, the doc told Michael that if Todd was careful, it should heal with time. He was going to wait a couple of days for the swelling to go down before putting on a more permanent cast.

The door to the office flew open, and Suzette rushed inside. "Michael! Michael!"

Michael had just stepped outside the examining room, leaving Todd in the doc's capable hands, and caught her in his arms. "Suzette, what's wrong?"

"Mrs. Archer says she can't get the silk for my dress in time for the wedding. What am I going to do? I insisted she hasten the order, but she says that since it was coming from Paris, it will take months." She wrung her hands. "This is just not acceptable. I cannot get up in front of everyone in town and wear a satin gown. Can you believe she suggested satin? That is so out of style, and I refuse to wear such peasant garb."

"Suzette——"

"What are you going to do about this?" She rested her hand on her hips, and a frown lined her lips.

"I can't worry about your dress right now."

"Of all the——" she sputtered.

"Todd fell out of a tree and broke his arm."

She flicked her hand. "I'm sure Tom has it in hand. Boys will be boys. They fall, get hurt, and get back up again. He'll be fine."

Michael shouldn't be surprised, but every single day, he was flabbergasted by Suzette's disregard for the children in her care. It was a wonder she hadn't left her children to fend for themselves, although he wasn't too sure she wouldn't do that if it didn't suit her in the moment.

"Now, about my dress." She stalked across the room and plopped into one of the chairs Tom had scattered around the room for anyone seeking his doctoring services. "I cannot accept what Mrs. Archer said. You need to talk to her and express to her how important this is. She'll need to send a telegram and explain that it is completely necessary that the silk gets here immediately."

"Fine, Suzette. I'll talk to Mrs. Archer, but I don't think I'll be able to do anything."

"You have to, Michael. It will not do for me to be in anything less than what I deserve. You promised that I would have the wedding of my dreams, and this is part of it. I cannot walk down the aisle in a flour sack."

He chuckled.

She slapped the table next to her. "Don't you dare laugh at me. There's nothing funny about this."

"I wasn't laughing at you, Suzette. I chuckled because you won't be wearing a flour sack. Mrs. Archer won't let that happen."

"She doesn't care about what I want. She is heartless." Suzette blinked, and tears fell from under her thick lashes.

She was nothing but predictable. Suzette could produce tears in an instant. It was as though she practiced so she could have them whenever she needed them. If he didn't know better, he'd think she was an actress on the greatest stage in America.

"Suzette." Tom walked out of the examining room. "Todd's awake and is asking for you."

"I can't handle his hysterics right now, Tom. Michael." She took his arm. "Please go to him. He doesn't need me. Besides, I need to speak with Mrs. Archer."

"I thought you wanted me to--"

"Men just can't deal with these things appropriately. I'll just demand that she do as I bid or that the Seymours will use none of her services in the future. Considering I need a full trousseau, she'll realize it's in her best interest to make you happy."

With that, she patted his cheek as though she were placating a young child and then flounced out of the doc's office like she had a mission. A mission to spend his money as fast as possible.

Michael sighed and rubbed the back of his neck. She was going to be the death of him, and he had to tell Todd that his mother didn't want to see him. Not that he would tell him that.

"Are you sure you know what you are doing, Michael?" Tom asked.

"Some days I wonder, but when I look at Todd and Natalie, then I know I'm making the right one."

"But living with her––"

"Will be an adventure, but we agreed it will be a marriage in name only."

"That won't keep you warm on cold nights." Tom pulled on the stethoscope around his neck and avoided looking at Michael. "Look, she's Janie's sister and is family, but I'd be remiss if I didn't tell you she has little care or regard for anyone besides herself."

"I'm well aware of who she is and what she'll be like, but I've made my choice, and I'll live with it."

"I'd hate for you to make a mistake. She doesn't care for her children and has only one thing on her mind, and it isn't well-intentioned."

Michael recognized he was likely setting himself up for a miserable existence. "Those children deserve so much. I can't break their hearts."

"I appreciate that, but you can't fix what she has broken, and she––"

"She's gonna be my wife. I'm sure she'll be more bearable once she gets the house she wants."

"And then she'll want something more. She'll bleed you dry." Tom's eyes were solemn.

"You don't like her much, do you?"

Tom laughed low. "No, not particularly. I've had to put up with her because she's Janie's sister, and occasionally, she is kind, but those moments are rare. She drove her parents to send her here ten years ago, hoping we could get her to become less selfish, but that didn't work. She put your brother through hell too, don't you forget."

Michael couldn't and wouldn't. Suzette had been conniving and manipulative. It'd only been because she'd run off with a man before Ben proposed that had saved his brother from marrying her. And then Michael had fallen into her trap, although he had gone into it with his eyes wide open and was aware of what he was getting.

"I'm afraid she's after you for your money."

Hearing Tom remind him of the havoc Suzette caused gave him pause, but all he had to do was think of Todd and Natalie, and his path was clear.

"I'm well aware she's after my money, but I have little. What I have is tied up in my livery and smithy back in Helena."

"Does she know that?" Tom picked up some folders on the desk against the wall and flipped through them.

"She does, although she thinks I'm holding something back and that we'll probably get something from Ben once we marry. But that won't happen."

"I'd hate to see how she'll react when she discovers that." Tom placed the folders back on the desk.

"I'll worry about that then." Michael wasn't looking forward to her reaction, but he had been honest with her and hadn't hidden a thing. What she chose to believe was up to her.

"You're a braver man than me," Tom said. "Do you want to go talk to Todd and tell him his mother has disappeared, or do you want me to do it?"

"I'll do it. Better for him to hear it from me. Can he still go to the town dance tonight? He was looking forward to it. Both he and Natalie were."

"I'd rather he rest, but it'll be good to have something to lift his spirits. Let me put his arm in a sling, and if you promise to get him home at a reasonable hour, and if he promises to take it easy, then I don't see any reason why he shouldn't be able to go."

"Thanks, doc. I'd hate to disappoint him. I just hope he's up for it."

"Hard to say, but just keep an eye on him. I'll give you a packet of aspirin to give him if the pain becomes too unbearable."

Michael shook the doc's hand. "It surely took a few years off my life when I saw him on the ground and that broken branch next to him."

"I've seen way too many broken bones from children climbing trees. You can't stop them from having fun and exploring, but I sure wish they wouldn't get hurt in the process."

"You and me both, but I suppose it's what keeps you in service."

The doc chuckled. "It surely does. Now, go see him before he wonders what we've been up to."

Michael rubbed his eyes before he plastered a smile on his face. It wouldn't do for young Todd to see how exasperated he was with his mother. Better for Todd to believe his mother hadn't even been at the doc's office than to know she had left without a care for his well-being. Todd already believed his father hadn't cared for him. Michael certainly didn't want Todd to believe his mother had the same disregard.

Thirty-One

Marie pushed open the glass doors and stepped outside to get away from the hustle and bustle inside the theater. The heat in the room had become overwhelming, but the stale air outside did nothing to eliminate the sweat that had gathered on the back of her neck and down her back. It had been a blazing hot few days, and there was no breeze to cool things down. August in Montana was sweltering at the best of times, but today was unbearable.

The women were anxiously getting ready for their march to the capital the next morning, and she should have been excited. They had over a thousand women who had signed the petition, and even more were expected to march in solidarity. They were building signs and banners, so they could present the legislature with their demands. It was an uphill battle, but they had to start somewhere, and the women were brimming with enthusiasm.

Marie had kept busy the past few months trying to keep her thoughts at bay, but she couldn't find joy or satisfaction in her goals, not any longer. She couldn't stop thinking about Michael and wanted to know where he had gone. She was too afraid to ask

Anne or his brothers, and once Anne had left for home, Marie had been left with so many unanswered questions.

Even her brother would've been too inquisitive if she'd asked him if he knew where Michael had gone. Walter was oblivious to her unhinged thoughts about Michael. He thought Michael had left because he was helping a friend and had never questioned her part in his leaving. The last thing she wanted was for her brother to know the part she had in driving Michael away.

Marie tried every morning to convince herself that Michael's leaving had been for the best, but at night, when she climbed into bed, she would remember the look in his eyes and the utter devastation she had caused without meaning to. She would then toss and turn for hours before exhaustion finally took hold.

Laughter and boisterous voices bellowed out of the large theater. It comforted her to know that so many women were on her side and were willing to put everything on the line to work toward gaining equal rights for women. She just wished she felt better about her life and the decisions she had made. Unfortunately, she questioned everything she thought she held dear.

"Hey, stop!"

Marie started to turn when a man pushed past her and shoved her to the ground. Rocks skidded into her palms, and her knees hit the ground hard. Pounding feet ran past her, but someone stopped, their heavy breathing mixed with shouts and yelling from others.

"Ma'am, are you all right?"

She looked up into the eyes of one of the new deputies of the night watch.

"Yes, yes, I'm fine," she said, although her hands might've argued otherwise.

The young man reached for her elbow and helped her stand.

"What's going on?" She picked at the rocks lodged in her palms and tried not to wince at the sting.

"Nothing to worry about, ma'am. We have it under control."
He lifted the brim of his black bowler hat.

"I can see that," she said. "Who was that?"

"No one you should concern yourself with." He rocked back
on his heels, barely giving her a glance. His gaze was focused on
another deputy running down the street, chasing after the man
who had pushed her aside. He clearly wanted to be in the fray, but
his sense of duty kept him by her side.

She bristled under the deputy's brush-off. "Do I need to warn
my colleagues of a dangerous element here in town? We want
tomorrow's march to be peaceful."

"Of course not. We have it under control." He looked down
his nose at her. "You hurt? Do we need to send for a doc?"

"No, I'm fine."

Gripping the sides of his vest, he said, "Good, good. Well, then,
I best be––"

"Can you tell me what is going on?"

He stared at her for a long moment, as if trying to decide what,
if anything, he could tell her.

"Young man…"

He bristled and straightened his spine with indignation.
"Nothing you need to concern yourself with."

"I am a reporter for the *Helena Gazette.* If there's something
dangerous happening, then the citizens of Helena have a right to
know." Luckily, Water was nowhere near her and couldn't dispute
her claims. Besides, he'd forgive her if she managed a scoop for the
front page.

"Sorry, ma'am, I'm not authorized."

"Then who do I talk to? Who is authorized?" She couldn't
figure out why she was being so stubborn. Normally, she wouldn't
be asking these types of questions for Walter's paper, but she'd
been out of sorts and needed something to distract her.

Before he could respond, another deputy peered around the
corner. "Arthur, let's go. We got him."

"Ma'am." He bobbed his head and hustled down the street and around the corner, joining his colleague before she could respond.

Marie blew out a frustrated breath. Even though she wasn't truly a reporter, the fact that the young whippersnapper didn't believe she was one infuriated her. She picked up her skirts in one hand and hurried down the street after them. If they wouldn't tell her what was going on, well, then she would find out for herself.

She reached the corner and peered around it, carefully watching as the deputies cornered a furious and belligerent man against the building's brick wall. He was spewing ugly words and fighting them with every breath. One deputy grabbed him, but he twisted away. His long, scraggly hair and thick beard only accentuated the evil in his eyes. He started to escape when another pushed him to the ground and subdued him.

"Marie! Marie!"

She turned and found Eloisa and Greta running toward her. Their eyes were wide and their mouths open in dismay. Their white gowns and purple sashes bounced from their erratic movements.

"Is everything all right?" Marie was concerned something had happened in the theater while she'd been outside ruminating about the man the sheriff's deputies had caught.

"You missed all the excitement." Greta peered over Marie's shoulder. "That man"--she pointed to the man the deputies were dragging down the street--"burst into the theater, yelling and screaming and saying he was going to end your life."

Marie took a step back. "I--"

"Luckily, one of the sheriff's deputies was keeping an eye out, saw what was happening, and tried to stop him."

"He didn't hurt anyone, did he?" Marie asked.

"No, thank heavens," Eloisa said. "He ripped up a few signs and smashed a chair into one table, but luckily, no one was close enough to get hurt. The deputies tried to stop him, but he escaped out the front." Eloisa took a big breath, waving her hand near her chest. "And it looks like they've caught him."

"Did you see the deputies catch him?" Greta asked.

"No." Marie's hands still smarted from hitting the ground. "He rushed past me, and I fell, but before you ask, I'm fine."

"You poor thing," Eloisa said, looking at Marie's hands. "We need to get your hands cleansed as soon as possible. I wonder what he wanted with you. Do you recognize him?"

"No." Marie glanced over her shoulder. The deputies had pulled him from the ground and marched him past them. The man's glare was ominous, and a chill ran up her spine. "I've never seen him before."

"Well, he certainly was determined to hurt you." Greta wrung her hands in her skirt. "I'm concerned he'll come after you again, Marie."

"The deputies have him well in hand," Marie said. "I'm sure they'll take every precaution and put him behind bars where he belongs."

"But don't you want to know why he was after you?" A frown marred Eloisa's pale cheeks.

Marie studied her hands and the scratches and cuts the rocks had made. "You're right, Eloisa. I should go to the sheriff's office and see what they can tell me."

"We'll both go with you." Eloisa took Marie by the arm. "You'll need our support."

"Yes," Greta said, grabbing her other arm. "You will."

Marie yanked open the door to Walter's newspaper office and ran up the stairs. She'd been at the sheriff's office for hours and had never expected to hear everything the man confessed. To say they'd been surprised at what he'd said had been an understatement. He had been one of multiple masterminds behind the attacks against

Marie. She had just assumed it was men who'd been angry with the suffragists' progress, and while that had been part of that, he'd also confessed there had been something even more disgusting.

"Walter! Where are you?"

Her brother appeared in the doorway, his black hair sticking up in various places. One end of his white shirt was untucked, his black tie was askew, and a handful of loose papers were in his hands. A scowl was on his lips. "I'm right here, working... Which is something you should consider."

Marie was shocked. He wasn't thrilled when she interrupted his work, but he rarely spoke to her in that harsh a tone. She wouldn't let it bother her, though, because she had more important things to consider.

"Do you know where Michael disappeared to?"

Walter walked back into his office. "I don't have time for this," he called over his shoulder. "I've got a deadline, my typesetter just quit, and I don't have a headline for tomorrow's paper."

"Just tell me where Michael is." She sounded like an ill-tempered child, but she was past worrying about how she sounded. She had to find him and warn him before it was too late.

Walter dropped the papers and ran a tired hand through his hair. "Go home, Marie."

"Just tell me where he is."

A young boy ran into the office and skidded to a halt. "Boss, Frank says we've got to have that final copy or we ain't gonna make it."

Walter mumbled something under his breath, rifled through his papers, and yanked one from underneath the pile. He held it out to the boy. "Give 'em this. It wasn't what I wanted, but it'll have to do."

The boy took the paper and ran out of the room, sweeping past Marie as he scurried down the stairs, his clomping footsteps fading away.

Walter fell into his chair and dropped his head in his hands.

"Go home, Marie. It's been a long day. I'm tired, and I need a drink."

"Have you always been this contrary?" she asked.

Walter didn't respond.

She sighed. "I might have a story for you, if you tell me where he is."

He slowly raised his head, and his red-rimmed, glassy eyes stared at her hard. "Why are you looking for him now? He's been gone for months."

Heat climbed up her neck. He was too perceptive, which was what made him the reporter he was. There were times she wished he were more like everyone else, but he wasn't.

"I made a mistake, and I need to talk to him."

Walter's expression softened. "You're too late."

Her shoulders stiffened, and uneasiness filled her limbs. "Too late for what?"

He braced his hands on his knees and stood. A moment later, he rested his hands on her shoulders as though he were preparing to tell her something she wouldn't want to hear.

"Is Michael all right? Has someone hurt him?" After what she'd found out tonight, he could be in danger if that nasty woman had gotten her hooks into him.

"He's fine, as far as I'm aware."

"Then what are you trying to tell me?" she said, panic starting to set in.

"Why don't you sit for a minute? I'll get us a cup of coffee, perhaps a bite to eat--"

She yanked away. "Don't try to distract me, Walter Marcus Owens. Just tell me."

"Are you--"

"Dammit, Walter. Tell me now!"

He sighed. "Michael's getting married."

She stumbled back a few steps and crashed into a bookcase.

Books and papers fell to the ground behind her. "No," she whispered. "Tell me it isn't to *her*."

Walter tilted his head. "Who?"

"Suzette."

He frowned. "How did you know?"

"No! No! No!" A loud, ringing noise roared in her ears, her vision narrowed, and she choked back a scream.

What have I done? She was too late. Suzette had hired someone to target her, all so she could get her claws into Michael. He was going to marry someone who had schemed and planned to hurt Marie and was the cause of some of the vicious attacks to get exactly what she wanted, and Marie had let it happen. If she hadn't been so stubborn in determining the path her future should take, she wouldn't have ruined what could've been the best thing in her life.

Marie had gotten what she'd wanted. She was alone and would be for the rest of her life.

Thirty-Two

Marie held her sign, marching alongside the hundreds of women who had joined her early that morning. It had taken everything in her to get out of bed, but she'd made a commitment and wouldn't let these women down, no matter how much she wanted to crawl into a hole and hide. Her spirits were not where they should be, but she mustered a smile and marched steadily toward the capital. No matter the choices she'd made, this was what she'd been working toward, and she wouldn't give up now.

The women around her crackled with determination, enthusiasm, and joy. The air was filled with the cheers and shouts of their demands. The wind ripped across the purple and white banners and flags, and their feet stomped on the ground as they moved like an avalanche down a mountain. Nothing would stop them. They were going to have their say.

More women had arrived than the organizers had expected. The streets were packed with women in all stages of life. Young women on the cusp of marriage, older women proud that their daughters and granddaughters would have more opportunities than they did, young girls looking up at the proud women around them in awe and envy, and even babies in carriages whose mothers would proudly tell them they had been a part of a magnificent movement.

"Marie! Marie!"

She looked around, but the crowds were thick, and she couldn't tell who was calling her name, but it didn't matter. She couldn't stop and talk to anyone even if she wanted to. If it was important, whoever it was would find her later. For now, she lifted her sign higher and chanted with everyone else.

Someone touched her shoulder, and she practically jumped out of her skin. Swiveling her head to see who it was, she sighed with relief. Even knowing they had finally caught the perpetrators didn't make her completely without unease. It'd likely take time before her nerves calmed. Once the man had started talking, he had told the sheriff there were a number of men involved, as well as that horrible woman. Hopefully, it was finally over.

"Anne," Marie said. "I didn't expect to see you."

Anne wrapped her arm around Marie's free arm. "I couldn't miss this. I had no idea you had garnered so many women for the cause. I wish I had gotten involved sooner, but…"

Marie squeezed Anne's hand. "You're involved now, and that's all that matters. I'm surprised you're back in town."

"I told Ben and Elizabeth there was no way I was missing this. I wish I would've come sooner, but with Michael leaving, I wasn't sure you'd want me to be here."

Marie's spirits sank. She hated that she'd made any woman feel like she couldn't be a part of this momentous time in history. She had to make it up to Anne.

"You're here now, and we are on the cusp of a new world. When the men in the legislature see our demands, they won't be able to ignore us any longer. That amendment will pass in September, I'm sure of it!"

This day was for all women, and seeing Anne reminded her

that even though her life might not be what she wanted, she was proud of the fact that they had come this far.

She tightened her hold on Anne. "Let's go get 'em. They can't ignore us now."

The women moved together as one, marching shoulder to shoulder until they reached the steps of the capitol building.

"Women's rights!"

"Women's rights!"

"Women's rights!"

If the legislature didn't see their determination, then they were living under a pile of cow manure. Their wives, daughters, mothers, aunts, and neighbors wanted the right to vote, and it was time for Montana to allow women those God-given rights.

Hours later, Marie and Anne returned to Luke's house. They had presented their demands, and while the women wouldn't know for a bit if they had succeeded, it felt like a success, and there was a sense of accomplishment among all of them. They had every right to be proud and would hold that accomplishment close to their hearts.

It was warm outside, and the house was right stuffy. Marie left the front door and the kitchen door open to hopefully catch a cross breeze. She dropped her banner and sign onto the kitchen table and pulled open the icebox to grab the pitcher of lemonade she had made the night before. It would be nice to have a cool glass after being out in the heat of the day.

"Would you like a bite to eat?" Marie washed her hands before splashing cool water against her flushed face. She had lost her hat at some point, and her face and neck were warm. She had gotten too much sun today, but it'd been worth it.

"Yes," Anne said. "I'm fairly famished and could eat a horse."

Marie chuckled. "I don't have any of those available, but I do believe we have some cake left from the other night. We have cheese and bread as well."

"That sounds delicious. How can I help?" Anne removed her hat, placing it on the table. She grabbed an apron and threw it around her waist before washing her hands.

"Sit," Marie said. "You've had a long day."

Anne pushed a strand of her dark blonde hair behind her ear. "And so have you." She grinned.

"You're right, we both have, but it was a good day, don't you think?"

"Yes, it was. All those women"--Anne fiddled with the pearl button at the nape of her neck--"were inspiring." Her eyes were wet with unshed tears. "My life has changed for the better since you came into it."

Marie halted as she stared at Anne in disbelief. She wasn't anything special and had done nothing more than encourage Anne to join in the fight.

"I've embarrassed you, haven't I?" Anne asked. "I'm sorry. I didn't mean to do that."

"No, no," Marie said, finally finding her voice. "I'm honored that you would say that, but I haven't done anything special."

Anne took Marie's hand and squeezed it affectionately. "You gave me a purpose. And now since we've gotten that mushiness out of the way, let's get that food on the table and eat. I'm starving."

Marie chuckled and surreptitiously wiped away the tears from her eyelashes.

An hour later, the two of them leaned back in their chairs, having fully satisfied their appetites. They laughed and giggled and analyzed everything that had happened.

"Thank you for today," Anne said. "I had so much fun and am going to pray hard that our state congressmen do the right thing."

Marie waved away the thanks. "It's so hard to wait, but we will continue to fight regardless of what happens. Each state has to change its constitutions, so it'll likely take years, but it will be worth it."

"I agree," Anne said. "But can I ask you something?"

Marie shifted in her chair, watching as Anne's expression grew serious. "Of course. You can ask me anything."

"Will you go with me to Michael's wedding?"

Marie looked at her hands, her throat thickening with emotion. That was the last question she expected Anne to ask her. "Why would you want me to come? He made his choice."

"Because... because he's making a huge mistake. I'm hoping that if he sees you, he'll change his mind."

Thirty-Three

"Michael!" Todd yelled. "I can't wait for you to be my pa."

Michael grinned, his heart tugging at Todd's enthusiastic reception, and crouched in front of the boy. Todd wrapped his arms around Michael's neck and squeezed tight.

"I love you," Todd said.

Michael blinked. He loved this boy and was just as excited to become his pa, to become a pa to both Natalie and Todd. The two children had burrowed deep into his heart over the past few months. He wished his affection for their mother was as special as it was for them.

He had plenty of doubts, but he had made a commitment to the children, and he wasn't about to disrupt that. He could live with Suzette. She wanted a husband. He wanted to be a father. It worked for both of them, although her behavior had worsened since they'd announced their engagement. She reminded him more and more of the girl who'd tried to ensnare Ben into marriage, but his doubts no longer mattered. They were getting married this Saturday. It was too late to back out.

"I love you, too," Michael said. "Where's your mother? We need to leave for the party."

Todd scrunched his nose and dug his toe into the wooden floor, avoiding Michael's gaze. "She's still getting ready."

"Oh, is she?" Michael ruffled Todd's hair. "Is something wrong?"

Todd shook his head furiously. "No."

Michael looked at Todd carefully. He didn't want to interrogate the boy, but he could tell something was bothering him. "If there's something--"

"No," Todd said. "Mother said to tell you she'll meet us at the hotel." He grabbed Michael's hand and started to drag him toward the front door.

Michael carefully extracted himself from Todd and knelt in front of him. "Why don't you get your sister and go to the hotel? I'll find your mother and meet you there."

Todd's eyes filled with tears, and he furiously shook his head. "No, please, Michael. Come with me. Mother won't be happy if we stay here."

"Hey, buddy, it's all right. I promise. Go get your sister."

Todd dragged his feet across the floor and kept looking over his shoulder, clearly torn, but something in Michael's tone must've convinced the boy to do as he asked. A moment later, Todd held Natalie by the hand, and they left through the front door, leaving Michael alone in the house Suzette was renting. Several trunks sat near the front door, ready for their trip back East. Suzette wanted to go to New York, so they were taking the train and would spend two weeks there before returning. The children were going with Ben and Elizabeth back to the Thundering Mountain Ranch so the two of them could spend time alone.

Suzette was purely excited about the trip, and Michael was happy to give her what she wanted. It would quiet her complaints about the new house not being built yet. He'd run into a few issues and hadn't been able to secure the plot of land they'd wanted, but he was still looking and was bound to find something soon.

Ben had asked him if she was marrying him for his money

just the day before. While he'd been furious with his eldest brother for even asking, he had no delusions about why she was marrying him. He wasn't about to admit it to his family, especially since maybe, just maybe, he'd been impetuous in proposing to Suzette.

He strode down the hallway until he reached the stairs. He grasped the banner and looked up before climbing them to the second floor. Michael had to brace himself for whatever she might be up to. Something was wrong from the way Todd was acting, but he couldn't imagine what she'd done now. The last two weeks had been tumultuous, to say the least. She'd been angry and out of sorts, yelling at the children at the drop of a hat, and snapping at him when she didn't get her way. He wasn't sure what their life was going to be like, but if this was the start of it, he could only imagine how worse it was going to get.

Reaching her bedroom door, he knocked.

"That better not be you, Todd," Suzette yelled, irate.

"It's not," Michael replied. "Can I come in?"

The door swung open, and Suzette stood clad in only a chemise, tangled blonde curls hanging across her shoulders. She leaned against the doorway, crossing her arms over her chest, which pulled the shift tight across her breasts. Suzette was trying to be beguiling, but he wasn't interested and hadn't ever been. She was only getting uglier because there was something angry inside of her that just built. One day, it was going to blow, and he was, unfortunately, going to have to deal with it. In the beginning, he'd tried to love her while trying to forget about Marie, but now, it wasn't worth the effort. It was a problem for the start of a new marriage, but he'd make it work.

When he didn't respond, as she clearly wanted him to, she huffed and swung around. She snatched her wrap from the bed and wrapped it around her slim frame. "What are you doing here? I told Todd I'd meet you at the hotel."

"Is that any way to greet your future husband?" he drawled.

"Let's not play games. We both know you don't want to marry me."

He thought he was the only one who had concerns, but maybe Suzette had them as well.

"But you will marry me, and I'm counting on that." She turned her back to him and stalked to her dressing table before flouncing into the seat.

"Excuse me," he said. What in the hell was going on?

"My children need a father, I need a husband, and you need a wife, so *we* are doing this." Malice and anger were in her tone.

Dread tingled the back of his neck. "Has something happened?"

"No, nothing," she snapped, slamming a hairbrush onto her dressing table. "But you've been distant, and you're only interested in Todd and Natalie's happiness, certainly not mine."

He contained his frustrated sigh. "That's not true. We're going to New York, and I'm going to build you the house you want next summer. What more do you want?" He cringed internally at how materialistic that sounded. But he couldn't give her more than that. It just wasn't in him.

"You don't love me." She pouted. "Maybe you don't love my children as much as you've claimed. Perhaps I should take them and leave."

His heart nearly stopped in his chest. He did not want to lose them. They were the only reason he'd been able to put one foot in front of the other when Marie had denied him. Making those two children happy was the only thing that mattered.

He strode to her, placed his arms around her waist, and pulled her to him before he nuzzled his lips into her neck. She liked that, and he would do whatever it took to make her happy, for his happiness was reliant on her becoming his wife.

"I'm sorry, Suzette. I don't want to see you unhappy. What can I do to fix this?" He placed a kiss against her ear. She shivered, and he tightened his arms around her waist.

"Just don't leave me, please," she murmured. "I want to make you happy, but you haven't seemed like yourself since your family came into town."

"You're right, I haven't." He was completely and utterly embarrassed that he was marrying the woman who had caused so much havoc in Ben and Elizabeth's lives, but he wasn't going to say that to Suzette.

"Ben and Elizabeth don't want you marrying me."

She was right, but he didn't need to tell her that. He wasn't about to ruin the peace such as it was. "That's not true."

"It is true," she cried. "I've changed, but they don't see that. They only remember what I was like all those years ago. Having children changed me."

Michael didn't disagree about that. She was worse. Sometimes, she appeared mature, but it was completely overshadowed by her complete and utter disregard for her young children and anyone around her. She thought of herself first, and everyone else was secondary.

"You *are* different, and they'll eventually see that. Give them time." He hugged her tighter, trying to placate her as best he could.

She twisted around until she faced him. "I just want us to be happy."

"We will." He kissed her softly. "I promise."

The ache in his heart grew even larger with that lie because she wasn't the woman he wanted, but she was the woman he'd have.

Marie stepped off the train in Spring Creek, Montana, with Anne by her side. She couldn't believe she'd actually agreed to Anne's scatterbrained plan. She wanted to mend things with Michael but was afraid she was too late, regardless of what Anne thought. If he were getting married in two days, then there wasn't anything she could do. The last thing she wanted was to cause a scene, and she was afraid that would be exactly what would happen, but at the same time, he deserved to know what Suzette had been up to, even if the sheriff wasn't entirely convinced she was involved.

The sheriff said they didn't have enough evidence to arrest her, especially since the man had recounted everything the next morning, claiming he'd been drunk and out of sorts. Marie didn't believe it for a second. Suzette had been up to something from the moment she came to town. They knew Suzette hadn't been involved in all the accidents since some of them had happened before she arrived, but the latest ones had been too personal. The man had been clear as could be when he explained Suzette's involvement until something had changed his mind the next morning.

"Maybe I should go back to Helena." Marie grabbed her bag from the porter.

"Absolutely not," Anne said.

"Here you go, miss," the porter said, handing Anne her bag.

"Thank you." Anne gave the porter a few coins from her reticule around her wrist. "We are *not* going back to Helena until you speak with my brother."

Marie followed Anne as she marched across the wooden platform. She was a woman on a mission. Too bad it was a mission that Marie was going to regret. She'd had doubts when they'd climbed onto the train in Helena, and now that they were there, she had a sinking feeling that her arrival was going to be a disaster of epic proportions.

It was hot, the sun high above them, but Anne looked like a fresh daisy on a spring day, while Marie felt like she was a hot poker stuffed deep in the fiery embers. It was likely stress from the thought of seeing Michael again. She'd rather go jump in an icy bath than face him, but she'd promised Anne she would, even though she seriously regretted the decision at that moment.

"What if he won't speak to me?" Marie hated the way she sounded. She sounded forlorn, and she supposed she was. If she had a chance to win Michael back, she wanted it, but this was a fool's mission. There was no way Suzette was going to let Michael out of her clutches. Based on what Anne had told her and Marie's limited experience with Suzette, coming here had been a mistake.

"We'll make him." Anne took Marie's arm. "Now, let's go find Ben. I sent him a telegram, and he should be waiting for us out front."

But when they found Ben and Elizabeth, they shared a glance that made her uncomfortable and told her it had been a colossal mistake in coming to Spring Creek, but it was too late.

She stood in her hotel room staring in the mirror. Her heart pounded something fierce. She'd never be able to compete with Suzette. Not that it was a competition. Suzette had already won and had Michael locked in as her future husband.

They were going to dinner in the hotel dining room, and Michael and Suzette would be there. Marie smoothed back stray strands of her hair, the purple ribbons she tied that morning holding it at the nape of her neck. She fiddled with the belt around her waist and sighed. There was nothing more she could do. She had to pretend to be Michael's friend and not the woman in love with him who'd rejected his proposals because she had been misguided in her goals.

Her heart rate increased when a loud knock on the door startled her. Marie wasn't ready for this, but she couldn't turn back. She was here and had to go through with it--if not for herself, then for Anne. She didn't think she had enough sway with Michael to get him to end things with Suzette, but perhaps she'd have a chance to at least tell him she was sorry. Maybe, just maybe, they could be friends again.

She opened the door and found Anne on the other side. Anne's smile should have calmed her nerves, but it only worsened them.

"Are you ready?" Anne tugged at the sleeve of her blouse. She took one glance at Marie and grimaced. "Oh no, you look like you're about to face a firing squad."

"Does he know I came to town?" She drummed her fingers against the doorframe, anxiety prickling her skin.

Anne looked away. "Not exactly."

She gulped, and her heart started to race. "Anne, you told me you were going to tell him."

"And I would have, except he hasn't arrived yet. Ben told me he was supposed to be here early, but for some reason, he was delayed. Suzette's son said Michael would bring his mother soon."

"This is a bad idea. I don't want him to be surprised that I'm there."

Anne pulled her from the room. "You're a family friend, and there are plenty of people who've arrived that weren't invited. It's like the who's who of Helena downstairs. Once word got out that Michael was getting married, our friends and family showed up in droves."

"But I'm not a friend--"

"Of course you are. You're my friend." Anne led them down the hall to the main staircase.

"But I'm not Suzette's friend. Or Michael's, for that matter."

Anne halted when they reached the first floor and turned toward her. "You *are* Michael's friend."

"No, I'm the woman who turned down his multiple proposals."

"And you're the woman he loves."

"I'm not. He's marrying Suzette." Marie raised a hand to her lips, trying hard to keep the tears from falling. "He hates me and wants nothing to do with me. I hurt him one too many times."

"Maybe, but he's not in love with that woman, and if he sees you--"

"He'll likely escort me out to the pasture. He won't be happy you brought me here."

"Well, I'm not happy he's marrying that conniving, spiteful woman."

"Ummm," a deep voice drawled.

Marie died inside. Michael stood behind her with Suzette hanging onto his arm. Marie's face flushed hot with heat. This was not how Marie wanted to see Michael again, and his scowl told her it had been a huge mistake. She should've never come to Spring Creek. Michael was in love with another woman, and he'd never be hers.

Thirty-Four

Michael couldn't believe she was here. It had taken some effort, but he had pushed Marie out of his mind and moved on. He was marrying Suzette, but to see Marie standing in front of him, next to his sister, of all people, he felt as though his life had been turned upside down and thrown into the nearest manure pile.

Marie was just as beautiful as she was the last time he'd seen her, but he couldn't do this. Anne was trying to stop the wedding, but it wouldn't work. Suzette would be his wife in two days, and nothing Anne said or did, including bringing Marie here, would stop it.

"Michael." Anne pulled him into a hug. "I didn't expect to see you so soon."

Anne wasn't sorry she'd been overheard. Michael could tell by the impish grin on her face. While it was nice seeing her, he didn't appreciate her trying to stop the wedding.

"Anne," he said. "I didn't think you'd be bringing a friend."

Anne stepped back and grabbed Marie by the arm. "Marie was kind enough to travel with me. I didn't feel quite so comfortable coming on my own."

He scowled. Anne was not afraid of traveling, but he'd be a fool to say otherwise. She had been through a lot in the past few years, and if she claimed she was uneasy, he'd be best to keep his mouth shut if he didn't want to bring down Ben's wrath.

"Suzette," Anne murmured. "You're looking well."

"Thank you." Suzette preened next to him, holding his arm like a fishhook. "I didn't expect you to arrive so early for the wedding."

"I couldn't wait to come and celebrate." Anne's tight smile said otherwise.

"Shall we go on to the dining room where everyone has gathered?" Michael needed to get away from Marie, and the quicker they retreated to the dining room, the better.

"Of course, darling," Suzette drawled.

Suzette pulled him toward the hotel's dining room and away from Marie and Anne. She was furious, even though she'd plastered a smile on her face. Suzette's lips were tight, forced, and she dug her fingers into his arm. It took everything in him not to release her fingertips. He'd likely have bruises in the morning if something didn't distract her and soon.

A moment later, they stepped inside the elaborately decorated dining room. Pink and purple flowers were on the tables. She had gone overboard with her decorations, and he cringed at what the bill was going to be. She had no concept of money and spent it faster than he could bring it in. He was running through his savings fast, and at the rate she was going, he wouldn't have enough to build the new house she wanted or pay the rent on the place she'd secured.

Friends and family filled the room, and while he appreciated they'd come to celebrate the nuptials, he wasn't looking forward to the side-eyed looks and forced smiles his brothers and sisters would send his way. No one was happy with his choice and didn't understand why he'd proposed to Suzette.

Many uncomfortable congratulations were uttered as he and

Suzette walked around the room. Suzette tittered and giggled while he thanked everyone who offered their best wishes. She lessened her grip as people greeted them and gave her the attention she sought.

A waiter walked by with a tray of champagne. Michael grabbed two flutes and handed one to her.

"Thank you." She took it and downed it in one swallow, dropped it onto the waiter's tray, and grabbed a second one before he took a drop of his.

It was going to be a long night.

When she went to grab for a third, he said, "Should you eat something first?"

She looked at him from under her thick black eyelashes and then downed the third glass of champagne. "I don't need you telling me what I should or should not drink. We aren't married yet." With that last ominous set of words, she flounced toward her sister, leaving him blessedly alone.

He breathed a sigh of relief. Her anger over Anne's comments was still simmering beneath the surface, but if she talked with her sister, perhaps Janie could calm her nerves. The last thing he needed was for Suzette and his sister to be at odds.

"Michael," Anne said, appearing next to him. "I fear I might have caused an issue, although... to be honest, I'm not sorry. I don't like her, and you're making a monumental mistake."

He stared at Anne, stunned. He shouldn't be surprised by how she felt. Everyone in his family felt the same way, but they'd kept quiet for weeks, other than Ben, who had already confronted him.

"She's going to be my wife. You don't have to like her, but you will treat her with respect."

"She doesn't automatically get my respect because you're foolish enough to marry her. You have to earn my respect, and she hasn't done that. She's not the woman for you, and you'll regret this if you go forward with it." Anne placed her hand on his arm. "I love you, Michael, and the woman for you is not her."

He shrugged her away. "I won't regret anything. Those children need me."

"Is that the only reason you're marrying her?" Anne's eyes were sad and full of sorrow.

He hated seeing her look of pity, but he was determined to protect those kids. At least then he'd have a family.

Thirty-Five

"Why are you marrying her? You don't love her," Ben said, his eyebrows pulled together tightly.

Michael said nothing. They'd already had this argument, and he wasn't going to do it again. He brushed white lint from his black suit jacket and straightened his gray tie. They were in the reverend's office, waiting for the signal to proceed to the chapel of the small clapboard church. He should've been nervous, but instead, he felt nothing. It was as though his body was empty of anything and everything of substance.

He should be a happy bridegroom, but the mirror's reflection showed sagging shoulders, stilted movements, and pain-filled eyes. It was as though he were attending his funeral instead of what was supposed to be the happiest day of his life.

Shoving down the weight of a life not as he imagined, he smoothed down his hair and turned. "Shall we go? It's time."

"Please think about this. You don't have to marry her. It isn't too late." Ben's brown eyes, the same color as his own, were filled with pity.

Michael bristled with irritation and brushed past him.

Frustrated, Ben grabbed his arm. "I can't let you do this."

Michael yanked free. "There's nothing you can do to stop me."

With that, he strode to the door, opened it, and stepped out into the front of the chapel in Spring Creek, Montana, where he would wait for his future bride. Guests filled the room, and the pungent smell of roses, lilies, and the undercurrent of sweat permeated the air. It smelled like a heavily laden funeral, and in a way, it was.

Thirty-Six

M ichael stood at the front of the church. The reverend kept looking at his pocket watch, concern growing on his face. Michael should be worried, but he wasn't. Suzette was never on time, so the fact that she was late for their wedding was not a terrible surprise. He smothered a yawn and tried to look like he cared, but he really didn't. The life he imagined was over, and he was resigned. At least the children would lift his spirits.

The vestibule door opened, and the pianist began playing the wedding music. But instead of a vision in white coming down the aisle, Janie hurried toward them. Her face was grim, and her movements were brisk.

Michael frowned. He wanted to get this over with and get his monkey suit off. He would have been perfectly happy to get married in his work trousers and chambray shirts, but he'd given in to Suzette's insistence on an elaborate wedding with all the bells and whistles to show everyone in town she was marrying a Seymour.

Although he may not love Suzette with the same fiery passion he felt for... No, he couldn't think of her. She was no longer for him. Her devotion lay elsewhere, and he offered nothing she didn't already have. She claimed she didn't need a husband, and after the last rejected proposal, he'd finally given her what she wanted and had left Helena and her behind.

Janie reached them, but she avoided his gaze and instead approached the reverend. Unease crept up Michael's spine as the crowd started to whisper. It was one thing for Suzette to make a grand entrance, but it was quite another for her to send her sister up the aisle in her stead.

Janie whispered something in the reverend's ear. He frowned and shook his head, but Janie appeared insistent. Finally, the reverend nodded and then glanced at Michael. Had something happened to Suzette? He reached to stop Janie, but she skirted from his grasp and hurried back where she came from. A moment later, the door snapped shut with finality behind her. Michael looked to the reverend, who approached him carefully as though he were a delicate vase that would break with one sharp glance.

"Michael, can we step outside? I need to speak with you." Concern filled his eyes.

"What's going on?"

"Please." He fiddled with his collar, his agitation noticeable.

"No," Michael said. "You can tell me right here. Is Suzette all right?"

"Yes, she's fine, but..."

"But what?" he snapped. The reverend reached for Michael's elbow as if to lead him away. Michael wrenched away. "No, tell me what's going on."

"Let's step outside where it's quiet, and I'll explain." The reverend's voice was low and serious as he tried to avoid a scene, but Michael didn't care if he caused a ruckus. The days of being kind and courteous had disappeared the moment Marie broke his heart.

Ben rose from the front pew. "Michael, do as the reverend says. He'll tell us what's going on. People are whispering."

Michael couldn't care less what the people in the congregation said or thought, but to spare the reverend any embarrassment, he turned and walked to the side vestibule door, leaving Ben and the reverend to follow.

They stepped into the hallway. The reverend closed the door behind them and led them down the hall to his office, where he gestured for both Michael and Ben to enter.

"All right, reverend, we've left the hall. Where's Suzette?" Michael was tired of the wedding spectacle of the year. Clearly, Suzette wanted something grander and more ostentatious. She was going to be a drain on his pocketbook, but he no longer cared. Let her have his money. It wasn't worth all the fuss.

The reverend walked around his desk and placed his Bible onto the scarred wooden surface. "I'm not sure how to tell you this, but there won't be a wedding today."

Michael scratched behind his ear. "Has something happened to Suzette? Is something wrong with her dress? She told me yesterday the seamstress was still working on it. You can tell her it's fine if her dress ain't perfect. I don't mind."

"Suzette is perfectly fine, but there will not be a wedding today or any other day." The reverend fidgeted and was uncomfortable with whatever information Janie had shared with him.

"Is she outside?" Michael sighed. "I'll go talk with her."

"I think it's best if you don't." The reverend sat heavily in his chair and unbuttoned his suit. "Why don't you sit and I'll tell you what I know?"

"This is ridiculous. I'm sure if I talk with her, I'll get her to calm down, and we can proceed." Michael grew irritable. What was the problem? Why wasn't the reverend telling him where Suzette was hiding?

The reverend cleared his throat. "She can't marry you."

"Of course she can," he snapped. "She likely just needs reassurance or a piece of new jewelry. That always seems to satisfy her latest complaint. Just tell me where she is, and I'll get this resolved in a quick minute."

"She..." The reverend stopped and wiped away the sweat lining his forehead. The room was hot, stifling almost. It was the middle of August, and the heatwave was uncomfortable, to say the least. "She's left with her... well, with her husband."

"Her what?" Michael couldn't have possibly heard right. Suzette was not married. She was a widow.

The reverend gazed at his Bible before raising his head. "I'm sorry. She *is* married, and her husband has arrived to take her and their children back to San Francisco."

"Wait... What? I don't understand. Her husband passed away." His heart beat erratically in his chest. This couldn't be true. There was some mistake, a misunderstanding, but as he stared at the reverend, the truth of his words crashed into him. All of his hopes of becoming a father had just been yanked away. The fact that he wasn't sad that Suzette was gone told of his disgust with the woman, but he didn't want to lose Natalie and Todd. They were the only reason he'd been able to put one foot in front of the other after Marie had permanently dashed his hopes of a future with her.

"Apparently, he is most alive and well, and is anxiously waiting to bring her home."

"No, that isn't right. Something's not right here. Suzette has been a widow for over a year."

"Suzette has left and will not be returning."

"I don't believe this. She wouldn't have lied to me." Michael slapped his thigh.

Ben placed his hand on Michael's shoulder. "Are you sure she wouldn't have?"

Michael gulped.

Ben sighed. "You know her past and what she did when she and I..." He stopped when he caught Michael's glare.

Ben had been proven right, and that was a hard pill to swallow. While most times Michael appreciated his brother's wisdom, today wasn't one of those days.

"Of course, I'm sure," Michael lied, because deep in his heart, he wasn't. "She means the world to me." Shame filled him for the falsehood he just uttered.

"There won't be a wedding today. I'll inform the congregation if you want to head back to the hotel."

His future had just changed once again. Although he hadn't had a burning and passionate love for Suzette, he had been thrilled with the idea of having a ready-made family. And that had just vanished. He had lost everything.

Marie sat at the rear of the church, her wide-brimmed hat shadowing her face. She sat in the corner, hidden behind an elaborate bouquet of white lilies. The smell was overpowering and only exacerbated her need to throw up. She shouldn't be here and didn't know why she tortured herself, but she couldn't help it.

Michael was no longer in love with her. She'd ruined her chances of being with him due to her relentless determination to gain women the right to vote above everything else. All of her grandstanding about what women should have as their God-given rights had done nothing but leave her lonely and afraid. It had been too late once she realized what she had lost, and the man she loved was marrying another.

As the time grew past when the bride was to walk down the aisle, the crowd started whispering. Where was Suzette? What was holding up the ceremony?

Marie had heard the rumors and the stories about how Suzette had caused quite the stir in town when she arrived six months ago. It matched her actions while in Helena when Marie had first met her. She certainly liked to cause commotion, it seemed.

When Suzette agreed to marry the younger brother of the man she had once strung along, the gossips' tongues in Spring Creek had waggled quite furiously. It hadn't taken but a few words to the right people for Marie to learn all that had transpired and how manipulative Suzette was. The cook at the hotel had been positively gleeful in telling Marie everything about Suzette and how there were numerous bets in town that the marriage wouldn't last but a few weeks, if the marriage took place at all.

Finally, the rear vestibule door opened, and the music began, but instead of the bride, another woman went down the aisle. She spoke with the reverend for a moment and then left. She avoided looking anyone in the eye and hurried out of the church as though a pack of wolves was chasing her. Ben approached him, and harsh words were spoken before the reverend, Michael, and Ben stepped out of sight of the congregation.

The crowd was restless, and the heat in the hall was thick and muggy. Sweat rivulets ran down her back, and she wanted to rip off the black hat and netting around her face and run out of the church, but she wouldn't cause another scene. She had already embarrassed herself in front of the town quite effectively the day before when she had begged Michael to listen to her.

Marie had never thought he wouldn't believe her when she told him that Suzette had been behind some of the attacks.

"Are you trying to ruin what I have with Suzette and her children?" Michael's voice had seethed with fury.

They'd stood in front of the hotel after she'd gone for a walk yesterday morning. She had been trying to gain the courage to talk to him when she ran into both Suzette and Michael coming out of the hotel. Michael had confronted her and asked why she was in town, and she had blurted out what the sheriff in Helena had told her. Marie had meant to talk to him in private, but his disdain had pushed her to say more than she'd planned.

"No." Marie shook in response to the anger he displayed. "She isn't what she seems, Michael. The man said she was behind the attacks."

"I certainly was not," Suzette drawled. "From what Michael has told me, you'd been experiencing incidents long before I arrived in Helena. It makes no sense that I'd be involved." She ran her gold necklace through her fingers. "What would I have gotten from doing something so cruel? I was trying to help you with the suffragists' cause, if you remember?" Suzette's tone was condescending and positively gleeful.

The smirk on her face told Marie all she needed, but Michael had barely looked at the woman hanging onto him like glue to a child's painting.

"The sheriff said he confessed she was behind everything." Marie's voice broke.

The look on his face was not encouraging. In fact, it was quite disdainful. She was heartbroken. Tears bloomed and threatened to fall. She was a pathetic version of herself.

"Then why isn't he here to arrest Suzette?"

Chagrined at his condescending tone, she wanted to run and hide, but she stood her ground. "The man recounted everything the next morning, but I believe--"

"That's enough, Marie." Suzette stepped forward as though she had to put herself between Michael and Marie. "It's clear you're jealous of Michael's happiness and are just trying to ruin our special day. Why don't you return to Helena and leave us in peace?"

Refusing to let the tears fall and give Suzette any more satisfaction, Marie had scooted around them and run up to her hotel room, hiding there until that morning, when Anne had convinced her she needed to go to the church for the wedding.

Anne hoped Michael would change his mind, but considering they were waiting for Suzette to walk down the aisle, it was clear nothing Marie said had changed anything. Instead, she had made a complete and utter fool of herself.

Marie looked around, trying to see if she could leave the church unnoticed, but she couldn't without everyone knowing it was her. As it was, she wasn't sure if a few of the townsfolk hadn't already recognized her. If she got up to leave, it would only cement her humiliation.

She shouldn't care, as she wasn't from here, but she *did* care about humiliating Michael any further. He planned on living here and making a life for himself. And although he would never be hers, she couldn't make him a laughingstock where he planned on living for the rest of his life.

Ben walked back inside the hall and stood at the front to address the crowd. The whispers slowly died as he stood waiting for everyone's attention.

"Sorry, folks, for the unfortunate delay." Ben's voice was loud as he talked over the remaining twitters from those who hadn't seen him or who were still gossiping about what might be happening. "There's no point in sugarcoating this. There'll be no wedding today."

The room burst into a chattering cacophony of voices, all confused, concerned, and, of course, tittering with anticipation over the potential gold mine of juicy gossip.

Ben waved his arms to quiet them. "I realize this is quite the inconvenience for most of you folks, but our family wants to thank you for coming to support Michael and Suzette, but they won't be getting married. Please feel free to go to the tent outside and enjoy the food and drinks. We don't want it to go to waste." He pulled at the collar around his neck, clearly agitated but trying to make a horrifying situation bearable. "Please remember to take the gifts you thoughtfully brought, but they won't need 'em. Again, we're sorry for any inconvenience. Thank you."

With that, he quickly left the hall, not waiting for the mountain of questions forming on the townsfolk's lips. Marie sat, shocked. What had just happened? Was Michael all right? She wanted to run after Ben to find out, but she was stuck in her seat with nowhere to go. She couldn't force her way out, for then she would be discovered, but she was desperate to go to him, even though she would be the last person he would want to comfort him.

It appeared Suzette had left Michael at the altar, but it made no sense. Suzette had made it abundantly clear that she had won. Regardless of what Marie said, Suzette had known how much Michael loved her children and had used that to her advantage.

And now, with his wedding to Suzette up in the air, he likely still wouldn't give Marie the time of day. Marie had ruined any chance she had of spending the rest of her life with him. It was all her fault, and she would never forgive herself for her stupidity and lack of self-awareness. Her single-minded focus had ruined any hope for a happy future.

Thirty-Seven

Michael strode out of the church and toward the house Suzette had been renting. With any luck, he'd catch her before she left. Something was not right, and he had to fix it. She'd told him that her husband had died tragically. Even Todd had said his pa was gone and was never coming back.

Suzette had told him one evening that she was afraid of her deceased husband's family. They blamed her for his death and had threatened to take her children. She had left San Francisco in the middle of the night so they wouldn't try to take them. The only thing that made sense was that someone from his family had tracked her down. Perhaps they had threatened her. She wouldn't leave without telling Michael.

Reaching the house, he bounded up the front porch stairs and pushed open the door, but all was quiet. Not a sound. Nothing.

"Suzette," he yelled. "Where are you? Todd? Natalie?"

No one responded. He ran up the stairs, pushed open Suzette's bedroom door, and skidded to a stop. The wardrobe doors hung open. It was completely devoid of clothing and shoes. Her dressing table was empty of bottles of perfume, hairbrushes, ribbons, and the various figurines she liked to fiddle with. Everything was gone save for a lone shoe on the floor next to the open window, the yellow lace curtains fluttering from the wind.

He turned and ran toward Todd's and Natalie's rooms, but they, too, were empty of everything. It was as though they had never been there. Every trace of them was gone. How could they have disappeared so fast? It was as though Suzette had planned this. She and the children were gone.

His future had once again disappeared like a flame snuffed out by a harsh winter's breeze. He was alone and would never have the wife he wanted or the children he adored. Everything he had put up with for the past few months had been for naught. He collapsed onto Todd's bed and held his head in his hands.

"Michael, are you here?" It was Ben.

Michael didn't want to face his older brother. Ben had warned him that Suzette was devious and manipulative, but he had been determined to prove them wrong. Unfortunately, he had only been shown to be a fool, but he wasn't sad that Suzette was gone, and that therein was a problem. He shouldn't have been willing to marry a woman just to become the father to her children.

He pushed off the low bed and went into the hall, his footsteps slow and sluggish. A moment later, he reached the first floor. Ben was in the front parlor, along with way too many other members of their family. He wasn't up for this, but they were concerned. And he understood that, but it didn't mean he had to like it.

Elizabeth pulled him into a hug. She cupped his cheek for a moment and then stepped back. "I'm so sorry, Michael."

He nodded, but they weren't truly apologetic. None of them liked Suzette and hadn't been shy about telling him so. They might have been sorry he'd been hurt, but nothing more.

"I'm sure you're thrilled there's no wedding today." Michael was angry and had every right to be. His fiancée had left him at the altar.

Elizabeth and Ben exchanged a glance, which infuriated him further.

"We aren't thrilled," Ben said. "No one wanted this to happen."

"No, you would've rather I never proposed to her." He undid the buttons of his suit jacket and yanked it off his shoulders.

"Michael." Elizabeth's tone was soothing and apologetic. "She might not have been what *we* would've chosen for you, but if you loved her, then that was all that mattered."

But he hadn't loved her, and it pained his soul to admit it. He was more concerned about the safety of Todd and Natalie. "Her deceased husband's family was after her children. What if they are in danger?"

"It wasn't her husband's family that came." Ben ran his hands through his hair. "You heard the reverend. It was her husband." He put his arm around Elizabeth's shoulder and pulled her near. "She's still married, and it's a good thing he arrived. Otherwise, you'd be married to a bigamist."

"I'm not convinced it was her husband," Michael said. "She said he died."

"Then she lied." Anne's voice was scathing. "She's a liar and a manipulator. You're better off without her."

Michael glared at Anne. "She *had* changed."

Why am I continuing to perpetuate a lie when I know she really hasn't? I've only been choosing to believe she changed so I could justify to myself that marrying her was the right thing to do.

"Clearly not, if her husband showed up after she claimed he was dead." Anne picked at the bouquet she held. They'd been meant for Suzette, but now they'd die, just like what remained of his dreams.

"Maybe it was someone pretending to be her husband." The words sounded untrue even to his ears.

"It wasn't." Elizabeth placed her hand on Ben's chest. Their love was as strong today as it had always been. "I talked with Janie after everyone left the church. She'd met him years before when

Suzette first married. She was just as shocked as the rest of us, but it was Suzette's husband."

"I don't believe it," he muttered. Although, if he were honest with himself, there had been holes in her story, but he'd chosen to ignore them.

"Suzette left him last fall, angry because he'd reduced her allowance. He'd lost his job, and his parents were supporting them, but Suzette continued to spend recklessly. When he told her to stop, she took the children and disappeared. It took him months to discover where she had gone. It wasn't until his brother got a letter from Todd that he figured out where she had gone."

"I don't believe it. She wouldn't do this to me." Michael was ashamed he had ignored the warning signs. "I'm going for a walk."

"Michael," Ben said, but Elizabeth stopped him with a hand on his arm.

He snatched his hat from the hook next to the front door and went to the barn, saddled his horse, and moments later, galloped down the street. Maybe he could forget about what had happened if he ran fast enough, but he doubted it. His life was a mess, and it rested solely on his shoulders.

Marie found herself behind the church once everyone had left, the gossips grinning from ear to ear, clearly wanting to tell their friends about the events that morning. Watching Michael almost marry Suzette had been far more difficult than Marie could've ever imagined. He had to be devastated, and she hated seeing him in pain. Marie wished she could comfort him.

Marie wasn't sure Michael would ever forgive her. She had hurt him one too many times, and having this happen to him with her watching had to be embarrassing. She shouldn't have come here. Having her watch his humiliation was likely to have added more to the burden he carried.

The day was warm, but a cool breeze blew off the pond behind the church. Marie found a large tree, settled on the ground, leaned against the trunk, and stared at the blue sky. She watched the white clouds ebb and flow across the expansive sky, wondering how her life had come to this.

Marie had lost the man she loved, and having him look at her with scorn and derision had broken something inside of her. Her goal of getting the women of Montana the vote was not looking promising, even with the petition and rally cries throughout the state. She had met with Eloisa and Greta before she left for Spring Creek, and they had told her what they'd been hearing. If the measure didn't pass, then she had failed even that part of her life. While she wouldn't give up, it was still hard to accept that they might not have won this time.

She pulled her legs up to her chest and wrapped her arms around them, resting her chin on her knees. A horse neighed behind her. Marie didn't turn and groaned inwardly. She hadn't wanted company. She would've rather wallowed in her misery alone.

Leather creaked behind her, and she shoved her face into her knees. It was just her luck that someone would interrupt her solitude. Maybe if she pretended she hadn't heard them, whoever it was would go away.

A whisper of a body settled next to her, but she didn't raise her head. She didn't have to. One whiff of his scent told her who it was.

Michael.

His scent of burnt metal mixed with sandalwood was unmistakable. Not to mention her body sang with an undeniable desire that she no longer ignored. The minutes ticked by, but he didn't move. He softly breathed, and occasionally a flutter would whisper across her skin, but she wasn't about to face him. She had come to Spring Creek unannounced and had likely been the reason Suzette had left him at the altar. Although to say that would indicate she had that much power over the man sitting next to her.

"You can't ignore me forever," he drawled.

"Yes, I can," she mumbled into her skirt. Heat flared up her chest and into her cheeks. There was no way she could face him.

He chuckled.

"Why are you laughing?" she asked. "There's nothing funny about this day."

Silence greeted her. When she couldn't take it any longer, she slowly raised her head and looked at him.

But he wasn't looking at her and stared straight ahead. One knee was bent while he fingered a piece of grass. His hat was pulled low across his forehead, and she couldn't see his eyes.

"Are you all right?" she whispered.

"Yes," he said. "Likely better than I should be, since I was left at the altar. Not exactly how I thought this day would go."

"I'm sorry she humiliated you."

"Nothing I won't live through." He scratched at his chin. "It won't take long for people to forget all about it. I'll move back to Helena and blend in with the crowd. I never wanted to leave Helena as it was."

A tiny kernel of hope bloomed inside of her. If he came back, maybe she could convince him to forgive her. "Why did you?"

"Many reasons, I suppose. Plenty of 'em likely done in anger and frustration, which is *not* how I should make decisions." A smirk lined his lips.

Marie's heart hurt. She'd been part the reason he'd left his home. "I'm so sorry, Michael."

He didn't respond for a long moment, and silence stretched painfully between them. So many things needed to be said, but she didn't know if she had the courage to tell him how big a mistake she had made.

"Why did you come here, Marie?" His voice broke, but he continued to stare into the distance, avoiding her gaze.

"I..." She was pitiful and a disgrace. "I wanted... I wanted... I don't know what I wanted, but I didn't want you to get hurt. I also thought if I told you what the sheriff said, you'd... Oh, I should be honest. I never liked Suzette, and I didn't want you to marry her. I'm so sorry she broke your heart."

He scoffed and flicked the piece of grass away. "She didn't break my heart. My heart was already broken."

She stiffened. He was talking about her and what she did or didn't do.

"Besides, I should've listened to what you said about her involvement in the accidents befalling you. I should've never ignored you. She likely was involved up to her eyeballs in the trickery. I'm just glad you weren't hurt with her scheming," Michael said.

"I never meant to hurt you." She pulled her knees tighter against her chest. "I thought I knew what I wanted. When you blew into my life like a tornado--"

"A tornado? Didn't realize I had that much of an impact." He laughed.

She hid her face in her knees. "I didn't understand my feelings. Not sure I do now."

He shifted on the hard ground next to her, his body heat sending a pang of longing through her heart. "I didn't exactly make it easy on you, that's for sure."

"No, you didn't," she murmured. "But I didn't give you a chance either."

"It doesn't matter now, does it?"

"Of course it matters," she said. "But because of my actions, I pushed you into her arms."

He stiffened next to her. "You don't have that much power over me, Marie. I fell in love with those children when I realized you didn't love me."

She loved him, but she couldn't get the words past her lips. To say them now would seem almost insincere, and she didn't want that to be how she told him.

"I thought I was finally going to have the family I always wanted, but a part of me knew I'd never be happy with her. I guess I thought if I had a ready-made family, I could look past all the things that didn't sit right."

There was nothing she could do to ease his pain.

"I loved 'em," he said.

Taking a chance, she placed a hand across his, squeezing gently. He stopped moving and then suddenly turned his palm up and returned the squeeze.

"They'll be forever blessed to have known you," she murmured.

"I don't know about that," he said. "Whatever game Suzette is playing won't end well for them."

"That's not on you to solve," she said.

His hand was heavy, warm, and comforting inside hers. She didn't want to ever let go, but at some point, he would realize she was hanging onto him like a bird on a tree limb and would pull away. He had no reason to stay with her, no matter how much she wished otherwise.

"Maybe, maybe not, but if I'd been more aware, maybe I could have..."

The pain in his voice was her undoing. She turned toward him and pulled his hand to her chest. She couldn't let him leave, not until she told him what was in her heart. If she could ease his pain in any little way, she had to do that.

"You did everything right." She removed hair from his cheek, resting her fingers against his chin before removing them. "I don't know what her plan was or why she left. That isn't any of my concern. But those children were lucky you were in their life, no matter how short it might have been. You can't predict what will happen, but that is on their mother, not you."

"I just hate that I couldn't even say goodbye. What if they believe I don't care?"

"I'm sure that isn't the case. They know you love them, as I'm sure you showed them every moment of every day."

"Why couldn't you have been their mother?"

Marie froze.

He pulled his hand away. "That's not fair. I should've never said that, but--"

"But I hurt you, and you'll likely never forgive me for that, will you?" she said.

"There's nothing to forgive. You did nothing wrong. I pushed and didn't understand what you wanted."

Is this my moment to fix everything? "I was so confused about what I wanted, Michael."

"Have you figured that out now?" His gaze was piercing and direct, as though he could see everything inside of her and found her wanting.

The words stuck in her throat. Now that she had his undivided attention and he was no longer talking about his missing fiancée and children, did she have the strength or the courage to tell him how she felt?

"I'm sorry," he said. "I shouldn't have asked. You didn't come to Spring Creek to... Well, I guess I'm not sure why you came."

"Anne asked me to come."

He shook his head and stood. "Let me take you back to the hotel." He held out his hand.

An ache filled her heart. She had done something wrong once again. *Will I ever make things right between us?* She scrambled to stand and bowed her head to avoid his penetrating gaze.

"You can never accept my help, can you?"

"What?" She snapped her neck to look at him. "I didn't..."

His hand was outstretched, looking forlorn and lonely, and in her normal way, she had failed to take the innocent help he'd extended.

"You didn't take my hand. Is my helping you such a horrible thing?" He dropped his hand to his side. "It's the same as before. Everything is on your terms, the way you want it, and you'll never let me be who I am with you, will you?" He turned to walk away, clearly angry and determined.

"No, Michael, that isn't true." But he didn't turn and didn't stop. "Don't go."

He ignored her and continued to walk away. She had to stop him. If she let him go, she might never get him back.

She ran to him and pulled on his arm to stop him. He halted but kept his head turned. His neck was stiff, and his lips were pulled tight. She had caused this mess, and she had to fix it.

Breathing hard, she wanted to take her time, but time was not on her side. It was now or never. "You're right. I do have a hard time accepting help. It isn't you, it's me. I just do things by myself without even thinking about it. I didn't mean to ignore your hand or intentionally ignore it. I just do it without thinking."

He didn't budge, except to cross his arms over his chest. He was more unapproachable than before.

"I'm sorry, so sorry. I've made such a mess of things with you. I didn't know what I'd lost until you were gone."

"You sent me away."

"You're right. I did. And I was wrong. So wrong."

He relaxed his arms and turned to look at her, but kept quiet. He was leaving everything in her hands to fix or make worse, and the last thing she wanted was to worsen them.

"I'd convinced myself years ago that having a man help me in any way would be like I was letting myself down. As though the only way to move forward was to be a suffragist only and that my mission had to be in getting women the vote. What I didn't realize is that I can't do this without you."

She swallowed. The suffering she'd put them both through because she'd been stubborn had been unfair, and she didn't know if he would ever forgive her.

"I can only ask if you could find it in your heart to forgive me. I've realized that if I can't get women the right to vote without you by my side, then I have nothing, and the fight won't be worth it."

His gaze softened, and his shoulders relaxed before he held out his hand.

She looked at it and then into his eyes. The love shining from them filled her heart with joy. Perhaps he would give her a second chance or maybe a third, considering she'd hurt him more times than she cared to admit. She would give anything if he let her in his heart again.

She carefully placed her hand in his, and he wrapped his fingers around hers. The movement was slow, careful, as though they had to navigate the hurt to get to the joy. He took a step forward and gently pulled her close, holding her hand next to his heart. His free hand rose to her face, and he cupped her cheek, his thumb rough against her skin.

Her heart jumped into her throat, and anything she wanted to say was stuck with no way to be released. She prayed this was his way of saying he'd give her another chance, but it was his turn to forgive her or let her go forever.

"You are the most exasperating, cantankerous, difficult..."

A sharp pain hit her. He didn't love her anymore, not with those words. Tears threatened to fall, and she pulled away, but he didn't let go. Instead, he tugged her back.

"... and the most beautiful, delightful, inspiring, courageous woman I have ever met. I love you, Marie, with all my heart, and I'm hoping you love me, too."

Tears leaked from underneath her lids, but with a shaky and determined breath, she said, "I love you more than life itself. I'm so sorry--"

He placed a finger against her lips to stop her. "No more apologies. We both made decisions that were not in either of our best interests, but maybe we can work together to fix what we broke?"

"Yes," she murmured. "I want to do that more than anything else in this world. I love you, Michael Seymour."

"I love you, too."

And before she could take another breath, he leaned forward and placed a gentle kiss on her lips. A kiss so sweet and special, it made all the heartache worth it. If this were a chance for them to begin anew, she wouldn't do anything to ruin it. She wanted a future with this man. He would make it easier and more special to fight for what she believed in, for he would be by her side, supporting her, fighting with her for all their dreams to come true.

Epilogue

November 3, 1914
11 years later

The doors to the state capitol building burst open, and a stream of women and a few men raced outside.

"We did it! Women have the right to vote!"

Marie stood next to Michael, her heart in her throat. The moment had finally come after years of fighting and never giving up.

Michael swooped her into his arms and swung her around. "You did it, love!" he murmured into her ear before placing a gentle kiss on her neck.

"No." She took his face into her palms and looked straight into his dark brown eyes. "*We* did it."

His charming smile sent a delicious streak of joy straight to her toes. He still made her blood sing and her heart race every time he looked at her. They had been married for just over eleven years, and the heat between them was still as strong today as it was the day she finally accepted one of his many proposals.

Screams of joy, cheers, clapping, and excited chatter were

around them. Banners and flags fluttered in the air around them. The steps and streets in front of the capitol building were packed with women, children, and the men who supported them. It was cold outside, but no one noticed or cared. The moment they'd been waiting for had finally arrived.

"Marie!" Eloisa waved to her from the steps above. "Marie, come here!"

Michael laughed. "She's impatient, but definitely enthusiastic. You better go up there before she falls down the stairs."

"Knowing her, she'll cause an avalanche of people falling."

"And she'll likely jump up, be perfectly unscathed, and ready to start her next adventure and try to drag you along with it."

She giggled. He was right. Eloisa was one of her closest friends, but she had no idea the havoc she caused. But her passion for the same causes made them the best of friends.

"Marie," Eloisa yelled again.

"I better go before she does something dangerous. You'll watch the girls?" She looked at their two daughters standing proudly next to their father. They were the spitting image of him, with the same dark brown hair and brown eyes. Marjorie was nine, and Cynthia was five. They were the apple in their father's eye, and if he'd had his way, she'd have five more just like them, but they hadn't been blessed again. After Cynthia's difficult delivery, the doctor wasn't convinced she'd be able to conceive again. They'd been disappointed but were grateful they had Marjorie and Cynthia.

"Yes." He kissed her on the cheek. "Go before she hurts herself."

She squeezed his hand, and then, picking up her skirts, she scooted around the various groups of men, women, and children until she reached Eloisa's side.

Once there, Eloisa threw her arms around Marie's neck and squealed. "This is so exciting!"

Marie grimaced at her screech but smiled when she extricated herself from Eloisa's embrace. Marie took Eloisa's hands to help contain her enthusiasm. If she didn't, there was no telling what would happen next. "Yes, it is. It took way too long, but I'm glad we finally were able to accomplish it. This is a new day and a great beginning for Montana."

"You should go up there and give a speech." Eloisa's sash blew in the wind. "All the women would love to hear you say something."

"No," Marie said. "This isn't about me. This is about all of us. Besides, Greta has everything in hand."

Greta was standing at the top of the stairs, waving her hands to quiet the crowd. A microphone was in front of her, and large speakers were set to the side. They had been set up in anticipation of finally passing the change to the state's constitution.

"Ladies." Greta's voice crackled through the large speakers. It was hard to believe how technology was changing their world. Who would have ever anticipated using a piece of metal to transmit sound so that large swaths of people could hear it? "Ladies and gentlemen, today is a momentous day in Montana's history. It has taken years for us to get to this place, and it will be a precious memory for all of us to remember. While we have accomplished this here in the great state of Montana, plenty of other states are resisting change. We cannot give up." She raised her fist into the air. "We have to continue to fight until there is an amendment to the United States Constitution that will grant *all* women the right to vote."

With that, the crowd erupted once again into applause, cheers, and whistles. The band began playing "March of the Women," a song that had become a symbol of their fight. The music was loud, and women's voices rang with joy and excitement, but it was a reminder that while they had won in Montana, there was still work to be done.

"Mother Marie!"

She turned and smiled. It was Todd and Natalie. She held out her hands as the two of them ran up to her. Todd had grown into a handsome young man, turning eighteen earlier that summer, and Natalie was going to be just as passionate, if not more so, than Marie had been in her causes. Marie would like to think she had played a part in encouraging Natalie to chase after her dreams.

When Suzette left Michael at the altar, they'd thought they would never see the children again. But Suzette had arrived a few months after Marie and Michael had married, this time running from the law after she killed her husband in a fit of rage. When the sheriff's deputies caught up with her in Helena, she'd begged Michael to take the children. Suzette had known that Michael loved them and had played on his sympathies, but Michael had been more than happy to step in. It was probably one of the only selfless things Suzette had done, and Todd and Natalie had become a part of their family almost immediately. It had been a rough few months when they first arrived, as they hadn't trusted that Michael wouldn't disappear again, but with plenty of love and patience, they'd learned to trust Marie and Michael.

"This is so exciting." Natalie was bouncing on her heels, her white suffragist gown swirling around her. It was the first real grown-up dress she'd owned. She'd been thrilled when they dropped the hems of her dresses when she turned sixteen just two months ago and even more excited to learn she could participate in today's festivities. "I love hearing the women discuss what's next and how this is an enormous change for us all."

"It is," Marie said. "While we have won here, there are plenty of places that are still not giving women the vote. We can't give up, have to keep trying, and eventually, your children and your children's children will have a better future than we have."

Natalie beamed with joy and excitement. Her future would hold so much more than Marie's had, and it brought such peace to Marie's heart to know that she'd been a part of enacting this change.

"Where's Father?" Todd asked. "I lost sight of him when the news broke."

"He was down there." Marie pointed in the direction she had come from. "But I don't see him any longer. He likely took the girls to get something to eat and drink. Cynthia was complaining she was hungry right before they announced we had won."

"Were they excited?" Natalie asked.

Marie smiled. "I don't know if they completely understand, but I'm sure they could feel the enthusiasm brimming among all of us. This day will be something they can tell their children about, just like the two of you." She cupped Natalie's cheek with affection.

Natalie would be a prettier woman than her mother ever was, considering her kindness and compassion far surpassed anything Suzette could have ever expressed. It was a wonder that both Todd and Natalie were as thoughtful as they were, considering how many years they'd spent with their spiteful mother.

Marie grabbed Todd's hand and squeezed. "We should find your father. I'm sure the two of you must be hungry as well."

"Who can eat on a day like this!" Natalie said.

"I can." An infectious grin lit Todd's handsome face. "I haven't eaten in hours."

They chuckled. Todd had an insatiable appetite, but he was a growing boy who was going to be a fine man, and Michael had everything to do with that. His compassion and love for Todd and Natalie were just as deep and pure as what he had for the children he shared with her.

"Let's go find them," Marie said. "Eloisa, we'll meet up later?"

"Yes, go! Enjoy the day! We will talk later." Waving goodbye, Eloisa moved like a tsunami to another group of women.

There was no shortage of welcoming women on the steps of the capitol today. It was a day of love, hope, and a brighter future than they'd had the day before.

Marie, Todd, and Natalie maneuvered their way through the crowd. Marie searched the area, looking for Michael, and found him sitting at a small table in front of a bakery. Cynthia's face was smeared with chocolate, but she bounced on her father's knee, her smile the spitting image of her father's. Marjorie stood next to Michael, whispering something in his ear.

Marie's heart was full. She had four wonderful children and a husband who loved her more than life itself, and she had finally achieved her goal of participating in the momentous occasion of ensuring Montana gave women the right to vote.

She had been wrong to think she could've done it on her own. Michael's support and unwavering love had made all the difference. They were better together and would be for the rest of their lives.

My Dear Readers,

I hope you enjoyed the latest installment of my *Thundering Mountain Ranch* series. This was an extremely fun book to write and I hope you found as much joy in reading it as I did in writing it. The next book will feature Anne Seymour and her road to her happily ever after. Turn the page for a sneak peak of *Thundering Sunrise(book 7)*.

If you'd like to learn more about me and my novels, please sign up for my newsletter at www.nicoleneiswanger.substack.com.

All my love, Nicole

Thundering Sunrise

BOOK 7

"Did you hear that?" asked Elizabeth, looking up from her needlepoint.

Anne glanced up from the floor where she was playing with Tommy and Vicky. "I didn't hear anything."

Elizabeth dropped her needlepoint and stood, a frown pulling on her cheeks. She walked to the window and pulled back the curtain.

"Oh, no!"

"What's wrong?" Anne said, scrambling to stand.

"Fire!"

"What--"

"Stay inside with the children. I need to alert the men." Elizabeth picked up her skirts and ran from the room, the door slamming behind her. Anne gave both Vicky and Tommy a reassuring smile. They had startled with the noise and Vicky started to cry when her mother rushed from the room.

"Hush now, Vicky. Your momma'll be back soon. Why don't you and Tommy build a fort."

Vicky smiled. "A fort?"

"Yes."

"But momma doesn't like it when we do that."

"Well, today is a special day."

Vicky scrambled to her feet and grabbed Tommy's hand pulling him with her to the chest behind the settee. They laughed and eagerly opened it, pulling out thick blankets and colorful quilts.

Now that they were occupied, Anne headed to the window to see how bad it was and was startled at the inferno roaring out of the barn. Men were running this way and that, grabbing buckets, pulling out horses, forming a water line.. The house had grown eerily quiet that a shiver ran down Anne's spine.

Sarah whimpered and Anne let the curtains drop before hurrying to her side. Picking her up, she checked on Jimmy but he was fast asleep, his little fist curled up under his pink cheek. Bouncing Sarah in her arms, she murmured into her ear when a loud banging on the front door startled her. Sarah screeched in anger and Anne shushed the little one in her arms. Whoever it was would just have to wait, she had four children she had to attend to and besides, couldn't they tell there was a fire roaring outside?

After a few moments of silence, the banging started up again and this time more incessantly. Muttering under her breath, she looked at Vicky and Tommy, but they were busy building their fort and were clearly undeterred. Anne decided to leave them for just a moment while she answered the door. Whoever was outside was not going to go away. The banging continued as Anne approached.

"Coming," she said, unlatching the lock when it was shoved open and a tall, bear of a man pushed his way inside. Before she could stop him, he grabbed her arm and slammed the door shut behind him.

"What are you doing?" she said.

"Where are the children?" he asked. His voice was curt and his fingers dug into her arm.

Was he a new ranch hand? But as he dragged her down the hall looking into each room her trepidation grew. None of her brother's ranch hands had ever put their hands on any of the women in the family. She feared he wasn't someone who should be there. They reached the parlor and the man pushed open the door. Seeing the children, he pulled her inside.

"What's going on?" she said. "Who are you?"

"Tommy," he said loudly, his voice carrying across the room like a sharp roar.

Tommy's head shot up, his eyes wide with fright.

Who was this man?

"Come here," he said.

Tommy stood slowly, his thumb going into his mouth. He didn't move toward the man and the man abruptly let go of Anne and in two strides was at Tommy's side. He pulled Tommy up into his arm's and before Anne realized it, he was reaching for Sarah.

"No," she said, her voice shrill with fear and anger. "Who are you?"

"Give me the child." he said, his dark eyes menacing and full of hate.

"No," she said again, this time turning to the side to prevent him from taking Sarah from her arms.

He again tried to reach for the baby, but Anne wasn't going to let him have her. She opened her mouth to scream but he suddenly dropped Tommy and grabbed her around the waist pulling her to him, his other hand clamping over her mouth, her nose, stopping the scream from forming. His filthy hand smothered her words, smothered her from taking a breath. She couldn't breathe, but kicked at him, trying to wiggle free but his grip was firm, unrelenting. He wouldn't let go.

He bent his head, grabbed her chin, and forced her to look at him. His dark eyes pierced deep, and he whispered in her ear, "If you want the other children to live, you'll give me this child."

She shook her head.

A door slammed and footsteps pounded down the hall. He cursed, abruptly let her go, and in three large steps reached the door as it opened. Sam, her brother's oldest foreman, rushed inside.

Before she could warn him, the intruder slammed a lamp against the back of Sam's head. Sam slumped and dropped to the floor, his head hitting the ground with a loud smack. Anne watched horrified as the man dragged Sam away from the door. Before she could do anything more, the man snatched up a crying Tommy, grabbed her around the waist and pulled her with him.

"You've given me no choice, lady."

"Let me go," she shrieked.

"If you say another word, I'll kill the other children and you along with them," he said, his voice low. Anne looked at him wide-eyed with fright. She couldn't let him harm Vicky or Jimmy, and if she had to go with him to keep Sarah and Tommy safe, she would do so.

~

My Dear Reader,

I don't have a release date yet for *Thundering Sunrise*, but I will let you know as soon as I do. Anne has been waiting for her time to tell her story and with any luck you'll enjoy her story as much as you have her brothers.

If you'd like to learn more about me and my novels, please sign up for my newsletter at www.nicoleneiswanger.substack.com.

All my love, Nicole

Author's Note

In Chapter Eighteen, I included a quote from Susan B. Anthony. If you want to read more about her, check out this website https://www.history.com/articles/susan-b-anthony.

In Chapter Twenty-One, I included a quote from Emmeline Pankhurst. She had no connection to Montana in 1901 but she was a leader in the suffragist movement in the United Kingdom. I took a little bit of liberty in placing her in Montana during that time frame, but I felt her quote was powerful. If you want to read more about her, check out her autobiography *My Own Story*. It was originally published in 1914.

About the Author

Nicole is a Senior Business Analyst by day, a reader during meal time, and a writer while watching historical dramas. She rediscovered her passion for writing during a summer vacation when her husband's truck died. While being stranded for five days with nothing to occupy her time she began writing. She writes American Western Historical Romances set in the heart of Montana and Idaho with swoon-worthy cowboys and feisty, independent women.

Please get in touch
www.nicoleneiswanger.substack.com
nicoleneiswanger@gmail.com

Help other readers find this book by writing a review with your favorite retailer or by sharing on your favorite social media platform.

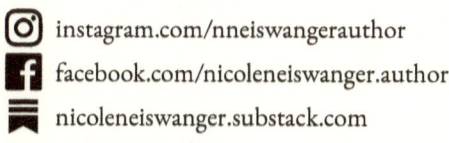

instagram.com/nneiswangerauthor
facebook.com/nicoleneiswanger.author
nicoleneiswanger.substack.com

Also by Nicole Neiswanger

Thundering Mountain Ranch Series

Beneath the Thundering Sky

Thundering Mountain

Thundering Meadows

Thundering Ridge

Thundering Snow

Thundering Sunset

Thundering Sunrise - coming soon

www.ingramcontent.com/pod-product-compliance
Lightning Source LLC
Chambersburg PA
CBHW030639020726
47493CB00006B/1789